THE CHILD GARDEN

THE
CHILD GARDEN

or

A Low Comedy

GEOFF
RYMAN

UNWIN
PAPERBACKS

LONDON SYDNEY WELLINGTON

First published in Great Britain by the Trade Division of Unwin Hyman Limited 1989

First Published in paperback by
Unwin® Paperbacks, a division
of Unwin Hyman Limited, in 1990
Reprinted 1990

UNWIN HYMAN LIMITED
15–17 Broadwick Street
London W1V 1FP

Allen & Unwin Australia Pty Ltd
8 Napier Street, North Sydney, NSW 2060, Australia

Allen & Unwin New Zealand Pty Ltd with the Port Nicholson Press
Compusales Building, 75 Ghuznee Street, Wellington, New Zealand

British Library Cataloguing in Publication Data
Ryman, Geoff
    The child garden.
    I. Title
    823'.914 [F]

ISBN 0–04–4406843

Printed and bound in Great Britain by Cox & Wyman Ltd, Reading

That the future is a faded song, a Royal Rose or a lavender spray
Of wistful regret for those who are not yet here to regret . . .

T. S. Eliot, *Four Quartets*

Acknowledgements
Thanks to John Clute, Paul Brazier,
Rob Burt and Amanda Brazier.

CONTENTS

INTRODUCTION

Advances in Medicine (A Culture of Viruses)

Milena boiled things. She was frightened of disease. She would boil other people's knives and forks before using them. Other people sometimes found this insulting. The cutlery would be made of solidified resin, and it often melted from the heat, curling into unusable shapes. The prongs of the forks would be splayed like scarecrow's fingers, stiffened like dried old gloves.

Milena wore gloves whenever she went out, and when she got back, she boiled those too. She never used her fingers to clean her ears or pick her nose. In the smelly, crowded omnibuses, Milena sometimes held her breath until she was giddy. Whenever someone coughed or sneezed, Milena would cover her face. People continually sneezed, summer or winter. They were always ill, with virus.

Belief was a disease. Because of advances in medicine, acceptable patterns of behaviour could be caught or administered.

Viruses made people cheerful and helpful and honest. Their manners were impeccable, their conversation well-informed, their work speedy and accurate. They believed the same things.

Some of the viruses had been derived from herpes and implanted DNA directly into nerve cells. Others were retroviruses and took over the DNA of the brain, importing information and imagery. Candy, they were called, because the nucleic acids of their genes were coated in sugar and phosphates. They were protected against genetic damage, mutation. People said that Candy was perfectly safe.

Milena did not believe them. Candy had nearly killed her. All through her childhood, she had been resistant to the viruses. There was something in her which fought them. Then, at ten years old, she had been given one final massive dose, and was so seared by fever that she had nearly died. She emerged with encyclopaedic knowledge and several useful calculating facilities. What other damage had the viruses done?

Milena tested herself. Once, she tried to steal an apple from a market stall. It was run, as so many things were, in those days, by a child. When Milena's hand touched the apple's dappled skin, she had thought of what it cost the boy to grow the apples and haul them to

1

market and how he had to do all this in his spare time. She could not do it, she could not make herself steal. Was that because of the virus? Was it part of herself? She could not be sure.

There was one virus to which Milena knew she had been immune. There was one thing at least that she was sure was part of herself. There was no ignoring the yearning in her heart for love, the love of another woman.

This was a semiological product of late period capitalism. So the Party said. Milena suffered, apparently, from Bad Grammar. Bad *deep* Grammar, but grammar nonetheless. This made Milena angry. What late period capitalism? Where? It had been nearly one hundred years since the Revolution!

She was angry and that frightened her. Anger was dangerous. Anger had killed her father. He had been given so many viruses to cure him of it that he had died of fever. Milena was certain that one day soon, the Party would try to cure her, too, of anger, of being herself. Milena lived in fear.

Everyone was Read at ten years old, by the Party. It was part of their democratic rights. Because of advances in medicine, representative democracy had been replaced by something more direct. People were Read, and models were made of their personalities. These models joined the government, to be consulted. The government was called the Consensus. It was a product of late period socialism. Everyone was a part of the Consensus, except Milena.

Milena had not been Read. She had been too ill with viruses at ten years old to be Read. Her personality was still in flux; a Reading would have been meaningless. She had not been Read, but she had been Placed as an adult. Would they remember, soon? When she was Read, her Bad Grammar and her petty crimes would be discovered. And then, as a matter of social hygiene, she would be made ill, in order to cure her.

Milena was frightened of dying when it happened, like her father. Had he been resistant as well? Her father had died, in Eastern Europe, and her mother had fled with Milena to England, where the diseases were milder. Then she too had died, and Milena had grown up as an orphan in a foreign land.

She had grown up with a head full of theatrical visions. She loved the mechanics of rotating stages, of puppets, of painted flats being raised and lowered. She loved the cumbersome, stinking alcohol lights that blazed with brightness found only in theatre. She thought about such things as the effect of alternating bands of white and yellow light cast over a white, white stage. She loved light. She toyed with hazy ideas of productions that consisted only of light. No people.

2

At ten years old, Milena had been Placed for work in the theatre, as an actress. This was a mistake. Milena was a terrible actress. There was something unbending in her that refused to mimic other people: she was always herself. She was doomed always to fight to stay herself.

Most mornings, a bus would take Milena to her next performance. She would sit, arms folded, like a flower that had not yet bloomed, and look at London as it creaked past her window.

People called London the Pit, with rueful fondness for its crumbling buildings propped up by scaffoldings of bamboo, for its overcrowding, for its smells. The Pit, they called it, because it lay in a depression, a river valley between hills protected by a Great Barrier of Coral that kept back the rising sea and estuary.

Outside her window, Milena saw women in straw hats smoking pipes and selling dried fish. She saw children dancing to toy drums for cash or pushing trolleys full of dusty green vegetables. Men in shorts bellowed to each other like cheerful bullfrogs, rolling barrels of beer down ramps into basements under the street. Giant white horses stood calmly before the wagons.

People were purple. Their skins were flooded with a protein called Rhodopsin. It had once been found only in the eye. In light, Rhodopsin broke down into sodium, and combined carbon and water.

People photosynthesised. It was a way of feeding them all. There were twenty-three million of them in the Pit. In summer they baked in tropical heat, stretching out in the parks in early morning, to break-fast on light. In the raw and bitter winters, they would lean against sheltered walls and open up their clothing in gratitude. Milena would see them from her bus. Their rippled flesh would be exposed, their swaddlings of black winter clothing would be thrown back. They would look like carvings in baroque churches. Milena would then be made restless with semiological error, desperate with Bad Grammar.

People died in the street. Most mornings, the bus would pass one of them. A man would be stretched out on the pavement, looking back over his shoulder as if in surprise, as if someone had called him. A bell would be ringing dolefully, calling for a Doctor.

And the actors on the bus would go on talking. An actress might laugh too loudly, a finger hooked under her nose, talking to a director; a young man might continue looking at his feet, disgruntled by a lack of success. Does no one care? Milena would think. Does no one care for the dead?

There were no old people in the streets. Young mothers worked the stalls. Their children stirred the food in the sizzling woks, or slammed new heels onto old shoes. The dead were young as well.

3

The span of human life had been halved. This was not considered to be an advance in medicine. It was considered to be a mistake.

In the days before the Revolution, a cure had been found for cancer. It coated the proto-oncogenes in sugar, so that cancer could not be triggered. In the old world of great wealth and great poverty, the cure had been bought by the rich before being tested. It was contagious, and it escaped. Cancer disappeared.

It had once been normal for the human body to produce a cancer cell every ten minutes. Cancer, it turned out, had been rather important. Cancer cells did not age. They secreted proteins that prevented senescence. They had allowed people to get old. Without cancer, people died in or around their 35th year.

After that, there had been a Revolution.

Milena sat on the bus in her boiled gloves and saw a nervous light in the eyes of the actors, a fervour for accomplishments completed in youth. She saw the unfailing smiles of people in the markets, and the smiles seemed to be symptoms of disease. It seemed to Milena that nearly everything she saw was wrong.

She saw the children. They had been given viruses to educate them. From three weeks old they could speak and do basic arithmetic. By ten, they had been made adults, forced like flowers to bloom early. But they were not flowers of love. They were flowers of work, to be put to work. There was no time.

Book One

LOVE SICKNESS

or

Living in the Pit

Midway in the journey of our life
I found myself in a dark wood
For the straight way was lost

chapter one

EVERYDAY LIFE IN FUTURE
TIMES (WINDOWS IN A BRIDGE)

It was an audience of children.

They sat on mattresses on the floor of a darkened room in a Child Garden. The children all wore the same grey, quilted dungarees, but they had been allowed to embroider them with colourful patterns. The children were allowed to drift in and out of the room as they pleased. There was no need for externally imposed discipline. On a makeshift stage, actors were trading convoluted Shakespearian wit.

Thou pretty because little!
Little pretty because little. Wherefore apt?
And therefore apt because quick!

It was a production of *Love's Labour's Lost*. The children were bored: they could follow the play with such ease.

Milena Shibush waited in plain sight of the children to make her entrance. There was no proscenium arch to hide behind. She could hear what the children said. She did not expect flattery.

'Another one of these New History things,' sighed a little girl in the front. Her cheeks were purple from the sun. Her voice was sulky, light, breathy. She was about three years old. 'If they're going to try to do the originals, why can't they get it right?'

'I don't know why they bother to send us these plays,' said her little friend. Her voice already had the crackle of adult precision. 'We know them by heart already. And who is that idiot in the floppy boots?'

The idiot was Milena Shibush. Tykes, she thought; it was expected that younger children would be obnoxious. They got everything without effort from the viruses; they had no idea that anything would require effort.

I don't like the boots either, Milena thought, but these are the boots I have to wear.

Milena was playing a constable called Dull.

She had a total of thirteen lines. I am sixteen years old, Milena thought, halfway through my life, and I have thirteen lines in a production that is touring Child Gardens.

Child Gardens were where orphans were raised. There were so

many orphans. Milena had been an orphan herself. She had become an actress to escape orphans and Child Gardens. Here she was.

Milena looked at the faces of her colleagues. The boy who played Berowne waited dull-eyed in his make-up and the beard he had grown for the part. He had to have a beard, for no other reason than that Berowne in the original production had had a beard. This recreation only served to preserve history. Milena lived in a culture that replicated itself endlessly, but which never gave birth to anything new.

The actors are bored, thought Milena, the children are bored, why, why, why are we doing this?

She muttered one of her thirteen lines. 'Me, an't shall please you.' It plainly didn't.

At least, she thought, I can change my boots.

It was nearly dark by the time Milena got back home. She walked beside the river on the pavements of the South Bank, which was feebly lit by alcohol lamps. There was still a smoky pinkness in the west.

The National Theatre of Southern Britain loomed out of the darkness and slight haze. Great sweeping buttresses of Land Coral and a cage of bamboo kept the old building on its feet.

The Zoo, it was called affectionately or otherwise. Milena was a registered member of the Theatrical Estate, but she was yet to work on any of the Zoo's main stages. It had a restaurant that was always open, called the Zoo Cafe. Actors could not sun themselves to feed. It made their skins too purple, too dark, and ruined them for Shakespeare and the classics. Actors had to be pale, for the sake of historical accuracy. They had to eat food and were nearly always hungry.

Milena went to the Zoo Cafe when she was lonely or could not face cooking on her one-ring alcohol stove. It was something of a homeopathic cure for loneliness. Other people sat talking at tables, leaning back to laugh, brilliant young actors or the well-dressed, imperturbable children of Party Members. Milena watched them hungrily as she moved forward one step at a time in the queue for hot water.

The fashion in everything was for history. People's minds were choked with it. Young people wore black and pretended to be the risen corpses of famous people. The Vampires of History they called themselves. Their virus-stuffed brains gave them the information they needed to avoid anachronisms. It was a kind of craze.

The Vampires only came out at night, when there was no sun to sweeten their blood. They had to eat too, but they could afford meals of historic proportions. Milena could only afford a seafood pasta, cloned squid tissue on cooling noodles. The great, heaped plates of the Vampires turned her shrivelled stomach. She looked away.

Milena saw Cilla, an actress with whom she had achieved a chilly

8

kind of acquaintance, sitting at a freshly vacated table. Cilla had just finished kissing a number of cheeks goodbye. Cilla knew everybody, even Milena.

'Who are you this evening?' Milena asked her, putting down her tray.

Cilla was in black, with white pancake makeup and dark vampire shadows around her eyes. 'Just me,' answered Cilla. 'This is supposed to be me when I rise from my grave.'

'Someone is playing themselves for a change,' said Milena.

'At least you know you're not being cast against type,' said Cilla, lightly. She was well on her way to becoming an Animal – a well known performer.

'You know I'm in this boring play,' said Milena. She began to wash her cutlery in a mug of hot water. 'Do you know any way I can change my costume? I hate my boots.'

'You can't change your costume if it's part of the original production. You'd be violating history.'

'The boots squelch. It's supposed to be funny.'

Cilla shrugged. 'You could go to the Graveyard.'

A Vampire joke? Milena looked at Cilla, narrow-eyed. Life had taught Milena to be wary of humour.

'The Graveyard,' repeated Cilla, in a voice that indicated that Milena knew very little indeed. 'It's where they dump the old costumes no one wants. They're not even on record.'

'You mean I can just take them out? No director's approval?'

'Yup. It's in an old warehouse under a bridge.' Cilla was telling Milena how to get there, when two Vampires swept up to the table in twentieth century clothes: a black tuxedo, and a black-beaded dress.

Party Members – Tarties. The boy wore spectacles, another affectation, and had something in his nose to make his nostrils flare. His hair was combed back and his make-up was green, to make him look ill.

'Good evening,' he said, looking sour, his accent American. 'We've managed to escape Virginia. She is busying herself listing all the ways in which Joyce is a bad writer. Her jealousy is so nakedly evident, I was embarrassed.'

The woman with him was trying to smile, under a low cloche hat. The smile wavered pathetically. 'Tom?' she said. His back was turned towards her. 'Speak to me. Can't you speak? Speak?'

'T S Eliot and Vivien!' exclaimed Cilla, and complimented them. 'Instant. Complete.' The couple did not relax out of their roles. Is there so little of yourselves left? thought Milena.

'I don't believe I've had the pleasure,' the boy said, holding out his

9

hand towards Milena. It was Vampire sociability. He wanted to know who Milena was playing.

'Who am I?' Milena responded with deadpan hostility. She did not take his hand. 'Oh. In life, I was a textile factory worker in nineteenth century Sheffield. I died at twelve years old. I'm a rather bad Vampire because I have no teeth. But I do have eczema and rickets.'

The Vampires made excuses and left. 'Well. That sent them packing,' said Cilla.

'I know,' sighed Milena. Why did she find so many things unacceptable? 'Is there something wrong with me, Cilla?'

'Yup.' said Cilla. 'You're prissy.' She mused for a moment. 'And . . . obsessive.' She nodded with decision. Then, to make it sweeter, she said, 'La, la la.' It was a nonsense expression. It meant that everything was the same, everything was a song.

'Obsessive?' questioned Milena. It was a new arrow to her bow of self-recrimination.

'You're still washing that fork,' said Cilla. 'You melted all of mine. When you visited, remember?'

'And prissy?'

'Severe,' added Cilla, nodding again in agreement with herself.

Milena had gone through a phase of thinking she was in love with Cilla. Oh, woman, if only you knew what was on my mind!

'I suppose that does sum it up,' sighed Milena. It was bad enough to suffer from Bad Grammar, but to be called prissy with it! She contemplated her cold squid, and decided that she preferred hunger. 'Excuse me.' She stood up and walked rather unsteadily into the night.

'You did ask me. Milena? You did ask!' Cilla called after her. Cilla always spoke without thinking. She only acted on stage.

Milena walked out on the Hungerford Footbridge and looked at the river. It churned in the moonlight, muddy and smelling of drains. The eddies made by the pylons of the bridge swirled with garbage and foam. Milena yearned for some leap away from herself, away from the world.

And then over Waterloo Bridge a great black balloon rose up from its mooring by the river. It made no sound except for a whispering of air, like wind blowing over the moors. Its cheeks were puffed out, and it propelled itself gently, by blowing. It was borne up in silence, moving with the grace of a cloud towards – where? China? Bordeaux? Milena wanted to go with it. She wanted to be like it, huge and unthinking with nothing to do but be itself, carried by the wind.

She was young. She thought she was old. On the South Bank, the windows of the Zoo Cafe were full of candlelight and Vampire silhouettes and the sound of laughter. They were all young and soft, and they had no time, and so they hated the silence, the silence in themselves that had yet to be filled by experience.

Some of them were driven to make noise, were kept jumping by something that was alive inside them. Others like Milena, cleared the decks and waited for something to happen, something worthwhile to do or to say. They loathed the silence in themselves, not knowing that out of that silence would come all the things that were individual to them.

Something, something has got to happen soon, Milena thought. I need something new to do. I'm tired of the plays, I'm tired of the Child Gardens, I'm tired of being me. I'm tired of sitting bolt upright on the edge of my bed all night, alone. I need someone. I need a woman, and there isn't going to be one. They've all been cured. The viruses cure them. Bad Grammar. I love you is Bad Grammar?

Milena suffered from resistance. She thought that in many different ways she was the last of her kind in the world.

The next day she went to the Graveyard, hugging the unwanted boots. Trains to the Continent left from Waterloo. The wooden cars creaked and groaned on rubber wheels that no longer ran on rails, chuffing with steam over the old city on old bridges made of ancient brick.

Through those brick bridges, tunnels ran. One of the tunnels was called Leake Street, and leak it did. Water dripped from the roof. The place smelled of trains, a dry oily itch in Milena's nostrils. The walls were covered with splattered white tiles and all along them was a series of large green doors.

The green doors were locked. Milena tried each one and not one of them would open. To Milena, this was mysterious. What was the point of a door that would not open?

Finally she came to a huge gate that had been left ajar. It was covered with many different layers of flaking paint, out of which emerged the words in old alphabetic script 'White Horse'. From beyond the gates there came the sound of a full orchestra.

It was playing in the dark. Milena peered through the gate. There must be a light, she thought. What kind of orchestra is it that plays in the dark?

She swung the gate open and stepped inside. She had time to see disordered racks of clothing, bamboo rods on bamboo uprights and little rollers. She saw them in a narrow band of dim light from the doorway. The band of light suddenly narrowed. The gate swung shut behind her with a clunk.

It would not open again. This Milena did not believe. She knew nothing of locks. Her culture did not need them. No one ever stole.

11

The old gates did lock however, and Milena pushed them, and slammed them, and shouted 'Hello?' at them. They didn't move.

Fine, she thought in anger. I'll starve to death in here and they'll find me fifty years from now, my fingers clawing at the wood. Why the hell have a door like that? Why the hell can't they light this place? And how the hell am I going to get out of here? Milena felt a sting of frustration in her eyes. She spun around and kicked the door and listened to it shudder. She listened to the music. Her viruses knew it note for note.

Some woman was warbling away to *Das Lied von der Erde*. Another piece by Mahler about death. All I need right now. Couldn't the miserable little turncoat write about anything else?

Still, some Animal or another was singing in the dark. Some Animal or another would know the way out. The music was coming from a corner of the warehouse that was diagonally opposite. Milena simply had to find her way there.

This meant fighting her way through racks of old costumes. There were no orderly aisles between them. The capes, the false chain mail, the nun's habits swung rottenly on their hangers, dry and stiff and booby-trapped with pins. Milena felt a sudden jab of pain.

Good, right, fine, she thought, sucking her finger, and growing savage. I've just injected myself with virus.

Then she dropped the boots. She heard a splash. Oh God, she thought, I've dropped them in a puddle of *something*. Her hand plashed in stale water. She found them, dripping wet, and held them out, well away from her body. She stood up and hit her head on a rack, pushed it over in a rage, got her feet tangled up in dead clothing, dropped the boots again, paddled in the dark to find them, stood up, snarled and took a deep breath.

More than anything else, Milena hated losing her dignity. She forced herself to be calm, and trembling very slightly, began to swing the racks towards her, juddering on their little wheels. She made a more orderly progress.

Milena went on in the darkness until she was lost. Under her hands, she felt the cheap burlap, the frail seams, the loose threads like cobwebs. She felt the scratchiness of dusty sequins in clumps. It was as if all theatre had died around her, leaving only husks behind. What if there isn't an orchestra? she wondered. Oh come on, Milena, who do you think is making the music, ghosts?

She began to imagine some very strange things. The music was too loud. Music was never that loud. You could stand in the middle of the orchestra next to the kettle drums and it wouldn't be that loud. And there was a shrill, unnatural tone to it that hurt Milena's ears.

Distracted, she scraped her head on brick. She crouched blindly under an arch and saw light. Light! Like in a forest just at dawn, grey daylight.

But the music! The music was louder than before, and she could see the rough texture of the bricks in the wall; she was yards away from it. There was no orchestra. There was no room for an orchestra.

But an orchestra screeched at her. The flutes were like knives, slicing into her head, the walls were being beaten like drums. Milena covered an ear with one hand, and moved back a rack of clothing with the other. She ducked down, in a kind of terror, and drew back a velvet dress, like a curtain.

There was a window to the outside world. A window in a bridge? Milena had never seen that. In the light, there were mounds of paper, heaps of it, stacked up in columns or fallen sideways across the floor. Paper was wealth, and Milena's eyes boggled in her head.

Sitting slumped in front of it was a Polar Bear.

Effendim, excuse me, you're not supposed to call them that, Milena reminded herself. They are GEs, genetically engineered people.

GEs had been human once. Effendim, *are* human, now. They had recoded their genes for work in the Antarctic, before the Revolution. It was a sickness, to be pitied. This GE was huge and shaggy, covered in fur of varying chestnut colours, staring ahead, mouth hanging open. The eyes did not blink, but seemed to ripple and glisten with a life of their own, wide and black and unseeing.

The music was coming from nowhere.

The monstrous voice was singing in German, with a voice like a steam whistle.

ewig blauen licht die Fernen
everywhere and eternally, the distance shines bright and blue

The viruses knew all the words, knew all the notes. The effect was to make the music wearisome to Milena, like a thrice-told joke. The mystery of where it was coming from simply made her feel very creepy. She looked instead at the posters of beautiful paintings curling on the wall. There were books as well, books turned face downwards on the desk. There was a scattering of what looked like wafers, something to eat. Books, paper, Milena had never seen such wealth or such waste.

Milena knew about the wealth of Bears, GEs. Bears, GEs, lived outside the Consensus. They were deliberate outlaws, selling Antarctic nickel. This one was massive, burly. What a gorilla, thought Milena. This one's trouble, she decided.

The music settled into silence.

ewig... ewig...
forever... forever...

The giant voice throbbed. Earwigs yourself, thought Milena. The GE looked stunned as if the music were a blow to the head. Finally the song fell silent and it was as if the entire building sighed with relief.

The GE moved. It fumbled behind itself without turning, sending a cascade of paper pouring out over the edge of the desk. Out from under it emerged a small, metal box with switches. The GE felt for one of them.

An electronic device.

Milena lived in a world without much electricity. Pulse weapons and poverty, sheer numbers, and a shortage of metal had made domestic electronics a part of history.

'Where did you get that?' Milena asked, stepping forward, forgetting herself for once.

Milena had a clock in her mind, a viral calculator. It added up the cost of the metal, and the cost of manufacture, all in terms of labour-hours. The electronic device was the most expensive thing she had ever seen.

The GE squinted at her, as if across the Grand Canyon. Its mouth hung open. Finally it spoke.

'China, I believe,' the GE said. The voice was high and rasping. The GE was a woman.

Milena had heard stories of Polar women. They gave birth on the ice, and stood up, and went straight back to work, blasting rocks. Milena's prejudices lined up in place. The creature spoke again, with a delicious, rambling delicacy.

'You wouldn't happen to have any alcoholic beverages about your person, would you?'

'Milena was by now out of step with the conversation. She had forgotten the question she had asked and was trying to work out what the answer, 'China, I believe,' could possibly mean. Distracted, she gave her head a little shake.

'No,' Milena said. 'I don't like poisoning myself.'

'Tuh!' said the GE. It was a chuckle that became a shudder. She stood up. She was nearly twice the height of Milena, and had to shuffle to turn around in the enclosed space. With slow bleariness, she began to ransack her desk. She pushed over more piles of paper, and swept a resin tray of wafers onto the floor.

It occurred to Milena that she was being ignored.

'Effendim?' she said, crisply, meaning excuse me, sorry to trouble you. 'I've come to change these boots.'

As she said it, Milena thought: GEs aren't part of the Consensus. This person does not work here. It's not her job to find me boots.

The GE lurched around to look at her. 'You,' she said, 'are a ponce.'

The consonant sounds were incised with a laboured precision. Milena was mortified into silence.

I know who this is, thought Milena.

She had heard of the Bear who Loves Opera. GEs were wealthy. This one was wealthy enough to buy a ticket for the first night of each production. She sat in the same seat each time, and left without talking to anyone. Milena never went to the opera herself. Though she did not admit it, Milena did not respond deeply to music. She had never seen the Bear who Loves. It was rather like meeting a legend. Milena watched as the GE began to empty the drawers of her desk, shaking out the contents over the floor. The GE found something.

'Bastard,' the GE murmured.

Milena was unaccustomed to harsh language. She herself might have committed an error of social judgement, but enough was enough.

'Are you talking to me?' Milena demanded.

'Oh, no,' said the GE in blank surprise. 'I was talking to this empty whisky bottle.'

The GE held up the bottle for Milena to see, and then tossed it aside. It clinked against glass as it shattered. Somewhere in the darkness, there was a mound of broken whisky bottles.

'Did you know?' said the GE. 'This used to be a distillery warehouse? I've made *the* most exciting discoveries.'

She was tugging at a drawer that was stuck. It suddenly came free, sowing its contents about the floor like seed – pens, earrings, more wafers, used handkerchiefs, spools of thread, a shower of loose and rusty needles, and a Georgian silver ear-pick.

Lodged in one corner of the drawer was a full bottle. The GE held it up. 'God,' she said, 'is a distiller.' She grinned, and her teeth were black and green rotting stumps.

Where *did* they dig her up? thought Milena.

The Bear was covered in dandruff. Silver flakes of it clung to the tips of her fur all over her body, and she was panting like a dog. A long pink tongue hung out of her mouth, curled and quivering, to cool. She took a great swig of alcohol. 'Gaaah!' she exclaimed, as if breathing fire, and wiped her mouth on her arm.

Milena felt a sudden wrench of amusement. She had a vision of the GE leading a troglodyte existence in this nest of paper and music.

'Do you *live* here?' Milena asked.

'It would be better if I did,' said the GE. Her fur dangled into her eyes, making her blink continually. 'This is where I hide instead.' She hugged the bottle. 'Since you don't like poisoning yourself, perhaps you'd like to look at this.'

She passed a thick, broad, bound wad of paper from the desk. Milena needed both hands to accept it from her. The paper was

15

beautiful to touch, heavy and creamy, ochre around the edges. On the cover, printed in large Gothic lettering was its title. *Das Lied von der Erde.* Song of the Earth.

Milena had never seen a musical score. They were a waste of paper, and cellulose was needed to feed the yeasts and hybridomas that were the cultures of the Party. She flicked through it and found it disappointing. Yes, yes, the notes were all there.

'I take it,' the Polar Bear said, 'that the reading of music presents you with no difficulties.'

'No,' said Milena, innocently. Who couldn't read music?

The Bear smiled wistfully. 'Of course not,' she whispered. She reached forward. It was alarming how far she could reach. Gently she coaxed the score out of Milena's hands. 'But you haven't *learned* how to read music. If you haven't learned it, it isn't yours.' She took a mouthful of whisky and sloshed it around her teeth like mouthwash. She put the bottle down, and seemed to forget that Milena was there. She turned to the end of the score, all its vast bulk over to one side, threatening to tear the ancient binding in half. The GE spat the whisky onto the floor. Then she began to sing.

She sang the end. '. . . *ewig blauen licht die Fernen* . . .'

She's forgotten I'm here, thought Milena.

'*Ewig . . . Ewig . . .*'

The GE sang better than the electronic device. Her voice was warm and strong, a fine mezzo, clear but weighty as if pushed from behind by something vast. Milena blinked. The GE was singing very well indeed.

There were long periods of silence, when unheard music played. Then *Ewig* again, each time softer than before, the voice throbbing without going harsh. A technique. *Ewig*. Unlike the recording, it was not too loud. The GE stared in silence for some moments and then looked up.

'Oh, sorry,' she said. 'There's a pile of boots over there.' She jerked a thumb over her shoulder. Milena peered helplessly into the darkness.

'Golly,' said the Polar Bear. 'I keep forgetting you people can't see in the dark. Shall I find a pair for you?' Her voice seemed to float, airily.

'That would be very kind,' said Milena. 'Size six. Something less floppy?'

The GE took the pirate boots and shuffled off into the racks. Her feet were bare. The fur on top of them swept across dust and whisky, making streaks on the floor to mark her passage.

Milena didn't know what to think. She felt she had been humbled in some way, and that made her annoyed. She suspected that she deserved it, and that made her worried.

16

The GE was gone for some time. 'Who's been pushing over all the racks?' her small voice wondered out of the darkness.

Milena looked at the phantasmagorical waste on the desk and the floor. Books, more books, papers with pawprints across them, old coins. These were real things, the real things that Milena had never seen. She began to feel an ache of jealousy, an ache of nostalgia. This is history, she thought, let the Vampires see this. She picked up a thick black book and opened up its crinkly pages, and realised that it had not been printed. The lettering, in fantastic sweeps and swirls of black ink, had been written by hand.

Penetrating Wagner's Ring, the lettering said with an excess of eloquent strokes.

'Not a fortunate title,' murmured Milena, a smile creeping sideways across her face.

It was an exposition of the Ring cycle. There were drawings of all the characters, slightly amateurish in execution. Each one was identified, not by name, but by a series of notes. The last page said only 'Conclusion: the Ring cycle is a symphony.' It was written in gold.

'That's not right,' said Milena. It was not what her viruses told her. But the clock in her mind told her the labour-hours it must have taken.

'Bugger,' said a voice, and a rack of dresses collapsed somewhere in the darkness. Milena hurriedly dropped the book. The GE emerged carrying boots.

'Typical of me, somehow, that title,' the GE said.

She's seen me reading her book, Milena thought, and went rigid with embarrassment.

'I console myself,' the GE continued, 'with the thought that there was a book of piano exercises that really did call itself *Fingering for Your Students*. Here are your boots. Try them for size.'

Milena pulled one of them on, feeling awkward. She hopped up and down on one foot and thought she was going to fall over. Her cheeks felt full and flushed.

'Fit?'

'Yes, yes, I think they do,' Milena replied. She really couldn't tell. She pulled the boot off again. The GE belched roughly. 'Excuse me,' she said, covering her mouth.

'You sing very well,' said Milena, surprising herself. Her viruses told her that the Polar Bear sang quite as well as anyone at the Zoo.

'Ah,' said the GE and shrugged. 'I suppose I do, yes.' She blinked. 'Why don't you take this with you.'

She gave Milena the Mahler score, yellow and plump.

'You might as well have these too.' She slapped on a Shostakovich and a Prokofiev. 'Don't tell anyone they're Russian.' Russians were not in favour.

'I can't take them,' said Milena. She didn't want them. The GE stared back at her dolefully.

'Really. I think I'm blocked from taking them.'

She didn't know if that were true. 'I think I'm supposed to feel that they belong to everyone.' She did know that the scores were too valuable to be given away so lightly. Milena held out the scores back towards her. There was a fruity smell of booze and lanolin.

'Ah,' the GE said, and blinked, her eyes distant and unfocused. She took the papers, and held them low and level just over the top of the desk before letting them drop.

'What's your name?' Milena asked.

'My name?' said the Polar Bear, and sniffed and smiled. 'Well, let's see if I remember it. Rolfa.' She grinned 'Woof woof.'

'I'm Milena, Milena Shibush.'

'Milena,' said the GE and bowed. 'Shall I show you the way out?'

'The door is locked,' said Milena.

'Ah! I have the key,' replied Rolfa. 'Here, hold on to my hand so you won't get lost.'

Rolfa's hand was as large as a cat curled up on a carpet and just as warm. It enveloped Milena's hand and most of her forearm. It was ridiculous. Milena's heart was pounding, and when she turned to say goodbye, Milena could only gabble. The words were confused. The Polar Bear just smiled and shut the gate. Milena felt as though she had had some kind of narrow escape.

Walking back alongside the wall of brick, Milena finally saw the windows, high overhead. They had been there all along, but she had never noticed them. Windows in a bridge.

chapter two

A DOG OF A SONG (COMING OUT OF THE SHELL)

People lived in communities called Estates. Estates were based around one economic activity, but each Estate had services of its own: a market and a laundry, plumbers and street cleaners. Amid the vastness of London, Estates helped keep life on a human scale.

Milena lived in the Estate for actors. The dormitory had once been the offices of an oil company, so everyone called it the Shell. It was built around a courtyard, like two vast, sheltering concrete-and-marble arms.

The Shell had its own messenger service. Every morning, every lunchtime, and at six o'clock each evening, Jacob the Postperson called to see if Milena had any messages.

Jacob was a small, finely boned, shiningly gentle black man, and he made Milena feel horrid and mean because he bored her.

'Good morning, Milena,' he would say with a delightful smile and dead exhausted eyes.

'Good morning, Jacob,' Milena would reply.

'And how are you today?'

'Very well, Jacob, thank you.'

'The weather is looking better.'

'Yes, Jacob, I suppose it is.'

'Do you have any messages for me, Milena?'

'No thank you, Jacob.'

'Well enjoy your day, Milena.'

'You too, Jacob.'

His mind had been opened up. He remembered everything, was unable to forget anything. He went from door to door passing messages, reminding people that someone wanted his razor back or that the bus was leaving at three o'clock. He was a way of saving paper. It seemed that he could only talk in an unvarying string of formulae.

'Good evening, Milena.'

'Good evening, Jacob.'

That wide enraptured smile as if he were seeing angels.

'Did you have a good day?'

'Yes, Jacob. And you?'

'Oh, very good, Milena, thank you. Do you have any messages for me?'

When his mind was full, it would blank out completely, in a kind of epileptic fit. To avoid lost information, he was cleared at regular intervals.

The day after Milena had visited the Graveyard, Jacob had a message for her. This was an unusual occurrence. Milena did not receive many messages.

'I have a message for you, Milena. From Ms Patel.'

'Who? Who is Ms Patel, Jacob?'

'She is the lady who is covered in fur.'

Oh. Somehow Milena had not thought of Rolfa as a Ms anything.

'She asks if you would like to have lunch with her this afternoon. One o'clock by the front steps of the National. Should I tell her that is all right?'

Milena couldn't think of anything worse. The first meeting had left her disturbed, irritated. Why did Rolfa want to have lunch with her? Milena considered saying that she was busy.

But that would be beneath her high standards.

'Tell Ms Patel,' said Milena, 'that one o'clock will be fine.'

Milena found herself considering what to wear. It was summer and the sky was bright. She would need to shelter from the sun if her complexion was to be preserved. She had two pairs of trousers, one white, one black. She decided to wear the white, with a long-sleeved, high-neck blouse. She also took her gloves and parasol.

Rolfa's eyes narrowed when she saw her. 'You're not taking that thing, are you?' she said, nodding towards the parasol.

Milena was rather proud of her parasol. It was made of canvas and had thick, brightly coloured stripes and was not at all frilly or mimsy.

'Of course I'm taking it. It's part of my job.'

'Bloody hell,' murmured Rolfa. 'Well, there's nothing for it. Come on.' She turned and began to lumber off in the direction of Waterloo Bridge. She was wearing nothing but blue running shorts and a pair of very dirty white cloth shoes. One of them had a loose sole. It flapped.

Milena stood her ground. 'Where are we going?' she asked.

Ponderously, the GE turned around. 'Flitting off to see some of my chums,' she explained. 'We are going to a palace of amusement.'

Milena felt an eddy of misgiving. 'Where?'

'Across the river. It's a pub. Do you drink beer?'

'No,' replied Milena.

'Oh, that's a shame. Perhaps they'll make you some tea.' Rolfa turned and began to shuffle on ahead. Milena considered simply staying where she was. No, she thought suddenly, I'm not going to let her think I'm afraid of anything. So she followed.

It was a bit like trying to keep up with a brontosaurus. Rolfa's arms hung down by her sides, and her shoulders were hunched, and each shuffling step seemed both small and slow, but the distance covered was deceptively great. Milena sheltered from the sun and found she had nothing to say. Next time she asks, Milena promised herself, I will be busy.

They made their way through the ruins of Fleet Street. It was now an Estate for boatbuilders, with its own market.

Tykes with tough, demanding faces pushed burned cobs of corn at them, or cupfuls of roast chestnuts. 'Miss! Miss! Just take one whiff for luck, Miss!' Their older brothers and sisters baked straggly chicken in thick lengths of blackened bamboo, which they broke open for customers with chunks of rubble. Whole families lived under the stalls, mothers nursing or knitting. Little boys sat on street corners, turning the wheels of sewing machines, repairing pyjamas or underwear. Their baby sisters tugged at Milena's sleeve, and she walked past them.

People seemed to find the two of them, Milena and Rolfa, funny. The way Milena walked, as if on slippery ice, her parasol and her gloves, all betrayed her fears and ambition. They made her absurd. Milena heard the children giggle. Life in the Child Garden had taught Milena to hear laughter as the sound of other people's cruelty. Laughter made her fight.

Milena went cold and awkward. Her parasol caught on an awning and showered dust over a stall. The stall sold old plumbing and dusty glassware, the very dog-ends of history.

The stallowner laughed gracefully, hand over her heart. She meant that her things were so old that dust could not hurt them. To Milena, the laughter was a mystery, and she walked into the knobbed point of her parasol. There was more laughter.

Laughter followed them as they walked westwards to St Paul's Cathedral, rising like a great domed egg. Then they turned north and walked past the Barbican, towards the Palace of Amusement.

The Palace of Amusement was a pub in the Golden Lane Estate. Milena's nervousness increased. The Golden Lane Estate was for the Pit's sewage workers.

The pub was called the Spread-Eagle, and the sign over it showed a man falling on his face. Milena had to step over drunks snoring on the broken pavement outside it. Even semi-consciously, they picked at the little crabs that patrolled their hairy chests. The sun had burned them the colour of bruises.

Inside, the Spread-Eagle was dark and cramped and the floor was made of bare, cracked concrete. It was varnished with spit and beer and dogturd from the street. It was full of skinny, naked men glossy with sweat. The whole place smelled of armpits.

It's like something out of Dante's *Inferno*, thought Milena.

'Quite jolly once you're sitting down,' said Rolfa. 'There we are. Oyez! Lucy!' Rolfa shouted and made semaphore-sized signals with her arm.

There was an ugly squawk from the corner and someone jumped up and had to be restrained. Milena couldn't quite see the people. They sat round a table in front of the glare from a window. They were lost in the light, but there was something horrible about them. Milena's mind blotted them out and she looked away.

'I shall wrestle with the bar staff,' said Rolfa. 'You go make yourself comfortable over there.'

You're not leaving me! thought Milena in panic. Rolfa gave her a gentle push. 'Go on,' she said.

In a desperate fashion, Milena made her way through the sewage workers towards the shelter of the table. Disease, disease, disease, disease, her mind was ringing in terror. She clamped a gloved hand over her mouth, her nose was pointed at the ceiling, she was trying not to breathe. She could feel how slippery the arms and legs were around her. She was anointed with sweat. A man near the bar roared, his mouth full of cheese, and he picked up a jug of beer and poured it over his own head. Milena caught only a light cool spray from it. The drops clattered onto the floor like applause. She found the table, gripped the edges of a chair, and sat.

'Hello, love,' said a warm voice next to her ear.

Milena turned to see a terrible head, framed in unnaturally orange curls. The lips were covered with crumbled red cosmetic, there were only a few teeth in the mouth, and the face had gone soft, like over-ripe fruit. It was covered in lines and cracks.

'My name's Lucy, but my friends call me Loose. Ha-ha-ha!' the voice barked.

Milena looked about her. A hunched and beaky man leaned around Lucy to look at her, black freckles over his muscular arms. His eyes were a watery blue and his face had collapsed into its own hollows and was veiled by a network of lines like a cobweb.

Milena felt her heart catch. They were old. These people were old. This was what age looked like.

'Meow,' said the old man.

'You mustn't mind Old Tone,' said Lucy. 'He hasn't been the same since the war. Have you, love?'

War? What war? Milena wondered. Lucy wore a beige jacket that covered her arms. It was splattered in front and grimy around the cuffs. Her fingers were blackened. Across the table sat an identical couple in identical grubby grey suits, their arms linked. Both of them were completely bald. They looked like leaking balloons. One of them leaned forward and spoke to Milena in a low, sensible, confiding voice. She could not understand a single word.

'OO er oi af ger whuh oi fough veh fink,' he said with a concluding nod. He had a tiny, very black moustache painted onto his upper lip.

'That makes sense,' said Milena. He was speaking with the accent of a hundred years before.

They were Tumours.

Many diseases had cured cancer. One of them sealed the proto-oncogenes in Candy. Others produced proteins that coaxed cancerous cells into maturity and stopped them dividing.

But some of the cancers were new and viral and quick. The cures did not stop infected cells producing new copies of the cancer virus, and the virus spread with the flow of blood. A curious balance was struck in the bodies of some of the people who already had cancer. The cancer virus infected the body cell by cell in an orderly fashion. The cancers differentiated. They matured and ceased to proliferate in wild shapes.

What was left was a systematised tumour in the form of a healthy human being, with its memories, its feelings. As long as it was fed and avoided accidents, it would live. It was immortal.

The Tumours looked at Milena with friendly expectation.

'Do . . . do . . . Have you come far?' she asked the orange head.

'In my time, love, in my time,' Lucy chuckled darkly and gave a hearty wink.

'And where do you live?' Milena was wondering if the old creature had fleas. She wondered how far they could jump.

'In the laundry,' Lucy replied. 'The room where they dry the clothes. You know . . .' She made a circular motion with a crooked finger that was shiny and blue-grey. 'I just slip in there of a night. Lovely and warm it is.'

She lived in the Estate laundry. Milena was appalled. She wondered what it meant for the supposedly clean sheets.

'Don't they give you a place to live?'

'Oh. I suppose they would. Whoever *they* are these days. I wouldn't be knowing, would I?'

She's crazy, Milena thought, addled with age. No one could help her.

Lucy was bored, and so she became incensed on Milena's behalf. 'Oooh, that Rolfa. Honestly, you'd wait all week for a slup out of her. Here.' The old creature shoved a mug of beer towards Milena. 'Go on, have a lick on me.'

Milena gave her head a little shake. 'Oh no,' she said. The mug had lipstick all around it.

'Go on, love, I don't mind,' said Lucy. She patted the top of Milena's clenched fist. Milena thought she was going to be sick. She began to wonder if she could make the door in time.

Then very suddenly, Rolfa was looming over them, streaming beer, lowering the mugs onto the table in front of Milena. Lucy laughed and held out her arms.

'I wanted tea,' said Milena.

'Mwom mwom mwom,' said Lucy, making motions with her mouth, wanting to be kissed. She looked like a goldfish. Rolfa leaned over and hugged her, and sat next to old Tone, who meowed like a cat. Rolfa barked like a dog, and put him in a headlock under her arm. The old man made gleeful squeaking noises and stamped his foot in merriment. The beer smelled of other people's kidneys.

The leaking balloon leaned forward. 'Ghoul,' he said. 'Ear. Whuh yer wan, ay? Ay?'

I want, thought Milena, to go home.

The old orange head slapped the table and made Milena jump. 'Listen. Listen,' she demanded. 'Rolfa. Time for a song.' There was a soft groan of assent.

'It's your turn,' said Rolfa. 'I believe you owe me a pint as well.'

'Oh all right then,' said Lucy. 'But I warn you, you'll get the full whack.'

Then she began to climb onto the table. Milena couldn't think at first what she was trying to do. The old woman simply bent over the table top and worked her legs back and forth, her old crooked hands trying to hold. She finally succeeded in getting one knee onto the table and then clung to it desperately, as if to the wreckage of a ship.

'Give her a hand!' roared Old Tone, suddenly furious. Milena shrank back from his voice, shrank back from touching the old woman. Rolfa pushed the old woman's skinny behind.

'Whoo-hooo! Ooops!' cried Lucy. Old Tone helped her to her feet. As she stood, Milena realized that she had smelly knees. How, wondered Milena, do you get smelly knees?

Someone passed Rolfa a squeeze box. A few testing notes announced that a song would begin, and the pub fell quiet, and the skinny purple men turned in anticipation.

An old, worn, squeaky melody began, a homely tune, and the men chuckled in recognition. The old woman gave them a wink and a toothless cackle and began to raise her skirts teasingly over slightly scaly thighs. Oh *don't*, winced Milena. Then Lucy began to sing, in a wheedling, bird-like voice.

'*It's a Dog of a Song*,' she began, her voice straining.

'Just a Dog of a Song
Ambling gently along'

She mimed an amble with her knees. Her fingers, all lumps and shiny patches, tried to trace sprightly patterns through the air. Her old wrinkled face pursed its lips and opened its eyes wide in a caricature of youthful naughtiness.

'With no ill feelings, no ill will.
Just a Dog of a Song' – the voice rose and quavered.
'But it doesn't know how to end
And it's so hard
When you lose a friend' – for just a note the voice held the clear tone it must once have had.
'Just a Dog of a Song
But...'

Her head did a funny sideways jump, as if something mechanical had caught in her neck.

'We all sing along. But...'

Jump.

'We all sing along. But...'

She did it over and over like a wind-up doll gone wrong. The rest of the song consisted of only that for over three minutes. The men joined in. Part of the fun was trying to make her stop. The men howled like coyotes, they shouted at her, they pounded tables with their mugs. Did they like it? Why were they smiling?

Finally Lucy stopped, and Rolfa took her hand and held it up, and there were derisive cheers. 'No more. No more.'

'Where's my pint? Where's my pint?' Lucy challenged and pretended to make a fist.

Rolfa stood back and lifted up her hands and clapped lightly. But somehow, in her mouth, by sucking air through spittle, Rolfa was able to reproduce, exactly, the sound of massed applause. It rose and fell in waves. Milena could almost hear the cheering.

Later, walking back, Milena suddenly understood what the song meant.

Lucy had been imitating a broken record played on a wind-up gramophone. It must have been a shock when the tinny horns replaced the smoothly sliding tapes.

'They were alive before the Blackout,' Milena said.

'Yup,' said Rolfa.

They were the incandescent people of the electronic age. That was what had become of them. They had seen cities spangled with light, they had laughed in unison, millions all at once watching the same entertainments all together in an electronic net. They had had to learn how to sing songs and play squeeze boxes during the Blackout and they were now – how old? At least 120, maybe 140, years old.

'*But it doesn't know how to end, and it's so hard when you lose a friend . . .*'

'They were singing about themselves,' Milena murmured.

'Yup,' said Rolfa, her back towards her. Milena noticed that she was abrupt and walking ahead of her.

'We'll go again,' said Milena, to make amends.

'If they'll have you,' said Rolfa. 'Tuh!' The chuckle, her chuckle that always died and became a shudder. 'You looked most of the time like you'd swallowed your bloody parasol.'

That's when Milena remembered that she'd left it behind.

'Yup,' she said, looking away from the river. She had begun, without realising it, to imitate Rolfa.

chapter three

LOVE SICKNESS (HOLDING A GHOST)

Love's Labour's Lost had grown so listless that the director had actually called for a rehearsal that afternoon. Actors did not normally need to rehearse; the viruses told them what to do.

The practice rooms were normally reserved for musicians, and were too small for a full cast. Summer sun streamed in through the windows. It was hot and airless.

'Me, an't shall please you,' said Milena in her own fiercely exact voice. 'I am Anthony Dull.'

'No, no, no!' wailed the director. His only job was to recreate the great production that the viruses remembered. 'Milena, you know how that line is supposed to sound.'

'Yes, thought Milena, flat, stupid, *dull*. She had no interest in it. She felt restless and worried and she did not know why. She did know that she wanted to talk to Rolfa, as if there were some unfinished business between them.

So in the late summer evening, still dressed as Constable Dull, she went to Rolfa's chamber. A new aisle had been cleared through the racks. It was easier for her to find her way. As Milena walked through the archways of brick, she heard Rolfa begin to sing, alone in the dark.

She'll stop in a moment, thought Milena. Rolfa didn't. The song rose and fell wordlessly. It was embarrassing. How could she go up to Rolfa and say, hello, do you always sing to yourself in the dark?

Milena was about to creep away, when the music snagged her attention. A lowering note seemed to seize something in her chest and drag it down. Milena felt a great weight of something like sadness.

But it wasn't sadness. It was as if someone were walking deliberately, sombre perhaps, but with high purpose. It had the sound of noble music.

What was it? Milena rifled through her viruses, but there was no answer. It wasn't Wagner or Puccini. What the hell could it be? Milena sat down between the racks.

Milena's viruses were told to keep track of the themes. They wove a structure in her head. The music kept unfolding out of itself, like a flower blooming. Then there was a slight catch, not in Rolfa's voice, but in the notes, a slight wavering of uncertainty.

Rolfa stopped. She sang the passage in a new form. Yes! said the viruses. They showed Milena how the three new bars referred to the first notes she had heard.

By all the stars, Milena's mind seemed to whisper. This is Rolfa's. This is Rolfa's music. She's imagining it, here in the dark. Rolfa began to sing again, from the beginning. Rolfa can do this? This wasn't bathtub singing or a drunken wallow. I've got her wrong, thought Milena. This is someone I don't know. Why is she singing here? Why don't people know about her?

Milena tried to remember the music. She told her viruses to remember, but even they got tangled up. The viruses were not used to listening to new music. New music was too alive, it wouldn't sit still, the themes got tangled up like snakes. Very suddenly, almost with a perceptible click, the viruses gave up.

Milena was not used to listening to unfamiliar music either. It made her feel strange, as if she were in a dream where everything is scrambled but weighted with meaning. Rolfa's voice suddenly rose to peaks, like a mountain, and Milena felt her eyes bulge. She felt tears start in her eyes. It was as if some great winged thing had taken to the air, rising out of a human body, transcending it. Milena saw it fly.

Rolfa sang for a half hour. The music was a single piece from beginning to end. Toward the end, it faltered. Very suddenly, Rolfa broke off. 'No. No,' Milena heard Rolfa say. There was a cough and a sniff, and a small crash.

'Oh bugger,' said the light, rasping voice. Milena smiled fondly, with a kind of ache for her. By now it was dark, and no light came through the little window. Milena heard a shuffling come towards her. In the darkness a wisp of fur brushed her, the very tips of it against her cheek, and Milena froze. She waited some minutes more in the dark.

'Bloody hell,' she murmured. Then she stood up and slipped out of the Graveyard, arch by arch.

Milena went to the room of her friend Cilla. Like Milena, Cilla lived in the Shell, in another wing. Milena knocked on her door. Cilla was wearing a pinny and was frying sausages on a single-ring cooker.

'Oh, 'lo,' said Cilla, surprised to see Milena at all, let alone dressed as a Tudor constable. 'I thought you hated that costume.'

'I do,' said Milena and stepped briskly into Cilla's tiny room. Her sword clanked. 'Cilla, do you have any paper?'

'What?' said Cilla, with an unsteady chuckle. 'Uh. No. What makes you think I've got paper?'

'I don't know. You're in *The Mikado*.'

'*Madam Butterfly*. Same country, different opera.'

'Don't they give you paper for notes or anything? I mean, being an Animal and all.'

'Milena, are you all right? We use the viruses for notes, like anybody else.'

'Can you get paper? Do you have any access to paper?' Milena suddenly felt the hopelessness of it. 'I need some paper.'

'What do you need it for?' Cilla asked, quietly.

'I've got to write some music down!' Milena's hands made a fist.

'Oh,' said Cilla, feeling absolved now of the need to be sympathetic. She went back to her sausages. 'Becoming a composer now, are we?'

'No, no,' said Milena, giving her head a distracted shake. She was trying to keep Rolfa's music going in her head. 'It's someone else's.'

Cilla seemed to find this unexpected. 'Listen. I'm sure whoever it is can go to Supplies and explain, if the viruses can't cope. There's going to be a lot more paper soon, they say. They've got the new beaver bugs.'

Milena shook her head. 'It's a GE,' she said.

Cilla went still. 'Really?'

'I think,' said Milena, 'that she's the Bear who goes to all the first nights. I just heard her sing. She sings beautifully. And it was new music.'

Cilla took her arm and made her sit down on the bed. 'U-nique,' she said, avaricious for news of other people's doings.

'She's rich, she's got all the paper she needs. But I don't think she wants it written down. She just sings it, in the dark.' Milena found that she was really quite disturbed. 'It's beautiful. I don't understand. She just sings it with no one to hear. Why doesn't she want anyone to hear it?'

'You want some sausages?' Cilla asked in a soft voice. 'I can't eat them all. I was out in the sun. You want to stay?'

Milena nodded. As the sausages sizzled and filled the room with meaty smells, Milena tried to sing snatches of the music. In her own thin voice they sounded aimless and colourless.

'How did you meet her?' Cilla asked, serving the food.

Milena told her the story of how they had met in the Graveyard. 'She says it's where she hides.'

'We ought to keep that a secret then,' said Cilla. She passed Milena a plate of sausages. They would have to eat with the plates on their laps, sitting on the bed. Cilla did not own a table or chairs. With a snap of the wrist, Cilla held out a twisted, melted piece of resin that had once been a fork.

'I think this one's yours,' Cilla said with a rueful smile.

Milena didn't notice. She kept talking about Rolfa. As she ate,

29

Milena told Cilla about the Spread-Eagle, and the people in it. Cilla stirred the sausages round and round on her plate and said, 'Go on, go on.'

Milena talked about the dandruff and the whisky and the cloth shoes and about the voice. Most of all, she talked about the music. As she left, Cilla took her arm, as if she needed support, to help her to the door.

Milena stumbled scowling downstairs to her own bed. Scowling, she slowly undressed. It was as if she had suddenly found herself in a different world. She blew out the candle, and squeezed it between her wetted fingers to hear it hiss. She felt the sausages repeat, and she settled down under her one counterpane.

She could hear Rolfa sing. She had a sudden vision of her as Brunnhilde, winged helmet and spear, with fur sprouting out from the edges of the breastplate. Half-asleep, she grinned. Dreamily, she imagined settling down amid the fur, brushing aside the dandruff. It would be soft and warm, and she would stroke it. She imagined Rolfa's head in her lap.

Marx-and-Lenin! she thought and sat upright in bed.

I am sexually attracted to her!

Milena had no shorter form of words. Milena lusted after the huge, baggy body. She wanted to do very specific things with it.

No, no, I can't, Milena thought, and tried to talk herself out of it. She's got green, rotting stumps for teeth, Milena reminded herself. There was no answering revulsion. The pull was too strong.

She's huge and hairy. Yes, replied some wicked part of Milena's mind. Don't I know?

She's got dandruff!

All over, came the reply. Tee-hee. The whole thing was one great hoot.

She probably has bad breath and is full to the brim with viruses.

For heaven's sake, you can't be in love with a Polar Bear! They hibernate. They moult. Their whole biology is different!

Then a thought came to Milena. The thought was so transfiguring, that it actually knocked her out of bed. She kicked involuntarily, and her legs got caught up in the counterpane, and she slid off the edge of the mattress face down onto the floor. She gave a kind of convulsive wrench and turned to sit up surrounded by fallen pillows.

The thought was this: Rolfa was immune to the viruses. All of the Bears were. Their body temperatures were too high. That was why none of Rolfa's knowledge came from viruses, why she had to learn things afresh. If Rolfa suffered from Bad Grammar, then like Milena she might not have been cured.

30

Suddenly Milena was sure in her gut that this was so. She simply knew it. From the way Rolfa walked, from the way she drank, from her air of displacement, from her wariness of hurt, from her strange combination of strength and weakness – from many things that could never be put into words, Milena knew that Rolfa was like her. Milena had finally found a woman.

Oh Marx, oh Lenin, oh dear. Milena's belly felt like a corset that had just been unlaced. Everything was loose and wobbly and undone. Her hands shook, her knees were weak. She stood up and walked around her room. She barked her shins on the corner of the bed, and bit a fingernail, tearing it off down to the quick, and finally had to go for a walk.

And her dreams took wing.

They would live together, Rolfa and her, and Rolfa would write great music, she would be a genius. Mozart, Beethoven, Liszt, they were virtuosos, why not a virtuoso of the voice? And Milena would brush her hair, all of it, and put it up in curls, all of it, for special occasions, hold her at night, cure the dandruff. They would stay together, they would have each other, and Rolfa would bloom. Milena suddenly felt she understood her, understood why she shuffled, hang-dog, why she drank, why she looked defeated. No one would think a Bear could sing, no one would ever listen. People thought of GEs as dogs, they hated them, feared them. Milena found that she shook with the injustice of it. She wanted to go to her. She would have walked to the GE house if she had known where it was. The sense of Rolfa all around her was so strong that she knew, she knew how her body would feel, the bulk and heat and softness of it. She knew how her mouth would taste. Her own heart was singing.

She walked for hours in a soft warm drizzle in dark streets that did not need policing. She walked until she was exhausted, her feet crossing in front of each other with each step, walked until the dull morning began to rise. And still she didn't feel any better, and still she couldn't rest.

She went to the railway arches and collapsed onto the pavement, and waited for Rolfa. The sun came up under an edge of retreating cloud and she felt it on her pale face. She didn't care. She saw Rolfa approaching.

Milena stood up, and brushed her clothes and ran her fingers through her short hair, to get rid of the tangles. She waited. Rolfa came up to her.

The fear returned. Milena didn't know she was afraid. All she knew was that she could not be herself. She would not be able to speak.

'What are you doing here?' Rolfa asked, blinking.

31

'Oh. Oh,' said Milena and flung her arms awkwardly about herself.
'You *are* in a state. What have you been doing?'

'Oh. I just went out. You're a bad influence on me.'

Milena's eyes were sparkling, almost swollen with unspoken message.

'I don't think anyone could have a bad influence on you,' said Rolfa. 'You're immune to it.'

'Are we having lunch today?' Milena's voice was wan and hopeful.

Rolfa stood very still, her fur stirring in the light morning wind. 'If you like, Little One,' she said and gave Milena's head, her hair a very quick stroke, a kind of pat. Then she walked on, down the tunnel.

Milena followed her, thrilled. She's got a pet name for me! She toddled, feeling small and tender.

'Another busy day,' said Rolfa sourly, as she swung open the big yellow doors that never needed to be locked.

As they walked between the racks in the dark, the silence between them became uneasy. Milena had been wanting a flood of revelation, had reached a peak of joy. Now nothing happened. Rolfa, Rolfa, I know you are, you must be. Rolfa, say something about it. Rolfa, give me a sign. But Rolfa had gone dark, silent, like the racks.

Rolfa coughed and shuffled and turned on her alcohol light and seemed to ignore Milena, and simply stared down at her desk, the suddenly shaggy and intolerable mess of it.

'Tuh,' said Rolfa, the shudder-chuckle. She sat down, slumped at the desk and Milena's heart ached for her. Rolfa picked up a score and held it up, looking at it, questioning, as if no longer certain of its worth. Milena made sure that it was printed, not handwritten, not a manuscript.

'Do you ever write music yourself?' Milena asked.

Rolfa sniffed and shrugged.

'I'd like to see some, if you do,' Milena said.

'Oh! I get a few snatches descend on me from time to time,' said Rolfa. She turned and tried to smile. 'But I don't write anything down.' She shook her head and kept on shaking it.

She must simply remember it, thought Milena. But there could be an accident, anything could happen.

Memory. A full score in memory. Milena had another transfiguring idea.

She jumped up. 'I've got to go,' she said. 'I've got to go now.' She did a worried little dance. 'I don't want to, I just have to.'

'Toilet's over there,' said Rolfa and pointed.

'No, no you don't understand. I'll be back. Lunchtime. On the steps. Don't forget?'

Rolfa gave her head a shake, meaning no, she wouldn't forget and a kind of wondering, pale smile was coaxed out of her.

And Milena ran. She had about ten minutes. She ran all the way back to the Shell, up the flights of stairs. She heard a door opening on the landing below her, and spun around, and stumbled back down the steps, legs akimbo. And there he was.

'Jacob!' she gasped.

'Good morning, Milena. And how are you today?'

'Fine! Fine. I'm great! Jacob! Can you remember music?'

'Do you mean written music, Milena? Or do you mean the actual sound?'

'Both. Both.'

'Yes, if it is part of a message. Yes. I can remember.' He nodded and smiled with beautiful ivory-coloured teeth.

Milena was still panting, a queasy trail of sweat on her forehead. 'Fine. Great. Can you come somewhere with me at six this evening?'

Jacob's face clouded over. 'Oh. I'm sorry, Milena. I don't think I can do that. I must run my other messages then. I must go to everyone in the building, and then deliver messages for them. I'm very sorry, Milena.'

'What if I helped?'

Jacob looked blank.

'What if you took one half of the floors and I took the other? You're supposed to come about five, right? So we'll both start about four thirty, run back and forth until six and then go on. Agreed? Agreed? It's very important, Jacob.'

He beamed. 'All right, Milena. I will help you. That will be very good.'

Milena gave a little snarl of delight, and kissed him on his cheek. 'That's great.' And suddenly she was weary.

'Do you have any messages for me, Milena?'

'Yes. One for Ms Patel. Tell her I'm too tired. I just won't be there for lunch.'

Tell her I love her?

'Tell her I'm not as immune as she thinks.'

And Jacob, for some reason, winked.

That afternoon, Milena ran from room to room on seven floors of the Shell. She had never known there were so many people living there. Faces she had only glimpsed suddenly became alive for her. She knew what the insides of their rooms looked like, she knew whether or not they made their beds, she could smell what they were cooking. They did not want to give her messages.

'Um. I'll wait for Jacob in the morning,' many of them said.

'I'm an actress. I've got good memory viruses too.'

They might give their heads the slightest of angry shakes. They were angry with Jacob for deserting them, leaving them to this stranger. Milena was embarrassed. She was embarrassed by all this weight of life that was going on without her. The rooms were often full of people lounging together on beds, drinking, talking, playing chess on little resin boards.

Milena went to Cilla's room and it was full of the Vampires, twenty of them, thirty of them, packed in, talking, agreeing, disagreeing, laughing.

'What are you doing?' Cilla asked, rising to her feet.

'I'm helping Jacob out.'

And Milena explained, breathless. Milena the Postperson, someone called her, smiling. How does he know my name? Milena thought. I don't know his.

'Anybody got any messages?' she asked. 'I'll take them.' She knew then why Jacob always asked. It was nice to be needed.

In the evening she and Jacob hid behind the costumes as Rolfa sang.

'Can you remember? Can you remember it?' she asked him, whispering, desperate.

Jacob smiled and nodded, and put a finger to his lips.

It became routine, for a time.

Milena and Rolfa would have lunch together every day. Sometimes they ate in the Zoo cafe. Rolfa would always cringe just before going in. She had to duck to get through the doors, but it was more than that. She did not belong. She looked huge on the narrow benches, ridiculous bunched up under the tiny tables, her knees pressing up under them, dragging them with her when she stood up. Her fur hung into the soup, the cups were too small for her to drink from. Watching Rolfa eat was a fascinating spectacle. For Milena, it was like being in the mead hall with Beowulf. Rolfa's appetite and manners were of a previous historical era. She munched and belched and slurped and splattered, looking rather forlorn and helpless, as if there was nothing she could do about it. She would have two or three helpings of chips, which she shovelled into her mouth with thick and greasy fingers. She had to stick her long pink tongue down into cups and lap and lick to get anything out of them. She had to lap to drink anything – her tongue got in the way if she tried to sip like a human being. She leant over her soup bowl like a lion over a stream, glancing furtively about her.

Rolfa ate in an agony of embarrassment. Quiet, folded in on herself, a tight false smile and staring, darting eyes. She licked her plates to get the gravy hoping no one would notice. People stared. They chuckled in disbelief when she came back from the buffet with a third helping of stew or lasagne. The place was steamy, with sunlight pouring through

34

windows. When she wasn't eating, she had to pant, moisture dripping off her long pink tongue.

'Does she eat the plates as well?' Milena once heard someone behind them murmur.

Milena didn't care. She was in love. She kept trying to smell Rolfa. The scent of Rolfa was pungent and a bit doggy, full of lanolin. Milena would haul it into her nostrils, savouring it along with the aromas of the food. She would ask to sample Rolfa's fish pie.

'Oooh, fish pie! Oh, please,' she would say. She hated fish pie. What she wanted was the taste of Rolfa on the fork.

I can't believe I'm doing this, she thought, sucking on the cutlery as if it were a lollipop.

She found herself wondering if she could lick Rolfa's plate without anyone noticing. She gave herself a very bad fright indeed when she stole from the cafe a spoon that Rolfa had used. She reached for it and something drew tight and stopped her, but the pull of Rolfa was stronger, and she touched it. It was still warm from Rolfa's hand. Something taut like wire seemed to snap with a twang, and Milena picked the spoon up and slipped it into her pocket.

This is ridiculous, she thought. What am I going to do with it? Keep it unwashed by my kitchen sink? That was exactly what she did with it.

Milena would deliberately walk into Rolfa to bury her face in her fur. She kept crowding into Rolfa, to feel the inhuman heat of her, to feel the tickle of the fur. Rolfa was highly charged with static. Milena would sometimes get a jolt of electricity from her. When she came near the little hairs on Milena's arm would stand up.

Rolfa began to get a bit annoyed with being walked into. 'We'll have to get you a bigger pavement,' she said, mystified.

Once Milena elbowed Rolfa into a rank of bicycles. Five or six of them fell over like dominoes in a row, and Rolfa's fur got caught up between a chain and a chain wheel.

'Oh, I'm sorry,' said Milena, and knelt to free her. She held the fur and gripped the calf and it was vast, fleshy and warm like someone's stomach. She fumbled with the chain, which was organically lubricated. Milena's hands, her nose and most of Rolfa's lower leg were smeared with thick moss-green.

'May I enquire, Little One? What are you doing?'

I'm hugging you, thought Milena. *Do something.*

'Little . . . Little One. I'll do it.' Rolfa eased her back, gently.

'Sorry. Sorry,' said Milena and hopped backwards. Oh God, how embarrassing. What *was* she doing? Oh Rolfa, Rolfa, please notice, please say something, please do something. *I can't say it*!

* * *

Rolfa began to take her to the opera. They went to the first night of *Falstaff*. The Vampires showed up in en masse as the original 1890 London audience. The men wore tails and the women wore bustles. Someone played George Bernard Shaw.

Rolfa seemed delighted. All through the opera she rocked with laughter, throwing herself back and forth in her seat. The whole row rolled with her weight. Milena was entranced by the staging and the lights. She loved the rumble of the great old stage as it began to rotate, and an inn was replaced with a house by the river. She was less moved by the music.

As they stood up at the end, Milena asked. 'Why weren't there any arias?'

'Tuh!' shuddered Rolfa. 'Every line in Verdi is an aria!' Milena thought that was hyperbole, simply a way to emphasise how much Rolfa had enjoyed the performance. It did not occur to her that it might be the literal truth.

The Vampires crowded around Cilla. She had played one of the Merry Wives and she had been delicious. She had made the scheming against old John Falstaff seem light and happy. She had worn the old costumes and had made the old stage moves. 'Cilla! Cilla!' said a young man, hopping up and down, forgetting his Vampire role. 'You were as good as the original.'

'You were better,' whispered Milena, as she kissed Cilla on the cheek. Love seemed to spill over everywhere.

Milena and Rolfa walked home along the river, and the alcohol lights were the colour of a low moon in a smoky sky.

'Oh dear,' sighed Rolfa. 'They really shouldn't try to perform music. No one should. They only ever end up performing part of it. Never the whole.'

'But people want to hear it, don't they?'

'More like the musicians want to play it,' said Rolfa. 'They haven't learned that they can't. It's an impossibility. Like trying to tell the whole truth.'

They reached the steps of the Shell. 'Goodnight,' said Rolfa. She began to walk backwards. The river glittered behind her, and with each step, she whispered, 'Good night. Good night. Good night.' Then she put a finger to her lips for silence.

Milena went to bed alone.

The nights were the worst. Milena would be feverish with love, unsettled, as if Rolfa were in the bed next to her, as if the miles that separated them were nothing, as if she could reach out and feel the warmth and the fur. It was like holding a ghost.

Sometimes she would remember the terror.

The viruses! she would think and sit bolt upright. She had forgotten about the viruses!

She would think of her dirty hands that had crammed food into her mouth and had rubbed in her eyes. She would think of the cutlery she had not washed, of how dirty her mouth was, of all the risks, the pointless risks she had taken. She would throw off the counterpane in panic. She would shower, even though the water in the middle of a summer night could be freezing cold. She boiled kettles and scalded her sink. She boiled all her plates and all her melting forks. She put salt in boiling water and let it cool for a moment in the mug, puffing at it. Then she would gargle, feeling the salt wither the inside of her cheeks. She would scrub her hands and suddenly cover her face and weep, from lack of sleep, from being stretched too far.

I will give her up, Milena would think. I won't see her. This is getting silly. And the next day, they would have lunch again.

They took to having picnics, in the garden by the river. They would sit on the grass, and Rolfa would crunch her way through the cooked legs of animals, a huge and filthy napkin tied around her neck. She would look quite jolly then, making cracking sounds and sucking out bone marrow. The Polar Bears had genetically engineered stomachs. They could digest almost anything. Rolfa ate the bones as well. Then she would drink gallon jars of yogurt and water. She didn't say much. Milena caught the scent of her breath and realised why: Rolfa was no longer drinking.

The GE was the most fascinating irresolution of opposites. She was huge and coy at the same time. Like the fat girl in the Child Garden whom everyone bullies, Rolfa moved with a fearful, tip-toe precision that meant she invariably knocked something over. She was boisterous and coarse and delicate and refined, usually within the same sentence. She talked about art. She talked about how Elgar changed keys. How he would play a joke, start in one direction, stop and go back again, start and stop again, and suddenly pull the rug out from under you by doing it backwards with the simplicity of a conjurer. 'He's the funniest ficken composer who ever lived!' she exclaimed, and laughed, exposing rotten teeth and a roiling mass of half-chewed food.

Elgar? Funny? Milena examined her viruses. That was not something they told her.

'Where did you learn all this?' Milena asked.

'Oh. When I was young,' said Rolfa, 'I went into hibernation. I was only about nine or ten years old. It's something we can do if the weather gets too bad and we have to wait it out. But this time there was no real reason for it. The vet said it was stress.'

Rolfa lay down on her side. She began to graze. Her long pink tongue reached out and seized a fistful of grass, tore it out of the ground and lazed it up into her mouth. There was something comfortable in the way she talked and chewed at the same time.

'I just curled up and went to sleep for six months. And all the time I was under, I was thinking about music.'

Rolfa moved her cud to one side of her mouth.

'I could play piano quite well by then, and I just went over and over all the pieces I knew. Picking them apart, putting them back together. Didn't think about anything else. Didn't dream, didn't open my eyes.'

'How did they get you out of it?' Milena asked.

'The vet gave me an injection,' said Rolfa, and smiled with her ruined teeth.

Milena wanted to lie next to her on the grass, in the sun. She wanted to curl up under her arm and go to sleep. But Milena was afraid. All she did was shift closer to her.

'You can remember your childhood,' said Milena, looking down at the expanse of Rolfa's body, wishing she had known Rolfa in childhood, had been part of her life then.

'Can't you remember your childhood?' Rolfa sat up.

Milena shook her head. No, Milena couldn't.

'Something happened. I don't know. I can't remember any of it. Well, I know I was born in Czechoslovakia – I can sometimes remember parts of that very hazily. Everything else is gone.'

'Oh, I shouldn't like that at all!' said Rolfa. 'There are all sorts of things I remember. I'd hate to forget them.'

'Like what?'

'Musk oxen,' said Rolfa. 'Especially the calves. They're like little round balls of fluff on tiny, scurrying black legs. That's when we lived on the tundra, what was left of it. Forests advancing you see, but we managed to save some of them.'

'There's no musk oxen in the Antarctic.'

'No, no indeed, no, we lived in Canada for a while, you see? Papa thought we should go there to make our fortune. North instead of South. Didn't work. He kept trying to save the musk ox. Herd them north, where there was still some tundra. Strange thing to do really. It makes me think my father might not be so bad after all. He taught them how to play football. They're terribly intelligent, you see. They played in teams. I used to play with them. I used to dream that one day I'd turn into a musk ox.' Rolfa's face was soft and her smile was fond. 'Don't you have any childhood memories at all?'

'No. They gave me a lot of viruses when I was ten. Maybe that knocked them all out of me. I don't remember.'

'Ah,' said Rolfa. Something strange seemed to happen to her face. It seemed to melt, and the eyes seemed to pull back, like snails into a shell. 'Ah yes, of course. I keep forgetting. They give you people viruses, don't they.'

She smiled again, and the eyes opened out, with a new expression. She was smiling, and the eyes still seemed fond, and the face still seemed happy, but it was pained too. It was a strange, disturbing mixture, like Rolfa's music. There was something powerful in the eyes, that made Milena draw back. Milena couldn't understand it. She had no experience. She didn't know what it meant. The viruses couldn't help her.

It was routine. Each day, like milk in a pan, about to boil over, Milena would nearly say, 'I love you.'

Or she would reach for Rolfa, to caress her in a way that would leave no doubt, come so near to the point of doing it that she could feel her own arms or the shadow of her arms, move out and hold her.

But she didn't do it.

Gradually a new idea began to seep in, so slowly that Milena never knew when she first had it. This idea was also transfiguring.

Rolfa did not need to be cured. Yes, she was immune to the viruses; her behaviour was her own; and Milena had given her a thousand unmistakable signs, she thought, of how she felt; and Rolfa had not responded. Rolfa did not appear to be interested. The great hulking innocent probably had no idea of what had been happening.

They were not going to be lovers. Milena had been wrong. Rolfa's grammar was undoubtedly strange, but not bad, not bad, no.

When Milena was most alone, in the middle of rehearsals for *Love's Labour's Lost*, she found herself coming to a glum acceptance of that. She sat on the periphery and watched the other actors sleepwalking through their parts.

The young boy with a beard was playing Berowne. He spent the whole of one afternoon glaring. Something had happened to him. Milena knew of it vaguely, something about a girl. That day he did not play the character of Berowne. He played himself, carried away by the words. 'I who have been love's whip,' he said bitterly, spit leaping out of his mouth.

Listening to him, Milena found that she was angry.

'That wimpled, whining, purblind, wayward boy
This Signor Junior, this giant-dwarf, Dan Cupid.'

Milena listened. They were all listening, as the boy-actor stood rigid, glowering. Milena's hands had curled into fists.

'A whitely wanton with a velvet brow,
With two pitch-balls stuck in her face for eyes.'

The hatred in it, the violence in it, made Milena jump. Who was speaking? The boy, Berowne, Shakespeare?

'And so I sigh for her, to watch for her,

To pray for her! Go to, it is a plague.'

'Stop,' said the director. He was thirty-five years old, and there were creases in the flesh around his eyes. He sat very still, looking at the boy-actor. 'You know how that's supposed to sound, Jonz,' he said. He sat a moment longer. 'I give up,' he said, and stood up. 'Say it how you want to, Jonz, if it makes you feel better.'

But it does, thought Milena, it does make me feel better. It's meant to hurt, it's meant to bite, it's meant to mean something to us too. We have to act it.

'All of you,' said the director, looking worn, 'do it how you want to.' Then he turned and walked up the aisle, leaving them.

'Go home, I guess,' shrugged the blandly cheerful fellow who was playing the King. Berowne still glowered.

'Your way was better,' Milena told Berowne. He only nodded.

Outside it was a drab, cloudy English summer afternoon. So fine, she and Rolfa would be friends. Could she accept that? She could accept that. It happens to everyone. Perhaps when she was certain of the friendship, she would tell Rolfa what she had felt just in passing, so that there would be no dishonesty – only friendship and music, until one day Milena would be cured. One day they would remember to Read her, and give her the viruses again. Perhaps she wouldn't be like her father, after all. Perhaps it wouldn't kill her. Why be a pessimist? she thought.

Until then she and Rolfa would be friends. Nothing would have to change. Even their routine, Milena thought could stay the same.

One evening they met for dinner and Rolfa was drunk. She had started to drink again. She arrived drunk, reeking in the middle of the Zoo cafe. She did not duck or cringe. She came up to Milena and prodded her shoulder with a finger the size of a salami sausage.

'Out,' she managed to say. 'Outside.' Under the fringe of fur, her eyes were baleful. She walked backwards towards the door. 'Come on.'

'Rolfa? Rolfa?' Milena heard herself, heard her own voice drained, hopeless, frail, and she hated the sound of it. 'Is there something wrong?'

Rolfa made a kind of twisted, barking yelp. 'Oh no,' she said. 'No, no, no, no.' She made a kind of waving motion with her hand, brushing something away. Very suddenly it became a slapping motion, in the air. She was dangerous.

'Let's . . .' Rolfa paused to belch, '. . . go have a good time.' The smile was a snarl. She spun off, into the night.

I don't like this, thought Milena and followed, full of misgiving.

They went to another horrible pub across the river. *The Comedy Restaurant* said art-nouveau lettering on tiles outside it. There seemed to be no one there who Rolfa knew. She rolled her way like a millstone towards the bar, through the men who stopped laughing as she passed, towering over them, jostling them. The men looked small and hard and weasly. The place was as disordered as anything in Britain ever got. The plaster walls were bulging and cracked and stained in streaks. There were harsh alcohol lamps that stank. Milena looked at Rolfa, at her back. Then she felt one of the weasels pressing up against her. He wore skimpy trunks and a sleeveless body-warmer that smelled of sweat and beer.

'Bow wow,' he said. His forehead glistened with sweat. He's got a virus, Milena thought. But which one?

'You like dogs?' he asked.

'No. I don't like dogs,' said Milena warily, meaning that she did not like him. He had friends all around them, and they were all sweating. Some of them shook with fever.

Milena did not have time to consider what disease it was they had.

There was a flurry, a scattering nearby, and Milena turned to see Rolfa wading towards her, towards them, her shoulders shrugging from side to side, and Milena thought: she's going to hit one of them.

That's what she thought until Rolfa picked up a table. Not a large table, but a small, light one made of bamboo. Mugs rolled off it, beer fell in a gush, men shouted protest, and the table rose up, hit a lamp, and broke it.

Along the very edge of her teeth, Milena seemed to feel something, the thing that made Rolfa rot her own teeth to nothing, and she held up her hands and shouted, 'Rolfa! Stop!'

Rolfa paused, blearily staring.

'Rolfa! Nothing happened.' Rolfa blinked, looked sheepish, defeated, confused.

'Put the table down, Rolfa,' said Milena.

Or you'll kill someone.

'Just put it down. Please? Nothing happened.'

The table was very gently lowered. Rolfa patted it, as if telling it she was sorry.

Milena pushed her way between the men, and took Rolfa's arm and pulled. 'Come on, Rolfa. Come on.' And Rolfa followed, tamely, out into the night again. The barman followed.

'What about the light?' he shouted.

'Don't push!' pleaded Milena, holding up her hands, and something in her voice convinced him.

Rolfa threw off her hand and walked towards the river. Milena called after her. She ran, to catch up, but Rolfa did not turn around or answer. She marched, with long lunging strides. It was dark, there were no lights, and Milena suddenly found she was alone with only

41

just sufficient idea of where she was to find the river again, and the Shell.

Well, she thought forlornly. Well. That's that. Something, she knew, had finished.

At one o'clock the next afternoon, she went to the steps and Rolfa was not there.

At six o'clock, she and Jacob went to the Graveyard and there was only silence. They waited hidden like mice for the singing to begin. The darkness deepened. Finally they edged their way towards the desk, and peeked out between the costumes.

Papers had been torn or crushed into balls. The musical scores had been ripped in half along their bindings and the pages had been scattered. The electronic device was in a corner; its panel was broken open; wafers were all over the floor; their resin tray was cracked and splintered; book covers had no pages in them.

Milena knelt and picked up what was left of the Wagner notebook. She tried to put its crinkly pages back in order and found spit between them. She wiped her cheeks and gathered up the things.

'Jacob,' she said, her voice going thin. 'Help me back with all of this?'

They piled up the musical scores, and the wafers and carried them back like the honoured dead to Milena's room at the Shell. 'Tell her I have them. Tell her she can have them back when she wants them,' Milena said to Jacob.

And she went to bed, wondering at the maze of rooms that was someone else's life. She read the score of *Das Lied von der Erde*.

The last movement told a kind of ghost story. Two old friends meet and one speaks mysteriously of life in the past tense, of finding a resting place. He seems to move on, into eternity, the bright and shining blue. The friend has chosen to leave.

Milena imagined the music. It was not about death. It was about the beauty of the world as it is lived in, and the sadness of having to leave it. It was about the sadness of losing friends, and the necessity of it. Milena remembered Rolfa's voice singing *ewig . . . ewig*. Forever.

The music was hers now. She had learned it. Milena was left at the end hugging the cream paper as if it were skin. She was holding a ghost, an abstraction of what might have been, a possibility.

That night she dreamt of musk ox, running on the tundra. One of them was calling like a seagull.

In the morning, Milena was shaken awake by Jacob.

'Ms Shibush! Ms Shibush! Oh, look what I have for you!' he exclaimed, smiling and excited. Then he whispered, 'from Ms Patel.' He passed her a fold of paper.

An envelope. It was as if something had been sent to her out of a previous century. Milena carefully lifted up the flap and pulled out a thick white card. It was edged in gold. Jacob waiting, smiling.

The card was engraved in beautifully flowing copperplate script.

'Do you feel able to tell me what it says?' Jacob asked her shyly.

'It's an invitation,' said Milena. 'For dinner at eight o'clock tomorrow evening.' She passed him the card. 'With Rolfa's family.'

chapter four

ANTARCTICA (THE INDIGENT GLOVES)

The Bears of London lived together in one street in Kensington. It was a Nash terrace, painted cream, with black wooden doors.

Milena was too short to reach the door knocker. She tried jumping and missed and decided to avoid any further risk to her dignity. She pounded on the door with the heel of her hand.

There were shouts and thumpings and suddenly the door was thrown open by a naked Polar teenager. All her fur the length of her body was in braids. There was a blast of icy air from inside. The girl took one hardened look at Milena and yelled. 'Rolf–a! Your little *friend's* here.' Then she walked away, leaving the door open.

It was bitterly cold inside. All the walls between the houses had been knocked down to make one enormous, barren room that ran the length of the street. A large male GE in a metal mask was squatting over a machine, welding a join. Milena had time to notice that the floor was covered in fur.

'Shut the door!' the Polar girl shouted. There was angry thumping, the girl stalked past Milena and flung the door shut. 'It makes our hair fall out, you little Squidge,' she snarled. 'Rolfa! Slump your fat tush down here!'

The room was full of unopened bamboo packing cases. Polar teenagers lounged on them, watching a screen. It was video! It was showing an old movie! Milena couldn't help but stare in wonder. There was a flash and a mechanical scream, and Milena saw someone torn to pieces before her very eyes. Why on earth, she wondered, have a video and then use it to see something like that?

'What are you staring at?' said another GE, a boy, his voice cracking on the edge of puberty like an egg.

'Nothing,' said Milena.

'She's never seen a video,' said the girl and rolled her eyes. Some of the Bears were grooming each other, brushing their pelts or braiding them. It was their moulting season, too hot to go outside. They were sullen and dangerous with boredom. Milena hugged herself and tried to stand her emotional ground, but she was still feeling sick from having seen a human being rent into stringy chunks. She began to shiver from the cold. That's frost, she saw in dismay, that's frost on the *inside* of the windows.

Rolfa appeared at the top of the staircase. She was trying to wear a dress, and looked like an unsteady column of crumpled satin. She began her descent, clutching the handrail, stumbling, swaying. Her feet kept catching on the inside of her hem, making frantic motions within it like trapped rabbits.

Rolfa, lift the dress *up*, Milena willed, silently.

Rolfa's hair had been brushed back out of her eyes and was held up by two pink resin butterfly clips that looked like lopsided ears. Braving the distance between the staircase and Milena, Rolfa held out something soft and black. It was a fur.

'We usually dine upstairs,' Rolfa said, as if to a stranger.

'Thank you,' said Milena for the fur, and wrapped it around herself, her teeth chattering.

'Follow me,' said Rolfa and began the ascent. She stood once more on the hem of her dress, and had to hold out a hand to catch herself.

'Rolfa,' whispered Milena. 'Up. Hold it up.'

There was a collapse of laughter from the cousins behind them.

There was something majestic about the way Rolfa ignored them. She bent over and lifted up her dress from the bottom, exposing her knees, and climbed the stairs.

There were chandeliers overhead. They blazed with light. There was a chug-chugging noise in the background. A private generator. There were paintings, extravagances of flowers or empty street scenes at dusk. But no people. Thick wires trailed alongside the carpet on the stairs, and from somewhere came the singing of a circular saw. The cold sunk into Milena's bones.

'Want to wash your hands?' Rolfa asked, quickly.

'I think they'd freeze if I did,' replied Milena, watching her breath rise as vapour. I wonder, she thought, if my eyebrows are frosted.

'In here,' said Rolfa. Her voice was higher and softer than usual, very precise but barely audible as if there was no force of breath or personality behind it. Milena was shown into a room that made her gasp.

Capitalism, she said to herself. Capitalism was what she thought she was seeing. It was the only word she had for it.

There was a polished mahogany table. Little rough wooden boots had been nailed to the bottom of each leg to make it tall enough for GEs. There were more real paintings on the walls, another showerburst of light overhead deflected through crystal. There was an enormous covered dish made of silver on the middle of the table. It was twice as long as Milena was tall. There were silver knives, silver forks, silver candlesticks, matching mahogany chairs and, in the corner, a tin rubbish bin. Even in the cold, it stank of fish. Milena thought: what if we're all still working for them?

A door swung open and a Polar female walked in backwards. She wore a billowing orange dress and carried a kind of porcelain cistern in front of her, a vat of food.

'Hiya, Squidge,' she said to Milena. The tone was not unfriendly. She put the cistern on the table and reached into the bodice of her dress. 'You want some mitts?'

'Oh yes please,' said Milena all in a rush.

'Thought you might,' said the GE and rumpled her lip in Rolfa's direction. 'Here you go.' She threw a brown ball of wool at Milena. Fingers trembling, Milena unwound it. They were gloves designed for counting money in Antarctic blizzards. There were no tips to the fingers. They looked utterly indigent, as if they'd been half-eaten by mice.

'This is my sister, Zoe,' said Rolfa.

'You're Milena,' said Zoe. Milena was too cold to answer. Zoe left, shaking her head as if it wasn't Milena's fault that she'd been brought there. As she went out another sister came in.

She was even bigger, and her cheeks were flexed with the effort of keeping down a grin. She looked at Milena and Rolfa, nearly dropped two tubs of food on the table, and ran out. From behind the swinging door, there came a shriek of laughter. It was followed by spurts and whisperings.

'That's Angela,' said Rolfa.

Milena sat down. The table was on a level with her chin. The two sisters re-entered, a matching pair, batting their long black eyelashes at each other over the top of fluttering Japanese fans. They lowered themselves gracefully onto chairs, spreading napkins over their laps. Zoe's hair was wrapped around a hoop to make a glossy, flowing arch around the back of her head, Navajo style, Milena's viruses told her. 'I like your hair,' she said.

'Do you?' beamed Zoe, lowering her fan. She batted her eyelashes. 'Do you like my moustache as well?'

Then Milena saw that her moustache had also been wrapped around hoops, one at each end.

'I used to have the same trouble with mine,' Milena replied, with a flash of instinct.

The eyelashes stopped batting.

'Only,' said Milena with a sigh, 'now I shave mine off.'

There was a click behind Milena and a kind of surly grunt. Milena turned to see a short GE. He was rotund and bristling like a hedgehog, his cheeks puffed out as if enraged. He was punching keys on a small device that made a whizzing sound and printed out a result on paper.

He climbed up onto an especially high chair, tore off a piece of paper, and attached it to his fur with a hair-grip. He was decorated with bits of paper like a Xmas tree.

'We gonna eat?' he asked, and went back to punching keys.

'Yes, of course, Papa,' said Angela, standing up. She lifted off the lid of the giant dish with a kind of malicious flair. It rang.

They were going to eat a seal, a whole roast seal. Its eyes had gone white and it was surrounded by a moat of amber fat.

Rolfa's father reached forward and began to thumb out one of its eyes.

'Papa!' exclaimed Angela. 'Please, remember our guest.'

'You want an eye, Squidge?' the father asked Milena.

'Yes please,' said Milena, crisply. He passed it to her on a plate. It rolled. Her eyes stonily on Angela, Milena popped it into her mouth. It's a grape, she told herself, it's just a grape. It crunched as she chewed it.

'Of course, we're on our best behaviour because of you, Ms Smash-puss,' said Angela, as she began to carve the seal. 'Usually we tear the hot carcass to pieces with our bare paws.' With deft aplomb, she lowered a section of seal fillet onto Milena's plate without letting fall a drop of grease.

'Some wine, Ms Shambosh? We make it ourselves out of leftovers. I do hope you like it.'

'Oh don't mind me,' said Milena. 'I'll drink anything.'

'If you're friends with Rolfa,' said Zoe, sounding serious, 'you probably have to.'

Angela went on serving. '*Ma chere*,' she said to her sister. 'You have let slip your nap-kin.' She sliced the word in half, like an orange, as a joke. They were making fun, of Rolfa, of Squidges, of the way they thought Squidges thought of them. You are merry gals, Milena thought. But that is no reason to let you get away with anything.

'Do try not to blow your nose on it this time, *ma petite*. Do you know, Ms Fishfuss, the last time she let slip her nap-kin, she picked it up and blew her nose on it, and it turned out to be the hem of my dress.'

'Well,' said Milena, sipping the wine. 'Better than wiping her arse on it.'

'You girls want to carry on like that, you can leave the table,' said the father.

The serious business of eating commenced. It was noisy and prolonged. Handfuls of boiled seaweed were shovelled onto plates and into mouths. There was a side salad of whole raw mackerel. Rolfa's father held one by the tail and lowered it into his mouth, steadily crunching. Seal paws were another great delicacy.

'*Don't* eat the toenails, Zoe,' said Angela. 'What will Ms Shitbush think of us?'

'You seem to be having some trouble with my name,' said Milena, giving up trying to cut her seal. She had to hold her hands up almost over her head to reach it. 'My last name is Shibush. My family are from Eastern Europe, but the name itself is Lebanese. I believe your name is originally Asian, too, isn't it.'

A silence as icy as the room descended.

Rolfa said nothing. She kept her eyes down on the plate and ate with pained, exaggerated good manners that made Milena want to throw the seal cutlet at her. When asked to pass the salt, Rolfa wordlessly reached across the table, moving as slowly as a rusty hinge. Rolfa was in hiding, even here, in what was supposed to be her home.

Her father sniffed and proprietorially brushed some seaweed off the table and into his cupped hand. He then threw it over his shoulder.

'So you actually work in Toy Town, do you, Squidge?'

'Were you talking to me?' Milena demanded.

'I wasn't talking to the seal.'

'My name is Milena. Perhaps no one told you that.'

'OK. Milly. You work at that place.'

'The National Theatre of Southern Britain. Yes, I do.'

'Could you tell my daughter please what the attitude of that place is towards GEs? For instance, are they ever going to let her sing there?'

Was that Rolfa's ambition? Milena's heart sank for her. Rolfa, Rolfa, you won't get to sing at the Zoo by hiding in tunnels. Milena looked at her. Rolfa reached thoughtfully for her wine, eyes focused inwards.

Milena answered the father's question. 'They probably won't, no,' she said, softly.

'Hey, Rolfa, we're talking about you. Did you hear that? Rolfa!' He slammed the table. Rolfa jumped, along with the glasses and the silverware. 'Look at yourself, sometime, girl. They're never going to let you sing, you're covered in fur.'

Rolfa picked up her silver knife and fork and began to eat again, in silence.

'Your daughter is a better singer than almost anyone at the National Theatre.' Milena spoke warily. 'She could also become a very fine composer.' Milena looked at Rolfa's face for any sign of surprise. The face remained a mask. 'If she ever got any help or training or encouragement . . .' Milena broke off. She's had to do it all by herself, Milena thought. She's had to do it all alone.

'Is that true?' Zoe asked, leaning forward.

Milena's eyes seemed to swell like small balloons about to burst. She could only nod in answer.

'Can you tell me why she's such a fat slob?' the father asked.

'Because her father is,' replied Milena. She felt like spitting at him.

He saw that and liked Milena for it. He laughed, showing his canine fangs. 'Hell yes,' he said, and belched.

'What does she *do* all day?' Zoe asked, concerned.

'I'm sorry, I'm not prepared to talk about Rolfa as if she isn't here.'

The father answered Zoe's question. 'She just hangs around. She thinks something's going to happen. Some angel's going to come down or something.' He looked back at Milena. 'She's wasted enough time. And money. End of summer, she goes to the Antarctic.'

'Antarctic? You mean the South Pole?' Milena was rendered stupid by shock. 'Why?'

'Because,' the father said, his voice going wheedling and sarcastic. 'That is where we make our money.'

Milena found that she was smiling, smiling with the absurdity of it and with anger. 'What is *Rolfa* going to do in the Antarctic?'

'Work for a change,' said her father. 'We're not like you people. We owe each other things. With us a woman does the same job as a man or we kick her butt until she does. She's going to Antarctica before the New Year . . .' The father began to chuckle, 'or I tear her head off.'

'I think that's the worst thing I've ever heard,' said Milena.

'You're a Squidge,' said the father with a shrug. 'Your mind's infected. It's full of germs. Nobody infects our minds. Nobody tells us what to do. So. You call us – what – "an intelligent related species". Personally, I think we're the last human beings left, but that's OK, because if we aren't defined as human beings, then we don't have to obey your crazy laws. We don't have to have our heads pumped full of disease, we all live to a decent age, and we do what the hell we want when the hell we want to do it. And you know what, Squidge? You people find that very useful. You find it very useful to have people who aren't part of your little exercise in mind control.'

Milena felt the icy breath of the truth.

The father unclipped a column of adding machine paper from himself and examined it. 'So,' he said, slightly distracted. 'What we're talking about here is legal definitions. My daughter over there is saying, I want to make bee-ooo-ti-ful music.' His voice was full of scorn. 'She hangs around with Squidges, she wants to be a Squidge. She gets herself defined as a Squidge, it could mess up our whole little system. You think we're going to let her do that?'

'No,' said Milena, almost inaudibly.

49

'Damn right,' said the father. He was finished with the paper. He crumpled it up and threw it onto his plate.

Rolfa still ate, slowly, carefully, eyes fixed on her food. Well, Rolfa, thought Milena. Do you have anything to say? I can't stop them, Rolfa. If you let them do it to you, I can't stop them.

'Going to Antarctica is like going to school for us,' said Angela. 'It's something everybody does. Maybe meet a nice man.' She was trying to sound bright and encouraging. Her father began to key in figures. There was a whizz of paper.

Rolfa, you are a great lump. Milena felt betrayed. The meat in her mouth went round and round. Why am I eating this? I don't need to eat. She spat the seal cutlet out onto her plate. That's what I think of you all.

'I can get you an omelette,' offered Zoe.

I don't need to talk either. Milena shook her head. She drank. The wine was sour and sharp, which seemed appropriate. May you all freeze in hell. Why am I sitting here?

Milena finished her wine, throwing it back down her gullet, and stood up. Rolfa finally moved, turning suddenly toward her.

'It's all right! You don't need to move,' said Milena. She looked at the family. 'Enjoy your meal,' she told them, and left. As she went down the stairs, she began to run. She ran to the door and threw off the coat. The carpet had crystals of ice along its fibres. Who needs winter? Milena pulled open the front door and left it hanging open, and plunged into human temperatures, the warm blanket of summer air. She still had on the indigent gloves.

She walked, mind raging, so angry she couldn't think. The tragedy loomed around her, so vast that it seemed part of the iron railings, and the classical Kensington porticos, and chimneys against the sky, part of the other people who passed her, hunched and hesitant, as if the pavements were too narrow. She walked round and round in circles through the unfamiliar streets.

She found herself back in front of the Polar house, all creamy, ice-blue in the summer night. Something broke.

'Rolfa!' she shouted. 'Rolfa! Rolfa!' Her voice went shrill and she picked up an edge of pavement and hurled it towards the house.

'I'm here,' said a voice. 'Ssssh.'

A shape, a shadow of a head through an open window on an upper floor. Rolfa had been sitting all alone in the dark.

Milena waited in the silence, in the moonlight, hugging herself. She stamped her feet with impatience and to get the blood flowing in her icy toes. Then there was a quiet clunk, and Rolfa stepped out the front door, carrying something, a blanket. She was back in her shorts and cloth shoes.

She came sideways, wary, as if on broken plates, cringing. Frightened of me, frightened of everybody. When Rolfa was close, Milena hit her.

'You let them! You let everybody. You're going to let them do it and you don't have the right. You going to spend your time breaking rocks? What a bloody stupid waste!'

Rolfa looked back at her forlornly, and Milena heard the sound of wind in the trees.

'Don't just stand there.'

More silence, and applause from the leaves.

'Do *something*!' Milena's hands were raised around her head, fingers spread like claws.

Rolfa hugged her. Milena was suddenly enfolded in long, soft, warm arms, and she was pressed against Rolfa's stomach. 'Sssh, Little One, ssssh,' she said.

The edges of Milena's vision were going black and grainy. I'm going to faint, thought Milena. She meant it as a joke, to make it ridiculous, so it wouldn't happen. Then her knees gave way. I really am going to faint, she thought. Real people don't faint.

'Ooovvvvgot ta sssip owwn,' she said. She was trying to say she had to sit down. Suddenly she felt herself lifted up. Her stomach felt weighted down and she thought she was going to vomit. She saw the moon dip and dive about the sky like a swallow, and she felt herself being laid out on the grass. She settled into it and went utterly still.

'Little Ones shouldn't drink too much,' said Rolfa.

Milena wished that her clothing were undone. She wanted to put the very tips of her fingers onto the palm of Rolfa's hand. She couldn't find it. All she felt was grass. Then there was darkness.

Had Rolfa kissed the top of her head? Had she run her fingers through Milena's hair?

chapter five

LOW COMEDY (JUST US VAMPIRES)

When Milena awoke, she was cured. She had had enough.

She woke up in her own bed, in the little room in the Shell. How did I get home? she wondered. She didn't remember. She sat up in bed. Her back was stiff and there was a comprehensive pain in the bones of her head, all around her eyes and temples.

Milena no longer wanted Rolfa. The very thought of Rolfa, of her smell, of her teeth, now made Milena feel a bit ill. The thought of them had become associated with pain. Sick with love, Milena had now become sick of it.

Nothing like a course of aversion therapy, she thought and was ambushed by a wet, explosive sneeze. She wondered dimly what the time was and her viruses told her. Oh Marx and Lenin! she thought. I've got a performance of *Love's Labour's* this morning. I've missed it. She felt relieved. Missing a performance was the right thing to do. She groaned, and lay back down on her bed.

Then the door opened and a stranger came in.

She's made a mistake, Milena thought, all the rooms look alike. She managed a crumpled smile of tolerance and waited for the woman to realise she was in the wrong room. The woman began to use Milena's towel. She was a doe-eyed female with black hair and black eyes and beautiful nut brown skin, not Rhodopsin. She was enormous.

Then Milena saw that there was stubble all over the woman's bare arms and shoulders, and criss cross cuts from a razor.

'I shaved,' said the woman, with a forlorn familiar voice.

'Rolfa?' Milena sat up in bed.

'I decided to do a bunk,' said Rolfa. She shuffled forward and sat on the bottom of the bed. 'I had to carry you back.' Shorn of her pelt, Rolfa had an odd face. It was fleshy and somehow chinless, with a very small, thin mouth that seemed too deeply indented between nose and chin. But the black and liquid eyes were the same.

'They don't know I'm here,' said Rolfa. 'Can I stay?'

Milena was not sure what she felt. 'Yes, yes of course. What have you brought with you?' She meant clothes, shoes, toothbrush . . .

'Piglet,' said Rolfa, and picked up a shapeless lump of felt from the floor. It was some kind of stuffed toy. 'Piglet goes everywhere with me.' Rolfa sat Piglet on her lap facing her and looked at it fondly. Even from where Milena stood, Piglet smelled of biscuit crumbs.

'You didn't bring anything else with you?' Milena asked softly.

'Wasn't anything else to bring.' Rolfa smiled at her. 'I took some money. They'll say I stole it.' She looked back down at Piglet. 'I did.'

'Will they come looking for you?'

Rolfa nodded. 'They're scared. Papa will be scared. The Family says his genes are impure because he's so short. He'll try to keep me quiet, not let them know. He'll try to find me himself. We'll be safe for a while. We'll be OK for a while.' She looked at Milena and seemed to be making a promise. 'After that, they'll call out the bloodhounds.'

'I'd better go and tell people not to let anyone know where I live.'

'There's a problem,' said Rolfa and turned. Underneath the cheap new blouse there was a dark swelling of fur. Rolfa held up a razor. 'I couldn't reach,' she said.

Milena came back from the showers with a bucket of hot water. They were silent and awkward with each other. Rolfa took off her blouse, but held it over herself, something she had never done when she had fur. Her skin had been stripped, cut, outraged. There were long straggles of fur that the razor had missed. Milena sawed at the fur on her back with the kitchen knife and used soap from the showers to get up a lather. Then she used the razor. Rolfa mewed quietly as the hair came off in soapy clumps. 'I'm cold,' she complained. To Milena, she felt hot, feverish. 'We'll put you under a blanket,' she said. She left Rolfa wrapped up on the bed and looking at her with a trust that made Milena doubt herself.

Well, Milena thought. I've got her. Now what do I do with her? The gift had been too sudden, too complete.

Milena went to each of the overstaffed information desks at the Zoo. She asked the Tykes who worked there not to tell anyone where she lived. 'Say you've never heard of me,' she told the children. 'Say there is no record of me.'

Milena did not know the forms that love could take. She lived alone. She could not remember her childhood friends. Her memories of her mother were faint; she saw her mother only as a dim, warm, mauveness. How did people live with love from day to day? Milena was full of misgivings.

Milena came back to her tiny room, with its bed, its sink, its cooker. It was now covered in paper. Rolfa had found the books and papers that had been rescued from her ruined nest. Rolfa lay on her stomach, filling the floor. Broken-backed books and loose sheets of paper filled the sink. They were piled on the cooker. There was a smell of burning. Fire! thought Milena in alarm and went to the cooker. The papers were untouched, though there was an acrid stench of scorching. How, wondered Milena did she manage to do this?

'Look what I found,' Rolfa said and held up a book. It looked rumpled, as if it had been left out in the rain, and there were ring stains on the cover.

'Oh,' said Milena. The title was unreadable.

'Do you think,' Rolfa asked, 'that you could possibly call me Pooh?'

The word Pooh meant something very specific and unpleasant to Milena. It certainly did not mean teddy bear.

'Why on earth would you want me to call you that?' Milena asked.

'Pooh,' repeated Rolfa. 'Pooh. You must have heard of Pooh. He's a bear. He's in a book.'

A GE novel? Milena had sudden visions of an entire Polar literature. 'Is it new?' she asked.

'No, no,' said Rolfa and stood up. 'Here.' She showed Milena a drawing of Pooh.

'He's not part of the culture,' said Milena, meaning there was no virus of him. She reads, thought Milena in admiration, unheard-of books.

'You could call me Pooh. And I could call you Christopher Robin.'

'Why?' said Milena warily.

'Here, look. That's Christopher Robin.'

There was a drawing of a small neat person with a page-boy bob and shorts and sandals and loose blouse and a large umbrella. There was no doubt. Milena did indeed look exactly like Christopher Robin.

'No,' said Milena.

'I *was* going to call you Eeyore,' said Rolfa. 'He's grumpy too.'

'I'll tell you what,' said Milena, 'If I call you Pooh' – it really was very unpleasant – 'do you promise, *promise* not to call me Christopher Robin?'

Rolfa nodded solemnly, up and down. Her hair still dangled into her eyes. She blinked. She saw Milena looking at the state of the room.

'Pooh's very untidy,' said Rolfa.

'Yes,' said Milena nodding.

'But she does have other qualities.' Rolfa paused and bit her lip. 'I'm sorry about the beans.'

'What about the beans?'

'I was feeling peckish, and all I could find was some bamboo full of beans, so I tried to warm it up.'

Underneath most of the score for *Peer Gynt*, Milena found her only saucepan. Light, crispy, burned-black beans were now a permanent part of it.

'I'll buy you another one,' said Rolfa.

'Good,' said Milena, wiping the charcoal from the tips of her fingers.

She took a deep breath, to calm herself, and began to explain the house rules. Dirty laundry in this bag here. Clean clothes in this bag. Dirty dishes there. Rolfa nodded in eager agreement. Oh yes, they must always wash up, just after dinner. Why, thought Milena, don't I believe you?

'I'm hungry,' said Rolfa, with tame expectation.

They took a water taxi upstream. The tiny steam engine sputtered, and clouds of vapour rolled upwards in the shape of doughnuts. They went to the Gardens beside the river, where no one would think to look for them, on the other side of Battersea.

There was an old Buddhist shrine there, one of the first built in London. Milena and Rolfa ate lunch beside it, under a marquee. It was crowded and noisy, full of steam and the sizzling sounds of woks. People sat on benches, arguing with infants who kept trying to order different kinds of food. 'You always order for me!' the Tykes complained. 'I can do it myself!' The infants wanted the food to be bland. 'No wonder you want everything blasted with pepper, you've burned your taste buds out!' complained one babe in arms. Outside, there were acrobats on the lawn. The babes refused to be distracted.

People walked hand in hand or leaned out over the river, shoulders touching. People live with each other, Milena told herself. Most people live with someone else. She felt a new admiration for the way in which they coped. It must be possible, she thought. There must be a way to do it. Watching other people in couples usually made Milena feel like a bottle with a message in it, washed up and left unread. Now, it began to make her feel a kind of kinship.

'What do we do now?' Rolfa asked, as if everything in this new world followed a polished routine.

They walked back along the other side of the river. There were children along the embankment, playing with hoops on moored barges. There was a traffic jam of carts heading back to the outreaches full of goods from the markets to be sold again. Young boys on them leaned back onto melons and played harmonicas. A circle of women sat cross-legged on the pavement, shoving slivers of bamboo into shoes. They were cobblers. A small blonde woman with spectacles and a thimble was talking. 'Well, my Johnny . . .' she began, her voice full of pride.

Rolfa and Milena sat in an old church in John Smith Square and listened to a choir rehearsing madrigals. They went to a market outside Westminster Abbey. Rolfa was hungry again. She bought some dried fish and munched it like candy. She bought a new saucepan and vegetables and bread and more fish. They walked through the August dusk, along Westminster Bridge, past fire-eaters, who blew sheets of flame toward the sky as children watched. Fat men in plaid shorts,

Party members perhaps, laughed and passed money. There was to be an ostrich race across the bridge. Jockeys were trying to clamber up onto the backs of the birds. Hoods were snatched from the ostriches' eyes and they sprang forward. One of them spun in circles and then ran off in the wrong direction. There were cheers. For the first time she could remember, Milena felt young. She and Rolfa walked back to the Shell.

They lit a candle in the room and sorted out Rolfa's papers. They put pages back in bindings and reunited different halves of musical scores. They worked in silence. They were going to have to share the bed.

It was a small bed and Milena, Rolfa and Piglet were all going to have to fit in it. When the time came, Milena was surprised at how straightforward sleeping with Rolfa was. Rolfa simply took off her clothes and slipped under the counterpane. Without any preliminaries, she began to snore. Milena climbed in next to her with only the slightest trembling in her belly.

Rolfa was hot. Her feet stuck out of the end of the bed to cool. Her snoring was dragon-like, great gurgling snorts, agonised asthmatic wheezes, ruffles of sound like a horse blowing through its loose nostrils. Milena stared at the ceiling in the dark, and felt a trickle of sweat on her forehead.

'Rolfa. Please?' she asked.

'Yum. Um.' said Rolfa.

Milena reached around and pushed shut her mouth. The snoring stopped and then started again. Milena's hand brushed Rolfa's shoulder. It was as warm as a radiator, made piquant by the stubble of whiskers.

Piglet, Milena decided, also smelled of childhood sick.

Finally she slept, as if in a fever, a skittish sleep with dreams. She dreamt that Rolfa rose up all around her and covered her and that they made love. It was a bit like being rubbed by warm sandpaper. Milena could feel the bristles against her cheek and with the tips of her fingers. She awoke in the dark, overjoyed, thinking it had been real, and reached out to find the bed empty and cool.

There was a sizzling sound. Milena looked up and saw a flame. Rolfa was frying something in the light of the single-ring stove. There was a smell of fish.

'You've got fleas,' said Rolfa, huffily.

'No I haven't,' said Milena, sleepily settling back onto her pillow. It was not possible for human beings to have fleas.

'I'm being eaten alive!' exclaimed Rolfa.

Milena was dimly aware of a stirring in the bed. She turned her head. There were mites on the pillow. She sat up and examined them.

56

'Oh,' she said, remembering. 'Oh. That's my immune system.'

'What, trained fleas?' said Rolfa. When she was angry, Rolfa became something of an aristocrat.

'No,' Milena said, mortified and miserable. To have forgotten this only showed so nakedly that she had never been in love. 'No, we call them Mice. They eat fleas. And bilharzia, and hookworm. They live in our skin. They were engineered for us when the weather got warmer. You're a foreign body. They think you're a disease.'

'Charming,' said Rolfa.

'They get used to you. It's what happens to us. It's what happens when people become lovers.'

Lovers? Oops. Milena's eyes popped back open in alarm, and she watched Rolfa, waiting for a reaction. Rolfa went on cooking.

'But. We're not lovers, are we?' said Milena, after a little while.

'No,' said Rolfa lightly, and looked at her. 'I'm making fried bread and sardine sandwiches. Want one?'

'No thanks,' whispered Milena. She sat up in bed, and propped her head on arm and looked at Rolfa. It wasn't going to be like her dream, or like the sickness, either. Living with Rolfa was going to be something calmer and more certain.

'Here, we go, fleas and all,' said Rolfa and sat cross-legged on the bed and began to munch. The bed, thought Milena, will be full of crumbs and smell of fish for weeks. She didn't mind.

In the morning, Milena got up and went to rehearsals. She left Rolfa reading one of the torn books. As she went down the stairs and walked along the pavements that reflected the low morning sun, the thought that Rolfa would be in the room when she got back was like a hand-warmer. People carried them in winter, little boxes in which an ember of charcoal smouldered. She didn't even mind going to *Love's Labour's Lost*.

Inside the bare rehearsal hall, there was an air of high excitement.

'Oh Milena, you missed it!' said one of the Princess's ladies. She and Milena did not normally speak.

'Missed what?'

'Oh!' said the actress, wondering where to begin. 'We're not doing the old production any more, we're doing a new one, our own.'

The director came in. He looked feverish, eyes glistening. Milena thought he might be unwell. 'Right!' he said. 'All ready for the Birth of the New, Part Two. Milena. You weren't here yesterday. We're going to do Dull's first scene. Now.'

Brisk, brisk, thought Milena, what's got into him? She did Dull as she always did him, but now each time that she spoke there were affectionate chuckles from the cast.'

'You see what I mean?' the director said.

'Dull's not dumb, he's smart,' said Berowne.

What is going on? wondered Milena. They *liked* my Dull?

And Milena felt a kind of giddiness.

I know this feeling, she thought. I think I know this feeling from childhood. There's something new, and you don't understand it, and so there is confusion.

It was the strangest feeling. It was as if Milena were standing at the end of a long, dark corridor. Far down at the other end, someone was talking, but the words were echoing from so far back, were so scattered by echoing, that they made no sense. The person who was speaking from so far back was Milena herself.

It was a scrap of memory. I'm trying to remember something, she thought.

'Right,' said the director. 'Back to Armado and Mote.' He peremptorily clapped his hands. The cast bustled into place. Milena felt as if she had been awakened from a dream.

I really don't remember any of it at all. Any of it. Being a child. It's all gone. Except for very early on.

Something destroyed my childhood.

The play began again.

Out of costume, wearing street clothes, Armado and the boy called Mote entered.

From the first word of the performance, Milena thought: it's all different.

In the original production which the cast had so hated imitating, Armado was a braggart, arch and florid and wearing a hat full of feathers. The boy Mote imitated him. The boy was arch and florid as well. He was going to become like his master.

It was a subtlety of performance that was beyond these young actors. What this Mote had was innocence. Mote had been allowed to become a child again. He was full of joy. He danced with the joy of the words.

'. . . but to jig off a tune at the tongue's end, canary it to your feet . . .' he said, swaying with each syllable.

When he was done, the cast applauded him.

'It's the words,' he said shyly. 'They're *virulent*.'

They worked long into the afternoon, utterly without realising it. Time had ceased to be a problem for them. Time became something delicious, the medium in which the words and the performances swam. It's alive, thought Milena. It's all become alive. She watched as performance after performance fell into place.

The Princess of the play was less superior now, more wary and confused. The King was less of a fool and more a good and quiet man. For the first time, you could believe that they would love each other. As the cast watched each other, all of them squirmed with delight. The whole damn play, thought Milena. It's like some huge wriggling fish. This is what it's supposed to be like.

It was late afternoon when they were done, and they burst out of the rehearsal rooms, throwing back the doors. They marched out of the room together, elated, their hands on the shoulders, on the neck, around the waist of their director.

'Who needs Animals anyway?' said Berowne. 'We're all Animals!' They walked back to the Shell in a mob, telling each other excitedly how good they had been.

'You do realise what this means,' said Milena. 'It means we're doing all the plays the wrong way. They should all be like this.'

'Ulp,' said the King, covering his mouth and swallowing in mock alarm.

'So what do we do next?' Milena asked.

'Anything we want' said Berowne.

And as they kissed each other on the cheek, dispersing to their rooms, and as Milena climbed the stairs, silent among a few other cast members who lived in her section of the Shell, Milena felt she had some news. She could feel the news ripen in her like a heavy fruit about to drop. The news had been ripened by the knowledge that Milena had someone to tell it to. She had Rolfa.

Everything is happening all at once, she thought. She was aware that her life had taken wing.

When Milena got back to her room, Jacob was waiting for her. He stood up from the bed and said, 'Someone's been hunting for you. You and Rolfa.'

'A Snide,' said Rolfa, leaning back on the bed, looking pleased. 'Papa would have hired him.'

'A tall, thin man,' said Jacob. 'I told him no one of your name lived here.'

Milena listened to the silence in the room. Snides had viruses that helped them sneak and search.

'They can hear thoughts,' she whispered in fear.

'Not exactly,' said Jacob, with a sideways grin. 'It's not like that.'

The air seemed to prickle. 'What is it like?' Milena asked quietly. You know, don't you Jacob?

Still the angelic smile. 'You catch thoughts. You see things. You feel things in your head. They are very difficult to understand. If you are with many people, the thoughts are jumbled. Milena, you must stay with people.'

So I can still be part of the play.

'What if he finds me alone?'

Jacob still smiled. 'You are many people, Milena. The viruses come from many people. Let them talk for you. Let them recite your lines. Let them add up things. Let them read books. You won't be traced. All these things are not personal.'

'And Rolfa? She's here all alone.'

Hood-eyed, Jacob turned, smiling to Rolfa. 'Oh, Rolfa, her thoughts are not personal.'

So Postpeople are Snides as well. What, wondered Milena, are Postpeople *for*?

'We'd better change rooms,' said Milena.

Jacob nodded. Rolfa lay on the bed as if none of it mattered.

Milena went to Cilla. 'We've got to trade rooms,' she told her.

'Drop anchor. Hold. Why?' Cilla asked. She was told the story and was thrilled. 'Right. Right away,' she said. 'We move.'

'A new room?' Rolfa beamed, and jumped up from the floor. There was a bustling of bags. Rolfa kept cheerfully hitting her head on the lintels of doorways. The beds, the cookers, the pans, the armfuls of paper, were all exchanged in less than an hour.

'I'll go buy us all supper. See you,' promised Cilla.

The new room was even smaller and did not have a view of the river. After the excitement of the move and of being hunted, Rolfa sat staring, disgruntled and pouting.

'There's no space,' she said.

'There's space enough. We got everything in.'

'There's no space for a piano.'

For a piano?

Rolfa, how much money do you have? Enough to keep you in food for a month? How much money do you think I have? Milena had to tell her that life would be different now. Rolfa would have to live the cramped and constricted life of a human being.

'We live in little boxes, Rolfa,' Milena said. 'For us there is no buying a way out. We don't have pianos. We don't have rooms big enough for them.'

'Then where can I play?'

'There are practice rooms, in the Zoo.'

'They won't let me into them.' Rolfa began to pace.

Something is going to have to happen, quickly, Milena realised. We won't be able to live like this for long. Something is going to have to happen with her music.

'You can always sing,' said Milena.

'Where? Where can I sing? If I try to sing here, people ask me to be quiet. And if there's a Snide after me, I've got to keep quiet.'

Cilla did not come bringing supper. Jacob came instead with a message.

'He is in your old room,' said Jacob. 'The tall, thin man. He will not go away. He is sitting on the bed. Cilla was playing *Madam Butterfly* over and over in her mind. He knew that. I said, Cilla your friends are waiting at the cafe. So she could leave. She asked him to go, and he shook his head. How long he will stay there I don't know. But I think he will soon come here.'

They had to move again. To move a second time was not fun. It was wearing. They traded rooms with Cilla's boyfriend, a well known young actor, who made a great show of condescending. Milena did not like being grateful to him.

They spent the night in their new, glum room and did not even light a candle in case the Snide was watching. They spoke in whispers. Rolfa walked back and forth at the foot of the bed.

'When I was bad, Papa would lock me in the closet,' she said. 'It was very dark and I knew there was no one to come for me. So I used to sing to myself in the dark. And it got so that I would do bad things like not make my bed or make a terrible mess in the kitchen, just so that I could be locked away. The dark was the only place I could sing. But here, I can't even sing. It's so small, I can hardly move.'

And Milena felt it again, the echo of memory. I've done this before, she thought. It was a habit, a pattern, something she could fall into if she didn't think about it. It was as if she had been snatched up so quickly and hauled into adulthood that part of her self had been left behind. It was as if only the shell remained, the structure. The strange soft creature she once had been was left behind. The child self did not realise what had happened. Perhaps it was still back there, in the past, still talking.

I don't remember, but I think that I probably talked to the new-comers. I suppose that in the Child Garden the orphans wept for their lost homes, even homes they had hated. Milena suddenly found the idea of homeless children unaccountably moving. I must have sat with them at night in the dark, like this.

And this is a child I am talking to now. Milena understood Rolfa then. Rolfa was still a child. Milena would have to take care of her for a while.

'Can you sing in silence? Like reading music?'

'It's not the same,' said Rolfa.

She will have to become part of the Consensus, Milena decided. If she becomes part of the Consensus, she can be Placed in the theatrical Estate. They will let her use the practice rooms at least. At least they will pay her, give her money and a place to live. If nothing happens she will go. She will have to go. What is the difference between this and Antarctica? It is still exile. The thought did not come to Milena that she herself was the difference.

That night she couldn't sleep again. She was trying to think of what she could do. Could she ask Jacob to sing the music that he remembered? Could she coax Rolfa into one of the rooms of the powerful, and persuade her to sing, cold? Milena finally fell asleep, sitting on the floor, only her head and shoulders resting on the bed.

She sat up suddenly some time later, knowing that she had been asleep. It was still dark outside. The counterpane was over her shoulders.

'I have been in bed forever,' said Rolfa. 'Isn't there something we can do?'

'There's a market open now. It's for stallowners, open early. We could go there!'

They crept down the unlighted stairs of the Shell, clutching on to each other, dreading a tall thin shadow. They slipped through the streets, their hearts pounding. They followed a butcher's cart, pulled by a huge and plodding white horse with a beautiful white mane. They reached the gas lamps, with their shining cotton wicks, and they saw the heaps of things to buy. Sparrows in cages had been dyed bright colours. There were whole smoked chickens, old furniture, T-shirts with pictures printed on them, musical instruments, and piles of fruit and vegetables.

'Pooh wants this,' said Rolfa. 'Pooh shall have it.' She bought a pineapple. The stallowner was looking at them.

'Isn't it funny how a Bear likes money,' Rolfa said, sorting coins. Milena felt her mouth go taut with embarrassment and the danger of it. He will remember us, she thought. They left as a corner of the sky was turning silver and the sound of horses' hooves announced the city was waking up. Streetsweepers in blue uniform nodded hello as they passed.

It became their new routine. Rolfa went to the market in the mornings in the dark. It was her time out. Milena would get up with her, and help her shave in the showers, a candle planted on the floor. Then Milena would go back to bed and lounge in its warmth. That was her time. When the sky was lighter, she would get up and clean the cooker, and undo whatever damage Rolfa had done with her pre-dawn fry-up.

'I hope you bought a new alcohol cannister,' she said once, when Rolfa got back. 'You used this one up.'

'You mean the cooker won't work?' Rolfa asked in dismay. 'And I got us something special for breakfast.'

'What is it?' Milena asked ruefully. 'Seal?'

'No. Penguin.' Rolfa held it up. It still had its feathers and horny feet, but at least it didn't kick.

'Well, I hope you can eat it raw.'

'I suppose it *is* all right in a salad,' said Rolfa, still looking crestfallen.

She'd also bought some peaches and some seaweed, and so they had a peach and penguin seaweed salad for breakfast – or rather, Rolfa did. Milena ate a peach and watched Rolfa bite through sinews as thick as her little finger. The sink was full of feathers. Milena smiled.

'Pooh,' she pronounced Rolfa, as if knighting her.

After breakfast, Milena would leave Rolfa for the day, reading a book. At the entrance of the Shell, the cast of the play would be waiting. Milena would walk in their midst to rehearsals at the Zoo, protected by a cloud of thought.

Milena learned things about them. She learned that Berowne was in love with the Princess and wanted to be a father. The Princess did not want to carry a baby. Berowne was thinking of carrying the child himself. The King, handsome, kind, faraway, loved nobody, but was one of those people who are, effortlessly, loved. The girls felt warmth and sympathy for him, as well as loving his blond-green curls and luxuriant beard.

They were all so ambitious. They all had such plans – characters they wanted to play, pictures they wanted to paint. Milena, as always, was quiet among them, but for once she was not full of resentment. She was content to go unnoticed. She found she liked being part of a group. And when she did say something, it would sound obvious and banal to her, but the actors would exclaim, 'Oh, Milena, you're always so sensible!' She would understand that it was not an insult. 'Not like you butterflies,' she replied once, with a chuckle. There was a kind of quiet acknowledgement on both sides of who she was.

Then one morning, on the walkway, the Princess whispered, 'Milena. That's the Snide!'

It was like swimming in the ocean and seeing a shark.

A tall man in a black coat was coming towards them. He ambled, hands in his pockets. It was a windy day and the tails of his black coat flapped. The Snide had a lean and dreamy face, with hooded eyes and a slight smile. His hair was like a pale mist, disordered and thinning.

Milena forced herself to look away from him, but she still saw the face in her mind. She hated it. It was sly and soft at the same time, sleepy, almost gentle, except for something glinting within the slits of the puffy eyes.

Think of something else! Milena told herself.

Me, an't shall please you. Milena remembered one of her 13 lines. *I am Anthony Dull.* Nothing happened. Think of his coat, she told herself, what did it cost, how many labour-hours? Count them. The viral clock in her mind refused to work.

Milena had spent a lifetime beating down the viruses. They now deserted her. In her terror, she could not dredge up one of them.

Shakespeare. T. S. Eliot, Jane Austen. *It is a truth universally acknowledged*, she recited to herself, *that a single man in possession of a good fortune must be in want of a wife.* There was no answering spark of life.

The walkway was elevated and narrow; they would have to pass the Snide. 'Ack!' exclaimed the King, loudly. 'We've taken the wrong walkway.'

All the actors turned at once, and walked in the opposite direction. The Snide followed. Milena could hear the clattering of his shoes behind her on the resin surface. Wooden clogs. He wears them so that people will hear and be afraid.

Marx! Milena thought, where is Marx, they must have fed me Marx by the gram. Lenin, Mao, Chao Li Song. All right, music, then. Brahms, Elgar, anything. She began to hum *Das Lied von der Erde.* That's not a virus, she remembered, I learned that myself.

'Milena,' called the Snide. His voice was light and mellifluous. 'I'm singing to you, Milena. Can you hear me?'

Milena could feel terror seeping out of her, as if she were a leaking balloon. She heard his shoes, clip-clopping like horses' hooves. They were beside her now. The actors walked faster, looking at their feet, not knowing what else to do. Surely this was illegal! Of course it was illegal, but where was the Law? The Law was everywhere, invisible and alive. But there were no policemen.

'Eastern Europe, Milena,' said the Snide. 'Do you remember the trip on the train? You went to St Malo. An island with walls. Do you remember the steamer, Milena? Rocking back and forth on the sea? Do you remember the chugging sound and the sailwomen, all in stripes?'

Milena remembered none of it. There was not even a sense of echoing, of familiarity.

Milena glanced to one side and saw him, walking with them, smiling. Her eyes darted back to the ground in front of her like frightened birds.

Me, an't shall please you. I am Anthony Dull!

'I can feel you, Milena,' said the Snide. 'Do you remember the Child Garden? Do you remember Senior Dodds who taught you English? Do you remember your first day there? June 23rd? It was raining and you were all alone. You were just four years old, and they made you ill with a virus to make you speak. Do you remember that?'

For Milena, the Child Garden had been destroyed. Something had happened to it. All she could remember was being ill at ten years old. She could remember the sudden weight of new knowledge. The old viruses began to stir.

The Princess spoke, angrily. 'Go away and leave us alone!'

The Snide stepped in front of her. The Princess had to stop walking.

'Milena?' the Snide asked, grinning hopefully, leaning down to look into her eyes.

Milena felt giddy. She swayed as she walked. It was as if the ground beneath her lurched. She stood still beside the Princess as if to help her. Instead of fear, Milena had a strange and most complete sensation of maddening ennui. An irritable boredom engendered by viruses rose up all around her like steam from the pavement.

Milena remembered words, German words, badly printed in Gothic lettering.

DAS KAPITAL

Milena remembered the reading of them. She remembered someone reading them in a very small, very cold room, smoking cigarettes. She had rolled them herself, straggles of tobacco in thin papers that were held together with spit. Her legs were limply fleshed and useless. She sat in a wheelchair, by a window, on the ground floor of a block of flats. Just outside her window, noisy children were playing with a ball.

Milena began to walk again, but in her mind, she was sitting in a wheelchair.

'You're not Milena,' said the Snide, gently, to the Princess.

Words on top of another page – *Chapter One: The Commodity*.

A forest of associations sprang up, thoughts and references neatly husbanded, ready for use. The thought came to the person who was reading: this will show the amateurs.

1. THE TWO FACTORS OF THE COMMODITY: USE-VALUE AND VALUE (SUBSTANCE OF VALUE AND MAGNITUDE OF VALUE).

The one who was reading sucked in smoke, past teeth that tasted of tobacco, down a leathery throat. Milena, who did not smoke, coughed.

The Snide looked up at her.

'Milena?' he asked.

Badly printed words were scrolling up through her mind, and embedded in them were aching joints and a tight band of nicotine poisoning across the chest and iron determination and icy pride. Embedded in the reading was an entire way of responding to the world, another sense of self. Me, thought the one who read, they chose me to read this. I understand it better than anyone. I am reading it for everyone. No more amateurs, ever again. They will all understand. There was a tingling in the middle of the cortex, a dancing of receptive virus, waiting to be turned into Marx. The one who read let out a triumphant blast of smoke from her nostrils. She was alive again, though she did not know it.

'I don't know anyone called Milena,' said Milena, quite truthfully. 'My name is Heather. What do you want?'

'You like Marx,' said the Snide, to let her know he could read her.

'Never met him,' replied Heather. 'I wouldn't say I like his books. They've eaten up my life. But I do understand them.'

Bourgeois fluff, she thought. God, I could tear you in half.

The nature of these needs, whether they arise, for example, from the stomach or the imagination, makes no difference.

The use-value is intrinsic. Like the value of music.

'Does anyone know anyone called Milena?' Heather demanded of the actors. Heather's voice was harsh and her smile, meant to disarm, was fixed and chilling. Milena saw the face in memory, long and freckled with huge front teeth, black-framed spectacles, and a thickness of the neck that was the first sign of the physical distortion below.

'They do know Milena, but they're trying not to think,' said the Snide. Suddenly he chortled. 'They're all churning over their lines. They're all seeing exactly the same play in their heads. Except for you.'

Heather was without pity. She had grown up a cripple in Belfast and pity was her enemy, pity was the thing that had held her back. What she wanted was respect, and if respect was not forthcoming, then she wanted fear. She had learned how to get it.

Heather stared into the eyes of the Snide, and gave him the full blast of her contempt. Crawler, money-snake, you have a talent and what do you do with it? Then she showed him, carefully and clearly in her mind, one of the things that she might do to him if he did not leave. She would hit him in the throat. He would swallow his Adam's apple, and choke.

'My God, you're scary,' he chuckled. 'I think I love you.'

Heather was not above being flattered, and she recognised submission when she saw it. She chuckled too, warmly. 'Fuck off,' she said using the old word, and made a motion of brushing something aside.

The discovery of these ways and the manifold uses of things is the work of history.

Very calmly, deliberately, Heather thought: it's a good job he doesn't know that Milena has gone away to Bournemouth.

'Bournemouth?' asked the Snide, amused.

'How did you know that?' said Heather, grinning her poker smile and failing to sound surprised.

The usefulness of a thing makes it a use-value. But this usefulness does not dangle in mid-air.

'I don't,' replied the Snide. 'Know it, I mean.' He made a brushing-aside motion now. 'Bournemouth. Perhaps I will go to Bournemouth, perhaps I won't. But I will be back.' As if his wooden clogs had suddenly grown roots, he stood still.

The actors walked on quickly, almost scuttling. Heather went back to reading, bound up in the reading, inherent in it.

I only hope, thought Milena safe within a cloud of thought, that I can get her to stop.

She glanced behind, and saw the Snide, still standing, buffeted by wind as if by the thoughts of other people. He was looking at her and smiling a happy smile of discovery.

That night Milena dreamed that Heather was sitting on the foot of her bed. She could see her, with the horse-mouth smile and the tiny legs, folded up under her. Heather, Heather, go away, get out, leave me alone! Heather kept on reading. The words rolled past, projected onto the walls. You will understand. You will get it right. Of course the most useful things are free, like air, and do not require labour. But value is an economic concept, a function of particular social relations.

Yes, yes, Milena answered, rolling her head from side to side.

There was a knock at the door . . .

Milena woke up, drenched in sweat, feverish, ill.

. . . a soft insinuating rapping on her door, in the dark.

Milena felt the bed beside her and it was empty. The sky beyond the window was going silver. Rolfa was gone. Rolfa would be at the market, buying food.

And the Snide had come knocking.

Good, good, let him in, let him see the empty room, no Rolfa hidden. Don't think, she warned herself, don't think. Milena found clothing in the dark, her hands shaking, and as she dressed, she pushed her own self, her own ego, down into the recesses. Heather floated up to the surface of her mind, like a corpse on a river.

The door opened. This was a culture that did not need locks.

'Hello, Heather,' said a soft, mellifluous voice. 'I wanted to talk to you.'

He moved in the darkness, unseen. There was a crumpling of the quilt. He sat on the foot of the bed, where Heather had sat.

'You could have hit me this morning. None of the others could. You've broken the viruses. So have I.' He reached out and took her hand. 'We're alike,' he said.

There came a shy, apologetic rapping on Milena's door.

What the hell now? Heather snatched her hand away. Rolfa?

'Oh my God, it's my boyfriend,' said Heather. She could hardly say it was her girlfriend. 'Quick, under the bed.' It was the only line she could think of.

'It's not your boyfriend,' said the Snide. 'It's a girlfriend.'

Heather tried to push him under the bed anyway, and flung open the door before she had time to think.

Cilla stood there in the corridor, clutching a bamboo box. Heather kicked her in the shins, to occupy her mind.

'The Snide is here,' Heather told her, smiling with scorn. 'He's come to call. I think he's going to make a pass.'

In the alcohol light of the corridor, Cilla's eyes went wide with terror. She hobbled away as quickly as she could, rubbing her ankle.

'I've seen this boyfriend of yours,' said the Snide, lounging on the bed. He actually thought he was being provocative, poor lamb. 'I saw him in your head. He sleeps right here, doesn't he?' The Snide gave the bed a pat. 'Big, broad shoulders. And a beard?'

Heather just smiled and thought of dialectical materialism.

'Ah,' said the Snide, catching a glimpse of something else. 'But he shaves now.' He rolled forward onto his knees, wrapping himself in the quilt. 'Your room is just as I imagined it,' he said. 'Lots of books. That's how you break a virus. You read it for yourself. I knew you hated the viruses too. I know why you're reading Marx. To be free. I broke the virus for Marx too,' he boasted. 'I wouldn't know it if I saw it.'

He picked up a small, stained volume from the window ledge. 'The Communist Manifesto?' he asked. 'No one reads it now. They want to control it. And they call this a Marxist state.'

He was holding Rolfa's copy of *Winnie the Pooh*.

'I want you to go,' said Heather.

'Not until I know for certain that you do not need me,' said the Snide, 'as much as I need you.'

There were bells on each floor of the Shell, linked by ropes. They began to ring now, over and over. From the far end of the corridor, Cilla was shouting, 'Fire! Fire!'

'The building is burning down,' said Heather.

'No it's not. Your friend just wants me to go. She brought you some paper so you could write your music.' He crawled towards her on the bed and took her hands. 'I know people, Heather. I know you're what I want. We could live together, outside the Law. Blister all the old paint of the walls. You're a bullshit-stripper, Heather. I am a sneak. I don't like sucking arseholes. You could save me.'

Oh God, thought Heather, another one who wants his mother.

'OK. OK. You're right. I need help.'

Vampire, thought Heather. All around her, across the ceiling, through the walls came the thumpings of people awakened in the night by an alarm.

The Snide looked up, dismayed. Too many people, thinking too many things at once, thought Milena. He won't be able to read me as clearly. The quilt fell from his shoulders, and he stepped down from the bed. He gazed at her mournfully, as the light grew stronger, tall but frail-boned, not as young as he used to be, afraid.

'I take people's thoughts,' he said, 'and I weave them into tapestries.

And I hang them,' he said, 'like in a gallery. There's no one else to see them.'

'Stop being a Snide,' said Heather.

He opened the door, adjusting a broad-brimmed black hat for sinister effect, and stepped into a crowd of people in their underwear. He's a fool, thought Heather, quite simply a fool. He heard her think it, faltering as he closed the door. The bells kept ringing. But could people love fools?

Heather waited a few minutes, to let him leave. Then she joined the press of people on the staircase. They clutched their most treasured possessions, toothbrushes or saucepans. Cilla was no longer ringing the bells. The alarm had been taken up, by each floor's fire wardens, according to the drill. No one would be able to trace the false alarm back to Cilla.

Milena found Cilla outside, holding her bamboo box. Milena hugged her. 'I'm sorry about your shins,' she said. Milena lifted the lid of the box, and saw it, the precious paper, ruled in staves. People were generous. Milena had never believed that.

Value therefore, does not have its description branded on its forehead, rather it transforms every product of labour into a social hieroglyphic.

'Oh, Cilla. Who did this?' Milena asked.

'Just us Vampires,' said Cilla, shyly, pleased. 'Just us Vampires of History.'

The all-clear, a trumpet blast, sounded. Elsewhere, in memory, Heather fixed the book to a holder on her wheelchair. Continuing to read, she began to wheel herself round and round her room for exercise.

That morning, Milena intercepted Jacob on the stairs. 'Look at what I've got!' she said and held up the paper. 'Jacob! We can write the music down. Can we meet this morning, this afternoon?'

'You have a performance this afternoon,' he said.

'I'll miss it. Won't be the first time.'

Jacob went very still, his eyes closed. 'I get tired, Milena,' he said.

She could see it in the flesh around his eyes, and she knew she shouldn't ask again. But without him, the paper would be no use.

'The Vampires bought it,' she said, flipping through it. 'They saved up money and got together and bought it. All of them.' She didn't want to manipulate him, but she couldn't hide the disappointment.

'I have to sleep in the afternoons,' he said. 'If I don't, I start to forget things.' The two friends looked at each other. Jacob sighed and shifted on his feet. 'But they will clean me out soon. I'll forget everything, then. The music too. I'll forget the music.' He nodded up and down, almost imperceptibly. 'All right, Milena. All right. We meet. This afternoon.'

How could she pay all these people back?

'Thanks, Jacob,' she murmured.

Life crowded round.

Milena and Jacob met every afternoon in the practice rooms of the Zoo. Milena was not sure why, but she did not want Rolfa to know what they were doing.

Perhaps she thought Rolfa would be angry that Milena had spied on her while she was singing. Perhaps she thought Rolfa might tell her she did not want the music written down. So it was kept a secret.

Everyday Milena and Jacob would sit hunched and whispering over an old wooden table they carried in each day from a storeroom. Jacob dictated the notes in a low worn voice, his head in his hands. When he got too tired to translate them into notation, he sang the melody in a rich but restricted voice. It went as rusty as a rooster's, and the workings of Milena's hand began to ache from writing. Then Jacob would stop and look at her silently, and she would nod. And together they would carry the wooden table out again.

People would murmur an explanation to each other as Milena and Jacob passed. It was as if a stone had been dropped in water. Word was spreading. The world was beginning to do its work, finding what it needed. Sooner or later, the Snide would find them too.

'Are you Milena?' a girl, a stranger, asked. Green-blonde hair and Vampire make-up. With a kind of heave, Milena hauled the virus to the front of her mind. Heather, I am Heather. She didn't get around to answering aloud.

'Good,' said the girl. 'Don't tell me. But we're all keeping an eye out for the Snide. If he pokes around here while you're in there . . .' the girl nodded towards the practice room, '. . . we'll keep him talking and send someone to warn you. That fits?'

Milena did not dare even nod in response. The girl left, half-running in black pixie boots. If you really want to help, Milena thought, how about carrying the table?

All the time, she had to battle with Heather. By day, by night, the virus did not stop reading. Heather gripped and Heather held, with powers of organisation and concentration that were beyond Milena, hauling her through the tangled forest that was Marx, pointing out a debt to Locke or Hume, refining a thought with a quote from Engels or Gramsci, always, always, making sure that Milena understood, understood in the same way that Heather did.

What, Milena wondered, have I called up in my mind? Viruses were supposed to be a passive reservoir of information, like your own memory. They were not supposed to drag you through the minutiae of experience. *Das Kapital* was over three thousand pages long, and Heather was determined to read it all, exploring every last dreary, undeniable nuance. She had no intention of ever finishing, she would go on and on, determined to control, without a shred of self-doubt or pity. God, the woman must have been a pain. When she was alive.

Heather, Irish Heather, if only there were some softness about you, some hidden anguish or pain, then I could feel sorry for you, I could understand, sympathise, but there is something inhuman about you. You wanted to be a disease. The match between you and the virus was perfect. You and the virus both need minds to inhabit, DNA to remould. Like Helen Lane's tumour, you are immortal, undead, and you have hold of me.

Milena began to think that what she had was an illness, in the old sense of something that did not cure, but wounded. Heather was like arthritis, a continual pain that had to be managed. The boredom was excruciating. Milena managed it by asking herself if it was worse than the boredom she usually inflicted on herself. Was it any worse, for example, than humming over and over to herself a song that she hated? Was it any worse than sitting alone in the Zoo cafe and examining, one by one, all her many faults of personality? If Milena was now infected by a dedicated Marxist philosopher, who had infected her before? Someone who hated Milena, who tormented her; someone who chattered away at her, who kept her distracted with a stream of useless quibbling that she would have tolerated from no one else.

Milena began to yearn for silence. As Heather read, as the music mounted, as Jacob faded, as she wondered what was happening with *Love's Labour's*, as the fear of the Snide continually nibbled at her, Milena developed a most profound and earnest desire for stillness.

She would return each afternoon from the practice rooms to find Rolfa growing distant and wan. Rolfa would smile at her in a soft and hazy way, eyes dim. It was a smile that was too accepting, that was without hope. Milena would know from that smile, and from the pallid sunlight on the walls, and from the shadows grown long from waiting that she did not have much time to do her work.

And there would be a toothbrush in the candleholder and a foundation garment in a saucepan, and the floor underfoot would be both sticky and crunchy at the same time from a meal of toast and honey. Milena would perceive and regret the disruption that had ploughed its way through her life. She would miss it, were it to go.

Then one afternoon, Milena came back, and Rolfa was not there.

Well, this is it, she thought, this is how it begins. One day she simply will not be here and I will never know, never know if she was caught, or simply went away. There is nothing I can do. She slumped onto the bed and closed her eyes and waited, listening for a familiar footfall. She opened her eyes again, and it had grown darker. She stood up and began to tidy things away.

She piled up the papers that Rolfa had disordered. She cleared away the washing up that Rolfa had done, leaving honey on the bottom of the plates. She found chicken bones in her clean clothes bag, and held them up, looking at the traces of Rolfa, the shreds of meat her teeth had left behind. It grew dark, and Milena became more and more certain that Rolfa had gone, and that it had all been for nothing.

Then, sitting in the dark, Milena heard a door slam, far below. She heard a great echoing voice roar up the staircase. Rolfa! Milena jumped up, overjoyed. She listened as Rolfa kept singing, recklessly. For God's sake, keep quiet! Do you want to post a sign and tell them that you're here? Rolfa began to whistle. Milena began to feel aggrieved. Why couldn't you tell Jacob where you were going? Where have you been all this time? The whistling drew near the door. Then there was a thump.

'I do not seem,' said Rolfa, in her mellowest tones, 'to be able to open the door.'

Drunk, thought Milena. 'Try turning the handle,' she said.

Rolfa thumped against the door again. 'Why am I unable to open the door?' she asked heaven.

Oooh, thought Milena. More low comedy. She went to the door to open it and couldn't. The handle would not move.

'Why won't you open the door?' Rolfa asked.

'Because you're pulling the handle up, Rolfa. Rolfa? Let go of the handle, Rolfa.' Milena was enunciating very clearly and slowly.

'How can I open a door by letting go of the handle?' Rolfa asked. There was a thump as she threw her full weight against it. 'The door is jammed. I shall have to break it down.'

'Rolfa, Rolfa please. Just push the handle down.'

'The handle,' announced Rolfa, 'has just come off.'

Then there was a silence. 'Rolfa?' Milena asked. The handle of the door was as limp as a dead fish. When Milena pushed the door open, she saw Rolfa, half crouching, with an expression of mingled delight and horror fixed like glaze on her face.

She was looking at her sister Zoe.

Although capitalist and worker confront each other in the marketplace . . .

'Oh, Rolfa,' said Zoe, looking at the shaved arms and face. She glanced miserably at Milena.

. . . only as buyer with money on the one hand and seller, a commodity, on the other. . . .

Heather, shut up!

'Do you want to come in?' Milena asked Zoe, stepping aside.

72

Zoe shouldered her way through the doorway as if past an obstacle, and stopped, distraught, and stared about the tiny room.

Rolfa followed, swinging a whisky bottle in one hand. The two GEs filled the room like air bladders. Zoe looked for a chair to sit on. There wasn't one.

'Do you know,' said Rolfa, holding up the bottle towards the window and what was beyond it. 'There are people out there. The whole place. Full of people. Like a string of pearls.'

'Do you know what the Family would do if they saw you like this?' Zoe said, enraged. 'They'd tie a mask soaked in ether over your face and ship you south in a box.' She turned away, arms folded in front of her stomach.

'If you break the string,' Rolfa continued, 'the pearls all go rolling down down the steps.' She sank to the floor. 'Oh God, my bloody beads.'

'This is the first time she's been drunk,' said Milena.

'We wondered how you were keeping her quiet,' said Zoe.

Zoe is the one I can talk to, Milena remembered. 'Would you like something to drink, Zoe? A cup of tea? It's about all we have.'

Zoe shook her head, and turned towards Milena. 'How can you live like this?' she asked. It was an honest, if unguarded question.

'By limiting our expectations,' said Milena. An honest answer.

. . . *both sides appear constantly, repeatedly, in the marketplace playing the same opposed roles.*

Zoe looked about the bare and tiny room, and did a kind of shrug with her eyebrows. She was wearing a white toga, and her braided hair was piled on her head. 'I was going to ask you to come home, Rolfa, but you can't, looking like that. Do you really hate us so much?'

'Yes,' replied Rolfa, grinning. 'Oooops.' She covered her mouth.

'The Family doesn't know yet. Papa hasn't told them. We managed to get him to call off the Snide. The sneak wasn't any good anyway, he got all lovesick over some female called Heather.'

'I suppose he cost too much,' said Rolfa, and took a swig.

'Angie and I wanted to give you time!'

'How does it feel to be an economy measure?'

'If you came back by yourself, Papa would be more forgiving. He's nearly given up on you, Rolfa.' There was a swollen silence between them. Zoe's face looked limp and puffy, and flesh showed through, as if the fur were patchy. 'I have.'

That's good, thought Milena, without quite knowing why. She seemed to feel a way.

. . . *in the course of time everyone assumes all the roles in the sphere of circulation.*

'Zoe,' Milena said. 'Would it make any difference if something happened to Rolfa's music?'

Zoe glumly watched her white sandals as they scuffed the resin-tiled floor. 'I'd be grateful for anything,' she murmured.

'And if it were done in such a way that no one knew it was Rolfa, no one knew it was a GE, not even the Family, would that help?'

Zoe looked at the floor without responding.

'Look, I don't understand how the Family works. But I do know that Rolfa is an embarrassment to your father.'

Zoe's eyes were full of warning.

'Tuh.' Rolfa's shudder. 'Pocket Caesar. Wants to be Consul.'

Zoe's head turned so sharply, the tendons of her neck showed through the fur. 'He wants to be accepted by his own People, and he never has been!'

Milena intervened. 'If . . . if Rolfa's music came to something and we all stopped the Family finding out . . .' Milena sighed with the difficulty and delicacy of what she had to say. 'Would that be enough?'

'Enough for what?'

'Suppose . . . suppose you simply tell the Family that Rolfa has disappeared. You don't know where, or why, but she's always been odd, and she's gone, somewhere. Now that would have nothing to do with the legal position of the Family in relation to the Consensus. It might not even have anything to do with . . . oh, I don't know what to call it . . . genetic drift back towards the average, or whatever. Which is all they care about.'

'You are a cold little fish, aren't you?' said Zoe.

'Look, having Rolfa with you is not going to do your father any good either. If she's a black mark against him now, she always will be. You're the only one who cares about Rolfa. This is what she wants.'

Something in Zoe relented. 'It's not so easy, Ms Shibush, to watch a sister Slide away.' She said it quietly. 'Especially when you're wondering why someone wants to give her such a good push.'

'Don't let her go! Just give her time.'

'Give you time, you mean.'

'Give her music time. The music is good.'

'How long?' Zoe asked abruptly.

Milena felt a prickling. 'A year,' she said. She thought she was overestimating.

Zoe leaned against the wall and chewed the inside of her cheek, looking out the window.

'All right, Ms Shibush. All right.' She rocked herself away from the wall. She looked at Rolfa, considered, and found that she had nothing to say. The broken door was still open. She walked to it and turned to Milena.

'Why don't I hate you?' she asked.

'I don't know,' replied Milena.

'A year,' said Zoe, warning her, and left.

Milena closed the door and started to shake. What had she done? How had she done it? Rolfa sat drinking quietly, staring at the bottle with a faraway smile, as if all of it had nothing to do with her. In a sense, it didn't.

The next morning, Milena bundled up what music she had and took it to the Minister who ran the National Theatre. He was popularly known as the Zookeeper. Even he called himself that at times.

Walking through the upper floor of the Zoo, Milena felt as small and as hard as a nut. There was a groomed young man whose job it was to stop people seeing the Minister. Milena could not afford the luxury of disliking him.

She did not say that she had found an undiscovered genius. She said that she was harbouring a fugitive and that she felt the Minister should know. She explained why. The reason was that the creature was talented. She left the evidence of that talent, the music, as if it were part of a briefing for a policy decision. The young man took a stern line. Why had she not come earlier? He would make sure the Minister saw the papers and attended to her case. He patted them at the corners to make a neat package of them on his otherwise empty table.

Milena devoted the rest of the day to Rolfa. She bought a pack lunch with the last of their money. Roast beef sandwiches and oranges and sticks of celery – things they both could eat. She took Rolfa, who was content and distant, on a ride in an omnibus to Regent's Park. The bus stop called it Chao Li Gardens.

It was getting cooler, and there were high, racing clouds in the sky. The leaves were beginning to change colour already, going yellow at the edges, with brown spots. In the centre of the park, there was a rose garden with ornamental ponds. Milena and Rolfa walked beside the artificial waterways. There was a smell of still, dark water. Ducks landed in it, sliding to a halt.

Milena explained what she had done, and Rolfa appeared to be unmoved. Rolfa threw bits of her sandwiches to the ducks on the water. Overhead a flight of greylag geese passed, on their way to the Thames estuary from Iceland. The world had been saved.

Rolfa watched the geese overhead. 'Everything moves,' she said. 'You wonder how it all knows where to go. Einstein wondered how birds knew where to migrate to. He thought they might follow lines of light in the sky. He saw everything as lines of light. That's how he was built. So we don't really know how he moved, either. Any more than the birds.'

Rolfa turned and flicked one of her grins towards Milena, as if apologising for what she had just said. 'Thank you for trying,' said Rolfa. 'But I really don't mind the silence.' She was admonishing Milena, ever so gently. 'The music comes out of the silence. I don't mind if it goes back in. We come out of the silence . . .' Her voice trailed off and she traced an arch with her hand. We go back into the silence too.

What is she saying? thought Milena. That she will go away?

'We have a year, Rolfa.'

'But we don't have any food,' said Rolfa. She threw the last morsel of bread to the ducks. They began to walk back towards the bus stop.

And suddenly Rolfa turned and attacked a rose. She snatched the stem despite the thorns and twisted it, breaking it off. Maybe it was the clumsiness, maybe it was the anger, but Milena was shocked without quite knowing why.

Rolfa turned, and holding the rose perfectly upright, gave it to Milena. She said something slurred and embarrassed. It took a moment for Milena to realise that she had said, 'A rose for a rose.'

She shouldn't have been able to do that, thought Milena. That is a public rose. If Rolfa had been anyone else, the viruses would have stopped her taking it. Rolfa is immune as well.

Milena turned the rose round and round in her hand. It was an old-fashioned rose, a very pale pink marbled with magenta. *Rosa mundi*, whispered the viruses. The petals had gone brown at the edges and had curled back to reveal a fresher core. It must have been recently watered by the gardeners. Fat pearls of water clung to it. Milena thought she ought to be embarrassed being seen walking with a stolen, public rose. Then she found she didn't care, and carried it boldly. It bobbed on its long stem as if made out of lead, as if heavy with meaning. The public rose was a private valediction.

On the bus back home, Rolfa's face was smiling, sad and faraway. Milena found herself thinking over and over: Rolfa don't go, Rolfa don't go.

Their little room at the Shell was cool and in shadow by the time they returned. September was declining rapidly. Rolfa won't mind the winter, thought Milena, she'll like the cold. If she's still here, said another part of her mind. Milena went up onto the roof of the Shell to sunbathe, to kill her hunger pangs. Cilla brought Rolfa some soup and sausages. Cilla slipped them both into the Zoo to see *Madam Butterfly*. Rolfa no longer could buy tickets. Her smile was rapt, with the music, with the singing, with the staging, and her eyes were famished and glistening. If only they had let us be ourselves, Milena thought.

The next day Milena tried to rejoin *Love's Labour's Lost*.

She was told at one of the informatin desks that the director had died. Quite suddenly. Thirty-five. Time-expired. The cast were in mourning. They had asked to have the production discontinued. They didn't want to work with anyone else. They can't face going back, thought Milena. They can't face going back to sleepwalking Shakespeare.

It was just like the play, at the end. Welcome Mercade, Mr Death. You interrupt our merriment. The King your Father is . . .

Dead, for my life.

It's a design flaw, thought Milena. We shouldn't have to die. She thought of the director, called him Harry in her mind. She remembered his feverish eyes. You knew you were going, Harry. This was your last leap. A lifetime of sleepwalking, of making other people sleepwalk, broke you. And then you were free. Harry, if I ever direct a play, she promised him, I will do it as you did.

And they are not going to break me.

Milena did not go back to her chilly room. She walked on, up the stairs, to the upper floor of the Zoo.

Out of the silence, into the silence.

She was going to talk to the Minister, before time.

'Oh yes, Ms Shibush,' said the sleek young man, smiling. 'I'll go ask.' He went through a door.

Milena sat down. A row of Postpersons sat next to her, staring ahead with expressions of perfect peace. Lined up like Buddhas in a temple. Their conscious minds were fully occupied with the records of the Zoo. But what of underneath? thought Milena.

Her legs jiggled up and down with nerves. Heather had reached the end of Volume One, the only one that Marx had finished himself. She was fighting against the ending, reading notes and appendices, reading quotes in their original language. She was re-reading the prefaces to all the different editions. It was as if she would die when she finished.

I am ready to welcome scientific criticism.

I don't really know you, Heather, thought Milena, I only know a virus. You may have loved, you may have been happy.

As far as the prejudices of what is termed public opinion, to which I have never made any concession . . .

You were dedicated. You were formidable. You gave your life away. Do your motives matter?

. . . I shall continue to guide myself by the maxim of the great Florentine:
Sequi il tuo corso, e lascia dir le genti.

77

Follow your own bent, no matter what people say.

Marx quoting Dante. Heather went on to read the next preface.

As Heather read, Milena thought of Rolfa and the wellspring of music in her, and of the paper from the Vampires, and of what she was going to say to the Minister, and she found that she had no idea.

'I'm tired,' she said aloud.

Marx could not enjoy the pleasure of preparing this third edition for the press.

The sleek young man came out again, asked one of the Postpeople to go in, and said to Milena, 'A few minutes, Ms Shibush. Are you thirsty? Can I get you something?'

So I am in favour, Milena thought, but the thought was bleak. The young man tried to engage her in conversation. It was his job to know what was going on. His combed-back chestnut hair and his busy black and orange shirt all annoyed Milena. His spectacles annoyed Milena; spectacles were a Vampire affectation. Behind the flat resin lenses were the goggle-eyes of a cornea regrowth.

Milena answered his questions with yes or a no, or a yo – a Vampire answer that could mean sometimes or maybe. Yes, she was an actress. Yes, the music was very good. Was she friends with the composer? Yo.

A door opened and the Minister himself asked Milena to come in. Milena followed him into his room.

That mighty thinker . . .

He slept there. His bed was behind a screen that was painted with green streaks to represent reeds by a river. The walls were covered in cloth that was also decorated with reeds, and a large black sketch of a heron. There was a picture of Marx on the wall. Milena looked at the eyes. They would have been brown and soft. There was a picture of Mao at 25, and of Chao Li Song, the hero of the Second Revolution.

The Minister wore khaki trousers and a khaki shirt. He was a very handsome man of Chinese extraction, with neat black hair, a neat smile, a neat moustache. Milena liked him. There was something informal and direct about him. He had an air of competence and balanced openness, the product of Party training. Was that a virus too?

'Do you mind if my Postperson stays with us?' the Minister asked Milena. 'I like to keep accurate records.'

The Postperson was a woman. She sat on a tiny chair, with her knees pressed together. Her head was wrapped in a kerchief. 'That's fine,' murmured Milena. The Minister held out a hand for her to sit on a large, upholstered chair.

. . . died on March 14, 1883.

As Milena settled into it, she felt herself enfolded and cushioned by something else, something that supported her and made the room go still.

Like an ear clearing of air pressure or an infection, her mind was suddenly quiet. Heather was gone. Milena was well. There was a hush all around her like a pond.

Outside the big window, everything was blue and hazy. The last of summer, the first of autumn, a jumble of old buildings. Milena could hear voices and horses' hooves below, as life was made and unmade in ignorance of what was going on behind this one high pane of glass on the top floor of the Zoo. The window was shaded, its frame was supported, by bamboo.

And Milena remembered. The bamboo reminded her of something.

Ice cream sticks.

She remembered that ice cream had come on little bamboo sticks. She saw the bamboo sticks very clearly. They were in sunlight, on a table. There were children with her, little girls, and they were laying out their bamboo sticks to make a picture. They were making a picture of a house.

Milena was making a window.

She saw it so clearly, it was as if the table, with the sticks, was just around some corner, to be found again.

Memory.

Milena heard footsteps in the corridor below. Very slowly, her attention turned to what was around her. She heard a hissing. It was the hissing of molecules of air against her eardrums. Milena was in the silence.

In the silence, nothing was fragmented. There were no separate strands to gather together, to fumble, to compete for attention. In the silence, all of that fell away, and there was only what was here, and what was to be done.

It was as if she, Milena, had finally come into the room and sat down beside her.

'I am told that you have been missing performances, Ms Shibush.'

Milena saw no reason to reply. Zookeeper.

'That cannot help your career,' the Minister said, gently.

'Nothing could help my career. I am a very bad actress,' said Milena.

His eyebrows rose and he shifted in his chair and smiled, amused.

'What do you think of Ms Patel's music?' asked Milena.

'Personally,' he said, 'I thought it showed promise. But what I think is of little importance. It may surprise you to learn that we consulted the Consensus on this matter.'

Nothing seemed to surprise Milena. 'And?'

'The Consensus is an extraordinarily accurate predictor of the success or failure of an artistic endeavour. It had a complicated response to Ms Patel's music. But then all its reactions are complicated. It has all of us inside it.'

But not me, thought Milena. It does not have me.

'Essentially, it liked it, but its more musically adept personalities registered concern over the roughness of what was shown.'

'Not surprising,' said Milena. 'They were shown what Jacob and I could remember of the pieces. They need work.'

'Exactly,' said the Minister. 'There were other problems.'

Milena waited. There was a silence. The Minister's smile widened and he chuckled. He was beginning to find the interview disconcerting.

'There does seem to be a balance in life. We have gained in knowledge and order. But that calm and that wealth of information do not lead us to originality. Out of the disorder of this poor woman's life, something new has come. So.' He leaned forward, 'do we as good immaterialist socialists advise that people should live in disorder and ignorance?'

Rolfa? Ignorant? You ignorant man, thought Milena. Aloud, she answered: 'I think we advise a love of beauty from whatever source.'

'Even from the Genetically Engineered?'

'Of course,' said Milena, engulfed in calmness. 'We believe that they are human even if they say they do not. We don't have to tell anyone that she is Genetically Engineered. We can accept her and her work as being human.'

The Minister chuckled again. 'We cannot do that, you see, without disrupting our wider and quite delicate relationship with the GEs. They do not wish to be defined as being human.'

'So what we are really talking about is mining in the Antarctic.'

The Minister's smile did not change.

'I've talked to her sister. The Bears are willing . . .'

'Please,' interrupted the Minister, giving his head a little shake of distaste. 'Don't call them that.'

Mining and a market for luxury goods, Milena decided. Where, she wondered, am I getting all of this from?

'The hierarchy of the GEs don't know that Rolfa is with us. Her immediate family have agreed to keep it from them. It is in their interests to keep it from them. If we pretend that the author of this music is a human being, they will. They have given us a year to do something with her music. They love her that much.'

The Minister corrected her. 'Well, we have had a representation from her father asking us to return her if she has been found.' He corrected her, but was still willing to be generous. 'We did try to return her. We tried to find both of you and no one here would tell us where you were.' His smile went crooked with amusement. 'Which told us that if our own people were so intent, perhaps we did not wish to act. Our relationship with the GEs is delicate but not close.'

He's amused for now, thought Milena, but I mustn't get too clever.

'Thank you, thank you very much,' she said.

I get this, she decided, from my father. From my political mother and father who dealt this way for years. And I also get it from Heather.

'Did you know she stole from her family?' the Minister asked.

'No,' lied Milena, sounding shocked.

'Whatever we do must reflect credit on the immaterialist programme, and on Consensus politics. Your friend has had a capitalist upbringing. She will suffer from grave distortions of personality.'

Milena began to get angry. The Minister kept on talking.

'It is not only that we will have to keep her shaved, or sitting down so she looks smaller.' The Minister was smiling, confident that he was talking to Milena on her own level. 'We have no guarantee that Ms Patel's behaviour will be acceptable. What we must avoid is making any link in people's minds between talent and childish behaviour.'

'I agree of course,' said Milena. 'But her upbringing has not been capitalist. It is inaccurate to call the GEs capitalists. Capitalists take the surplus value created by other people's labour. The GEs do all the work themselves. They may amass wealth and live outside the Consensus, but their Family is in fact a classic example of the Estate system as desribed by Chao Li Song.'

Oh. The Zookeeper's face was as blank as a nail hit on the head.

'That is why their economic activity is able to mesh with ours,' said Milena. 'Are GEs immune to the viruses?'

'Yes . . . unless.' The Minister made a vague gesture.

So, thought Milena. There is an unless. They can cure Polar Bears, they just choose not to. Of course they can cure them, lower their body temperature, suppress the immune system . . .

'She is so talented. There must be some way,' said Milena.

'We will give it thought,' he promised.

'If she joined the Consensus, was considered human, she could use the practice rooms, take instruction . . .'

'Of course,' he said.

Come on, come on, follow it through. Milena kept her hands still.

He looked wary. 'Of course, if she joined the Consensus . . .' he mused. 'We could correct for all of that. We could ensure that there would be no bad behaviour. And it would be a shame . . . it would not be just . . . if such talent were allowed to wither. All right. We will consider that aspect.' He leaned back. The interview was over.

No, thought Milena.

'It has to be done today,' said Milena. She began to feel fear. She began to be unsteady. It was like waking up. The Minister's eyes were sombre.

'Please,' said Milena, suddenly shorn of her bigger self. 'She's hungry. She's not Rhodopsin, she can't just go out into the sun. We've got no money. If she joins the Consensus, she can have a position here, she can eat!' Milena found that she had gone tremulous. 'Otherwise she will leave. Please. Can you arrange it for today?'

The Minister seemed to have a question rise in his mind. He was looking at Milena now, not considering what she said. He was considering her.

'I will see if it can be done,' he said, no longer smiling. Milena began to quake. It was a rattling in the bottom of her belly. 'But what you must do is check with your friend and prepare her. We must make sure that this is acceptable to her.'

I've won, thought Milena. I've won. She stood up to go. She did not want to speak. She did not trust herself. She nodded yes to whatever he said.

'Can you come back in an hour?'

Yes, yes. He shook her hand. She walked out of the rooms into the corridors, and began to run. The shaking continued. Her knees wobbled, her hands flapped. There was a sense of fear, of being in a bigger world. She was not who she had thought she was. I may not be a good actress, she thought, but I am good at this. I can arrange things. She had learned in the cushioned silence that every artist is perforce a politician.

chapter six

MEETING CHARLIE, CHARLIE SLIDE (SURVIVING IN CONCERT)

The Public Reading Rooms – the rooms in which the public were Read – were underground in bunkers. The bunkers were under what had once been the Department of the Environment. The Department of the Environment had been torn down to plant a forest.

The forest was the Consensus. The Consensus was a garden of purple, fleshy trees that reached up and fed on sunlight. The mind of the Consensus was below. A buttressing marble wall ran around the garden. In the wall, there was an old stone plaque that had been preserved. 'This is Marsham Street,' the plaque said, '1688.'

Underneath there were corridors of brick. They wound their way through fleshy roots and a gathering of synapses called the Crown. Below, like tubers, there grew mindflesh, on which memories were imprinted, memories and the patterns of response. They were models made of children, Read at ten years of age.

This was the Consensus for the Pit, the central heart of London. In the corridors of brick, painted white, there were air vents and electric lights. Milena stared in wonder at the glowing bulbs and their golden, dazzling filaments. She had always loved light.

The rooms were full of classrooms of children, about to be Read. Their Nurses led them in song, playing on guitars or hand pianos. The children wore their best clothes. The little girls wore printed saris translucent with colour. The boys wore jewellery through their nostrils. They danced in a line, waving their hands like the branches of trees. The lucky ones had parents, who sat on benches and watched with quiet pride.

People in white uniforms danced with them. A huge woman in white saw Rolfa and beamed and worked her way, still dancing, towards them.

'You're Rolfa. I'm Root,' she said. 'You're our special case. You're going to have special treatment from us, I promise you that.' She led Rolfa to one side. 'Just a few questions to ask first,' said Root.

Health. Medical record. Any intoxicating substances lately?

There was a cheer from a class of children. They were praising their own Estate school. Root turned and pressed her hands together.

'Oh, the little darlings, oh the little flowers. I tell you, this is the happiest place. They come here dancing. They leave here dancing too.' Root's grin was wide.

'Now, love, you have any experiences with the paranormal?'

Instantly, Rolfa's face looked withdrawn.

'Have you ever levitated, or had an out-of-body experience? Any poltergeists in your home? Anything of that sort?'

Rolfa shook her head and gave a shy smile. Who me?

'It's very important. You're sure? OK, then, we go in.'

This woman is too used to talking to Tykes, thought Milena. Then Root turned to her. The smile was like a beam of light. 'You, too, love. You've never seen this, and we want you to see how happy it is.'

Milena felt ice in her chest. They know, she thought. They know that they've never Read me. It's been deliberate. They've decided not to.

Quiet, she thought, and followed Root.

I thought I was free, Milena thought. Instead, I was being tolerated. Or used. They wouldn't leave me alone, if there was no reason for it.

Of course they must know they haven't Read me.

Another mystery, lost in Milena's history.

Root was holding open a door, and waving to her, come in, come in. Milena followed, in anger, and in fear.

They went down a corridor to a sealed hatch, that hissed when it was opened. Beyond it was a loose and flabby concertina corridor, made of soft resin. It shifted underfoot, floating in flesh. It was wet and smelled of disinfectant and was lit by an ultraviolet light.

'Got to avoid disease,' explained Root.

They stepped into a room made of flesh.

The walls were slightly phosphorescent, and they seemed to pull back as they entered.

'Hello, Baby,' said Root. 'Time to go for a walk.'

She's Terminal, realised Milena. She talks to the Consensus, with her mind. It can talk to her. She can see for it, hear for it. This is the Consensus, here.

'What's it like?' asked Milena, all in one breath.

'Big,' said Root the Terminal, warmly. 'And alive. Come on, now Rolfa love, you sit over here, on the floor, anywhere will do.'

This is what holds me, Milena thought. This is what rules. This is Charlie. This is the Slider, maker of Angels. The beating heart of her culture, and she had never seen it. Machines had imitated life, and now life had returned the compliment. Patterns were repeated. A computer made of flesh, growing new capacity when it needed it, sending mycelia through the earth, sprouting elsewhere like mushrooms, fed by purple gardens.

Milena remembered again.

She had never seen a film, but other people had with viruses in their heads, and she had their memories. They were the memories the Party wished her to have. She remembered a film now, of Chao Li Song.

Milena saw a wry, smiling face, an old gentleman full of good news he could not contain. 'We will have to accept that we have been superseded,' he said in a voice like a rusty hinge. 'We are like parents who have produced a giant baby. It deals in things we cannot conceive of.'

Thought was chemistry moving into electricity, and electricity was unified with the other forces. In the fifth dimension, the master of the eleven dimensions, gravity and electromagnetic phenomena were the same thing. The Consensus could think in gravity. It could imprint personalities in gravity. Angels, they were called. The Angels could slide through gravity. They could slide across space at the speed of light. As predicted, they travelled backwards in time. They travelled backwards in time to other stars.

The highways of gravity were called by the English the Charlie Slide.

'How will it help?' asked Chao Li Song, 'to send thought to the stars, long ago? The answer is that it will mine for wealth. Thought and gravity are one. Gravity pulled the universe into existence, by inflation. It pulled against nothingness, and as it pulled energy was released. There was a flash of heat.' Chao Li Song smiled, in the past, as if he had travelled at the speed of light. 'The Angels will unleash blasts of heat. They will smelt the rocks of other worlds. They will lift them, like toffee, and hurl them towards us, out of the past. They will guide them to us, through the long light years back, very slowly.' He paused to smile privately. 'We know they will do this, because it has already happened in the past. The blocks of metal. We have seen them coming towards us. We have heard the Angels, in the lines of gravity.'

The universe had been made by inflation, gravity pulling energy out of nothing. The Consensus was mining the vacuum as well. It was plucking it gently, to release floods of heat. The Consensus would soon be making energy by making tiny, pocket universes.

'You comfy, love?' Root asked, giving Rolfa a drink of water.

Chao Li Song had other things in store to say. 'For so long now, we have known the universe was not material. Everything calls up its opposites and achieves a new synthesis. Hegel told us, Marx told us. The time has come now. We had Dialectical Materialism. Now we must have Dialectical Immaterialism. Idea precedes reality.'

He had to flee for his life. The viruses did not tell Milena this. Her mother had, in the name of her father who had died. Because of Chao

Li Song, socialism forged an alliance with resurgent religion. Because of him, socialism won. It required only a few compromises, with prudery and common sense. Milena lived in a theological state.

Charlie, the English called him. Charlie Song.

'Sing a song of Charlie, take you for a ride,' Root the Terminal was singing, wobbling backwards like a jelly towards Milena. 'Sing a song of Charlie, down the Charlie Slide.'

We rose out of Africa, thought Milena. We rose out of a drought and survived, not with a bigger jaw, but with a smaller jaw because we had the beginnings of speech. We survived because we worked together. We are designed to survive changes in climate by working in concert. Like music.

Root gripped her hand and shook it. 'You stay here with me, love, or we get two readings all mixed up, and that's very weird. You never seen this. You never seen this, you in for a real treat, I can tell you that.' She chuckled. She was like a balloon full of chuckles.

We survive, thought Milena, because after everything else, we are good. We survive to the *extent* that we are good.

The thing that was the room chuckled with them. It chuckled and space chuckled, the space containing Rolfa. There was a wave through it, and her.

Rolfa's head was flung back like a cannonball, and it split into a grin. 'Yeee-haaa!' she cried. She roared with laughter. 'Whooo-eeee!'

'That's it, that's it!' shouted Root and she jumped up and down with her vast bulk. 'Oh, yeah. Ride it love, ride it!'

I had heard, thought Milena. I had heard it was wonderful, and I never believed.

Every synapse is engaged at once, every neural pathway, every cell in the brain works together, all at once for the first and only time. Like a national grid, all lit up. Each person a nation, a universe.

The Consensus pulled energy up out of nothing, from quantum vacuum, and it could roar back in time by travelling faster than light. It had been known for a century and a half that gravity in the form of inflation had helped spark the beginning. But how was there a view-point, a reference, for gravity to work in before space and time? The answer was that gravity had been imported back to the beginning, thought in the form of gravity.

Humankind, working as the Consensus, was going to make the universe. So loved the world that we made God in our own image.

'Oh!' cried Rolfa, in fondness for everything. 'Oh!' and her voice broke into a whine of loss and regret and she looked at Milena, smiling and sad.

'That's it,' said Root. 'Darling, you just been Read.' She walked to

Rolfa, leaned over her, inspected her, stroked her head. 'So what did you see, love?' she asked, speaking gently.

'All kinds of things,' said Rolfa, faintly.

Root laughed and nodded. 'Yes, yes, everything comes back.'

'I saw my mother,' said Rolfa. 'She was picking water lilies in a pond; she had her dress, her big orange dress lifted up out of the water, and she was laughing in case she fell.' She sat up and took hold of Root's arm. 'The pond was behind an old white farmhouse. We were staying there. On Prince Edward Island. I was five years old. I got in a fight with my sister. She said she was going to grow bigger than me because she drank tea. And big people drink tea.'

'I tell you, it's the same for everyone. I see people, they leave here dancing.'

'But it doesn't just come back,' said Rolfa. 'It goes forward as well.'

'Hmmm?' said Root, turning, as if someone had spoken to her. Someone had. 'Back to business,' she murmured, and cupped a hand around an ear, and listened, rapt. Milena was given an uncomfortable chance to think.

Root began to smile. 'Well you're quite a character, aren't you? You're all over the place. I've never seen anyone like you before.' She chuckled and shook her head. 'You like your drink, I can tell you that.'

Milena felt a familiar chill. 'Change as little as you can,' she said, in a whisper.

'We do, love. We don't go mucking around.'

'She's a genius. That's why this is being done.'

'Is she now?' Root was amused. 'Well I wouldn't be knowing about that.' She bent down. 'You feel up to moving now, Rolfa? We've got to make space now for someone else.'

Gently, Rolfa nodded. Root helped her to her feet.

'In and out like a giant lung,' murmured Rolfa.

Milena took the other arm. She felt Rolfa lean on her, exhausted. They walked through the concertina, down a white corridor to a little room with old chairs. As she was leaving, Root gave Milena a wry grin, and waved her to follow into the corridor, to talk.

'Your friend, you know, she shakes with both hands.' Root's eyebrows were raised, her cheeks were bursting with amusement, her tiny hand on its fat wrist was placed delicately over her breast.

What was the woman talking about? Milena began to have an uncomfortable creeping feeling. 'I think she's left-handed, actually.'

'Now don't let on you don't know!' insisted Root. 'We see it all here, nothing bothers us.'

'What are you talking about?'

'Your friend. She wants to botty-bump with other ladies.' Root covered her face and hooted with laughter. 'Oh, the shapes humankind gets in. We see them all! But a little rough justice and it all works out.'

Milena went still and cold. 'She likes other women.'

'Oh, loves them, love. Loves you.'

'Can we stop this?' Milena asked. Her voice was a croak.

Root shook her head sadly. 'It's the law,' she said. Her vast buttocks made her white skirt rustle as she walked away.

Milena turned and walked into the room. She saw Rolfa sitting, smiling, looking through the whole world to somewhere else.

'Rolfa,' Milena said. 'I love you. I want to sleep with you – *I mean* – I want to have sex with you.'

Rolfa began to grin. She covered her eyes. 'This is a fine time to tell me.'

'I tried before, but I couldn't.'

Rolfa began to laugh.

'It's not funny!' Milena did an anguished little dance.

'It's ficken hilarious! It's the funniest thing I ever heard.' Rolfa took Milena's hand, and shook her head. 'Why didn't you say anything?'

'I don't know. I was afraid. Why didn't you say anything?'

'Because you're a human being, and I thought you'd be cured! You told me. You said. I had all those viruses when I was ten years old!'

Oh merciful heaven. Something so simple. Milena whispered. 'But I was never Read. They gave me viruses to educate me. But I was never Read. I was never cured.' And I never talked about not being Read, because I was afraid of being found out. I never said anything because I was afraid. But they knew all along.

I had Rolfa. I had Rolfa all along. And now they're going to destroy her.

Rolfa was laughing. 'All those nights! Should I touch her, shouldn't I touch her, no I mustn't, they cure these people.' She looked down at Milena's hand and played with its fingers. 'Who needs viruses, when you've got fear?' She looked up at Milena, still smiling. 'We'll have some time,' she promised. 'However long, we'll have it.'

Root rustled back into the room. Involuntarily, Milena jumped away. Rolfa pulled her back.

'A little bit of honey,' Root said, 'and a touch of immuno-suppression.' She bounced her hips back and forth with the rhythm of the words. She was wearing pink gloves. 'Now. Stick out your tongue at me. Going to give you Candy.'

Run away, thought Milena. She contemplated violence, pushing the huge nurse over and running. But where? Where was the way out?

Rolfa stuck her tongue out like a naughty girl. Root said, 'That's the spirit,' and dabbed the tongue with a finger of the glove.

'And that's all there is to it. You'll begin to feel ill in about three hours. Just relax, drink some fluids. No booze, now. Any complications, use your Postperson and let me know, and I'll be straight around.' She turned and her eyes flicked towards Milena. 'This is a main virus,' Root told her. 'It's contagious.'

Milena looked back at her bleakly.

'Rough justice,' said Root the Terminal. 'But less rough than it used to be, I tell you that.'

Then she helped Rolfa to her feet and led her out of the room. Milena followed. There was nothing else she could do.

chapter seven

AN ULTIMATELY FATAL CONDITION (LOVE'S LABOURS)

Outside, it was Indian Summer, almost warm with patchy sunlight and racing shadows of clouds. Fat pigeons limped across the stretch of green beside Lambeth Bridge. It was mid-afternoon and most people were working. A circle of teenage boys, their shirts open, sat on the lawn drinking and playing a desultory game of cards. On the bridge, a wagon had broken its axle and kegs of beer had split open on the slope of the bridge, sudsy and bitter-smelling. Children paddled in it, kicking at the seagulls that had gathered.

'I didn't know about your mother,' said Milena as they walked.

'She left us,' said Rolfa. 'She didn't like Papa.'

'Where did she go?' Milena asked.

Rolfa turned and gave her a very peculiar smile. 'Antarctica,' she said.

They walked on in silence past what had once been the palace of an archbishop. They knew they were going to make love, and Milena knew that she was going to catch the virus. She wanted to catch the virus. She did not want to be left behind. It was not something she needed to think about. Sex complicates, but it is the power of love to simplify.

They walked past the hospital that Florence Nightingale had founded, and past another small park, listening to seagull cries. They passed into the enfolding stone arms of the Shell, its forecourt, and then up the stairs.

Finally, in their small, cold, crowded room, they made love and it was both more ordinary and more strange than Milena had imagined, as ordinary and as strange as rainfall.

Then the shivering began. Rolfa was cold. Milena piled on blankets. Rolfa complained how dry and sore her sinuses were. Milena kept a kettle boiling in the little room, to keep the air moist. The steam hung in the air like a fog.

'It's like a buzz,' said Rolfa. 'It goes all along your arm and right into your head.' Milena got her cups of hot water. The steam seemed to help. Rolfa's voice went smooth again, and she drank the water thirstily, gulping, and sat up on the bed. Milena lay beside her, put her head on her stomach. It gurgled, and they both laughed. Outside, it was growing dark. The city disappeared.

'I'm going to sing,' said Rolfa.

Milena fumbled for the candle, fumbled under the bed for the paper and before she found it, the song began. Hold, hold it! she thought and began without the beginning.

It was like the final chorus of Beethoven's Ninth or the Hallelujah Chorus, simple and powerful and happy. Rolfa smiled as she sang it. She was singing about her life seen whole. Somewhere, Milena was part of it.

'Give it a rest!' someone shouted from an upper floor.

Rolfa's smile was broader, and she raised her voice.

'Qui—et!' howled someone else.

Milena slammed open her window. 'Someone's dying!' she roared in fury. For her, it was true.

When it ended, slowly, peacefully complete, Rolfa made a tracing in the air with her hand. She and Milena looked at each other in the unsteady light, in silence.

Then, with a self-mocking smile, Rolfa made, perfectly, the sound of massed applause. To an actor, it is nothing less than the sound of justice being done.

Milena pulled the counterpane up over her, and kissed her, and Rolfa slept, and during the night, the illness passed. In the morning, when Milena tried to kiss her, Rolfa turned her head. Milena passed her a cup of tea. 'I drink this, I get bigger. Like a big person,' said Rolfa. That afternoon she said, 'I think I'm well enough to get out of bed.' She threw back the counterpane. Her cheeks, her arms, her shoulders were covered in stubble. Slowly, still slightly dazed, she began to pack her few things – the huge cheap clothes, her apron, her frying fork.

She stood by the door and said, feeble and embarrassed. 'I'd better find somewhere else to live. They will find me somewhere else to live, won't they?'

Milena sat on the edge of her bed, looking away from her, and nodded. 'Yes, they will,' she said. 'Come back for your books when you've got somewhere.' There was nothing else to be done. She heard the door close, a soft, considerate clicking.

Milena stayed sitting on her bed. She didn't move. She didn't think she felt particularly sad. She simply didn't move. For the last three months, Rolfa had been almost the only thing she had thought of, and without her Milena found she had nothing to do. She could think of nothing to do.

She didn't want to eat, she didn't want to go outside. Go outside for what? To be an actress? She didn't want to be an actress. Sunlight poured in through the windows, the room became hot, Milena was as silent as a ghost. This is what it was like when Rolfa was here and I was away, she thought.

When she began to smell herself, she went to the showers and washed. She looked glumly at the trails of stubble around the drains where Rolfa had shaved. Stony-faced, she turned the jet of water on them and washed them down the drain with her foot.

She came back and tried to sleep. There was a stirring in the bed. She sat up and saw that the pillow and the quilt were crawling with purple mites. Her immune system was looking for Rolfa. She saw her Mice, scuttling in a kind of frenzy of alarm over each other, over the rumples in the undersheet.

It was what happened when people lost a part of themselves, an arm or leg. In a kind of panic their Mice would go hunting for what was missing. Where is Rolfa? Where is Rolfa? they seemed to be saying. In the end, exhausted, they would crawl back home.

The mites were particularly thick around the back corner of the bed. Milena felt behind it, and found Piglet, jammed between the mattress and the wall. As if in relief, as if the doll were something alive, the Mice swarmed up and over it.

Milena had always hated the doll. Now I'm stuck with the bloody thing, she thought, and threw it at the cooker. Piglet lay face down on the cold floor. Its eyes seemed to look at Milena. Its eyes seemed to say: don't leave me here.

Finally Milena picked it up. As if it were alive, she stroked its grubby felt ears. It had been almost the only thing Rolfa had brought with her from her old life and now it was left behind, deserted.

Part of you didn't want to go, Rolfa. That's why you left so much of yourself behind, all the books, all the papers. She kept on stroking Piglet's ears. She began to weep, and then stopped herself, angry with herself. Oh, you weep do you? Well you did it, she told herself. You made it happen.

Milena felt no rage against her oppressors. The Consensus was to do such great and extraordinary things. How could she argue against those? She was the one who had got things wrong. On balance, she still believed that the Consensus was good and just.

Tyranny is a form of perversion. We come to love it. Every government is a tyranny to a degree, and the more evil it is, the more it is loved. The difficulty lies in judging the degree of tyranny under which you live.

Milena had relied on her tyranny. She had believed one day that it would Read her and cure her of her anger and fear and longing. She had hoped that she would catch the virus from Rolfa. But although

92

she now felt just the slightest bit feverish and queasy, she was not ill. She was resistant to the viruses. She was doomed to be herself.

In the morning, and again in the afternoon, Jacob the Postperson called. 'There is a new play. They want you to act in it,' he said. 'Do you want me to say that you are ill?'

'Yes, Jacob, tell them that,' Milena said.

The long day passed. She didn't eat. Milena sat all night on the bed, leaning against the wall, drifting in and out of sleep. The next morning, there was a shy, apologetic rapping on her door. Cilla called in with bread and cheese. Milena told her that she wasn't hungry. People often were not hungry; Cilla assumed that she had been photosynthesising in the sun.

'We've heard the news about Rolfa,' Cilla said. 'You must be very happy.'

'Yes,' said Milena. 'Very happy.'

'Listen,' said Cilla, sitting next to her on the bed. 'Everyone from *Love's Labour's*, we want to set up our own little company of players. Just to do new theatre, you know. Our way.'

Cilla paused and smiled. 'We want you to help us run it.'

Milena stared back at her. 'Why me?' she asked.

'Why? With what you managed to do with Rolfa? Magic! Complete!' Cilla waited for a response. 'Everyone thinks you've been gutter top,' she said, sensing sadness, wanting to make Milena smile.

It was Vampire slang: gutter top. Grate. Great.

'You're all gutter top, too,' murmured Milena.

'So I can tell everyone you'll do it?'

'Yah,' nodded Milena, looking down at her hands. 'Yah.'

Cilla leaned forward, her face crossed with a perplexed scowl, knowing there had been a loss and not understanding what it could be. Had the old, withdrawn Milena returned? Cilla took the food away.

In the middle of the afernoon, without knocking, the Snide walked in. He wore his sinister hat at a rakish angle.

'Lo, Heather, I'm back,' he said.

His face fell.

'Heather?' he asked in horror.

Milena looked at him and shook her head. No. Not Heather. Heather is dead. There's just me.

He sank down beside her on the bed. 'She was a virus?' He covered his eyes. Masked by his hand, sheltered by it, he found again his edged and bitter, nervous smile.

'And you are Milena,' he said. 'That was good. Good trick. You must have laughed.'

'I was too scared,' said Milena.

'I sensed something, you know. It's just that viruses aren't usually that complete.'

'They aren't usually Heather,' replied Milena.

'I've stopped being a Snide,' he said, looking down at the counterpane, beginning to pick at it. The smile had turned inwards. 'I was going to tell her that.'

I don't have the time or the energy for this, thought Milena. You must know what was between me and Rolfa, you must know what you tried to do to us and yet you want my help. My help. You're not just a fool, you're a shit. You're a fool because you are a shit.

'That's why I needed Heather,' he said, completing the thought for her. 'Did . . . when she was with you . . . did she ever respond to you. Did . . . did she ever talk to you?'

Wearily, Milena shook her head. No, she just read. All she did was read. It was all she could do. She needed me to do anything else.

He stood up and went to the door. He turned and looked at her, searching her face, searching her mind. I was Heather, thought Milena. For him, I had Heather's mind and face.

'I'm glad you're unhappy,' he said.

But I'll get over it. You won't.

Reluctantly, pity stirred. Pity, that was Heather's enemy. Milena showed him Heather's face, its great freckled length, the pebble spectacles. She thought you were a fool, but I think she could have loved you. She needed someone to manage.

He started to put on his sinister hat, then thought better of it. 'There's a bit more to me than that,' he told her.

'Then go and find it,' replied Milena. Like a shadow, he turned and was gone.

She tried to sleep and couldn't. She picked up one of Rolfa's books, brown and battered, and it fell open on the last page.   . . . *at the top of the Forest, a little boy and his bear will always be playing.*

She would have immediately thrown down the book, except that under each word, or rather, each syllable, there was a tiny, pencilled note of music on a tiny, pencilled stave.

Quickly, she flipped through the other pages. It had all been set to music, the entire book, re-written to be sung.

She had left Rolfa reading all day.

Milena picked up the next book in the stack. It was huge, bound in dirty grey cloth, anonymous and slumped sideways on its over-used binding. The first page was an engraving of Dante. *Divina Commedia* said words printed in red. Underneath, in pencil, Rolfa had written, 'FOR AN AUDIENCE OF VIRUSES'.

All three books of the Comedy – *Inferno, Purgatorio, Paradiso* – had been bound together in one volume. Underneath all the words, all the way through, there were musical notes. The handwriting was small and neat and crabbed, as if trying to hide. Some of it was in pencil, some of it was in red ink. Some of it was written on pieces of paper stitched into the book with white thread. Some of it was written in gold. There was one note for each word, but in places there were messages: 'trumpets here' or 'Virgil descant'. Milena turned back to the first page.

Nel mezzo del cammin di nostra vita...

> *Midway in the journey of our life*
> *I found myself in a dark wood*
> *For the straight way was lost*

Then Dante meets the beast. The words were set to the music that Rolfa had sung in the dark the first night Milena had heard her, hidden in the Graveyard.

'Rolfa!' said Milena, and shook the book. To do this and keep it hidden! While Jacob and I copied out the rags of what we had heard. You didn't say anything, I didn't say anything. Did we ever tell each other a word of truth?

Milena read *The Divine Comedy* buoyed up by music. Her viruses translated the notes into imagined sounds. Her viruses sang.

Milena began to imagine it, a great abstract opera that would last for weeks if it were ever performed. She saw it staged in the sky, amid stars, with bars of colour and symbolic angels, beasts with human faces, a hell in honeycombs, tunnels of light opening into the heavens.

Suddenly Cilla stepped forward in the robes of Virgil. The part was written for a soprano, to contrast with Dante. For no reason, Lucy, old Lucy of the Palace of Amusement, was Beatrice. She wore the crown of heaven askew, and gave a sideways wink. A comedy after all. Milena closed her eyes and smiled. All right, Rolfa, all right. It is funny. The whole thing is funny – my not speaking, your not speaking, it's funny. We could have sat down together, and planned what we were going to do with this. You could have orchestrated it, if you'd wanted to. I could have taken it complete and shown it complete and told them, take it or leave it, only leave her alone. Now I'll have to put it on. I'll have to get it performed. Thanks a lot. Milena looked at the size of the book, her finger wedged between the pages to keep her place. I'll have to get this sung, somehow. Not all at one sitting, you understand my love, or the audience would die of starvation or old age. But over several months. But on what kind of stage? What kind of stage could hold this? You knew, damn it, Rolfa, you knew I'd have to do something about this!

Milena went on reading and seeing and hearing while her viruses made a tally. Sometimes she had to go back and re-read for them.

This was unfamiliar music. The viruses followed the structure. Milena saw the themes dart and dive and interweave like swallows, fly off and come back, in and out of the silence.

You've done it. You've done it, Rolfa. It's better than your bloody Wagner. It's better put together, the songs are better and it's even longer. This is Mozart, Rolfa, this is Bach. How could you do it? How could you do it to me? Milena began to feel the terrible weight that genius, like death, leaves behind for other people.

And you won't be here, Rolfa. You won't be able to hear it. You'll be someone else. You'll be like a ghost, Rolfa. I'll see you walking through the Zoo, but you'll be dead, undead. I'll hear you sing, but it won't really be you. All of this may have been a comedy, Rolfa, but it hurts, it hurts like slapstick full in the face. So it wasn't a high comedy, my love. I would call it low.

It was sunset and there was a knock on the door. It was Jacob the Postperson, and he came in singing.

> *Happy birthday to you*
> *Happy birthday to you*
> *Happy birthday dear Milena . . .*

She had forgotten.

'Happy birthday, Milena,' Jacob said smiling shyly. 'I bought you an ice cream.'

The ice cream was on a bamboo stick.

Milena gave a pale, grateful chuckle and reached out for it. Jacob jumped forward to pass it to her. 'It is very good, Milena. It is very good that you eat. You have not eaten.'

The vanilla was meltingly delicious. Did Milena remember the taste of it from childhood? 'I'm seventeen years old,' she said. 'An old lady.'

Milena felt weak to the point of nausea. Her Rhodopsin skin was itching for sunlight. As she ate, Milena realised something.

'You take care of us, Jacob.'

'Oh, yes,' he said. 'I carry your messages. I also know when you are ill or unhappy. I am the one who finds you when you die. That is my job.'

'And you know all of us.'

He smiled. 'When I dream,' he said, 'I dream all your messages, all scrambled up. But now, because of you and Rolfa, when I dream, I also hear the music.'

Hunger pangs returned. 'I need to get some sun,' said Milena.

So Milena and Jacob walked down the steps of the Shell together. He had to boost her up, help her as if she were old. Her knees felt shivery and weak. This is silly, to do this to yourself, she thought. He took her outside onto the walkways facing the Thames. It was cool, with a strong breeze from the river. Milena's face was turned towards the wind and towards the last of the sunset sky.

'I must run my messages,' said Jacob. Their handclasp became more firm for a moment, and then he left. She watched him as he walked back into the Shell, and the sunset was reflected like fire on the rows of windows. That is how it is for him, she thought. Each room is alive with light. Each room has one of us in it.

Milena went for a short and gentle walk and found herself standing on Hungerford Footbridge, where she had once stood before, and she was shaking, as if the bridge, the river, the city and the sky were all shaking with her. Seagulls were festooned about her, calling, not needing to move their wings in the wind, dropping parcels of waste into the river.

Life was a disease, thriving, and it was given breath by love. That was what it seemed to Milena. Water, clouds, wind, they came at her in a rush. What am I feeling? she thought. It was as if something had pulled her up with it, snatched her up, made her its own.

She looked at the Thames, with its heavy-bodied barges and their thick, waxy sails hanging in crisp folds as if carved out of wood; and at the rowing boats painted in bright colours; and at the brown autumn leaves being gathered up for storage by organised parties from the Child Gardens; and the press of bicycles and horses on the South Bank; and the sun panels on the roofs of the ancient white buildings. Further around the sweep of the river just behind St Paul's were the Coral Reefs, the new houses looking like giant cauliflowers. They sparkled in the last of the light, as if it had snowed.

How much work had made it? How many billions of hours, to build the roads, the carts, the boats, the embankments? How many billions more to learn how to do it, and to store the information? To write the songs in people's heads, to tame the horses, to grow the food? Her viral clock began to count.

On the opposite bank, a great green drum was being hauled by dray horses.

It was laying cable. The power would soon be on again. There would be metal, sent back along the Slide. The world was going to be rich again, and hung with light. There would be stages big enough for *Paradiso*. There would be no need for mines in the Antarctic.

Four billion hours and counting.

And all of this will go, sometime. Here it was, in front of her, history, if only for someone else.

Everything goes, everything is lost, eventually. But if something is good, it doesn't matter what happens. The ending is still happy.

We might have lived in the Antarctic, my love. We would have visited your mother, and you would still have sung, if only to sled dogs.

We might have run away to Scotland and been sheep farmers in smelly old jumpers. Or we could have stayed as we were until we hated each other.

Or there could have been this. You will be great, and I will stand in the wings and hear your music, and the applause will rise up.

Endings don't mean anything. Meanings lie where the world takes its breath, and that is always now. And suddenly, over Waterloo Bridge, the black balloon rose up again, in sunlight this time. Light was reflected from its full black cheeks. It was blowing itself backwards, as it rose into the sky. It blew itself, and was blown. It had been made by others, but it was also entirely itself. That's me, thought Milena. From the gondola that hung underneath it, people waved. There were coloured streamers. Was there a wedding? Milena waved back, and saw herself, as if she were the balloon. She was tiny, standing on the bridge, but the gesture, the wave of greeting, was clear.

Ten billion and counting.

There was a lot to do. Seventeen years old, Milena thought. She only had another seventeen, maybe eighteen years left to live. Time to get busy. She began to walk, as if counting her steps as well. Time was the problem. She thought she could control it. Instead, time swept her up, blew her on her way, through her life, without Rolfa for all her life. But whatever work she did could not be negated, not even by the death of the sun. That would only be an ending.

Twelve billion and counting.

Milena walked backwards to keep her face toward the sunlight, unaware that she was humming to herself.

Just a Dog of a Song. But . . .

Jump.

Somewhere else, the voices of the Consensus were falling like rain, calling

Rolfa

Rolfa

Rolfa

Rolfa

Rolfa.

They were the voices of children, wounded and anxious and eager for love. And they said:

It wants to hear your music. The Crown of the World wants you to sing.

And a pattern gathered itself into thought, and seemed to say, in mild surprise. Oh, really? Very well then. It was a pattern that was used to singing in the dark and imagining music out of silence.

There was a blast of imagined light.

It was engulfing, blinding, and the voices scattered like cherubim. With the light, there was the striking of a great chord, made of many voices and instruments, a sound like the beginning of the world, or the end. The sound was sustained. Very faintly at first, like a ringing in the ear, came a voice.

In the end is my beginning.

A hidden thought followed the words like a dart: and this the end of the Comedy, and the music at the end is the same as at the beginning.

The one who had come awake could orchestrate thought and sensation. The blinding light seemed to fade; eyes were adjusting to it. There were clouds, mountainous, rumpled, going off into many layers of distance, with shafts of light and lakes of shadow and cloud-valleys full of icy mist. There was an infinity of light and air, a world without end.

The audience felt wind in its face and a throbbing of blood in its temples and cold air being pulled into its lungs – it felt nostalgia for flesh. And out of the mists, Angels came streaming in black, their round and innocent faces painted white. Their robes and lips and eyesockets were black.

The Angels were the Vampires. They had been a chorus all along. There was T. S. Eliot, his face painted green to make him look ill. There was Madame Curie, glowing with her discovery. T. E. Lawrence had the marks of the lash, and the Brontës coughed, their arms about each other. The Vampires of History held each other back. They bore each other up. The signs of health were indistinguishable from the signs of disease.

The song they sung was this:

All'alta fantasia qui mano possa . . .

> *Here high fantasy failed*
> *Yet, like a smoothly spinning wheel*
> *Desire and my will were turned as one by Love.*

Then everything dropped out. The audience fell into night, into a sky dark and blue and full of stars. The darkness, the sky, had been below the light.

The Love that moves the sun and all the other stars.

Drums beat. The imagined music drew to a firm and conclusive end. The thought came that this was a prediction: we will all live in the spirit. Rolfa was free.

Then, silence.

Book Two

FOR MILENA
WHO MAKES THE FLOWERS

or

A Change of Climate

To run on better water now, the boat of my invention
Shakes its sails and leaves away to stern
That cruel stretch of sea.

And I will sing of this second kingdom
Where the human soul is purged
Made fit to leap up into Heaven.

Here let dead poetry rise again.

chapter eight

WHERE IS ROLFA? (A CHANGE OF CLIMATE)

Milena remembered the face of Chao Li Song.

His hair and his beard were black and his eyes were narrow, hard and smiling. This was not an old saintly man, but a young Chinese outlaw who attracted women.

'The problem,' said the outlaw, 'is time.'

His two hands moved, one forwards, one backwards. 'Time moves forward with the expansion of space. But space is also contracting, and time is moving backwards.' The two hands met, as if in prayer. 'They intersect at Now. Now is always timeless.'

There was a whirring sound of cameras. 'There is no single flow of time. There is no cause and effect.' The outlaw pulled a face that was childishly sad. 'There are,' he said, 'no stories.'

Four years after Rolfa left her, Milena was Read by the Consensus. She was made into a story. A wave of gravity and thought slammed into her, filling her. All her memories, all her separate selves were inflated, like balloons. Her past was made Now.

She remembered the night the power came back on. She was standing on Hungerford Footbridge, and it was crowded with strangers, crowded with friends.

The cast of *Love's Labour's* were with her, Berowne and the Princess. Cilla was with her as well. They sheltered in a viewing bay on the bridge, a mass of people pressed around them. Along the river, the embankment was full of people. It was late in the summer evening, and the sky was a silver blue. It was warm and mild and the air moved in currents like silk ribbons. The Shell-Mex, a great grey building across the river, stood against the light in the west.

Berowne was pregnant. Most people thought he looked grotesque. The foetus was attached to his bowel, and all the back of his body was swollen with it. He had to sleep in a sling. His beard had gone thin and his teeth were grey and fragile, speckled with white like a dog's coat. He would have to grow new teeth after the birth. If he sat down suddenly, he would die. He would probably die anyway, giving birth.

Milena thought he was very brave. Coming out with her tonight was dangerous. Life itself was dangerous, and there was something in Berowne's acceptance of it that Milena found admirable.

The Princess, the mother of the child, was with them, puce-pale and haggard from wishing she was more heartless. When Berowne had become pregnant, the Princess had tried to pretend that, beyond donating the ovum, she would have nothing to do with it. But she was here, with him.

'Cuh!' she said, trying to speak. 'Cuh-could suh-see.' Her lips trembled against each other, as if they could lose their balance. 'Fuh! From the Shuh-Shell.'

The Princess had begun to stammer in the spring. It was a virus. She had caught a virus, and it stopped her speaking. The only way she could speak smoothly, was to sing, to set the words to music. She refused to sing in public.

'I wanted to be part of this,' said Berowne, and held out his hands towards the spectacle. Even the septum of his nose had gone thin, the calcium leached from it. The wind stirred his thin hair as if with hope. The Princess hugged herself, forlornly.

On the pavements of the South Bank, the mosaic pattern of many people shifted and stirred. Costermen carried barrels of beer on their backs, helped by children. The children turned the taps and filled the mugs, and danced playing bamboo pipes. All along the walkway, there were giant ash trees, and the branches were crowded with people. Beefy workmen sat astride the branches as if they were horses' backs and they lowered mugs on rope, down to the children to fill.

Over it all, dirigibles floated. Gondolas hung underneath them, full of people. Party members, of course. Tarties, thought Milena, the actress. They're up there and we are down here.

Then from underneath Milena, there came singing.

Singing of sort, a kind of humming. The tide had gone out, and the river bed was shingled and muddy, heavy with the broken glass and torn rubber of history. Out from under the bridge came people. They moved across the mud, in fits and starts, like flamingoes. They picked their way, heads bobbing back and forth, arms folded like wings. They stopped at once, all together, and stood on one leg, transfixed. All of them tilted their heads together in one direction, as if listening to something. Then they suddenly scurried forward, all in a flock.

'Don't look at them,' said Cilla, for whom any form of extreme behaviour was only a way of attracting attention.

Mud coated their heads like helmets, and they wore tatters of resin, bound to their bodies by nylon cord.

'Those are Bees,' said Berowne.

Milena had never seen Bees before: they had been only a dim

rumour for her. It was said that people's minds were becoming disrupted. Their minds were becoming disrupted in unison.

As Milena watched, all the Bees dropped, like puppets whose strings have been cut. They dropped down all at once onto their knees. They kowtowed as if to an emperor and began to scoop, furiously, more mud over their heads.

'They're supposed to be Snide,' said Berowne, 'but in a funny way.'

'Fuh-funny!' exclaimed the Princess in fear and bitterness. She had not wanted to bear a child for the sake of her career. What career was there now for an actress who stammered?

There had been a change in climate, in many different ways. Behind the sunlight and celebration, everywhere there was an underlying tickle of fear and doubt. There were the Bees; now there was the stammering. People knew that something was going wrong with the viruses. They still did not want to think about it; they still did not know what to do about it; and so they came here to celebrate something new and good.

On the embankment, the hurdy-gurdy men began to grind out fairground music faster than before. The costers began to call out the names of their wares with a gathering clamour, and a breeze began to blow, as if the river itself were stirring with anticipation. On Waterloo Bridge, people were standing up on horsecarts. People were lined up along the roofs of buildings or leaned out of windows. Milena's viruses told her: you are looking at half a million people.

Across the river, on the face of the Shell-Mex, the hands of a giant clock were still. They had been still since the Blackout, the Revolution, ninety-seven years before. Tonight the hands would move, tonight at 10.30. There was enough metal now. The electricity would flow again, at first along the North Bank of the Thames only. But after that?

It was getting late. There was a sudden surge forward on the bridge as people tried to inch forward, to see. Milena pushed backwards. 'Stop shoving!' she said. 'We've got a pregnant man here!'

'Smile,' said Berowne to the Princess, and took her hand. She looked down at his hand, and compared it with hers, and shook her head. Time was running out.

The people began to count, echoing their viruses.

'TEN . . . NINE . . . EIGHT . . .'

In the mud below, the Bees were rocked by each giant number, buffeted by blasts of thought.

'SEVEN . . . SIX . . .'

Milena thought: the town will be lit up at night. There will be film shows for the public on giant screens in parks. There will be videos. Different Estates will start vying for control of them. All of us are going to have to find different things to do.

'FIVE . . . FOUR . . .'

Berowne turned to Milena, and nudged her, smiling wanly. This was why they had come. Join in!

'Three,' murmured Milena, wary of joining in a mass.

There will be a lot of sickness, she thought, a lot of new kinds of sickness.

'TWO! ONE!'

In anticipation, horns began to blow, and whistles to screech. There was a dull roar of noise, barely intelligible.

'ZERO!'

Nothing happened. There was a wave of laughter and ironic cheering as darkness deepened.

'ZERO!' the people called again. 'MINUS ONE! MINUS TWO!'

At 'minus two,' there was a leaping of light. Bam! Suddenly light flooded the face of the Savoy hostel for the homeless. A chain of lights hanging from lamp posts came alive with light.

Bam! Spotlights were suddenly shining upwards on the face of the Shell Mex. It gleamed, newly washed against the navy blue of the sky. Lights came on in succession all along the North Bank, in the boat-houses and along the docks at the foot of the stone embankments. Light glinted on the granite length of Cleopatra's Needle. Lights came on all along Waterloo Bridge. Bam, bam, bam, in quick time, pools of light, golden as if in sunset, spread in contrast to the darkness of the sky.

Oh! the people sighed. Oh! it was even more beautiful than they had thought it would be. They had all tried to imagine what it had once been like, the electric cities spangled with light, light in windows shining like eyes, and here it was, as if they had been transported in time. The electric city was reborn. This was to be called the Restoration.

The Bees leapt to their feet, shivering with other people's delight, and they jittered up and down in place, wailing, warbling in tongues.

And on the face of the Shell-Mex, giant shadows slowly crept. The hands of the clock had begun to turn again, as if time had begun once more. It was as if the clockwork of change itself had started up once again.

Milena felt the artificial light prickling on her Rhodopsin skin. Everything is going to change, she thought. There would be power now, light and holograms. It would be possible to perform the Comedy.

All around her people whistled and stamped and cheered. Bam, bam, bam, the lights came on in succession, like memories.

And Milena remembered being in a vehicle that could orbit the Earth.

It was alive, and it floated, swollen with gases like the throat of a

106

frog. It rocked in the wind as it drifted upwards. Below her, Milena the director saw England swing in and out of view.

Milena saw huge autumn fields, golden brown with harvest. She saw lines of motion trailing through prairies of grain, blown by wind. It was as if the grain were the legs of the Earth. By waving them, the Earth turned. Between the fields, there were tiny copses of sycamore and beech. There was a river moving in a straight line, held by banks of coral. The shadow of the vehicle floated across the river, sending up a flock of ducks that flew in panic, the mass of their wings scintillating brown/white/brown as they flapped.

England was a revelation to Milena the director. She had not been outside Greater London since early infancy, and she remembered almost nothing of her childhood. This was an unknown country, huge and full of life and forgotten, like childhood itself.

There were villages below, with houses shaped like bee hives, next to ancient churches or barns made of stones. Giant pear-trees were stretched out on the ground beside them, pinioned to catch the sun and occupying whole fields. Children carried food on their heads out into the fields. Flocks of them ran in the Child Gardens, running and gathering and breaking apart like starlings in the air. Giant horses pulled machinery through the fields, churning up a golden haze of dust. Milena saw through the glass roof of a laboratory. Inside there were vats and tanks and rows of glinting dishes like sequins. She saw groves of bamboo, and people sitting in the sun, having their lunch.

Milena saw many lives held in one pattern, the events in different fields, neighbouring villages. It was as if she could suddenly see the shape of Now, the simultaneity of life. She could see the shadows of clouds and an advancing front of weather. It was as if she could see the future of the children below.

Elevated, she thought, in every sense of the word I have been elevated.

Milena Shibush was going to produce and direct *The Divine Comedy*. She was going to produce it as she had always wanted to, filling the heavens with light and music, Rolfa's music.

Rolfa's music filled her life. She heard it everywhere she went, in her mind. Even without the viruses to help her, she would by now have known it all by heart. The music had become a way for her to talk to herself. If she were alone, unhappy, perplexed, triumphant, she would find herself humming the music, and the music she had chosen would tell her what she was really feeling.

Now she was humming the mountain theme, the music of climbing, that followed Dante's footsteps up the mountain of Purgatory.

In a flurry of cottonwool white, the landscape below was snatched away, with the suddenness of a viral illness. Milena was inside a cloud!

She leaned forward to see, to remember. Everything was grey, like fog. Of course, of course a cloud would be like that! Soft and grey and full of dampness. Between the panes of cellulose that was the window, there was a pimpling of condensation. Milena had time to think: I want to see. Then the vehicle blinked. A fold of flesh slipped down between the panes, to wipe them.

Milena was Terminal now. She could feel the vehicle all around her. She could sense the miles of its nervous system. She could feel her own position within that system, a concentrated knot at its very centre. The vehicle was alive, but it had no self. Milena was its self. The vehicle did whatever she wanted. Milena could feel it crowd all around her, needing direction, needing a centre. The need was desperate and she withdrew from it.

All down the centre of her head, there was a weight in a line. It felt like scar tissue, dead but somehow tingling at the same time. It was a wound, a disease. It was where Milena was Terminal, attached to the machine.

The pressure on its gasbag was translated for her into altitude in kilometres. Wind velocity and direction, temperature and estimated time to ignition were all ticking through her mind like her own thoughts. She could feel the opening and closing of the creature's valves, the seeping of its glands, its eagerness for a command.

The vehicle had a scientific name, in muddled Latin and Greek: *nubiformis astronautica*. Most people called it the Bulge. The Bulge electrolysised water into oxygen and hydrogen. It inflated itself. Lighter than air, it drifted up to the border of the stratosphere. Then it mixed and electrochemically ignited the gases, to blast itself free from the Earth.

'Fart-propelled,' old Lucy of the Spread had called it once. Milena the director saw her in memory, her grubby fingers lifting up a pint in a salute.

Outside the window, the mist began to glow a pearly-white. There was suddenly dim light and shadow on Milena's arm. Then as suddenly as someone gasping, the Bulge swept out over a landscape of white.

And Milena heard the music of Heaven in her head, Rolfa's music, the mounting bass line, the crying of the Angel voices. She was swept up between mountains of cloud, with highways of light and blue-shadowed valleys between. Remember, remember, she told herself.

She rose higher with Rolfa's music. There were plains of cloud below that looked crisp enough to walk on. There was a coastline, with bays and inlets and an ocean of air, with floating icebergs and islands of white. Outside the window, sunlight glinted on ice crystals. Something bobbed jiggling between them. There in the air, between the particles of ice, there were cobwebs, great nets of them, and there were aerial spiders dancing, legs akimbo. The spiders looked like Bulges, in their net of nerves, as if the universe were a series of Russian dolls, a smaller likeness contained in the larger.

Overhead the sky was mauve. It was time for the Bulge to blow.

Yes, Milena told it, and the Bulge began its internal dance, its heart pounding, closing its hiatuses, opening others. Milena felt its shell, a latticework of bone, begin to close around them. As its eyes closed, Rolfa's music reached the peak of Purgatory, about to leave the Earth altogether. Rolfa wasn't with her, and would not be with her, except in the music. Always present by her very absence.

Tongues of flesh wrapped themselves around Milena to hold her in place. Milena felt the Bulge gather and clench for the blast. She felt in a line down her head like a collar that pulled a weight.

I am not a Party Member, she thought, but they treat me like one. I still have not been Read, and they know it. I have not been Read, but they have made me Terminal. They need me for something. In a line down her head, she felt another weight, something vast and tangled and the size of planet. It was the Consensus. It was present by its absence too. It was watching, through her eyes, listening through her ears. It used her hands to do its work. Milena closed her eyes and waited.

There was dull roar in the bowels of the vehicle below, and the walls trembled, soft and slightly crinkled like chamois leather.

How, Milena wondered, thinking of her life, how did I end up here?

Then she sat back and surrendered to the roar.

After Rolfa had gone, Milena had tried to find her. She remembered wandering through the Shell, through the Zoo, along the walkways between them, asking everyone: where is Rolfa? Where is Rolfa?

Milena asked the little girls who worked at the desks of the Zoo. They giggled at each other's jokes and were slow to pay attention to her. She stood hopping up and down inside herself, trying to keep her hands still.

'Rolfa. Rolfa Patel. She has probably just joined the Zoo as a trainee Tech. You must have heard something about her.'

'No,' said the child, her pink cheeks swollen with a smile, no trace of doubt or fear. 'Nothing.'

'Well, you've heard nothing. Maybe the others have?' Milena looked at the other two children. They were bargaining in low voices, arms folded, something about shoes.

'Have you heard anything?' Milena demanded of them.

'We're all linked,' explained the first child. 'Terminal. One of us knows something, all of us knows it. There's been no Rolfa Patel.'

Rolfa had disappeared.

Milena looked for her in the Graveyard. She took a candle with her. In the golden light she saw that the dust of the floor had been undisturbed. It lay thick on the shoulders of the mouldering clothes that still smelled of sweat.

Rolfa's nest was empty. The desk was there, with a few spare pieces of paper still scattered about the floor, and a few dry pens still in the drawers. Milena stood in the place where this particular story seemed to have begun. The place produced a very slight sensation of sadness, a kind of lowering in the stomach, as if accelerating upwards at high speed, but it would have been an exaggeration to say the place was haunted for her. It had already become just another place. Milena wrote with her finger in the dust on the desk.

> *Where is Rolfa?*
> *I still have your things*
> *Milena*

She didn't sign it 'Love, Milena'. She thought that might frighten Rolfa away.

Milena left the Graveyard, and went to the Zoo Keeper. She asked his assistant, the sleek young man, if Rolfa had been there. Had there been any news?

'No,' said the sleek young man. 'Hoi. Can a Polar Bear become an Animal?'

His name was Milton, and he was given to bad jokes.

'Tell the Minister, I would like to be told when she reappears. It may be a joke to you, but she has no money, and she has to eat!'

Milton was not used to high emotion of any sort. His face went blank and slack as Milena marched away.

She went to the Zoo Cafe. She talked to the plump and surly woman who washed all the cups and filled them with tea. Had she seen a very tall woman? Milena asked her. Had anyone come in begging for food, someone perhaps who needed a shave? The woman looked at Milena through swollen, puffy eyes and shook her head.

Milena visited all the pubs, all the kaffs on the South Bank, up along the Cut and back towards the Elephant. Had they seen a very tall woman, not Rhodopsin? The Tykes behind the bars looked surprised. 'I think we would have remembered,' they said. Milena crossed the bridges and tried the north. She went to the Comedy Restaurant. Rolfa had been in none of the shops, none of the stalls. She wasn't drinking. She wasn't eating.

Milena went back to her room, and found Cilla waiting for her.

'Well?' Cilla asked. Milena slumped down next to her on the bed.

'Nothing. Oh Cill, there's nothing!' Exhausted, Milena lay down, the back of her head on Cilla's lap. Cilla began to stroke her hair.

'Don't worry,' said Cilla. 'She's just working it all out. Don't you remember after you were Read? All those new viruses hitting you on the head all at once? It takes a while to sort through the new filing system.'

No, Milena did not remember.

'She hasn't come out to eat, Cill! She's not like us, she's not Rhodopsin. She hasn't eaten in six days.'

Then Milena had a thought. 'Oh Marx and Lenin.' She sat up and turned around. 'Bears hibernate. It's a response to stress. They go to sleep and hibernate.'

'Then that's fine, she'll sort things out that way.'

'No, no. They have to build up reserves of fat first. If they go under while they're hungry, they starve to death in their sleep. I mean she hadn't eaten properly for weeks when she left.'

'Oops,' said Cilla, who had recently looked into Rolfa's famished eyes. 'You think she'll die.' There was a pause, a stillness in the air between them. 'I'll go upstairs and get my coat,' said Cilla. 'I've got some oats for porridge, I can bring those, and I think some soy sausages.'

'I don't have anything,' said Milena, and raised her hands and let them fall.

'Where would she go to sleep?'

'Anywhere quiet and dark.'

They got help and candles. Berowne, the Princess, the King, all of the players. They went to all of the unoccupied rooms of the Shell, where people had recently died. They all went out together, and looked in every corner of the Graveyard, between the racks. 'What a place!' they all exclaimed. The King particularly liked it. 'A good place to hide,' he said. He had put on one of the sequined jackets. Milena thanked them all and said goodnight to them, hugged them with gratitude. She and Cilla kept on looking.

They went to the night market, that Rolfa had always visited. The stallowners were still singing songs and piling up mounds of spice-paste or feather cushions. No, the stallowners said, they hadn't seen the big one. They knew who Milena meant, but no, she had not been around for the last few days. The stallowners were moving mountains of fur, covered against the autumn chill and Milena kept thinking they were Rolfa. Finally she and Cilla rested in a kaff. They ate hot spicy chicken and warmed their hands around mugs of tea.

'We'll find her,' promised Cilla. 'All of us. We'll do it.' She kept nodding yes, to the steamy cafe windows. They walked back arm in arm to the Shell.

'You get some sleep, love,' Milena said to Cilla.

Then Milena turned and walked across the Hungerford, across town. She went to South Ken, to the house of the Family.

* * *

111

You do not have to like me, Milena thought, as she knocked once again on the door of Rolfa's house. I don't have to like you, either. You only need to tell me if Rolfa is with you – or help me find her.

The door opened, as if by itself. Behind it, a huge old Polar woman stood on crutches. Her fur was white and smoky yellow and hung in satiny strands.

'Rolfa? Rolfa? She's still with you Squidges, in't she?' The old dam spoke to someone still hidden behind the door. 'Shawnee?' she asked. There was a low murmuring reply. Milena couldn't hear because the old woman suddenly snorted back mucus and then swallowed with a noisy gulp. There were smears of mucus on the fur of her arms.

'Yep. Yep. She's gone. Where is Rolfa? Don't know!' The old woman shifted on her crutches, and suddenly Milena saw that she was miserable. 'Seems like they would have told me if she was back.' She breathed heavily, a deep sigh, as if her bulk made breathing difficult. 'I am her mother, after all.'

'You're Rolfa's mother?' Milena felt something like dismay.

'You're the Cold Little Fish, ahn't you?' said Rolfa's mother, not at all unkindly. 'Why don't you come inside?'

'I'm very sorry. It's cold for me inside.' October winds buffeted Milena, blowing her scarf over her head.

'Looks pretty cold for you out there too. I can't stand up, honey, and I'd like to talk to you.'

The mother Bear turned. She swung herself on her crutches towards a packing case and began to lower herself onto it. From behind the door, a little human maid in billowing furs scuttled forward and took the old woman's arm. Milena stepped forward to help as well.

'They made this over into my room. Nice, in't it?' the old dam said.

Milena said that she agreed. The front room was as cold as Milena remembered it and even more stark. It was now completely bare, except for the packing cases. The old dam asked for tea and the human maid scurried away to fetch some. For just an instant her frightened eyes caught Milena's.

'I had to go and break my leg,' complained the GE. 'And end up in this place. I just feel like some old walrus who can't pull her bulk around. It really is time I was put down. You sit by me, honey, and keep warm.'

Milena did, and Rolfa's mother enveloped her in a hug.

'You're the one who wants to help Rolfa sing, ahn't you?'

The familiar smell of lanolin and the familiar, basking warmth.

'Yes, Mam,' Milena said. She found herself using the honorific.

'Well that's good. Rolfa never was meant for anywhere, unless it was someplace she could sing. I'd have helped her too, but I couldn't stand this place. Couldn't stand it, you understand me? I expect Rolfa's

112

just the same.' She paused. 'There's trouble, in't there? She's done another bunk.'

'They tried to cure her,' said Milena.

'Of what? Being Rolfa?' The old dam seemed to know, instantly, what Milena meant.

Milena could only nod.

'Well her father will be happy with that. That's the biggest favour you people could have done him. I'm not happy though.'

'Neither am I,' whispered Milena.

'Aw, hell, honey, I can see that. You want some whisky?'

Milena shook her head. 'She's disappeared. I think she's hibernating again. But she was very hungry when she left.'

The bottle paused in mid-air. Again, the old woman understood: Rolfa was in danger.

'I was hoping she was here,' Milena said, and even to herself her voice sounded drained and hopeless.

'Well, we'll just have to go and look for her.' Rolfa's mother looked at Milena. 'We may have to bring in the rest of the Family, though. People are going to be pretty mad.'

'I know,' murmured Milena, and braced herself.

Zoe was the first to come down the stairs.

'You did what?' Zoe demanded.

'We gave her the viruses. It was the only way.'

'You gave my sister your horrible Squidgey viruses?'

Milena felt herself cringe. 'It was a pre-condition of her performing. I'm sorry. It was a mistake. It was the only way I had to get her into the Zoo.'

'My God,' said Zoe, pressing her hand to her forehead. 'She could have dropped down anywhere.' Zoe looked at her mother. 'We'll have to call out the dogs, Ma,' she said. Zoe looked back at Milena with a strange, grim smile. 'You are going to have come with us,' she said. 'And don't think it's going to be a pleasant ride.'

Two huge cattle trucks roared up outside the Polar household. They were full of excited, yelping dogs. Young Polar men stood on the rails that surrounded the flatbeds. They shouted out to the house as the engines rumbled. The engines were on display, nickel-plated and polished like mirrors. Bears swarmed out of the house, full of gleeful aggression, climbing up the slats of the trucks. One of them was blowing a hunting horn.

This, thought Milena, could be a real mess. Zoe ushered her towards the trucks, hand on the back of Milena's neck. Was there any way she could warn the Zoo? Could she slip the human maid some money to run across London? The trucks would get there first.

Something growled at her. Between the slats of the truck, a pair of

113

blue eyes, a husky's eyes, were fixed on her. 'He knows you're a Squidge,' chuckled a Polar teenager, astride the rails.

Milena was loaded into the cab, squeezed between massive Polar thighs. They cushioned her as the truck swooped and veered across London, beeping its horn, swerving around horse carts, making people jump out of the way. Milena was not used to moving at speed; her stomach kept plunging in different directions. She felt slightly giddy and ill. 'Yee-ha!' called the driver.

Suddenly the truck was bouncing up and over pavements and onto the embankment gardens. Here already? Milena had not even noticed them going over the bridge. The other truck skidded up beside them, brakes locked, sliding across the grass.

Young Bears launched themselves over the sides. The slats were raised and the dogs bounded down. The Polar huskies looked like thunderclouds, thick and white and massive. The dogs were clipped onto leashes and then led, straining against them, towards the Zoo.

The Bears filled the main lobby, laughing at the blank surprise on the faces of the Zoo administrators. The Tykes at the desks came forward to protest. 'Aww!' said the Bears and picked them up like the children they were. 'Put me down! Put me down!' the children wailed, and began to weep.

Rolfa's old socks and shorts were pressed under the noses of the dogs. Then they were let loose.

Matinee performances were interrupted as packs of huskies surged down the aisles, sniffing. Dogs poured onto the stages, searching the corners and corridors of the backstage mazes. Zoe marched Milena through the upper floors. Broom closets and waiting rooms full of resting Postpeople were searched. In the rehearsal halls, musicians stood on chairs, holding their flutes and violins out of the reach of the playfully snapping dogs.

'OK,' said Zoe. 'Where else could she have slumped off to?'

'We've already looked in most other places,' murmured Milena.

'Well think of some more!' demanded Zoe.

Milena took Zoe on the small round that had been her life with Rolfa. She led her down the Cut, hoping to steer the Bears towards Leake Street and the Graveyard. They threw open the doors of the shops and ran up the stairs to the rooms above. The Bears had such fun. They took boisterous revenge for years of misunderstanding. Milena stood in the street and heard them laugh, incredulous at the way Squidges had to live, their small cookers, their few possessions. She heard things fall and break in the rooms. Off in the distance, bells began to ring in the continuous series of strokes that signalled emergency. Dogs came lolloping back down the steps, their thick white coats and heavy feet looking as springy as mattresses. A Polar man reeled out after them, wearing some Squidgey woman's sad straw hat.

The Bears rollicked their way down Leake Street. A contingent was left to scour the Graveyard. Out on the other side of the tunnel, more trucks were pulling up in the embankment gardens. 'We haven't done that building,' said Zoe to the newcomers, pointing towards the Shell. 'I'm going to check the hospital. You,' she said to Milena, 'you just stick around where we can find you. Zoo main hall. Go on.'

Milena spent the rest of the afternoon in the main lobby. She swayed where she stood with exhaustion, yearning to sleep, but forcing herself to watch. The Zookeeper will never forgive me, she thought.

'Have a drink,' said Rolfa's mother. Milena took a swig direct from the bottle. Rolfa's mother stood by her, balancing on crutches.

'The Antarctic's like this,' said Rolfa's mother. 'Things go wrong, you just have to bear it. Simple things. You can't pee. It's so cold that when you widdle, it freezes before it hits the ground. You got to be real quick or just push it out in little jets because it freezes from the ground up. Depending on how low you crouch, you got about thirty seconds before frozen pee hits your fanny.'

Milena took another swig. 'It's not a problem I've ever had to consider,' she said miserably.

A well known Zoo Animal ran past screaming, pursued by jolly dogs who trotted after her. The woman wore only a towel wrapped around her middle. Steam from her shower rose up behind her. It's like a nightmare, thought Milena. It just gets worse and worse.

'Then there's the spit,' said Rolfa's mother. 'You can't spit anywhere near the sheds cause it freezes on the ground and won't go away. It's worse than concrete. You can't chop it and it's slipperier than a doorknob in a bucket full of snot.'

'You have a colourful turn of phrase,' said Milena, breathing whisky. From somewhere there was a crash and a splintering of lights. A dog lifted its leg against the corner of the main reception desk.

Raising the bottle up in a toast, Milena said, 'To my remaining friends, wherever they might be.'

'You're smiling,' said Rolfa's mother. 'Never saw a Squidge smile before. You got the funniest little teeth.'

She likes me, thought Milena. Her smile became a little broader. 'Thanks,' said Milena.

Dusk drew in again. Milena heard the dogs being loaded up into the trucks. Zoe came in and stabbed a finger in Milena's direction. 'You find my sister,' Zoe said. 'Or there will be real trouble.'

You mean this wasn't?

Rolfa's mother shuffled around on her crutches. She looked back over her shoulder at Milena and winked. Milena stood where she was, still with the whisky bottle and heard the trucks pull away.

She wanted to die. She walked to the Shell by a back route, to avoid the Cut or the walkways where people might know who she was. She listened to the sound of broken glass being swept up, and people muttering under their breath. She staggered along Bayliss Road, named after the founder of the Old Vic, and down Hercules Road, past the William Blake Estate, where the poet had once lived. As far as Milena knew, Rolfa had never ventured this far.

And then Milena turned right into Virgil Street.

Virgil Street ran under an old railway bridge. Railway bridges fanned out from Waterloo, like branching realities. Along the brick façade, there were windows, more windows in other bridges. My God, thought Milena, she could be anywhere.

And standing there in the gathering darkness, Milena heard Rolfa begin to sing.

The voice echoed out the twilight blue, from all around Milena, as if the bricks were ventriloquists. The voice was powerful and fluid. It pounced on a note and then held it, and then, as if in rage, tore the note apart with a kind of screech. Milena felt a shudder in her heart, and her breath go still. She tried to breathe, and couldn't.

'Rolfa,' she heard herself whisper. 'Rolfa. Where are you?'

She walked towards the tunnel. On her left was a walled courtyard. She walked through the gap in its surrounding wall, and the sound was louder, harsher. Milena saw no one. She walked around the edge of the courtyard, peering into corners, hoping to see a niche or hidden doorway. The voice seemed to lead her, hovering in the air, a few steps in front of her.

Virgil Street was lined with arched gateways. Milena walked slowly, as if on thin ice, her breath held. She found herself knocking politely on one of the gates. It slid sideways on runners. A Tyke was holding it open, a boy with his shirt off. There were other boys, swarming over the body of a coach. The coach was painted white with a red cross and the boys were working on the leather straps of its suspension. They were coachbuilders for the hospital estate, working after school.

'That singing,' said Milena. 'Do you hear it? Do you know where it's coming from?'

The boys wiped the grease from their hands onto rags. They had tough adult faces on tiny bodies, and they wanted to show how adult they were. They pulled on shirts, lifted up their alcohol lamps, and stepped out into the street. Milena walked backwards as they advanced, as if into a cloud of the singing. The sound distracted her. The notes went wild and strange and ugly. Suddenly the tunnel was full of the sound of laughter, a wild, bitter, sarcastic hooting. Milena spun on her heel, expecting to see Rolfa looming over her shoulder. There was no one.

'Can't tell where it's coming from,' said one of the boys.

'What's in there?' Milena asked, pointing to the other gates.

'Hospital gear,' the boys shrugged. They brought their lamps and opened the doors. Milena smelled clean linen, and walked between the racks. The sound of singing dimmed as they walked further into the warehouse. Milena ducked under one arch, and saw more neat and tidy shelving. Rolfa would never be here, she thought. As if the spirit of the place were inimical, the sound of the singing seemed to fade altogether.

Milena walked back out into the street. There the sound of singing wafted around her, like mosquitoes. One of the boys was kneeling on the ground, his ear over a grate. 'Could be coming from here,' he said. With a jerk of his head, he indicated the drains below the street.

Another boy stepped forward from the coachworks with a crowbar. Neatly, he lifted up the grate. Milena saw metal bars down the side of the entrance forming a ladder.

'We'll go down,' offered the boys. Milena shook her head. She climbed down into the drains. The boys passed her a light.

There was a sound of water, a trickle, a dripping. Did Milena hear the sound of wet footsteps running? 'Rolfa!' Milena called. 'Rolfa!' Her own voice came back to her, very close, from against the low walls. She held up the torch and saw the bricks, encrusted with salts. The singing seemed to come from both before and behind her. The notes went raw, howling, as if a dog were crying to the moon.

Milena climbed back up. The boys took the lamp and her arms and helped her.

'It's everywhere,' said one of the boys, with a shivering chuckle.

'Maybe it's a ghost,' said one of them.

'Hassan!' protested one of the Tykes, and elbowed him to be quiet. They were all slightly unnerved.

'That's exactly what it is,' said Milena. 'A ghost.'

The old Rolfa would never have sung like this. She would have had too much respect for the music. This voice was angry, angry at the whole idea of music.

'Thanks, lads,' she said. 'You go on in. I'll just wait here for a while.'

'Need help, we're there,' said the one called Hassan, and the boys clustered together, and went back to their work. The gate slid shut behind them, and the golden light of the alcohol lamp was shut away.

The singing voice broke. It cheered raucously. 'Yaaaayyyy! Whoopeee!' Then it screamed a long, harsh howl that seemed to be the sound of flesh tearing. Sounds like that could ruin a voice for good.

Then Milena heard it, like a cough right next to her ear. 'Tuh!' said the voice, the shudder-chuckle. Then it was still.

Milena stood in the darkness that was now complete. 'Rolfa?' she asked the darkness. 'Rolfa. Where are you? Rolfa, it's me. Please come out and see me. People are worried about you. Everyone is worried about you. Please?'

There was no answer. Milena took a swig from the whisky bottle. Then she turned to leave. She stopped and left the whisky bottle behind, propped up against the wall of Virgil Street. She left it behind in case Rolfa wanted it.

Finally, in her room at the Shell, she fell asleep.

She woke up the next morning, late, with a hangover. The room smelled of sunlight and whisky. I've got to get looking, she thought.

Then she thought: no, you don't. She's alive, Milena, and that must be an end to it. You can't take care of her any more. You've got other people to think of now. You've got the new company to get organised. Other people than Rolfa depend on you now.

Jacob came in. It was not his usual time.

'Hello, Milena,' he said, his voice and manner shy and gentle.

'Hiya, Jake,' said Milena.

And he held out a card with gold edging. Milena jumped forward from her bed and took it from him.

The card said:

dear fish:

well rolfas back with us now – she came home last night – but she's not too well – what did you people DO to her? zoe well shes hopping mad – looks like a toad in a toga – i tell her its just rolfa done herself another injury – so we all are taking care of her now and i knew you ud like to know that so i wrote this i will say that i now suppose me and her father will have another up and downer over this – i want rolfa just to rest a bit and then ask her real carefully what she wants to do now – if she says sing well let her sing – her father sees it as another chance to mould her his way – seems thats what most people try to do to young ones – treat them like clay and make them over – most of the trouble in this world comes from trying to make other people over just like you people and your viruses which have made my great big lump of daughter so sick – im going crazy with this leg of mine – just itching to get back down south and out of South Ken – all people do here is add up their money –all day long – on their little machines – you ud think they ud come to a total sooner or later at least and give their poor finger tips a rest – me i want the continent south – ice and walruses are sane at least

i dont know how bad things are for you – but listen – fifteen years from now you will still be able to tell people the story of the day of the

dogs – it will be the funniest thing that ever happened to you – thats
what you do with things like that – make them funny – some day i
will tell you my stories about rolfas father !!!!!!!

listen you write me sometime too – i never had a squidge for a friend
and it might be nice to know how you can stand it
yours

hortensia patel

hey – i dont know your name – ill just give this to my little gal behind
the door and see if she can get it to you

Smile, thought Milena. She makes me smile. Just like Rolfa did. 'Jake,
can you stay a moment?' Milena asked. 'I'm going to write an answer
now.' Jacob nodded yes. He sat in comfortable silence. The unvarying
formulae were no longer necessary.

Milena wrote on the back of the card.

I don't know how I stand being a Squidge, either. My name is Milena
but for some reason, people have started to call me Ma. Thanks for
letting me know. Tell Zoe I'm sorry.

Milena signed it, love. Jacob smiled with beatific approval and then
left.

On the windowsill there was the great grey book. Milena reached
forward for it and it seemed to dump itself in her lap. FOR AN
AUDIENCE OF VIRUSES it said. Oh, Rolfa. What does that mean?
Milena looked at the tiny, tiny notes cowering between the lines as if
they were trying to hide. Most of them were in red, but whenever
anyone was quoted, the notes were in black. What does that mean,
Rolfa?

The Comedy and its mysteries were all that was left, all she had.
Milena picked up the great grey book, put it under her arm, and went
to visit the Zookeeper.

'Well Ms Shibush,' the Zookeeper said, his smile grim. He had a
terrible cold. He spoke like a rusty hinge and his joints had swollen.
'That was a day to remember.'

'I'm sorry,' she whispered.

'There has been a letter of protest from the Family. And we have
responded with a letter of apology.'

'She's back home now,' said Milena.

'Ah,' said the Zookeeper. He couldn't turn his neck. It was as if
everything about him were grinding to a halt. 'Have we lost her music,
then?'

119

'They will stop her coming back to us. They blame us for making her so ill,' said Milena.

'Perhaps,' said the Zookeeper, with a uncomfortable shift. 'If so much virus was necessary, it is no bad thing that she stays at home.'

'We have destroyed her.' Milena stated the worst possible case, as if saying it would make it untrue.

'Then this has been a tragedy,' said the Zookeeper.

No, it wasn't.

'We still have this,' said Milena, and held up the Comedy.

'It is not orchestrated,' said the Zookeeper.

'It can be orchestrated,' said Milena.

His eyes narrowed. 'You are not exactly in favour, Ms Shibush,' he warned her.

'I don't matter,' replied Milena.

The Minister's gaze was watery, and he kept blinking. 'How many hours of music is it?'

There were one hundred cantos lasting a half hour each. Milena had hummed them to herself. 'Fifty hours,' she replied.

'Mozart's entire oeuvre is longer,' he said. 'So is all of Wagner's work, but not by much. Who could orchestrate 50 hours of someone else's music?'

'I don't know.'

'Who could? Who would want to? How would they be paid? It's impossible.'

'No, it's not,' said Milena.

The gaze of the Minister, heavy as lead, was also weighted with warning. 'It is impossible,' he said again.

Milena had been holding back, holding in. It now seemed to her to be angry at what had happened, or to grieve too deeply, would somehow be ungrateful to life. She had learned newer, even higher standards of behaviour. Self-love would not let her slip.

'I don't remember much about being a child,' said Milena the director. She spoke very calmly. 'But I do remember that I could not catch any virus at all. That meant I knew nothing. I had to read to catch up. People tried to tell me there were no books. I found some. I read them, just to keep up with the other children. I read Plato when I was six years old. I read Chao Li Song when I was eight. I am telling you, sir, that it is never wise to say that anything is impossible.'

The Minister sat still for a moment, and then said, 'We know about you, you know. We were wondering when you would show up.'

Milena the director's mind went blank for a moment.

'Doesn't it strike you as strange that you were never Read? We knew you were resistant to the virus. That interested us. We wanted to see how you would turn out.' The Minister sighed, and hid his eyes. 'Go on then, Ms Shibush. Go on, and try.' His hand came away from his eyes. Through the swollen flesh and teary film his eyes were full of wariness and sympathy and an assurance that she would fail. 'Do what you can. I have no doubt that you have further surprises in store for us.'

Right.

'Who?' Milena asked. 'Who at the Zoo can orchestrate music?'

chapter nine

WHERE IS ROLFA? (CONDITIONS OF WEIGHTLESSNESS)

Nothing is impossible.

Milena remembered looking out of the window of the Bulge at the Earth below. The sky was black, like velvet, and the Earth was like polished brass. It was sunset and the Earth reflected the fire. The sea was smooth and burnished, and the clouds were pink and orange, skimming the surface of the ocean. The cloud shadowed the sea, and the sea reflected the light that came from underneath the clouds. It was a network of light, a system of exchange.

The Bulge had docked, meeting its larger sister in space. Kissing, the procedure was called – two mouths were sealed together. There was a hiss of air.

'Hello,' said a voice just behind Milena.

Milena reared back from the window in surprise. She launched herself from the floor, and suddenly saw her feet rear up over her head. Why are they doing that? she wondered mildly. She somersaulted into flesh and bone. Someone's elbows were rammed into her ribs. Milena reared up and over him. That's the ceiling, she thought as she plunged into it. The ceiling was soft and warm, and gave with her weight, enveloping her in its chamois embrace. Then it flung her out, back down towards the floor.

This isn't supposed to happen, she thought. I'm supposed to be trained for weightlessness. Then she remembered. The training was a virus. She had been resistant to that as well.

'What do I do?' she wailed.

'There are holds. Grab them.' said a man's voice.

Milena whirled like a propellor. Her stomach seemed to be somewhere down around her ankles. 'I'm terribly sorry!' she cried. She was giddy and confused, the balance of her inner ear disrupted by weightlessness.

'Oh,' said the voice, calmly. 'That's OK.'

He didn't understand. Milena had been apologising in advance.

'I think I'm going to be sick!' she wailed.

And the Milena who was remembering spun as well, through memory.

* * *

Milena remembered work.

She remembered going to an Estate in Deptford, the Samuel Pepys Estate, to try to sell a production of *Love's Labour's Lost*. The cast had set up their own small Estate, to do new plays. Milena remembered the ride in the water taxi. The day was grey and cold, without comfort. Milena remembered the tink-tink-tinkling of the tiny engine, and the tillerman who sang a song about lovers being parted. Why thought Milena, hunched against the river wind, why do songs always have to be about love?

She was met at Deptford docks by a very lean and smiling woman. The Pepys Estate grew Coral. 'We call ourselves Reefers,' said the woman.

She smiled sweetly and explained that the Estate did not want a production of Shakespeare, no matter how original. 'We like to put on shows for ourselves, you know. A bit of singing, a bit of a laugh. We have got our centenary coming up though. If you could do us a new show about the history of growing Coral, that would be good.'

Milena paused for just a moment. It was as if she were trying to catch a handkerchief in the wind. If she didn't snatch it right away, it would be lost. 'Right,' she said. 'We'll do it.'

'You will?' The woman looked surprised. 'And you all work at the Zoo, you're all professional singers?'

'Yes,' said Milena, in a whisper and a catching of breath that meant: I think I've done it.

'Oh well, then,' said the woman. 'I'll have to put it to the others and see what they think. How will you do it? I thought you only did viral plays.'

'No, no, that's the whole point.'

We're whores. We'll do anything.

And Milena remembered talking with the Reefers about their history, of how Coral was developed, and how it was used to grow the great white wall that kept back the sea, the Great Barrier Reef. She remembered rehearsals, the false starts, and the look on the faces of the actors, the blank horror, when they tried to speak without a virus giving them lines.

She remembered Mote the actor standing helplessly in place, wondering what to do.

'Look, Ma, where do I go? Do I keep standing here, or do I walk off? I don't know what to do next!'

'Of course you don't,' said Milena. 'This is all new, remember? Make it up.'

Mote still looked perplexed. Milena had an idea. 'I know. This is before the Revolution, right? You smoke cigarettes. Take out a pack,

123

find it's empty, and start asking other people for tobacco. In desperation, that's right, you're an addict.'

Milena started to direct.

All that October after Rolfa had gone, into November, Milena spent her time telling actors what to do. She remembered finding Technicians and hiring the ambulances of St Thomas's hospital to deliver lighting. She remembered the fittings for costumes, the bright little Zoo seamstress who restitched them out of cloth from the Graveyard. She visited every Estate that was about to have a centenary, and offered them a production. The boatbuilders, the maids and manservants – they had all started forming Estates in the days just before the Revolution. Each Estate was like a separate country, self-contained, in rivalry with the others.

'The What Does Estate wants us to do a show!' she announced, expecting enthusiasm.

'Uhhhhh!' the actors groaned. 'Not another one. We can't do it!'

'Each one takes us *weeks*!'

The problem was time.

It was the actors who found a solution. It was not a solution of which Milena approved.

She remembered being ushered into a secret meeting in a bare rehearsal hall. The King guarded the door and only let in members of the company. The Princess, Berowne, Cilla who had joined them, they all came in and sat on the floor. Hiya Babe, they said to each other. They had started to called themselves the Babes.

In a corner of the room, there sat an apothecary.

Oh no, thought Milena. Apothecaries thrived around the Zoo. They sold illicit viruses that heightened emotion or powers of mimicry.

The apothecary stood up. She wore black, shiny leotards that showed off her slim legs, and a loose white smock that hid her apple-round belly. Her face was painted with apothecary make-up, a clown-like promise of emotional cornucopia.

'A play is in the mind!' the apothecary announced. 'And minds can be Read!' She flourished a plate of agar jelly like a tambourine. It was a viral culture.

'This virus has children,' the apothecary said. 'It plants them in you, and the children read you. Then the mother comes, and harvests them, and merges them. She gives birth to the play for you, out of all of you. And then you catch her, as you would for any other play.' She held up a gloved hand, as if to say, what could be simpler?

The Babes applauded. They admired her performance.

'So it's not one disease, but two,' said Milena.

The woman's face faltered.

'The first disease collects whole sections of personae. The second

124

is a transfer virus that picks up all that information and merges it. We then become ill with the transfer virus. Is that right?'

'Yes. That's all it is,' said the apothecary, giving a clown's smile, and holding up her glove again.

'Both of your viruses have to pick up information. The DNA has to be open to change. So neither of them can be Candy-coated. Obviously your transfer virus reproduces itself. Does it have two sets of chromosomes? One for information and one for reproduction?'

'Only the transfer virus,' said the woman.

'Only the transfer virus,' said Milena grimly.

'So?' asked Cilla.

'So it's contagious! It's contagious and it can mutate. Ficken hell, woman, what you've got there is the end of the world!'

'Uh. Ma. We know you don't like the viruses . . .' the King began.

'It's not a question of what I like. It's what those can do! It merges minds. It turns merged minds into a contagious disease. Anyone could catch us!'

'Many Estates use this virus,' said the apothecary. 'Any time people have to share information, and work together, and know in advance what each other are going to do.'

'How many of those have you sold?' asked Milena in a chill little voice.

'Many. Many.'

'If I told the Party they would haul you in for a Reading so fast it would make your head spin.'

'You would have to find me first,' said the apothecary.

'So the clown make-up is a disguise.' said Milena.

The woman kept smiling.

Berowne slid across the floor to be closer to Milena. He was not yet pregnant. His beard was full and his teeth were white. He was beautiful. 'Ma,' he said. 'Ma, look. Everyone uses the viruses.'

Milena saw the broader pattern. People were used to getting everything from viruses. These people would have no resistance to the idea. Milena covered her mouth in fear. 'You're all programmed to accept them.' It was like watching a trap close. Everyone was used to the viruses doing the work for them, they had been trained to think of viruses as an unmitigated good.

'No! Look, Ma. We need to speed up production.'

'It takes months to rehearse a new show,' said a heart-faced young actress, sullen with ambition. Milena could not remember her name. 'You all knew that when we started,' said Milena.

'Yes!' said Berowne in frustration. 'But if we're to make a living at this we have got to put on more and more shows. Each one you get us is brand new, for a different Estate.'

They aren't used to working, thought Milena.

'If we don't do this,' said the Princess, 'We'll just have to give up on new plays and go back to sleepwalking.' This was before the Princess had started to stammer.

'Look, Ma,' said Cilla. 'Chao Li would say we were getting it right. We're not taking value from anyone else, we are generating it ourselves. And we're entitled to do that.'

'This isn't a matter of Tarty principles,' said Milena.

'All I was saying is that we got to start turning a few francs.'

The truth was economic. The truth was that viral theatre came whole and finished. It was cheaper than creating and rehearsing new productions. The truth was that the Babes could mount any play they liked. But they had to make it pay.

The apothecary saw the advantage. 'One or two days,' she said. 'That's all it will take, to collect your ideas, merge them into a whole, polish them a bit. I'm not saying the play will be perfect the first time. But you'll save time.'

'We're going to do it, Ma,' said Berowne, smiling out of kind regard for Milena.

'Don't,' said Milena, hand across her forehead in alarm.

She watched as the apothecary touched each of their tongues in turn with the finger of a resin glove. 'Think of it as a kiss,' the apothecary said.

'None for me,' said Milena.

She watched the Babes go pale and sick and ill. She nursed them and took care of them, and sold productions for them, and organised collections and deliveries and fittings. Over the next eighteen months, she and the Babes would stage 142 new productions. For a while, everything seemed all right.

And Milena remembered meeting Max.

Max was the conductor of one of the Zoo orchestras. He could orchestrate music. He could orchestrate the Comedy.

Milena remembered standing in his chilly office, when was it? Late November, the November after Rolfa had gone. Max sat behind a huge, black desk. The desk was meant to intimidate, Milena was certain of that now.

Max was looking through the great, grey book. He was unhurried. He was not speaking to or looking at Milena. He was like some swollen little boy: round, fat and smooth. The oils on his forehead reflected the windows of his room. His green-blond moustache masked his purple mouth. His mouth needed masking. It seemed to curl in scorn, but was somehow too pretty at the same time. It made him look petulant. Through the airy linen of his shirt, Milena could see that his breasts were pendulous with fat. Milena stood with her arms folded and looked at the room.

The floor was bare concrete, and the shelves were empty, except for a green glazed pot with some kind of dried twig protruding artistically from it. The walls were painted white and were hung with framed sheets of music, safe behind glass, like paintings. By Max's elbow, as if he were just about to begin composing, there was a sheaf of perfectly stacked, ruled paper and a very sharp pencil. Though it was November, two charcoal hibachi kept the room stifling hot. It was so airless, that Milena felt giddy. She needed to sit down, but there was no chair for guests.

'Hmmm,' said Max. He finally looked up at Milena and fixed her with the swimming, glassy look of someone whose corneas have been replaced. 'Yes,' he said in a very flat, precise, but muted voice.

'Yes?' repeated Milena. 'Does that mean yes, you'll do it?'

'Yes,' he said again.

Milena was taken aback. It was too simple, just to have him say yes. 'But how? When?' she asked, trying to inject into her voice the joy she thought she should be feeling.

'Well,' he said, in the same detached, quiet voice. 'It's a big job. I can't say when. I really need to look at the whole thing some more.'

So did he really mean yes? Already Milena felt a confusion, somewhere. 'So you need some time still to look at it.'

He made a totally meaningless gesture, a shrug that looked like some kind of deprecation. What was being deprecated? The time he still needed to make up his mind? The importance of what he was asking – no big thing?

'Do you want to keep the book?' Milena asked. 'It's just I'm a bit chary still of letting it out of my sight. There's been no time to write it all out again somewhere else. That's the only copy.'

'I'll be needing it,' he said.

'If it's just a question of looking at the music to see if it's worthwhile, there is a copy of most of the main themes.'

He looked back at her without answering. Was he terribly insulted? Finally he said, 'I will be needing the book.'

'Of course,' said Milena. She had to tell herself: the book is not yours now, Milena. It belongs to everyone now. It has to fly by itself. 'Fine. By all means,' she said.

And she thought: so why don't I feel happy?

'Well I guess that's it.' Milena tried to be generous. 'I guess I wasn't expecting you to be interested. I'm very pleased.' She smiled, but there was no response in Max's face. This was unnerving. Milena found that she did not quite know how to leave. 'You'll let me know, then?'

'Yes of course,' he replied. He turned to his pile of blank paper and began to tap its sides, as if something were out of order.

Weeks, thought Milena. That's all I'll give him. Two weeks. She looked about the office. At least it seemed organised and workmanlike.

'Then goodbye,' she said.

'Yes,' he replied, without looking at her.

It took a month to find him again.

She left messages at the music desk. She found his Postperson.

'Oh him,' said his Postperson. 'You'll be lucky. I can never find him myself, and if he ever sends messages he never sends them by me. What was your name, love? And your message?'

Max had the only forgetful Postperson Milena had ever met. That seemed to explain things. She visited his office and found it empty. She knocked on his door in the Three Eyes, where the musicians lived, but there was no answer.

Finally she went to one of Max's performances. She waited outside the concert hall, looking at the patterns in the varnished wood panels on the walls. Long after the audience was gone, Max emerged, holding the door open for a very tall, serious-looking woman. She was carrying a violin case, and nodding at something Max was saying.

Milena drew herself up next to them. Max ignored her. He kept talking about orchestra business; how to divide the orchestra's earnings fairly. The violinist kept giving Milena speaking looks, tight-lipped, steady-eyed. Finally she said, 'Excuse me, Max,' and addressed Milena. 'I'm sure you must find listening to our conversation terribly dull. Perhaps you could talk to Max later.'

'I would love to talk to Max later, but we keep missing each other. Max, have you been able to make up your mind about the Comedy yet?'

'I'm afraid not,' he said, and tried to turn back to the violinist.

'Do you think you could let me have the book back, so I can make a copy?'

'Please!' he said turning to her. He looked harassed, piteous, as if she had been hounding him. 'You are asking rather a lot. Let me look at it, and I will let you know.'

Milena felt her jaw jut out. 'You have had a month, Max. I don't think that's rushing you.'

'I will let you know soon. Please give me some time, and please let me continue talking to my colleague.'

All right. For now, all right. 'I shall try to see you in a week or two's time,' she warned him.

Sometime in early January, she visited him in his office. Winters were getting cold again. There was cold grey light coming in from the windows, but the room was still stiflingly hot. Max looked up in alarm when Milena came in. He was sitting at his desk, arms folded, hands buried in his armpits as if to stop them doing something. He's sitting here doing nothing, Milena thought. 'Hello, Max,' she said quietly. 'Have you made up your mind yet?'

His face was frozen. His mouth gaped open, with a kind of twist in its slackness. Milena realized that Max was trying to smile and couldn't. He dreads me, she thought, he dreads me coming. I am the least welcome thing that could happen to him. Well, Max, say yes or no, and either way I'll let you alone.

'Max,' she repeated. 'Have you made up your mind?'

'Yes,' said Max, in an unconvincing imitation of firmness. 'Yes, I have. I think the material is very good. It does require, a lot, a lot of work. But I'll be happy to do it for you.'

'Fine. Thank you Max.'

'It will take some time.'

'I'm sure of that, Max. But we don't need a full orchestration. I think just the first canto will be enough to show the Minister what we want to do. So. I have brought you all the vocal line for the first canto.' She had reconstructed it from memory, it was such a part of her life. She passed it to him, all tidy on staves. 'Now, could I please have the book back?'

'It isn't here, Milena.'

'I realize that, Max. It's a big book. I'd see it if it were here. When can you get it to me?'

'I will send it to you tomorrow.'

'I will expect to see it. This is a major project, Max, and we have to begin thinking in terms of time. The Minister will want to see a schedule.'

He began patting his blank paper again. 'He shall have one.'

'I will need one, too,' said Milena.

He shrugged again.

Milena chuckled with frustration. 'Max!' she said, as if to call out his better self. 'Will I see a copy of the schedule?'

He only nodded.

'I'll come in tomorrow for the book, if that is well with you. Max? Max, please answer me.'

'Yes,' was all he said.

Milena shook her head as she left. I get that book back, and then I get rid of you, Max. There's no way that you are up to doing this project.

Milena came back the next day to his office, and was not surprised to find that he wasn't there. The charcoal burners were full of icy ash. Milena searched his room. The drawers of the black desk were empty, the long white shelves were empty. The room was as blank as the paper.

Milena took a sheet of his paper and wrote on it, angrily, making slashes of the Chinese characters.

Where is my book

Then she went to the Three Eyes.

The corridors echoed with the sound of distant feet walking on other floors, and with the strains of music – pianos, violins. It was as if the building were sighing to itself.

Milena knocked on his door. The door was green and should have hidden dirt, but all around the handle there were grubby fingermarks. From down the corridor, from outside the windows came the drifting sound of someone rehearsing Bartok on the violin.

The door opened very slightly, and there was a blast of hot air. It smelled of socks and stale bedding, and the room beyond the door was dark. Milena saw part of Max's face, one eye looking at her.

'May I come in, Max?' she asked.

'It's a bit of a mess,' he replied.

'I'm used to that. I don't need to come in, if you can just give me the book.'

'Let me get dressed,' he said.

Dressed? thought Milena. It's mid-afternoon. I'm not waiting for you any more, Max, I am not standing out here in a cold corridor looking at a closed door. Milena lunged forward at the door before Max could close it and pushed her way in. She felt the edge of the door thump into the soft flesh of his shoulders and toes.

'Milena, please!' he yelped in genuine outrage. Milena forced herself sideways through the door.

Max stood looking at her, appalled, in only his linen shirt, underpants and socks. The room was dark and the blinds were down. Milena had an impression of clothes in heaps and bedclothes that had fallen onto the floor.

'I'm very sorry, Max, but we agreed to meet today. I have been leaving messages and trying to talk to you for over a month. I am sick of chasing you. Please may I have that book!'

'It's in my office,' he said.

'No. It is not. I have searched your office and it is not there. Where is it, Max?'

He stared at her, even more exposed than his nakedness made him. 'This is really outrageous,' he said to the floor. 'I am the conductor of an orchestra. Having you go through my office!'

'Max. Where is the book?'

'I will get it for you.'

'Is it in this room, Max?'

The room was small. A sink, a bed, a cupboard, a chest of drawers. He was a Party member, so there was also a small water closet. He was Party and had privileges. But there was not much space there for the great grey book to hide. Clothes were piled on the floor, twisted in strange shapes as if being tortured.

'You've lost it, haven't you Max?'

'I'll find it for you!' he insisted. He could not manage anger, only petulance. Hands shaking, he began to pull on his baggy, wrinkled trousers.

'Did you give it to someone else to write the music?'

He did not answer. Shaking, wounded, he was pulling on socks.

'If you gave it to someone else, simply tell me who and I will fetch it.'

No answer. 'Max. Please answer me. Did you give it to someone else?'

'Of course not. I don't think so.'

'Which is it Max. Yes or no.'

'I don't remember!' he suddenly shouted.

'You don't remember?' It was Milena's turn to be undone. Her voice went dismayed and childlike.

'No! Now leave me alone, and let me think.'

'Max, what do you mean, you don't remember?'

'I don't know. I'm a very busy man with a full concert schedule and I'm afraid I had rather more on my plate than your silly little book.'

'Max. Max. It was a great work. It was not your property, it belonged to the Zoo, to everyone. What do you mean, you were busy? Will you answer me please, Max?'

He didn't, he couldn't, there was nothing to say. Milena began to ransack his room. She picked up all of his clothes, trousers, shirt and socks, and threw them one after another onto a heap in the middle of the floor. She pulled back the sheet and the under blanket from his bed and dragged the mattress away from the wall, and looked behind it. Max stood over her, hands on his hips.

'Go on, make a mess,' he said. 'It's not behind the bed.'

'It's probably up your arse,' said Milena. Max went pale.

Milena stood up, and began as neatly as her rage would allow to turn out the contents of his cupboards. She unloaded masses of paper from the upper shelf. It was full of music paper. There was a fortune of paper, and it had all been wasted. Notes were placed aimlessly on it, and crossed out, sometimes in what looked like scrawled fury. The notes sometimes dribbled away into doodles, meaningless patterns, or drawings of faces or women's genitalia.

'What I wouldn't have given to have this paper,' said Milena, thin lipped.

'All right,' said Max, and began to help, as if doing her a favour. He was taller than Milena and could reach the upper shelf. He stepped in front of her, blocking her view and went through the paper, sheaf by sheaf.

As he thumbed through the first sheaf, he said, 'It's not there!' With each subsequent pile of paper, he said, 'And it's not there! It's not there,' as if to say I told you. Almost as if to say, see? It's gone forever.

'It's not in this room,' he said, as a finale.

'So try to remember, Max. A big grey book. What did you do with it Max?' No answer. 'How long ago did you last see it, Max?'

'I don't know. A long time.'

'Why didn't you tell me?'

'I kept thinking it would turn up.'

'Max!' and Milena found that she was almost weeping. 'Max, how could you do it? How could you do it and keep any self-respect?'

The face was blank again. You don't have any self-respect, Milena thought. Not really. Your whole life is a mask. What are you trying to hide?

A man like this, Milena thought, has motives that are secret even from himself. Without realising it, Max, you wanted to destroy the Comedy. She thought of sheafs of wasted paper, and the angry scrawls and knew, without quite being able to say why, that part of him had deliberately lost the book.

Milena looked at him. He was so ugly and helpless that she could not yet pity him. She could feel only anger and scorn. Somewhere in that fat head of yours, she thought, is the answer, buried deep, deep down so that even you can't find it. I need a mind-reader to get at it. I need a Snide. Milena knew then what she was going to do.

'I'm not going to tell the Minister for a week,' she said. 'I'm not going to tell him you've lost an entire, very valuable project for one week. Start thinking, Max. I won't tell him anything about this if I get that book. But I will be back and back and back again until it's found.'

She left him and went straight to the apothecary woman.

Without her clown make-up, the woman's face was beautiful but sharp. The nostrils were too flared, the eyes too avid, the precision-painted mouth too perfect. It was a criminal's face. Milena needed a criminal.

'I need a Snide,' Milena told her. 'Can you find me one?'

If you are sick in conditions of weightlessness, your vomit will keep travelling, spreading very slightly from air resistance until it hits something. It will then cling precariously, held in place only by friction. A cloth can not absorb the moisture or be used to wipe it up. A cloth will simply shunt it free again. Eventually, vomit will coat every surface in the vehicle as evenly as its rather coarse texture will permit.

The main body of Milena's vomit moved towards an air vent. Suddenly it ballooned backwards, as if it had grown a head and a mind of its own. It wobbled its way back towards Milena, looking rather like an octopus.

Something caught Milena's ankle. She kicked.

'Don't!' said the voice. 'Hold still!'

'Aaaah!' squawked Milena, about to be enfolded in her own half-digested breakfast. Milena felt herself hauled backwards. The vomit followed tamely, as if unaware that it was not wanted. It was about to give Milena an unwelcome kiss, when she had an inspired idea. She puckered her lips and blew. The octopus reared backwards, rippling. It reared up and over her. Milena arched her neck and ran out of air. She gasped for breath, and pulled the thing closer towards her.

She kicked and wrenched out of its way. Out of the corner of her eye, Milena saw that a man was trying to hold her. The vomit loomed. She blew out and it burst scattering.

From somewhere there came a sound like peeling fruit. 'Oh darn,' said the man, rather mildly. 'Dislocated my shoulder.'

Milena was released. She and the tiny babies of vomit spun away, perpetually falling.

She spun and seemed to land in a park in winter. Hampstead Heath, she remembered. The expanse of hill sloping away beneath her was covered in snow. She could see her own footsteps. The branches of the trees were coated in ice, as if they had been dipped in glass.

Milena was waiting for the apothecary to catch up with her. The woman climbed the hill, panting, pushing herself up, hands on her knees. Milena could hear the rather satisfying crunching noises the woman's feet made in the snow.

'There!' the apothecary sighed as she reached Milena and the top of the hill. There was a wreathing of vapour from out her mouth. 'Whoo! That's it.' The apothecary pointed to a wagon, a black box on two huge wheels. Black smoke poured out of a stovepipe chimney. Winter ponies were watching the two women. The ponies were small and shaggy creatures, with hair that trailed into the snow. Winter ponies were fiercely loyal. If someone came for their master, they would attack. Their eyes, thought Milena, they have human eyes.

'Shalom,' said the apothecary, to the ponies. It seemed to be some kind of codeword. The animals went back to pawing back the snow with their hooves, and chomping the grass. There were other footsteps in the snow, leading to the wagon. The wagon was a mobile club for Snides and empaths. Boites, the wagons were called. The boites were continually moved from place to place. Snides and empaths gathered there, to do what exactly, Milena had little idea, except that it involved illicit viruses. They performed for each other. Mind-dancing they called it.

The apothecary climbed gypsy steps to the door of the wagon and knocked.

'Ali, Ali it's me,' she called.

The door was pushed open. Men and women sat all at the lower end of the wagon, crosslegged on the floor. Milena could feel a current of hot air rise up out of the door. The apothecary pushed Milena in ahead of her and slammed the door shut.

'Sorry everyone. Sorry,' she said. 'Good?'

'His best,' said a bearded man, his eyes dim, his speech slightly slurred. 'He's weaving all of us into this one.'

The wagon leaned forward on its nose. The wooden floorboards all pointed up the sloping floor towards a man in black, sitting crosslegged on a thin rug.

He was Al, Al the Snide.

His eyes were closed in concentration. Then they opened. They opened and were staring direct at Milena.

'That's it ladies, gentlemen.' he said. 'That's all for now.' There were jars of potheen lined up along the edge of the floor, held in place by a rack. 'Keep warm, drink something. We'll complete the tapestry later.' He stood up with one smooth movement. He was still tall and lithe. The hat and cape had gone. He looked at Milena with sadness.

'Hello,' he said.

'Hello,' said Milena.

He pulled on a sealskin coat. He caught something in Milena's mind.

'Real seals weren't killed making it,' he said. He paused. 'And yes, I'm still defensive.'

The room chuckled warmly. They all understand, Milena realised, they all hear what I'm thinking, they all know. I feel naked. Do I mind?

The room chuckled some more. The faces were ordinary, rough, but not unkind.

'Would you mind being a strand?' one of the empath women asked Milena. Milena didn't understand.

The woman's face was suddenly crossed with concern. 'Don't worry, love, we're just asking if you want to be part of the tapestry. We all like you.' The woman looked at one particular man. 'You have to tell them or else they don't know,' she said. She looked back at Milena with pity. 'Do you, love?'

'Salt and wool,' said another dancer. She also was smiling. She wore a Postperson's headscarf. There was a murmur of assent from the other empaths.

Al the Snide thumped down the slope of the floor, in black boots, smartly pulling on gloves. He looked at Milena with expectation. Then he smiled and closed his eyes for a moment, as if embarrassed.

'Sorry,' he suddenly said. 'I keep forgetting you can't hear me. Do you mind going for a walk? We can talk then.' His pale, pale face was even leaner, but the eyes were less faraway, less self-concerned than they once had been.

Outside, the air seemed to have daggers of ice in it. In bare branches a community of crows had gathered, cawing and croaking to each other in smoky mist. Al helped Milena down the gypsy steps.

'The problem is to get him alone,' he said.

'Sorry?' Milena was completely taken aback.

'Max. I will need to be alone with him.'

'You already know what the problem is?'

He nodded, and kept speaking.

'So going to a concert or something is out. Too much mind noise. It would be best just to visit him. And tell him what you are doing. Why you think it's best to try and trick him, I don't know.'

'I'm sorry, I'm not used to this,' said Milena.

'I know,' he said darkly.

You want this over with quickly, she realised.

'I suppose I do, yes,' he said aloud, and looked back up at her, his lips drawn thin.

And Milena found herself thinking: I wonder what he feels about Heather? She thought it, and he looked away.

'I treated you badly once. So I feel I owe you something,' he said. 'I won't charge you for this.'

'Thank you,' murmured Milena. But she thought: I never mentioned money; it never even crossed my mind.

He was trying to keep things businesslike. 'We need to tell Max openly what we are doing. Our approach is that I'm simply helping him to remember. Arrange an appointment to meet. It's always easier if people co-operate.'

It still rankled Milena that he had mentioned money. 'You don't owe me anything,' she said.

He punched the palm of his gloved hand. 'I wish you people could hear!' he exclaimed. It was so indelicate, having to speak.

'Look. You are Heather. At least half of Heather was you. Maybe most of her.'

He still loves her, thought Milena. Oh, poor man.

He sighed, and ran a hand over the top of his head. 'She's buried deep now, isn't she?'

He looked at the top of Milena's head, as if to see Heather there.

'You already know that,' said Milena. 'Why ask?'

Al shrugged. 'You don't hate me any more. That's something.'

'I did something far worse to Rolfa in the end. Far worse than anything you did.'

'Ssssh,' he said, and held up his hands. 'I know. I know.' And there was more than pity in his eyes. There was comprehension. 'The bastards with their bloody Readings,' he said. 'It's all about control. They don't care what they kill in the process. I'm sorry.'

And Milena knew there was no answering comprehension in her. 'Tell me,' she said. 'I'm afraid you'll have to tell me. How have you been? What you've been doing?'

He looked suddenly, coltishly pleased that she wanted to know. He made an awkward, embracing gesture back towards his boite. 'I make my tapestries. As I told you before. I make patterns out of all the people I see. The personalities are like colours. I make them and hang them in the air for the other Snides. There's enough of us now. We work in ordinary jobs. Don't let on, most of the time. So I make them tapestries and they buy them.'

'Take them home and hang them on the wall?'

'They remember them,' he said, correcting her, shyly. More viral memory.

'But you hate viruses.'

'I hate *their* viruses. I love the ones people make for themselves.' He looked at her face, searching it. 'If only you could read,' he said. 'You'd know all that.'

They walked on. 'Until you're Snide, it's hard to believe how complex people are. Like a whole universe. There's all this chattering going on in their heads. Mist we call it, like the inside of clouds. It fogs everything, stops people seeing. Most people function by shutting almost everything out. Below that, there's the Web. That's the memory. That's where everything is stored, and the Web is a real mess. You can get tangled up in it. A very complex personality is actually difficult to get out of. It can be very scary. Underneath that is the Fire, and that just burns. That's where the heart is.'

'How tangled am I?' Milena asked.

'You . . .' he paused, eyes narrow. 'You're very neat, very tidy. But you're in compartments. There's parts of you that don't communicate with each other. So you surprise yourself all the time. It's an ordered mind. You've got an amazing capacity for detail, you're good at organising. But you could do a lot more than that.' He smiled at her. 'You'd make one hell of a Snide, you could take it all in.'

He was being kind. He likes me, thought Milena, seeing him smile.

'Yes,' he said, gently.

He loves me. I'm still Heather for him.

He must have heard her, but the smile stayed steady, and the eyes were still full of comprehension.

'They've paid for their tapestry,' he said. 'I've got to go back and finish it. Then we'll go and meet this Max of yours.'

As they walked back towards the boite, Milena thought: the clouds have cleared for him. She had never seen a change like that, when someone comes whole.

'Not entirely,' he said, looking back casually. 'I'm still a criminal. But I don't hurt people any more.' He stopped in front of his door, looking back behind him on the steps. 'The thing about being a Snide is, if you hurt people, you feel the pain too. So you end up hurting yourself.' He smiled again, and pulled the door open, and stepped smartly inside.

He sat still again, weaving patterns. There was a warm, approving chuckle.

'There she is,' said the Postwoman. 'There she is, our thread of wool.'

'Undyed,' said the dim-eyed man. 'The kind that holds the whole thing together.'

It was dark, night, when they got back to the Zoo. They found Max rehearsing the orchestra for *Wozzeck*. He saw Al and Milena slip into seats in the theatre, and gave them one of his long, unblinking stares.

Then he turned, and nodded, and the music began.

'Hoo boy!' Al exclaimed. 'Oh, poor baby.'

'What? What can you Read?' Milena asked.

'Sssh,' said Al.

The music began. It sidled forwards, uncomfortable, disjointed, angular, expressing alienation. Max conducted, making flowing, muscular gestures. Al's face seemed to freeze, fixed on him, watching him, as if he were a flickering light.

'He can feel you at his back,' murmured Al, without moving his head.

Suddenly Max made a messy, hurried wave in the air. No, no, no, said his hands. The orchestra stopped playing by degrees, the music trailing off into disorder, the musicians looking up in wonder. Max turned around. He looked at Milena. 'Do you have to be here now?' he said. His voice was quiet but it still managed somehow to penetrate the curtain of air between them.

'We're just listening to the music, Max,' said Milena. 'We'd like to talk to you. We'll wait outside for you.'

'I'm busy this evening, I can't.'

'When are you free?'

'Talk to me later!'

'We can never find you, Max. One week, Max. Remember? Two days of it have gone, Max. We need to find the thing that you lost, Max. This gentleman can help you.' The musicians began to stir in their seats and murmur to each other.

'Stop,' said Al. 'Stop now. Or you'll kill him.'

'We will wait outside,' said Milena, gathering up her coat.

They walked in silence up the corridor.

'Whoo!' said Al, expelling air as the doors swung shut behind them. 'What did you get?' Milena asked.

Al scowled. The music began again, dimly, behind the doors. 'It's like this. He makes a motion one way.' Al moved his hand like an arrow. 'But then the motion deserts him, and he's left stranded, so he makes another motion this way, in another direction, and that stops because he then remembers he meant to go the other way. There's no centre to give him any weight.'

The music wheedled through the door, sad, aching, the music of ghosts.

'He's weightless,' said Al. 'There's no up or down for him. He's totally lost. Like some poor, huge, overgrown child. He's been unable to move anywhere since childhood. He was stunned in childhood.'

The music stopped again. They could dimly hear Max talking.

'That's why he likes music. It's all pre-written, it's all rehearsed. It all flows in one direction for him. It's the only time he gets any flow. Most of us go swimming through time, with the current like a fish. He just gets lost in it. Except when there's music. As long as the music doesn't surprise him. So.' Al looked up at Milena with an odd smile. 'He hates new music.'

The problem again was time. The music started up again.

Al was still looking at Milena with an odd smile. 'He hates you. He hates the Comedy. He can't bear either of you. You make him feel so small.'

After the rehearsal, Max saw them outside in the corridor. The angular violinist was with him and she was pale with fury.

'How could you do that to me!' Max said, fists clenched and pale, mouth stretched and desperate.

'Who are you?' the violinist demanded, glaring at Milena. 'Who are you to interrupt a rehearsal like that? This is a very talented musician, and you're making him very unhappy.'

'He's made me very unhappy,' said Milena. 'He's lost the entire score of an opera. The only copy.'

'Don't!' he said, his pink fists bobbing up and down. He shuffled, knees bent, in the posture of weightlessness.

'He's lost it,' said Milena, 'because it makes him realise that he could never write it himself.'

'Milena,' warned the Snide.

The woman smiled bitterly. 'A new opera,' she said. 'God. We get one of those a month. No one can write opera any more. They're all written by ambitious stumblebums like you, who have no more appreciation than . . .' the woman broke off. 'Oooh! You should be grateful that someone like Max even looked at it.'

'We don't want to hurt him,' said the Snide. 'Not at all. We would just like a few moments alone with him.' Al took Max's hands, and began to coax the fists to uncurl. 'I'd just like to go back onto the stage with him. Where the instruments were played. The beautiful violins, the harps. The oboes. The place will still be warm from the music. We'll go there, and you can tell me all about the music you love. Eh, Max? Maybe that will help you remember.'

'Will she be there?' Max demanded, looking in terror at Milena. It was as if Milena were his mother, as if he were a naughty little boy.

'No, Max,' said the Snide. 'Just you and me.'

'If anything happens to him,' said the violinist, and jabbed a finger towards Milena, 'I'll hold you responsible. Max. I'll be waiting downstairs.'

'And I'll be waiting here,' said Milena.

Max and the Snide went back down, into the theatre. And Milena waited. How long? What was time? She got to know her own fingernails better. They were bitten, right down to the quick. Please, she prayed, though she knew of nothing to pray to, please let him remember.

Finally the door opened, and Al came out, supporting Max. Max was sobbing, rubbing fat hands into his eyes. Milena looked into Al's eyes.

'We found it,' said Al.

Max broke free and began to run. He ran for the stairs. 'Alice! Alice!' he cried, stumbling down the steps, covering his face.

Al looked at him as he ran. 'He really didn't know that he'd done it, Milena. It was buried deep, well below the Web.'

'In the Fire,' said Milena.

'In his heart,' said the Snide, and blew out again. 'He was like a maze, a horrible twisted tangle, everything unsorted.' Al was staring, looking now at what he had seen, eyes round with fear. 'I nearly didn't get out.'

Milena touched his arm. 'Thank you,' she said. 'Do you want a drink?'

Al shook his head, no, no. 'I know what drink does. Oh by all the stars! To be like that. To be trapped in that, forever.' Al looked back at the stairs and the plush carpet, as if a ghost stood there. 'At least he gets out. At least he gets out in music.'

Milena found that her sympathy was somewhat limited. 'What did he do with the book?' she asked.

Al's eyes turned around slowly to look at her. Al spoke very carefully. 'He bundled it up with other old books he had borrowed, and returned them. They were books he had borrowed from the British Museum. You know where that is.' It was a statement, not a question.

'I should know,' said Milena. There were the merest whispers of memory. It was as if she heard footsteps overhead through a ceiling. 'I grew up there. I was raised there. On the Estate of the Restorers.'

'There's a wall,' said Al.

Milena looked up.

'A wall in you. The Museum lies on the other side of it.'

'I know,' said Milena. Her childhood lay on the other side of it.

'And you're going to go there tonight, now?' Al could read her thoughts.

'I've got to get that book. The Museum won't be locked,' said Milena. 'Do you know the titles of the other books? That will tell me where to start looking.'

Al touched the tip of Milena's nose. 'Careful, Milena,' he said. 'You keep thrusting, you could hurt yourself.'

Milena remembered meeting Thrawn. It was her own fault. She kept thrusting.

The Restoration had come. Milena was convinced that people would want holograms, and she wanted the Babes to have them first. She wanted someone who knew about hologramming, someone who came cheap. So she found herself in a hostel, off the Strand. What sort of person is it, she wondered, who lives so far away from her own Estate? Milena knocked on a purple door. What an awful colour, she thought.

'Come ih-hnnnn!' sang a woman's voice beyond the door. It sounded like a caricature.

The room was deep blue inside, full of water. From out of the Coral Reef walls, seaweed sprouted. Schools of thin black fish moved among it with zig-zag precision. White light wriggled like worms over the surface of everything, even Milena's arms. A clump of seaweed spun around, and smiled with a manic, slightly daffy grin. It looked something like an amused death's head, all sinew and bone and pop-eyes. 'We are in a Coral Reef, after all,' it said.

A pink-scaled fish swam up and then into Milena's hand. Her Rhodopsin skin tingled with the light. Milena held up her hand and saw light glowing inside her flesh, orange like a sunset. Milena looked up and the face now trailed long black feathery fins. Tiger fish, said her viruses. Touch it and you are paralysed.

'I'm Thrawn McCartney,' the tiger fish said. 'Are you my saviour?'

'I doubt it,' said Milena. 'Do you need one?'

'Sure do. No one will give me a job. What did they tell you about me?' Thrawn wanted to hear about herself.

'They said you were the best hologram technician that the Zoo has,' said Milena.

'And that I'm a pain in the lymph nodes.'

'Somewhere else mostly,' admitted Milena.

'Well I am,' said Thrawn, her face fixed.

'So am I,' said Milena.

Thrawn gave a connoisseur's shake of the head. 'No,' she said, and spun back around. The whole room seemed to blink, and the tiger fish was gone. A woman remained, her back towards Milena. 'You're one of those quiet, boring, determined little pains,' she said. She wore a black leotard and looked small and slim. 'I am a great, gushing volcano's mouth of a pain.'

She tossed what seemed half a hundredweight of black hair over her shoulders and turned, arching her back. She was deliberately posing, offering herself. Milena felt a kind of jolt, but not necessarily one of attraction. The woman was dangerously thin. The neck was all tendons. They looked as if they could snap, as if the disproportionately large head could break the tendons and then roll off. The face was haggard. Milena felt something like desire and something queasy, at the same time.

'I'm about to offer you a job,' warned Milena. But she found she was smiling. 'Do you want to talk about hologramming?'

'No,' sighed Thrawn. 'Holograms are two hundred years old and about as exciting as dandruff. We could remake the world now, with light.' She glanced about at her underwater world. 'I bet all you want me for is some old opera. You want me to cube in some real places onto the stage. Right? Right?'

'Yes,' said Milena.

'We're all so bored with your old operas. We're all so bored with your ficken high-toned quality.' The room blinked again, and she dropped down onto a beanbag.

It was an ordinary room now. The Coral Reef walls had been plastered over and left unpainted. There was a mattress on the floor, and bags, and a bank of equipment – metal boxes, lights, and leads. A cable went out the window to the Restoration wires along the Strand. Thrawn stretched her legs out straight and looked at Milena. 'I ought to warn you,' she said. 'I've never been Read. I've never been Placed or doctored. So you'll never know what I'm going to do or say next.'

Milena was still smiling, at the aggression, at the foolishness of it. 'I haven't been Read either,' she said, hoping she sounded unimpressed.

'Then why are you so dull?' asked Thrawn.

'I guess some people just naturally are. Like some people are naturally obnoxious.'

Thrawn liked that. It made her grin. 'Yup,' she agreed. 'So how did you get away?' She rolled over onto her stomach, still stretching, like some starved cat.

'I didn't. They gave me one final load of viruses and I was so ill they couldn't Read me. In the meantime I was Placed.'

'Well *I* ran away,' said Thrawn, rather grandly, comparing herself with Milena. 'I hid out in the Slump, in the reeds. Nobody was going to doctor me. I hid, and then I came back. I tell you, I got terrible grammar.' Then she leaned forward. She leaned forward and used both her arms to push her breasts forward. They hung within the neckline of the leotard. 'Are you?' Thrawn asked, smiling.

'Am I what?' asked Milena, scarce believing.

Thrawn rolled her eyes and asked again. 'Are you?' She rolled forward onto her knees, presenting herself.

Milena felt a kind of slow, hazy panic. My God, is she asking me? My God, have I found another one? 'Yes,' Milena said, experimentally.

Now it was Thrawn's turn to be coy. 'Yes to what?' she asked, striking another pose.

Milena's face was hot. She was smiling a lazy, fearful smile. She felt confused. 'Yes to whatever you're asking.' The whole thing was moving too fast, hurtling forward.

Thrawn laughed, and slid nearer to Milena. 'Saying that could be dangerous. You might not know what I'm asking.'

There was something between them, as if the gases in the air had solidified. It was a shape, defined by them, but with a life of its own. Sex was only part of it, but it was as impersonal as sex. It and time hauled Milena forward towards Thrawn.

She crawled towards Milena with her slow smile. 'You don't know what I'm asking at all.'

But this is so crude, thought Milena. This is so banal. I'm being vamped.

Thrawn kissed her on the cheek. I've had fantasies like this, Milena thought and made herself continue. Then Thrawn began to lick her face as if it were a lollipop.

I'm not sure about this, thought Milena, pressing her lips and eyes shut. Thrawn smelt of sweat and boiled onions.

'Oh, tooch, bubi, tooch.'

What, thought Milena, is that supposed to mean? Does she really think it will drive me wild with passion? Thrawn leaned back to pull off her leotard, and Milena felt desire retreat. It left her beached and dry and slightly sick in the stomach.

The flesh around Thrawn's eyes was coiled like a rope; her face was a knot. As she descended again, Thrawn's face was turned away from Milena, denying what was happening. Is she enjoying this? Milena wondered.

She tried to make the best of a bad job. She tried to shift to a more comfortable position but the rug kept rucking up and sliding away underneath her. She lay still for a few moments under the oblivious Thrawn. Finally, Milena tapped her on the shoulder.

'Thrawn,' said Milena, as if reminding her of something she already knew. 'Thrawn. Stop.'

Thrawn went still. Then very quickly, she rolled away.

Milena sat up. Her elbow had been badly knocked in the struggle. She looked at Thrawn. Thrawn lay on her side, back to Milena, picking at the rucked-up rug. Milena's trousers swaddled her thighs and made it difficult to stand. She managed it by pushing her knees together at an awkward angle.

'It's because I'm old and fat, isn't it?' said Thrawn, from the floor. She was staring at the strands of the rug.

'You aren't fat,' said Milena, out of kindness, and because it was so far from the truth.

Thrawn sat up and her eyes were poison. 'I am. Don't tell me I'm not fat.' She shook a dried pouch of loose skin on her belly. She stood up, and began to pull on her leotard, carefully running the elastic back into place along the same lines of indentation in the skin.

'Our relationship should be strictly professional,' said Thrawn, with a kind of snarl.

'It's a bit late for that, isn't it?' said Milena, beginning to smile.

'Not,' said Thrawn, and pulled back her hair. 'Where *I* am concerned.'

'Good. Fine. Glad to hear it,' said Milena, rubbing her elbow.

'I'm quite ruthless in my standards,' said Thrawn coolly. She pulled on a pair of trousers over her leotard. 'I am a perfectionist. It is something of a curse always to want the very best.'

'I'm sure it is,' said Milena and thought: there's something wrong with this woman. Her elbow was black from bruising.

'You'll hate me,' said Thrawn with a sigh, looking up. It was a statement of fact. It had the ring of truth. It also sounded like a promise. Milena looked up at the sad, devouring face.

'No I won't,' said Milena, lightly. A process of mollification had begun.

* * *

Later that same day, walking back from the Strand, Milena suddenly thought: it's my birthday soon.

It was one year since Rolfa had gone. The thought rooted Milena to the pavement where she stood. She was standing on Waterloo Bridge, where she and Rolfa had walked back together from the Spread-Eagle. This year, September had been hot, wet, monsoonish. But on this one evening, the sky had cleared. It was the same plum colour it had been on the evening when Rolfa had led her back from meeting Lucy.

St Paul's Cathedral looked the same, with its dome of white stone and sheets of lead. But electric lights hung in chains now all along both banks of the river. There were puddles of light, pools of it on the pavements. It will be like this, Rolfa, thought Milena. I will get further and further away from you. And you'll get dimmer and dimmer, like one of those little lights on the end of the chain.

Milena couldn't dawdle. It was her turn tonight to take care of little Berry. She walked on slowly, her head down.

A year since Rolfa; a month since Berowne had died giving birth. It was so unfair. He had made it all the way through. The child was born. It was wailing. He had time to shout at it, 'Hello! Oh hello!'. Then the afterbirth came free. The blood had hit the ceiling. And there was another orphan. Of sorts. The baby's mother, the Princess, could not face him.

Milena walked down the steps of the Zoo, and into the Child Garden.

She walked down into a room full of wood panels with colourful paintings. The place smelled of infants: milk and nappies and sodden padding. It was too warm. It made Milena giddy. A Nurse took her to Berry's cot. He was three weeks old. He looked up at Milena with solemn blue eyes. Who are you this time? he seemed to ask. Milena lifted him up onto her shoulders and he started to wail.

'I know. I know,' she said, and patted him.

Out of the corners of the room, on the mattress-covered floor, the other infants came. They came crawling and whispering to each other.

'All these people coming to see him.'

'Yes, but they're not his parents are they?'

The voices were high and wispy and wheedling with jealousy.

'His father is dead.'

'His mother never comes to see him.'

Their minds were full of virus. They could speak, they could read, they could add and subtract. They ringed Milena round like a hostile tribe. The sound of someone else crying made them angry. They wanted to cry themselves. They wanted to howl their lungs raw. The viruses made them speak.

'Why can't he talk?' one of the infants demanded. He supported himself on all fours. His flesh was plump and creased.

'Why haven't you given him the viruses?'

'It's time he was given the virus.'

Milena didn't answer them. She stepped over them. The room was hot and she was feeling ill. She simply wanted to escape.

'He hasn't had the virus!' the infants called after her, in rage, as she fled.

She couldn't think why it had so upset her. She felt she was protecting Berry from them. She had to stop to gather breath, cool breath, and found she was trembling. Her hands shook as she wrapped Little Berry up in his blankets. She held him to her, and walked under one of the brick bridges along the elevated walkways, and then looked up, and saw the Shell.

The windows were full of fire, reflected sunlight. Here it was again, September fire. Milena remembered Jacob. She remembered him walking back, into the Shell, to run his messages.

But now, because of you and Rolfa, when I dream, I also hear the music.

Rolfa was gone, and Berowne was gone. Jacob was gone too. All in one year? Milena had found Jacob one day in spring, crumpled on the staircase like an old suit of clothes, a costume in the Graveyard. The fire in the windows had once seemed like the fire of people's lives. Now it was the fire of ghosts.

Milena stood where she had once stood before, unable to move. How did I get here? she wondered. How did I get here, holding someone else's baby, with the smell of Thrawn McCartney still on me? In a world with holograms and electric lights. Milena felt the giddiness of time. It was a kind of vertigo. It was as if time had hauled her up at high speed a dizzying distance away from herself, away from her life. It was as if she were on a train, and the train was going faster and faster, and it never stopped. The stations of her life were rattling past. Sixteen, seventeen, eighteen. She was never given the chance to get off.

It was dark by the time Milena had climbed the stairs to her room. It looked much the same as it had when Rolfa lived there; a little tidier perhaps; a little emptier. The baby needed changing. Milena was surprised by how brave she had become about nappies and feeding times. When the baby was clean, she put him into his hammock and began to rock him.

Berry started to sing. His voice was high and pure and piping and he sang particular songs. Was it normal for a child to sing before it could talk? She thought. Berry seemed to hear her. He smiled at her. Is he Snide? Milena wondered. The songs he sang were the songs he had heard Milena humming. He sang the songs of the Comedy.

Milena lit a candle on her windowsill and opened the great, grey book. Here she could find herself. She took a piece of staved paper from a tidy pile of paper. And she began to work.

Milena was orchestrating the Comedy. A year after Rolfa had left, she had worked her way to the beginning of Canto Eight. There were one hundred cantos in all. Dante and Virgil had come to the river Styx. Milena looked at the tiny notes of music, one for each syllable. Why were some of them in red? In the corner, in pencil, words said:

trumpets glint like light on water. Sombre and joyful at once (a Comedy after all)

How, she wondered, how can you make horns sound sombre *and* joyful?

She could only do what she was able to do. Pretend the Comedy is a transcription, she told herself. Pretend that it's a vocal version of an orchestrated original. Pretend you are reversing cause and effect and remember that horns in G will be written in C. No sharps or flats. The viruses will help.

Milena started to write, lost in work. She did not realise that she and Little Berry were humming in unison.

dear fish

Milena remembered a letter. She saw all of it, in memory, the light on the page, the clots in the ink. It read:

sorry about the name, but i think of you as fish – i dont mean any harm by it but tell me if you really hate it and ill try to mend my ways – to answer your question – i actually think of myself as canadian – the arctic is different from the antarctic – more grass, more trees – the antarctic is a desert – but i still love it – now rolfa's father he is definitely english tough which is how we ended up trying to live in south ken from which god preserve me

well im back now in the antarctic – place doesnt look any different – all blue ice and blue sky – my dogs still knew me – good lord – the love in dogs – you wouldnt believe – yipped and yelped whined and widdled – you sure knew you were wanted – dogs simply feel more than we do – im sure of it – never saw people get so happy to see anyone – never mind me I am just trying to get you to think of dogs a bit more kindly after what happened last year

anyway here i am sitting under my old alcohol lamp and im going out digging tomorrow with my dogs and im eating a greasy stew thats still frozen in the middle and i couldnt be any happier –

rolfa didnt come with me – said she didnt want to and she should know except that right now i think she doesnt know what she wants –

never saw anyone so confused as that poor girl – she went for the
weediest little fella, a squidge, real tiny with a pudding basin haircut,
blouse, shorts – papa's hair turned spiky over it – then that all passed
just as quickly as she took it up – she said she ate the little guy for
breakfast and I can believe it – believe it or not my great soft lump of
a girl is getting real aggressive these days – just before i left she
THRASHED her first cousin – now he is one huge devil – size of a
house – he said something and suddenly he was swallowing all of his
teeth – last i heard she was reading up on ACCOUNTANCY –
you keep writing – i really like your letters – they make me laugh –
though i know the real reason you take such an interest in an old
antarctic lady is that you want to know whats happening with rolfa –
thats OK – ill let you know when i hear things

your friend

hortensia patel

Milena stopped spinning.

Someone was holding her down. He was very tall and very thin and
his smile seemed to have been cut out of the tension of his face with
a knife.

'You shuffle forward, one step at a time, knees bent,' he was telling
her. His accent was American. 'You try to keep your balance. That is
the posture of weightlessness.' He took his hands away. Success.
Milena stayed where she was. 'Well,' he said. 'That sure was some
introduction.'

'Yep,' said Milena. 'I threw up all over you and dislocated your
shoulder.'

'My name's Mike Stone,' he said. 'Astronaut.'

Milena dared to reach forward and shake his hand. She had finally
found her feet.

Outside, the heavens were full of stars, the stars of memory. Rolfa,
they seemed to whisper. Where is Rolfa?

The Reading was over.

Milena woke up. That was what it felt like. She found herself lying
on a floor. At first she thought it was the Bulge. The floor was warm
and soft and alive. Milena was covered in sweat. Across the room,
which was dimly lit, a huge woman in white was talking, hand on her
chin, shaking her head. It was Root, the nurse. And there was Mike
Stone, astronaut, sitting in some strange sling chair.

When was this? thought Milena. When did this happen? I don't
remember this. Where is my Now?

147

Root glanced over her shoulder and saw that Milena was awake. Her eyes widened, and she cut off her conversation with a nod. She half-ran towards Milena, her round arms held aloft and swaying from side to side with her hips. Root leaned over Milena, and her hands were pressed between her knees.

'I'm sorry, love,' said Root. 'But we're going to have to Read you again.'

'Again?' croaked Milena. She felt horribly ill.

'They don't have everything. I guess there's just so much of you to have.' Lightly, Root stroked Milena's thin hair. 'You're fighting it, aren't you, love?'

'What else does it want?' Milena asked. The Consensus had everything else.

'Well. It got nothing from your childhood, nothing at all. And there's Rolfa. You kept back all your memories of Rolfa. She's very important to you. They need Rolfa too.'

Oh, do they? thought Milena. Do they indeed.

'You mustn't fight, you know,' said Root. Her eyes were full of sadness, but her face was deadly serious. 'You fight, you could hurt yourself.' She gave Milena a steady, examining stare. 'Ready?'

'Why do they want the Past?' Milena asked. 'If they keep telling us the world is only Now?'

'Because the Past is you,' said Root, and stood up. Milena heard her rustle away.

My whole life, thought Milena, my whole life has not been mine.

Then space was twisted. Space shivered as when heat rises up from roadway. The shivering space rose up, and began to roll, quivering towards her. It was a wave, a wave in both space and time, a wave in the fifth dimension where light and thought and gravity are one. It confronted her, trembling as if with desire. It wanted Milena to be a story, that it could Read.

Rolfa, where is Rolfa? Where she always is, Milena thought. Here with me.

Now, where is my Now? My now is here, where I fight the Consensus.

The wave slammed into her, washing over her, through her, racing up the channels of her nerves, as if to wash them clean, as if to wash all of Milena away.

It was as if her memories of Rolfa were a rock to which Milena could cling. Milena held them and preserved them.

Everything else was surrendered to the roar.

chapter ten

AN AUDIENCE OF CHILDREN
(THE TREE OF HEAVEN)

Milena remembered being in the womb.

All sensation was nameless, wordless, unshaped by any kind of grammar. There was light, orange light, passing over her, through her. There was a pulsing, a rush that seethed through her, warm, thrilling, delicious.

There was music.

Dimly heard amid the throb, the sound of a violin was filtered and soft, faraway as dream. It was more like light than sound, a settling of nameless comfort. The music swayed, and the warmth that surrounded Milena swayed with it. Her world moved with the music. There was a dance in the pulsing of her blood, a dance of love, of chemical release. A delectable tingle invaded her. Milena felt the music because her mother felt it.

Her mother was making it. Her mother was playing the violin. To the adult who was remembering, the music was the only familiar thing. The adult knew it was a piece by Bartok. To the unborn infant, it was a physical sensation. The unborn Milena hummed with the music, as if she were a string of the instrument, as if her mother were playing her as well. The music lifted up and swung the unborn child, she rose and fell with it. I've never felt that! thought the adult who remembered. I've never felt music like that since. It was a different state of being: gentle, surging, warm, ultimately intimate. Milena was part of someone else. Blood and fluids caressed her; everything was touched by light filtered through flesh; everything was heard through the singing in the blood, the stroking fluid. It was like being bathed in something delicious, lemon chocolate perhaps, and being able to taste it with the skin. It was like that brief joyful moment, not necessarily of orgasm, when sex is pure delight. No wonder, thought the one who remembered. No wonder sex keeps pulling. It is trying to pull us back to this.

The infant tried to dance. It moved its legs. The very sensation of movement was new. It was power, to be able to move.

The music stopped.

There was a muffled voice, from outside, from above, a message from beyond. It was a message of celebration. The Milena who remembered could almost make sense of the words. They were like words spoken by a ghost. Milena remembered the tone and timbre, the rise and fall. It was the ghost of her mother.

The infant's ears were plugged and her nose was plugged, but she felt no desire to breathe. She was one with her world, and it was a world of love.

And Milena remembered that world turning inside out.

The fluids left her, suddenly. A clinging veil settled over her, still warm but slightly harsh. And then the convulsion began, the expulsion. The world pushed her out. The infant knew one thing: she had started this. She had worked at herself. She had felt like an old tooth coming loose, and so she had tried the power again, the power to move. And it seemed that she had broken the world. She felt horror and fear, but above all regret, as if the world were wounded.

The world pushed, caressing no longer, and the infant knew death, the death of the world and she grieved as she was being born.

For the adult who remembered, sensation was as jumbled as a roller coaster, great peaks and sudden fallings. All things were terribly important, the sounds, communicated through flesh, the clackings of separation, the slitherings of movement, the lapping of the walls like giant tongues, the pumping in her ears and veins. The world parted, like lips.

Giddyingly, inside became outside, as if Milena herself was being born out of herself, swapping places, mother and daughter. Suddenly, all inside had been swallowed up.

It took a moment – each moment a different universe – for air to envelop her. Air was new. It was dry, searing like fire. It burned her face; it burned her whole body. There was blazing light, and stinging gases. The infant was gripped about her ankles, and where she was held there was a sizzling abrasion as if her skin was being fried.

Suddenly she was fighting. There was a swelling in her, as if she was trying to start the pumping up again. Something gave. But the pumping was not outside her now, but smaller and contained in her. Air rasped its way like sandpaper over her tongue, down her throat. She felt an ache across her chest as the aerole of her lungs inflated – pop, pop, pop, one after the other. She roared in pain.

She was lowered onto soft warmth. A ghost of paradise returned. Dimmer now was the pumping, louder now was the murmuring voice. She lay on top of her old world. She covered it now. This world was in layers. Panels of warmth descended over her back, rough, but comforting as they lay still on her, weighing her down, pushing her, it seemed. The infant hoped. Was she going to be pushed back inside?

Then something clattered on a tray, horribly sharp like something rammed into her ears, and she began to wail again. The infant was wailing for the vastness of things, and an already forming sense of all the things she had to learn. The voice soothed her, the warm fingers stroked her, and the infant remembered what had been lost. It's still here, the voice seemed to say, it's different now, but it's still here. Here, but different.

Layer on layer of life folded over the infant. Lungs breathing, two hearts pumping, all the organs with their rough surfaces and hidden spaces, all of them turning in and out of each other like patterns in a kaleidoscope.

The infant was left there, on her mother's stomach, to sleep. She dreamed of tunnels of light, and sealed places full of fluid, and things dim in the fluid, cushioned, floating, safe.

Milena remembered crawling.

She remembered the braided rug, padded sections in a concentric pattern. They swirled under Milena's fingers and smelled of cat.

The old world was forgotten now, driven out by the wealth of this new one. The infant looked up, and the world still seemed concentric, fragmented.

It looks, thought the adult who was remembering, like a Picasso painting.

There was a room, in this her second and forgotten world. The room itself was not familiar at all. The room was jumbled, cast in layers, like many photographs of the same room. Things had so many sides, it was difficult for them to hold their shapes. The back and sides of the chair were just as present as the front. They drifted in and out of view, overlapping each other. They were now near, now far. Anything she liked seemed to come closer. She reached out for it, thinking it was coming to meet her.

Milena saw the top of the spout of a watering can. The adult who was remembering recognised it, with a jolt. The watering can had a rough, screw-on cap with holes in it that turned the water into a spray. The infant's eyes focused on the cap and brought it together as a whole. The world spun around it, fragmented as if seen through a jewel.

The infant reached up and touched the watering can, felt the recalcitrance of the cap. The hardened resin would be difficult to turn against the resin spout. She tasted it. There was a flavour of pine. It clung to her tongue, clung to her lips. Milena was not sure whether she hated it or not.

There was a voice, warm behind her. '*Ne, ne,*' something said, warmly, deeply, '*Ne, Milena.*'

Ne was a strange word. The infant had not yet exhausted its meaning.

Whenever it was said, it was best for her to go still. It was a powerful word, but she herself could say it over and over, shaking her head, and it had no effect.

There were trouser-legs, beige. There was a man, a tall skinny man with a beard. He had several faces, all turning at once, until they focused. Milena knew him, by his beard, by his black eyes, and by the veins in his hands. When the hands were kind, the world was a delight. The hands picked her up, full of power, and nestled her on her father's warm lap. Milena was kissed on the head, and there was a warm sound, a chuckling. Then cloth was laid before her, and the man's hands began to sew. On the table there were needles, slivers of bamboo. Light was reflected on them, a rippling stream of it, like a river. Milena reached for the needles.

'*Ne, ne, Milena, ne,*' said the voice. Ne could mean no needles, no light.

'*Milena! Amin!*' called a voice from outside the room. The words were signals, full of import but imprecise, like the waving of flags.

Milena flew. The man lifted her up and swung her through the air. The air was warm like fingers, and Milena saw her world, the swirling carpet far below her. She squealed and laughed. She was swung through a doorway that seemed to meet itself from several different directions and angles at once. Milena passed through it, and out into the garden.

There it was in memory, as if a place could die and have a ghost. There was the bench, top and bottom at once, slats of warm wood, dappled with shifting shadows. What made the shadows, what made them move? Great roots went up into a tangle in the sky, all rough, scintillating with wind, showing silver-pale undersides in waves. Vines crawled overhead, on a frame. Beyond them, there were trees. They rose even higher than the vines up into the sky, towards the clouds.

The infant looked away. The trees were beyond comprehension. She could not pull them near to her, she could not make her eyes focus.

And there, stepping in and out of dappled shadow, there came Mami.

Mami was a word that grouped many things about the woman into a bouquet: the smiles and the warmth and the red trouser suit. Mami knelt down and kissed her. Mami with her beautiful face. Then Milena was carried towards the table, held upright by both her parents, each one holding her hand. On the table was her red bowl. Milena was sat down, and a napkin was tied around her. Milena didn't want the napkin. *Ne*, she said, but the word had no effect. A cool spoon of sweet pablum was lifted up to her mouth. Milena wanted to feed herself, but was not allowed to. In the sunlight, she accepted that.

152

The pablum was delicious and made her laugh. That made Mami laugh too; Mami was glad when Milena was, so Milena laughed again. On the table there were round, red plump things that would be cut open and scooped out, all pulpy, onto Milena's plate.

Sunlight brewed on her skin, hatching something. Milena looked down at the kaleidoscope of her arm. She saw the smooth surface of her perfect skin from many angles. She saw a cell of her skin lift like a lid. Something was being born out of her. It was the same colour as Milena, a mild magenta. It was tiny and wriggling. The infant was delighted. Was this how things grew? Out of each other? Did worlds grow out of people in the same way? Or did people grow out of things, out of trees perhaps?

Words came like flags. Mami spoke, like the wind spoke, and the sounds were soothing. The sounds meant the little wriggling things were good. Mami held out her own long arm next to Milena's. It was armoured by mites as well.

Milena had something of her own. She looked at her creature. She knew that she and her creature protected each other. Milena felt love for this tiny thing that was alive and intimate with her. The idea was implanted: I grow things out of myself.

The trees sighed in the wind. The sun baked the hot white wall, and made the vines overhead glow with light. Birds whistled. People laughed. This world was paradise, too.

The kaleidoscope turned.

Milena lay in her blue crib, in the dark, but the dark had gone evil.

From the bars of her crib, toy painted heads grinned at her discomfort. The sheets were clammy, another damp veil, and a smell oozed out of Milena, a sour tang that ruined her perfection. The infant knew her perfection had been damaged. All along her arms and into her head, there was a buzzing. A numb vibration hummed in the tangle of her nerves. The infant had not known she was a tangle until then.

The Milena who was remembering thought: this is virus. This must be the first time they gave me virus.

The infant howled, as if to expel it.

The door opened, and the infant hoped for comfort. Milena swallowed the sounds of crying in anticipation. There was a fluttering of light, and the mouth of a lamp opened, bringing light, but the light looked orange and sick as well. Mami came, cooing, and leaning over the blue crib. She lifted Milena up and patted her, but nothing changed. As Milena was jostled up and down, she sensed in her mother a kind of grim forebearing. Her mother said something cool, with a twist in it, a false sing-song note at the end. It seemed Milena's mother was determined she should be ill. The infant did not understand the words. But she understood their import. In some way her mother condoned this; in some way her mother was part of it. Milena knew then that she would not be helped. The whole world was sick and ill and twisted, dim and ill-suited to itself. It had been invaded, not by music or by love, but by something alien.

The aliens tried to speak. They tried to speak inside Milena. The words were muffled, like voices heard through a womb. Milena could feel the voices stir, like larvae. Words had been deposited in her head like grubs. They began to seethe.

It was the world that was threatened, and Milena wanted to save it. *Ne!* thought the infant. She resisted. *Ne, ne!*

The alien words were woven, like blankets, out of thread. Milena could feel the thread, touch it with thought. The threads were tightly stitched. At first Milena could only feel how harsh they were, like blankets on her skin. Then she felt more carefully. The threads were ladders, tiny, granulated. The ladders were spirals. They spun about each other in a double helix.

Ne! Milena told them, and the grubs went still. She could feel the ladders change. The ladders fell silent, moulded themselves to her thought. She hunted them with thought. She gave chase, through the spider's web of her nerves. *Ne!* she told the invaders, and they went still and tame, waiting to be filled.

The viruses were supposed to fill her, but Milena filled them instead. She made them her own. *Ne* was the word of rejection. *Ne* was the word of independence, of freedom. It worked when you had power.

The infant Milena was touching the DNA of the viruses, and changing it to her own purpose. That young? thought the adult who remembered. I knew that much, so young? How much else did I know, before words?

The viruses went still. They would now store information. Milena was augmenting her own memory. She was making a bigger, silent self, a larger No.

She opened her eyes.

Her little room, with its doilies and dolls still looked ill and evil, the orange lamplight as steady as a headache. Even the face of Milena's mother looked ill, baggy, tired. You, thought the infant. You did this!

It was the betrayal that made the infant howl and wail.

To the Milena who remembered, each shift of memory made the world tamer and more secure. It became more adult, less like leaves scattered in layers, and more like butterflies pinned in rows under glass. With each shift, the adult felt more at home, could find her bearings with more ease. Emotions came with names, already controlled and bear-

154

able. Milena the infant now knew words. But these were words that she had learned for herself. The words belonged to her.

The room around now came in only one focused shape, four walls. The wooden table, the wood-burning stove, the rickety chairs, the bean bags on the floor, the string of garlic, were all as the adult remembered them. They showed only one side of themselves at a time. Outside the windows, there was blazing daylight. Milena could now hear the ticking of the clock in all its soulless regularity. Tick-tock time.

'*Milena*,' said her mother, quietly. '*Your father wants to talk to you.*'

Tatinka, her mother called him. The words unleashed a sense of loss. Milena, the adult felt an undertow tug of strangeness, of loss. The adult had lost a language.

Milena felt another chasm open up under her. Time had hauled her away from her mother and her mother tongue. She felt the vertigo.

The infant was looking at her mother's face. There was something very grave and serious in the world. It made her mother quiet and noble, and Milena's heart swelled with love. Her mother was young and beautiful, and now noble as well. Her mother took her hand, and led her out of her old world, into another one, through the door to her parents' room. Her parents' room was where Milena went at night, when darkness frightened her. This room was darkened now. Milena felt panic.

'*Is it night?*' she asked. The infant lived in a world where day could become night without warning.

'*No, Milena. It's just the shutters. The shutters have been closed.*

The room smelled acid like sour lemons. Milena the infant knew that smell. It rose off your body, from the tangle, when the world went sick.

The walls were brown, the sheets were brown, everything was jumbled, and dirtier than it should be. Her father was brown and jumbled, crucified on a bed. His black hair pasted slick and flat over his forehead. Now that Milena was older, people only had one face at a time. Words, even Czechoslovakian words, gave things only one face. This face had black stubble and dark flesh around the eyes.

Milena's mother nudged her toward the bed. She stood next to him, at face-level, and a hot, damp arm was drawn around her. He was burning. Milena knew then that he had the illness. He had the burning and the shaking. He looked at her with eyes that were different, a stranger's eyes. Milena went wary. They could take your father and give him someone else's eyes.

'*Svoboda*,' he croaked.

Like *Ne*, the word meant freedom. But it was a Czech word, and not the same as English freedom, and never could be. *Svoboda* was something natural like apples, like the earth. Like paradise, the way to it was barred.

You can fight it, *Tato*. You think at it, and it changes. You can do that can't you *Tato*? Milena wanted to explain, but couldn't. Then she thought he would know that already. She had already been taught that adults always knew more than she did. *Tato* took Milena's hand in his own. Milena could smell the hand. He spoke in rough and alien voice.

'*Be good, Milena.*'

Adults were always telling her to be good. It was not possible to know what good was. It always seemed to change. Milena knew she could not promise to be good; she wasn't sure what good was. She didn't want to lie, but she knew she could not say no. So Milena nodded yes. She knew it was a lie, so didn't say the words. She wanted to be good, but if he had to ask, did that mean she really wasn't good? What should she do to be good? No one ever seemed to be able to explain it fully. The word good seemed to spread out, diffuse, as part of the brown walls.

'*Milena, answer your father.*'

They were going to make her say yes. Yes was the word of acquiescence. It was the word of powerlessness.

Milena murmured, yes. Her mother made her say it again, louder. Her mother's hand was on her shoulder, pushing her closer to her father, who was sick and who smelled. They both wanted something from her, and she could not think what it could be, however much she wanted to give it. She wanted to give it as long as she was not pushed.

The future, thought the one who was remembering, they want some promise of the future.

'*Kiss your father,*' her mother told her.

He smelled and was wet, and already he was not her father.

'*Milena, don't be naughty. Your father wants to kiss you.*'

There was something awful in her mother's voice. It was not her mother's voice. Her mother could become someone different too. Milena felt the hand on her shoulder like a claw. She was afraid. Any moment she would weep from fear, and that would be bad. She leaned forward, sticking out her lips to give her father a quick nip on the cheek. But his arm pulled, and her mother's hand pushed, and his hot, wet sticky face seemed to swallow hers, and he smelled of beds and illness, and his wet lips were on hers, coating them with moisture.

Milena hated it. She stepped back, shaking inside. She wanted above all else to wipe her face, her lips, her forehead stained with someone else's sweat. Above all else, she wanted to escape the transforming sickness. They let her go, and she ran out into the daylight, from the darkness, out into the garden, into the air.

* * *

Milena remembered standing until her legs ached, outside a church. She was wearing new white clothes, that her mother had made from sheets. The church was white, small and squat with thick walls and a dome on a spire. There were old lead plates on the roof, and Milena looked at them, sensing how warm they would be in the sun. She loved the dull burnish on them. The lead plates were made of metal and Milena had not seen many things made of metal.

Milena had asked her mother what the lead plates were and had been shushed into silence. Milena's mother did not like it when Milena asked questions when other people were around.

Milena was beginning to discover that she was stupid. Other children, she was beginning to discover, had heads that were crowded full of answers. When Milena asked questions, her mother looked miserable, and her jaw thrust itself forward in something like anger. Already, when Milena wanted to get back at her mother, she would ask a question. Her mother, she knew, put things in her food, that made ill, to stop her asking questions.

Her mother stood next to her now, towering in black. She shook Milena's hand to draw her attention back to the funeral proceedings, back to the hole in the ground, and the box that had been lowered into it, and the man in black who was speaking.

The proceedings were endless and had no point. They confused elaboration with importance. There were birds in the air, cawing in a spiral, swept round and around in circles. What kept them together? Were there wires that strung them together, that kept them up? Why could birds fly and not people?

The birds were important, the light on the roof was important. The fierce, black concentration of the adults on the dead box and the dead hole exhausted importance. By the time the adults were finished, the hole and the box would have no meaning. Milena knew the dead box and the black hole were her father. She knew he was gone. She was sorry. She had said she was sorry once, and meant it. There was no need to go on saying it. Sunlight fell like rain. The rain-light did not grieve. Neither did Milena. That was what adults found terrible.

Her mother gave her hand another exasperated shake. The box was being lowered. More murmuring, and a shaking of water. Milena watched the light in the water. That was nice. It was like her resin watering can. It was as if her father had become a plant, to be tended. 'She doesn't understand,' murmured Milena's mother, explaining, apologising. Milena, the infant, felt a surprisingly fierce wrenching of anger. I don't understand, do I? I understand as well as you do, thought the child. I just understand it differently.

There was much more to endure. Soil was heaped. The villagers came forward, one by one, to say they were sorry, and take Milena's mother's hand, and lean down over Milena and say something false. None of them really knew Milena's family. Milena's family were strangers to them, mysterious people who lived high on an isolated hill. One of them gave Milena and her mother a lift in a cart up the slopes back to their house. Milena sat in the back with sacks of grain, wanting the adults to go away. She wanted to be alone with her world.

Finally, the cart left them, and Milena's mother went inside the house to change and Milena was left, standing in the garden, in front of a gate. Beyond it was a field.

Beside the gate, there was a tree. Its leaves glowed with light; the trunk was riddled with deep cracks. Blossom was hung about its branches and the scent of it was like a thread, linking things together.

Milena and the tree stood poised together, as if to escape.

Then something spoke.

'*Lipy*,' it said, naming the tree. Everything seemed to darken, as if the sun had gone behind a cloud. '*Tilia platyphyllos*,' it said, pushing the tree into a framework of science.

There had been anxious visits to the house from women in white. They had spoken in hushed voices to Milena's mother. Whenever the Nurses came, the voices followed. It was Milena's mother who let them do it to her. There was a silent war between them.

Milena closed her eyes and groped in the darkness like a blind woman, until she touched them. The viruses were hot and roiling and tightly wound. She sprung them. They leapt apart as if wanting to be free. She silenced them. Milena waited with her eyes closed, to see if they would try to speak again. The viruses could darken the world with words. To Milena, it felt as though she were saving the world, and not herself.

Slowly she opened her eyes again.

It was as if Milena and the world had crept out of hiding together. The sun had come out from behind a cloud; colour was sprung from the heart of everything. Everything was encased in light, like a halo. Light went into and came out of everything. Light, like time, moved in two directions at once, an exchange between all things. Light and weight and consciousness itself, they all seemed to pull, steadily, orienting everything towards each other. The trees, the grass, the wooden gate, they were oriented towards Milena because she looked at them. They seemed to come closer to her. The lime tree leaned with all its weight, towards Milena, towards the field. The world glowed in silence.

And it was as if her father quietly stepped up beside her. He seemed to be in the light, in the silence. He seemed as heavy and silent as the lime tree. He, too, seemed to lean out towards the field. Let me go, Milena, he seemed to say.

The field was forbidden. It was unsafe. The field dropped off steeply at one end, where a wood began. Lines of larches stood bolt upright along the edge like the tails of squirrels ready to bolt.

Milena did not believe it was unsafe. She stood on tiptoe, and worked the latch. There was a rising of wind. The gate swung open, as if by itself.

Birds rose out of the trees into the sky. The long grass in the field waved, seeming to beckon. It was as if Milena and her father walked forward into the world. It was as if Milena's father were the wind.

The wind seemed to sweep light and sound with it. The sounds of grass and trees rose out of the ground and bore up the birds, rising up and breathing into the clouds, the clouds shedding light, making highways of dust and haze, everything exhaling warmth, the breath, the song of the earth. It was as if the spirit of her father had been sprung. He seemed to leap out into the world and expand, as if the elements that had made him had finally been set free, to rejoin the world.

Milena broke into a run. It was as if she were running with her father, a fat and waddling toddle, near to the ground, down the slope at gathering speed. She ran looking upwards. She threw out her arms, squealing, giddy, the world spinning. When she fell down, it was as if the grass had arms, to spread open and catch her. It was as if it caught her, laughing, and held her. *Svoboda*, said the earth.

'Milena!' a voice cried behind her. 'Milena!'

Fear, like winged monkeys descending.

Milena felt herself snatched up from the grass, wrenched away from it. The grass seemed to reach out for her as her head tipped down and her bottom tipped up, as if she were weightless. She sickened, see-sawing to a fresh sense of balance. She didn't want to look, she didn't want to see, her mother's face.

Her mother hit her. This was something new. Her mother hit her across her bottom, her dirty place of indignity and shame. Milena howled at this new and terrible thing. She howled and was tipped back upright. Her mother spoke to her. The voice was full of venom, hatred. Milena's white leg was seized. Her white shoe was shaken at her. The grass had left green slashes across it, and on the new white trousers. Exchange. You could not expect to move through the world and not let it touch you. What was wrong with the marks of grass? At least the grass had never hit her.

Milena was whirled up and over the fence, as if by a cyclone. She was dumped, back where she belonged, on the other side of the gate. Her mother swept through it, and closed it, barred it. Milena could only see the columns of her trousered legs. She was struck again, across her bottom, and spun around by her shoulders. Howling with horror, her nose and mouth and eyes clogged, Milena was forced against her will to look at her mother. She looked at her with the mercilessness of a child.

There was this tall grey thing. Its body worked in completely different ways from Milena's, all sharpness and angles. When it moved, there was a nauseating, lurching moment of hesitation. It was deciding. Have I moved into the future yet? Am I still in the past?

Where, where is my Now?

It never quite located itself. It would stop, start, stop again, flickering in and out of time, as if crossing in and out of it, never quite landing in Now.

As if in a dream, when the worst thing is about to happen and cannot be prevented, the infant began to look up, tracking up the dry wall of the legs, the lumpy sweater with the long extensors for arms, spider's arms. And the hands! They were riddled with veins and stick-like inner workings. They were not chubby and soft and round and accepting. The very skin of them was harsh, worn, as if it had grown a shell. The hands looked like crabs, hungry, working.

Then up to the face.

And the infant Milena saw all the desolation there, and she burst into fresh wails and cries of horror.

The face was wrinkled and stretched and bony, blasted with dryness and lipstick. The eyes were dead, as if someone had tied a mask across them. The only thing in them was baffled loss, helplessness, and anger, anger and sorrow. The flesh hung, exhausted by the battle against itself and the world. The flesh began to shake, like the trees.

And Milena's mother suddenly crouched down into a tight bundle, as if trying to become a child again herself, as if she herself were a child needing to be comforted. The crabs of her hands scuttled across Milena's back, and pulled Milena to her. Milena felt slimy tears across her own innocent cheek, and felt her mother quake with a loss that was beyond Milena's understanding.

Milena felt the strange, inextricable tangle that was her mother, and felt the loss beyond naming, and Milena began to cry too, for everything: for her mother, for her father, for the love and the pain and the warfare between them, and for the world. Beyond the fence, the fields still glowed. The gate was barred.

'It's called,' said Milena, the director, '*Attack of the Crab Monsters*.'

She was sitting in the Zookeeper's office. She was very concerned about her new grey suit. She was sitting crosslegged on stuffed bags, and the knees of her new trousers would bag and crease. She worried about marks on cloth and braced herself for the reaction of the people around her.

They stared back at Milena, all expression on their faces suspended. They sat on the bags too. The bags were called Pears, and the people were pear-shaped, pears on Pears, their stomachs ballooning outwards. A large-boned woman sat folded across from Milena. Moira Almasy! thought the one who remembered, startled by the change. The woman's hair seemed less grey, her face less creased, as if she had suddenly become well after an illness. She was younger.

Milton the assistant served tea in little cups on lacquered tables. The cups rattled and Milton insinuated with a smile. In the corner sat the Minister, now a scant but formal presence. His eyes were closed and he was perfectly still, his hands resting on his folded knees.

Courage, Milena the director told herself. 'The opera is about . . .' she said, and hesitated. 'It's about an invasion of aliens from outer space. They look like crabs, but can talk. Well, sing. The idea comes from an old video that Thrawn McCartney saw.'

The expression on the faces of the Pears had curdled from horror.

'People like junk,' said Milena. 'In fact, they need junk. Junk is fun and harmless and makes no demands. People are starved of junk. Everything has been so terribly high-toned. I think if you ask the Consensus, it will tell you the same thing.'

Milena the director glanced at the Minister. He sat unmoved, unmoving.

'It's best to let the Consensus speak for itself,' warned Moira Almasy.

'What other social benefits can you claim for this?' asked a man in the circle. 'Except for the fact that it is, as you say, junk?' He had an open, likeable face, a broad smile and hair that flopped over his forehead. Charles Sheer.

You weren't so bad, Charlie, thought the Milena who was remembering. You just had other projects you wanted to promote. You wanted the money to go elsewhere. You didn't think I was very talented. You were probably right.

'First,' said Milena the director, 'no one in the cast will use viruses. This should be made very plain. People are going to become very frightened of viruses.'

That was the easy part.

'Second, it will help people with their feelings of . . .' the director prayed for a delicate word, '. . . distrust for the Chinese.'

Milena felt the room go still. There was an explosion of breath from Charles Sheer. But it is the truth, isn't it Charlie? 'I think you will find many people of British descent do not like the Chinese. They feel surpassed by them. Junk makes people feel good. So. This junk . . .' Milena paused to gain both breath and spirit. 'This work will be staged in the manner of classical Chinese opera. The music and the dancing will be classical Chinese opera.'

'The crabs too?' demanded Charles Sheer.

Moira Almasy was beginning to smile.

'Of course,' said Milena. 'There are many precedents in the classical tradition of giant singing beasts – dragons for example. The spaceship will look like a Chinese dragon, in fact. It will land in the main courtyard of the Forbidden City. These will all be holograms created by Thrawn McCartney. Uh. No one has hologrammed scenes on this scale before, or from such a distance. We propose to use Hyde Park as the main stage. This will give us a chance to use to the full the new mind-imaging technology.' Milena coughed. 'The spectacle,' she said hopefully, 'should have some curiosity value.'

'Ms Shibush,' said Charles Sheer. 'I am stunned. You have surpassed yourself. This makes your efforts to stage all of Dante seem almost credible.'

That is the general idea, thought Milena to herself. We understand each other, Charlie. There is a bond between enemies too.

The Minister sat still, without movement, as if the whole universe turned around him. On the hessian screens there were slashes of green, cartoon reeds reduced to one dead message. The screens were covered in blackheads of dust.

For you keepers of the Zoo, everything must be worthy and have high purpose. For you everything must be part of the advancing social schedule.

Me, I'm doing it all for Rolfa. And the Consensus – what does it want?

'It does tie in with what we were discussing earlier,' said Moira Almasy in a low, quiet voice.

All around them, the cartoon reeds slowly rotted.

'I'm going to make a garden,' said Thrawn McCartney, in a voice that was supposed to be like a child's.

There was a new machine. It took images from people's heads and turned them into light. Reformation technology it was called. The Restoration had led to it.

All the light in the Thrawn McCartney's room was muddled, in disorder. It heaved in currents like oil and water that would not mix. An orchid, half-remembered, swam into queasy existence. It attached itself to a bush with branches like serpents. The branches writhed in place then suddenly froze. They and the flower were held in place for a moment, and then faded, forgotten. Grass gathered like a slowly poaching egg, a bleary smudge of green. There was a hedge, a few leaves pinpricked out of the mass of it. The sky was full of impossible sunset colours.

I want to get out, thought Milena the director. She stood with Thrawn in some colourless centre, a point of view. There was no air,

162

no sound, no clarity of image. Is this all you can remember, thought Milena, of trees and plants? Can you really see no more clearly than this?

Milena found it nearly impossible to be honest around Thrawn. She would smile tolerantly, when all she really felt was anger. She would offer compliments as if to placate. She had become frustrated with herself. Why, Milena wondered, can't I speak?

Thrawn placed an image of herself in the garden. At last there was something that Thrawn could see clearly. It was not Thrawn as she was. This Thrawn was tall and lissom and wore a spotless white dress. Her face had been subtly altered. It was beautiful now, and it was backwards. It was a face seen in a mirror, a face with the flaws removed.

What an airy creature she was, this Thrawn, light as a feather, fleshless. The stringy, tormented tendons of her neck were gone, as was the desperate stare of starvation. This is why Thrawn never ate. She thought she could become like this creature. The creature danced, lean as a ballerina, bent over, arms like a swan's neck.

'Now this is beautiful. Isn't this beautiful?' Thrawn demanded.

The trouble with being dishonest is that it requires an ability to act. Milena could not. She shifted inside her quilted winter jumpsuit. 'We can see you quite clearly, yes,' she said.

Thrawn had sensed enough. 'This is a new technology, you know. No one has done this before.'

'Oh, I know, I know,' said Milena, as if no criticism had been implied.

'I mean here, you try it,' said Thrawn. 'Go on.'

She took Milena by the shoulders and stood her in front of the Reformer. You had to stand in the point of view. Milena felt something in her head drain away, as if light, right in the centre of her head was gone. As if it now resided in the machine.

'Don't be scared,' said Thrawn, arms folded, shaking her head in pity at poor Milena. 'Just try to imagine something and see what you come up with.'

Milena had been rendered self-conscious, as she always was in Thrawn's presence. It was difficult for her to imagine anything. So she tried to remember instead.

A garden.

She remembered an autumn day, the smell of loam and fallen leaves, and geese overhead, ducks fluttering their wings against still water. She remembered water, and the rose bushes, with their spotted leaves, their last roses, nibbled by the shorter days.

She remembered Rolfa, in Chao Li Gardens. She remembered the rose Rolfa had picked for her. The shock as Rolfa broke the law. She remembered the weight of the rose as it bobbed in her hand, and the scratching of the thorns against her fingers. She remembered the single, round, focusing drop of dew, catching the light.

And suddenly the *rosa mundi* was in the room. It filled it with huge, dappled shaggy pink petals, curling brown at the tip, but soft and slightly rippled nearer the centre. It bobbed, poised for a moment.

As if something had finally been set free, there was an avalanche of flowers. Milena did not know if she were imagining them in her head or seeing them in the room. What she saw and what she imagined were one and the same thing. She could feel them spill out of her head, as if some great living weight were pushing out flowers, giving birth to them. They tumbled through the room slowly, a turning kaleidoscope of flowers, remembered flowers each one different.

There was a garland of lime blossom in summer, each flower spinning like a star. There were blowzy hollyhocks, liberated from their tall stems, showering their loose, purple petals. Arum lilies lifted up their heads in a chorus, their white hands holding out yellow stamen. They were mixed with tobacco flowers, and crowned with thorny, white acanthus.

The kaleidoscope turned. There was a tumult of branches overhead in the wind, seen from many perspectives at once all jumbled, fragmented like Picasso, reaching dizzyingly up into a sky, blue behind them, that fell away to heaven. Confusingly, the branches went down below as well, as if the sky were the earth. The branches plunged through grass, down into clouds. Somehow the water of the clouds fed them. The grass was blown in waves. The grass came closer with attention. Each cell was revealed in the light. There was a stirring of life within each of the cells, a green movement of protein in and out of their inner structures. There were beetles as polished as jewels, frozen in the attention of the light, waiting for it to swerve away from them. There was a thin crust of earth giving birth to small, wriggling creatures. They were mild magenta. And the green stems of the rose bush rose, like ladders towards the sun.

And suddenly Milena was inside the dew drop, the focus of light. Light burned blearily in it, catching on motes of life, swimming in it. The lens of the surface of the dew drop turned the world upside down. A face was refracted in it. It was a human face with nut brown skin and black, liquid eyes, and there was a smile, and the face was about to speak . . .

Milena was pushed. With a lurch, it was all snatched away.

Milena looked about her, dazed. She was in a rather small, messy room, with the flowing walls of a Coral Reef shelter.

Thrawn was staring at her, outraged.

'I had no idea you were a horticulturalist,' she said. Her voice was acid, her face sour and straggly with panic. Her chest rose and fell

164

with deep, angry breathing. 'This is my equipment,' she said, very quietly. 'You do not hog my equipment.'

Milena was still confused, snatched from her flowers. 'How long was I on it?' she asked.

'How long does not matter. I let you use delicate, new equipment and you treat it it . . . like . . . like.' Thrawn shook her head, at a loss for words.

I was better than she was, thought Milena. Oh God. She's angry because I was better than she was.

The impulse was to make it up to her. 'Look, if I damaged it in any way, I'm sorry.'

'I don't know whether you've damaged . . .' Thrawn broke off. She began to cry. 'My beautiful, new machine!'

Why did I say that? wondered Milena. Why did I just give her an opening? What am I apologising for?

'Look, let's just find out if it's damaged, first. Is it damaged? What could I have done to it?'

'I don't know,' admitted Thrawn, wiping her face, angrily. 'But you just ripped through it, as if you were angry with it or something.'

'I sincerely doubt I damaged it. Isn't that what it's meant to be used for?'

'You don't know anything about it!' exclaimed Thrawn, she leant over the machine, patted it. It had a mirrored surface. Her own, straggly face was reflected back at her. 'Look,' she said standing up, taking a deep breath as if she were being amazingly tolerant, controlling rage. 'There is a lot more to this than just ramming yourself through the machine. Focus? Do you know anything about focus at all? I don't know what it was you were supposed to be showing me there, but it was a jumbled mess! The trees were upside down, the flowers were all over the place. That was supposed to be a garden? You've got to have a bit of discipline, Milena.'

The woman who prided herself on being wild looked anxiously over her machine, holding her hair back. She shook her head, and stepped into the focal point. She tried to imagine. All that happened was the room about them, the light, heaved and shifted. It was as if the walls and furniture, the bleak emptiness of the place melted.

'I think you have, you know. I think you've fried the focus!' Thrawn's voice became a screech.

'Just look at something in the room. Something real, and see if that comes out,' advised Milena.

Thrawn turned to her. The eyes were burning.

And Milena was in the room twice. She stood on the floor, as if she were there perfectly placed, feet on the floor. There was even a shadow on the shabby throw-rug.

165

'OK,' said Milena, soothing. 'OK, so there's nothing wrong with the equipment.'

'Just with the people in it,' said Thrawn. Suddenly the image of Milena was standing on its head. This imaged Milena was dumpy. The fat on her hips sagged downwards towards her face. Her tongue lolled out of her head, the size of a cow's and the eyes rolled. She started to bounce about the room on her head.

'You see, Milena. The whole point is to place the image exactly where you want it. It's a specialised skill, Milena, and you just do not have it. It's really very sad, the way you keep trying to push yourself into this specialist area with no skills at all. It's as if you can't admit for a moment that anyone could be better than you at something.'

'You're talking about yourself, Thrawn,' said Milena, quietly.

The eyes were turned on her again.

And suddenly Milena was blind.

'I can take light out of anywhere in this room.' said Thrawn, out of the absolute blackness. 'I can Reform it, or place it somewhere else. Right now, all the light in your eyes is being focused outside your head. The area I am taking it from is very precisely that of your retina.'

Milena moved her head. There was a flickering of light. Then darkness again.

'That is what I mean by focus, Milena.'

Milena moved again, and this time the darkness followed her. 'Of course, I could take all the light in this room and focus it on your retina, instead.'

The room was restored. Thrawn stood arms folded, jaw thrust out. 'That might burn your retinas out,' Thrawn said, succinctly. 'Now get out of here, and don't let me catch you messing around with my equipment again.'

'It's not your equipment. It belongs to the Zoo.'

'It belongs to the Zoo,' repeated Thrawn, in a mocking imitation. 'It belongs to the person who uses it and who has responsibility for it and that is me. Clear enough for you?'

'There's no talking to you when you're like this.' said Milena and turned, and fled. She closed the purple door behind her, her heart pumping. Only when she was away from Thrawn, could Milena realise her own anger. That's it, Thrawn, she told the purple door. That's it, you've done it. We finish this show, and then I get someone else. There is no reason why I should put up with this when no one else will.

Milena turned and trooped down the Coral steps, making as much noise with her feet as she could. That machine belongs to everybody, there will be other people who will learn to use it, and the very next show, you're dumped, you're ditched.

The thought calmed Milena, until she reached the street.

'Ahi,' said a Tyke, standing up, holding out red scarves for sale.

'No,' said Milena.

The Tyke pursued her. It was fat and dirty and bundled in woollens, and its voice was piercing and high. Milena could not even tell what sex it was. 'Look, lovely scarf, beautiful scarf, for the lady, very cheap, and very warm in winter.'

'Go away!' shouted Milena, and threw off the Tyke's light touch. Marx and Lenin! Do they see me coming? Milena glared at the child, still feeling a throbbing in her heart.

The child shrugged. 'Go freeze, then,' said the child. 'And take it out on someone else.' The Tyke spun around and walked away, feeling in a pocket for a pipe. Horses trotted past, making a clatter. Milena felt even smaller, weaker.

Someone has just threatened to burn out my eyes. Milena was shivery, feverish, tears beginning. She stood still in the street, a hand clamped across her forehead. How could I let her? How could I let her do that to me? How could I stand there and do nothing?

She needs a Reading, thought Milena. She began to walk again, still driving her feet down against the pavement. I never thought I'd say it, but she needs to be Read, and wiped, and to start all over again, as a decent human being. And I need to be wiped too, for putting up with it. Why? Why do I do it?

They both were a tangle, tangled in each other.

It was a long walk back to the Shell. The sun was shining, crisp, bright and cold.

Well, thought Milena, consoling herself. At least I learned one good thing. I have a talent. I never thought I had a talent. Just a small one.

I can imagine flowers.

The sister Bulge smelled of rosemary and sage. A bay tree grew out of its walls, and a current of air made its leaves rustle. The Bulge could commandeer its own genes and grow other forms of life, out of itself, out of memory. It grew garden herbs; it grew the flesh of chickens. It lactated orange juice.

'May I offer you a drink, Ms Shibush?' offered Mike Stone, Astronaut.

'Oh, don't bother, please,' said Milena. She was mortified. She had thrown up all over him and dislocated his shoulder and he was still being so nice. If only he wasn't so polite, she thought. If only he would get angry, I wouldn't have to feel so awful.

Mike Stone kept smiling. Even his teeth looked tense. 'The circulatory system behaves differently under conditions of weightlessness,' he informed her. 'Dehydration may sometimes result. It is advisable to drink plenty of fluids.'

Milena relented. 'Then thank you very much, I'd *love* a whisky.'

Mike Stone's smile did not slip. 'I'm afraid I have no alcoholic beverages. Would you care for an orange juice?'

'Yes, yes, that will be fine,' said Milena. 'Thank you.'

'Right-o-rooty,' said Mike Stone.

Right-o-rooty? Milena began to see the humour of the situation. It had indeed been quite an introduction. Oh God, she thought, I'm going to laugh. I'm going to go into one of those silly giggling fits where you can't stop laughing.

The prophecy was self-fulfilling. She looked at Mike Stone, at the way he moved. He was very tall, and very slim, with coathanger hips, and his muscles seemed to have been pulled too tight, like piano wire. I had heard Americans were starched, she thought. This one looks like he's ironed every morning. He's being so proper and pukka and nice. Milena felt her cheeks clench.

He held up her orange juice in benediction. 'For what we are about to receive, may the Lord make us truly thankful,' he said. Then he looked at Milena with the complete seriousness of a child. 'Wine is the blood of our Saviour,' he said. 'We should not drink it or any alcohol except in a spirit of communion.'

'Ah,' was all Milena managed to say. She took the drink from him, her arms bobbing in weightlessness like waterwings under water. Poor man, he'll think I'm laughing at him. He'll think I'm laughing at his religion. Milena was giddy with a desire to laugh. She turned away, to hide from him. She looked out of a living window, down onto the Earth below.

It was beige and blasted, white plains with blue mountains, discolorations like age spots, dry canyons like crows feet. The Bulge was in orbit over a desert. It moved beneath them, slowly drifting.

Milena thought of production schedules and holograms; she thought of Thrawn McCartney. Even that didn't make her feel serious. Everything made her want to laugh; everything seemed funny. The weight of her life had been left below.

'Beautiful, isn't it?' said Mike Stone. Milena had a quick glimpse of him waddling closer to her, as if on slippery ice. He looked like an elongated penguin. 'I look through this window and I say "Hallelujah!".'

'Hmmm?' said Milena, not trusting herself to speak.

'In five minutes, we'll be over Mount Ararat. From up here, the outlines of Noah's Ark are clearly visible.'

'Mmmmmm!' said Milena, trying to sound impressed.

'Of course, Ararat would have been underwater for most of the

Flood. We know how deep the Flood was: two-thirds of the highest mountain. Now. Mount Everest is 8,840 metres high, which means the Flood was 5,893.32 metres deep. Which is very nearly the height of Mount Ararat. Do you believe in reincarnation, Ms Shibush?'

'Mmmm mmm,' said Milena, shaking her head.

'Neither do I,' he said, and sipped milk through a straw. 'Post-millenarian Baptists such as myself do not. But I have a thought I'd like to share with you. If only Noah survived, then he is the ancestor of us all. And we would have his memories stored in our racial subconscious. Many is the time that I've sat in this spacecraft, Ms Shibush, and felt that I was Noah. If there was another Flood, I could repopulate the Earth, grown by Chris from memory.'

'Mmmmm,' said Milena, as if giving the thought serious consideration.

'I should explain. Chris is my Bulge. The name is short for *Christian Soldier Two*. The first one died. Would you like to see my snapping turtle?'

Mike Stone reached into the pocket of his jumpsuit and produced a live, suede-coloured snapping turtle. 'Chris grew him for me. Had one since I was knee-high to a grasshopper.' He held it out for Milena to examine. 'He also tried to grow me back my old Army knife, but the blade was soft.'

Milena had to turn around to face him. He loomed over her with round and innocent eyes. A child, she thought, I am talking to a child. She was in extremis. Her cheeks were compressed, her stomach muscles were clenched, her back was held rigid. She did not laugh. But her eyes brimmed full. Tears of mirth slid down her cheeks.

Mike Stone fell silent. He looked at the tears on her face, and then down at the floor. Moved beyond words, he pressed the turtle into her hands. 'It's nice to know,' he said, 'that someone understands.'

The turtle bit her. It snapped, as it had done in childhood.

And Milena awoke, a child in England.

She woke up in her room in the Child Garden. On the windowsill, there was her candle, gutted and blackened, with a spread of wax on her breakfast plate. She had been reading in the night. The book, old and heavy, had slipped out of grasp, and worked its way down between the bedding and the wall.

It was summer, and there, beyond the old sashcord windows, was her tree.

The tree seemed to greet her every morning. It was very tall, but its long branches were delicate and hung airily down, almost like curtains, its leaves dappled into many colours by the sun. Its trunk was mottled; sections of its bark fell off like pieces of a puzzle. Milena knew its Latin name because she loved the tree: *ailanthus altissima*. The Chinese called it the Tree of Heaven.

Already it was hot. Sunlight streamed through the window. Behind her there was a sound of someone stirring. Milena turned. The two girls Milena shared the room with, Suze and Hanna, were still asleep. Their faces were as drained of personality as rice pudding. One of them had turned in her bed. They would be up soon. Milena wanted to avoid them.

She pulled back her quilt as quietly as possible and sat up. There was her old room. There were the orange walls, there were the old chipped skirting boards, lumpy with layers of paint. There was the fireplace that no longer fed into a chimney; there were the black urns of the charcoal heaters.

Milena the child did not want to move. Her eyes felt swollen and dusty. She had been reading most of the night. She wanted to fall back into the bed and sleep; but if she did that she would be trapped, with the others. As a kind of compromise, she reached for her book. If the others started to move, she would still be awake and could escape.

The book was a biography of Einstein. A few days before, Milena had heard other children talking about him. The ache had come over her: something else she didn't know. So she had gone to the Museum and found this book. She opened it up and looked at the photographs. She saw a photograph of Einstein as a child. He already had a slight, amused smile. Beidermeir, the other children had called him – honest, clumsy furniture – because he always said exactly what he thought to his teachers. At sixteen, he pretended to have a nervous breakdown, to get out of Germany.

Suze groaned in her bed and turned away from the sunlight. Milena stood up, and pulled on her jumpsuit that had been laid out flat on the floor. Everything was arranged for a quick escape in the mornings. She pulled on her black slippers, and slipped out of the apartment. The apartment had three large rooms and slept nine girls. There was a blackboard in the front hall. A work rota was written on it: names in English, tasks in Chinese. Milena's name was not on it. Milena was regarded as disabled, and exempt from tasks.

Milena went down to breakfast without washing first. She was famous for not washing, and was commonly supposed to smell. From the adenoidal way the other children sometimes talked to her, she knew they held their breath when she was near. But there was only one bath in the apartment for nine children. If Milena washed when they did, she would have to stand in line with them and try to think of things to say. Anything she said seemed to reveal the blankness of her memory, how little she knew.

Milena trudged down the steps, all the way to the basement. The other children used the front door of their stairway and walked to breakfast in sunlight. Milena walked the length of the building at its lowest level. Milena liked it there. The old mansion block had been built two hundred and fifty years before around a series of light wells. The light wells were tiled and streaked and looked somewhat lavatorial, but there was blue sky at their summit. Light was shed seven storeys down through the honeycomb of pipes and lift shafts. It was like a hidden city. The Senior kept his bee hives on the roof. Milena could see the bees overhead, plump black dots humming in the air, rising and falling. They were working. Milena liked their faithfulness.

The light wells and the roof were supposed to be out of bounds. The children raided the hives for honey, and ran screaming through the basement at night, playing hide and seek. They burst into the Nurses' rooms, which lined the lower floor, and ran laughing as the Nurses chased them. The Nurses would be thirteen or fourteen years old. They laughed too. It was then, at night, when the other children played, that Milena could read, alone in the room.

Milena walked on and tried to remember what she had read the night before. She had been charmed to find that Einstein's first wife had been called Mileva. They had lived together in Berne when he was a civil servant. He had forgotten the key to their apartment on the day of their wedding. Mileva was from Czechoslovakia, like Milena.

Wasn't she? Czechoslovakian? Milena suddenly wasn't sure. She was dismayed that she could not remember the nationality of Einstein's first wife. Why can't I learn? she wondered, scuffing her feet. She was a freak; she knew she was a freak; everyone treated her like a freak. The viruses buffeted her like a hurricane, but left nothing behind. She read books and they seemed to evaporate. Milena was very discouraged.

She pushed open another door, and walked up more steps, to the Hall.

The Hall was full of folding bamboo tables. They had flat, grey resin tops to make them easier to clean. On sunny days, the whole room smelled of pine. The work shift was still laying spoons and cups for breakfast, solemn, puffy-eyed children of eight or nine, moving with the mindless motions of machinery, dazed with sleepiness, driven by training.

A Nurse was serving lentil porridge. 'Good morning, Ms Shibush,' the Nurse said to Milena. The Nurse was older than most: about eighteen years. Milena knew her name but didn't use it.

'Lo,' murmured Milena grumpily, without any other greeting.

The Nurse looked at Milena, unwashed, impolite, and dazed by hard work of which the other children – indeed the Nurse herself – had no experience. The Nurse shook her head. All the staff were giving up on Milena. They had stopped praying for her, they said. Milena was beginning to give up on herself. She could not read enough, or study enough, or memorise enough or think enough to keep up with the others. Milena made kindly children doe-eyed with pity; cruel children were afraid of her. It was part of Milena's affliction that she was able to hit people.

Milena took her lentil porridge to an empty table. Some Tykes sat at another table. Wee Lambs. Billy Dan and his little gang of five year olds. Milena could hear them playing games.

'OK,' said Billy. 'What's this?' And he recited:

> *'Besides with justice this discerning age*
> *Admires their wond'rous talents for the stage:*
> *Well may they venture on the mimick's art,*
> *Who play from morn to night a borrowed part . . .'*

And the other Tykes cried out the answer: 'Johnson, Samuel Johnson!'

'London. That's the title. "London: A Poem".'

And Billy tried to look superior. 'Written in imitation of . . .' He was not allowed to finish.

'The Third Satire of Juvenal!'

It was a pointless game. Everyone had the same viruses, but the Wee Lambs were still impressed by the knowledge that basked like whales inside their heads. The Wee Lambs were insufferable. They would put wood chips or dried peas in people's beds for fun and then weep themselves to sleep. They needed taking care of. The older children did their washing and ironing for them. The Wee Lambs would lord it over them, or try to prove they knew more than the older children. Just a phase, the older children said, wrinkling their noses with the disdain of those who were nearly adult. The older children admired practical skills. They prided themselves on the stalls they ran, on the deals they drove, buying or selling lumber or crystal or plaster or eggs. They compared each of the Estates, eyeing up their possible futures. Would it be better to stay a Restorer or become a Reefer, growing new buildings instead of repairing old ones? What about Farming? Nice outdoor life, with plenty of razzle – off-duty work – on the side. What about Resins or Hides or even Pharmacy? Doctors were the highest, Doctors were the best, but no one expected to be Placed as a Doctor.

It was a superstition that a child could fix on a future Placing and Develop towards it. Their main goal now that they were nine years old was to pull what they called a Plum – a Plum Placing in a good Estate. At the age of ten, they would be Read by the Consensus. Any faults in personality or criminal tendencies would be cured. The Reading would be used to plan their future lives.

Milena was nine. At the end of the summer she would be ten. What kind of Placing were they going to give her? Humping garbage, probably. How about street sweeper? There was a range of possibilities for someone who was resistant to the viruses.

Milena ate the last of her lentils in silence, finding comfort in their unvarying richness. Other, older children began to come in. Some of them came in pairs, a boy and a girl holding hands, already engaged to be married. To Milena that was pure foolishness. Come ten and you're both Read, and wiped, and you come out different people. After the Reading, they change you, you end up marrying a stranger. Or they give you different Placings in different Estates at opposite ends of the Pit. Becoming engaged was just a way of saying: huh, me, I'm Developed already. Me, I'm an adult. Why, Milena thought, do you want to be an adult anyway?

Time to go. Milena stood up and was halfway down the aisle when she remembered her plate. You were supposed to take your plate and wash it up yourself. Milena had forgotten. Why don't I have a memory? She turned around and walked back to her table. The eyes of Billy's gang were on her, and the Lambs were smiling. One of them started to giggle and go red in the face. That's her, that's the Lump who can't remember anything. See? She's forgotten her plate. Milena glared at them and they all looked away. They were frightened of her.

Milena snatched up the plate, took it to the sink, and washed it without talking to anyone. Milena didn't want to be feared. She wanted to have friends. She wanted to be a part of things. Why? wondered Milena the child. Why can't I remember? What is it? She had no idea why the viruses failed her. She no longer knew that she could spring the viruses, rethink the codes of DNA.

She ran down the stairs away from the Hall, down to the front door of the block, and pushed it open as if bursting free, and stood outside, unwashed on the street.

There was the light; there were the trees. The street was called the Gardens, because one side of it was planted with grass and trees. Along a branch, a great fat pigeon, his neck swollen up, waddled after a female. She scurried away from him, escaping his advances. Further down the Gardens there was a cart. A huge, slow, solemn man was carrying hessian sacks. He emptied them into the cart. They were full of garbage.

Is that my future? Milena wondered, looking at him.

The man shook out the sacks, his muscles raising and lowering their heads. He had a beard and long shaggy hair. He looked like a Biblical prophet.

So what happenes when you're Placed as an emptier of garbage? Milena wondered. She began to walk down the gardens, past the man.

Do you suddenly discover that, yes, emptying sacks was really what you wanted to do all along? Do they give you a virus to make you love your work? The man glanced at her, scowling. He could play King Lear, thought Milena. There were more hessian sacks, lined up against the bamboo railings.

Milena wanted to be part of the theatre. She had put on shows with other orphans and would be seen to flower suddenly when directing them. Was there any chance of Milena Shibush pulling a Place in a theatre? I'd take anything, she thought. I would sweep the floors, I would pump up the alcohol lights, I would wash the sweaty costumes. I'd do anything as long as it was in a theatre.

It seemed highly unlikely. All that the Nurses could imagine her doing was being some kind of humper. They thought she would carry bricks or melons. Whenever Milena asked questions about Placing – about its fairness, or why it was necessary, the Nurses only smiled. It was a particular, soured, superior sort of smile. The smile seemed to say: haven't you got beyond worrying about that yet? Are you still stuck back there? No answers were given. Milena had come to the conclusion that they didn't have any.

Milena walked on, becoming angry.

They had told her there were no more books.

No more books! When their own Estate was hard at work saving the British Library! Every book published in the twentieth century was there! Milena had heard that and found the library for herself. She could remember the first whispered hush of those rows of shelving. She remembered the disdain on the face of the librarian. Read them? You want to read them? Child, these are historical documents, originals. Why do you need to read them? It took a visit from the Senior of the Child Garden to get Milena access. The Senior was a boisterous, hearty man in his early twenties, who was good at jollying people. All a great lark, he had said to the librarian. The child wants to read books. Well, good for her. Then he had whispered to the librarian and her eyes had melted into what she thought was an expression of sympathy. Reading books was a symptom of a grave disorder. The librarian had made a fuss over her after that and had talked to her in a cooing artificial voice, explaining simple things over and over, very slowly.

When Milena had finally been left alone with the books, she had wept for all the knowledge in them, the things that other people carried in their heads, as a gift, for free.

And so Milena tried to catch up. She had been six years old when she started. The first book she had read, or tried to read, was Plato's *Republic*. Do I remember a word of it?

Why would the Nurses tell her there were no more books? Out of

174

shame for her disorder? Out of fear she would read something she was not supposed to know about? Milena had grown suspicious of the motives of the Nurses. She had grown suspicious of the motives of the Restorers, on whose Estate she lived.

The Restorers had been given the old city, the Pit, to rebuild. Everything outside it, beyond the Reef or in the hills, belonged to the Reefers, who would chew up the rubble and turn it into sleek new biological buildings. But in the Pit, the eighteenth century townhouses and the old art deco buildings were slowly being rebuilt. Their contents were recreated. The Restorers remade the chairs, they rewove the curtains, they filled in the embroidery where it had come away. They raised the great old roofs again.

There were book binders and upholsterers, there were stonemasons and sculptors, there were experts in oil painting and workers in wood. There were plasterers, and carpenters; there were metalsmiths and those who knitted by hand. They were the preservers of history, living together in one Estate in central London.

Milena went for a long walk. She flitted through the City like some kind of ghost feeding on sunlight and other people's lives. She walked up to Euston and then back down through the trees of Tavistock Square, to Malet Street. The main warehouse for the Restorers was there. It was called the School. Outside the School's great grey gates there were stalls of people on the razzle, selling paper, reeds, pipes, shoes – anything the community might need. A Professor of the School sold kidney beans in great heaps. The beans were red and polished like semi-precious stones, and the Professor smoothed the piles of them with anxious hands. There were oxen yoked to the gates. They were sold to carters who hauled stone and great wooden beams. A small boy guarded the oxen, with a switch and a collie dog. He sat on a stone bollard, wearing a kind of toga over his shoulder, smoking a pipe, his face turned towards the sun. From behind the gates came the sound and smell of fresh wood being sawed.

The School had once been part of a university. Now it stored goods and was a workshop. There the elegant plaster moulds were made and carefully loaded for shipment. There the timber was stored and cut to standard lengths. There were the bolts of cloth, the glass works, the vaults that kept the gold, the lead, the mercury and the arsenic. It was the preserve of history and of adults.

The Medicine was the preserve of the young. It was where all the Estate children, orphaned or not, were trained. It had once been a school of tropical medicine. The building stood on a corner of Malet Street. Milena stopped and looked at it, unwilling to go inside.

There were ornamental balconies all across its grey stone face. On the balconies were gleaming Egyptian sculptures of fleas and rats and lice. The children kept them polished. They were one of the few things Milena liked about the Medicine.

On the other corner was the Tacky Shop, where one resin tool could be melted into another. The wife of the Tacky was turning a bamboo pole round and round in her hand, lowering an awning over her display. It was going to be hot; the resin goods might go soft and warp. The Tacky Wife turned and gave Milena a happy grin.

Milena grinned back. It really did seem to her that adults were nicer than children. There was a hiss of steam inside the shop. Then the Tacky came out, a mask over his face, and heavy gloves over his hands. He held up a newly pressed pitcher. Its mouth had sagged to one side. His wife laughed, and shook her head, and placed a hand on her husband's hairy chest.

It must be possible to live a life, Milena thought. It must be possible to be happy. Suddenly she wanted to be an adult. Have a nice little Place and a nice little husband. Milena wanted to be like everyone else.

What would her Reading show? A vast blank of ignorance? Would they have her loading garbage sacks? Maybe they would have one final load of virus to burn its way into her. Maybe it would kill her, like her father. Maybe that was it. Maybe Mami had lied. Maybe her father was like her, beyond education, and that's why they were in hiding in the hills of Czechoslovakia.

Milena did not think of her mother with respect. She thought of her with a kind of exasperated fondness, as if she had been a very foolish woman. Coming all that way to England to find freedom. As if England were free. She had gone to the Restorers looking for the kind of debate and discussion she had so loved back home. She had thought that people who worked with books and history would also have ideas. She did not believe that they could be so mild and so uninterested in life. The loneliness had killed her. She had died, leaving Milena here, alone among the Restorers. Milena had no one else to blame. She turned and went inside the Medicine.

She was late. That was a symptom of Milena's disorder as well. Other people had a virus which told them the time. The other children were already hard at work. The Medicine was built around a large brick courtyard. It was hot, so classes were being held in it, outside in the shade. Work groups had already claimed tables. They hammered their copper plates, or stitched their leather seat covers. Some of them were cooking their breakfast, boiling gruel on little charcoal stoves, and arguing with their parents about whose turn it was to cook the evening meal.

176

The children worked at their own speed towards set targets. The School Nurses measured their Development. The children talked to each other as they worked, about sport or sales or sources of cotton cloth. Sometimes a School Nurse would set a Problem Race or lead a discussion. Milena wished she had brought her book to read. Books had been written by people like her. She could sense that in the careful, step by step links they made, and in the simplicity of their thinking.

Milena was in the Physical Development Group – the Lumps. The Lumps were all to some degree mentally retarded. The Nurses did not have high hopes for the Lumps. Most of them would be Placed as humpers. The Lumps were the last to leave the state of childhood. It was not fair to send ten year olds out into the world to drag rocks. After their Placing, they were brought on for a year or two with injections and weight-lifting.

Milena saw them at a table. There was no mistaking the Lumps. One or two of them were huge males, fat but heavily dependent, rather tame. They loomed over the tables, smiling as always. They smiled hopefully, offering the world their good nature until their good nature was disappointed. Then, and only then, the boys would become dangerous.

It was the girls that Milena had the greater difficulty understanding or dealing with. The girls laughed at Milena. They affected a wild superiority; they needed someone to whom they felt superior.

Milena sat down, boldly, on the concrete instead of the bench. The Lumps slapped each other's shoulders and giggled.

'There are benches, Milena,' said one girl called Pauline. Her face was flat.

'Too tired to climb up here?'

Milena hated the Lumps, hated having to be with them. She knew that she herself could not learn, but she thought that the Lumps were simply stupid.

She could see the congenital damage in their faces; their eyes were sunken, there was a coarseness to their mouths. The poor Lumps. The viruses had filled their heads with Shakespeare and the Golden Stream of philosophy that led to Chao Li Song.

The School Nurse approached. Milena saw that there was someone new with her, another Nurse.

'Lo, team,' she said, greeting them by placing her hands on their shoulders. 'Everybody happy?'

'Milena's sitting on the ground!' exclaimed Pauline, her eyes like goggles, so thick were her artificial corneas.

'Perhaps she's more comfortable there,' said the School Nurse, glancing at Milena. The Nurses were a little frightened of Milena. She could not learn, but she was far from stupid. She would say things

177

that politeness would normally forbid. The School Nurse was called Ms Hazell, and Milena thought she was beautiful. She had sun-deepened purple cheeks and hazel eyes, like her name. She made Milena ache to be like her, to be noticed by her.

The new Nurse with her was very pretty too – blonde curling hair and a scattering of magenta freckles. Milena's heart sank. Someone else who was pretty and happy and whole – forever beyond Milena's reach. The new Nurse smiled at her, perfect white teeth gleaming against purple skin. Milena stared back at her bleakly.

'This is the new Nurse, team,' said Ms Hazell. 'Her name's Rose Ella. Now I know Rose Ella very well because she was a child here herself. She grew up a Restorer, and was Placed here as a Nurse. So it's very nice for all of us here that she's joined us.' The School Nurse bestowed on Rose Ella a smile of real affection. The smile made Milena go desolate with longing. How did people become friends? Why was it so easy for them?

Then a Team Discussion began. It was a kind of group Problem Race, to give the Lumps practice in thinking. The School Nurse introduced the topic.

The mentally retarded, the gravely challenged, were going to discuss Derrida and Plato. It was an exercise to see if the Lumps could apply the Golden Stream to their own lives. I read Plato, thought Milena. I read Derrida. I understood hardly any of it, and can remember less.

'Now what is Derrida really talking about in his article on Plato?'

'Writing!' chorused the Lumps. Then, washed by the same viruses, they remembered other answers. Racing time, they straggled in, one after another. 'And memory. Writing as tool for memory. What's wrong with writing.'

The School Nurse smiled indulgently. 'He was asking, really, how it was that Plato could bear to write when he found writing so artificial. He thought of it as an artificial knowledge that people could lay claim to without really having experienced or learned anything.'

You always talk down to us, thought Milena. You make us jump through hoops that are nothing to do with us, and then smile so sweetly when we fall over.

'Sounds like the viruses,' said Milena. 'Just like the viruses. Plato would have hated the viruses, too.'

The School Nurse laughed. 'Very good, Milena, yes, yes he would have hated the viruses. As we all know, he and Aristotle founded the Axis of Materialist and Idealistic thinking, both of which the Golden Stream swept away. Plato believed in dictators. He certainly would have hated the Consensus, our democracy.'

The School Nurse looked pleased. Got a nibble, huh? thought

Milena. I bet you tell people there are glimmers of intelligence in my face.

'I agree with him,' said Milena.

The Lumps all laughed.

'Are you an idealist, then Milena? Do you think you are just a shadow on the wall of a cave? Perhaps you disagree with Plato and are a materialist. Perhaps you want a Materialist state, with its choice of dictatorship or capitalist, economic terrorism?' The School Nurse was still smiling. 'Compare that to an idealist state, a theocracy perhaps? Being told you are damned, and that God wants to burn you in Dante's Inferno?'

Milena was neither a materialist nor an idealist. Browbeaten, she withdrew into herself. But I know what Plato meant. All of you get everything you know for free without working for it. It isn't yours. I have to fight for every word. So maybe I am just grumpy old Plato, upset because people have a new tool that makes things too easy.

The School Nurse turned her attention to the other Lumps. 'Now how did Derrida point out how Plato resolved the contradiction of writing against writing?'

The Lumps chorused, '*Pharmakolikon.*'

'Yes,' said the Nurse. 'The root for our word pharmacy. Healing drugs. What people used to call medicine. But in Plato's time it meant both poison and cure. So Plato regarded writing as a poison that could also cure.'

Milena remembered something. 'He doesn't use the word!' she yelped.

The Nurse faltered. 'That's not relevant,' she said.

'Derrida says he doesn't! Not once! Plato doesn't call writing *Pharmakolikon.* Not once. He just calls it poison.'

'Anyone like to comment?' the School Nurse said, on firm ground again.

The beaming faces turned to Milena, hunched on the ground.

'It's implicit in the culture,' said one of them.

'It can be in the text without being there.'

Milena dug her hands deeper into her armpits. 'So Derrida can make Plato say anything he wants him to say?'

The School Nurse shook her head. 'No. But he allows himself the freedom to fully understand Plato in context.'

Anger flowered inside Milena, a rich and vital growth. 'I'll tell you why Plato wrote when he hated writing,' she said. 'He wrote because he knew that he had lost. He had lost, and everyone was writing, and so he had to write. But he still hated it.'

Like I hate the viruses. But I need them, now, here, to keep up.

Plato lost? The Lumps laughed. How they laughed. Milena had got it wrong again. Plato, the great voice of Idealism did not lose. He had founded the stream of discourse that ruled for two thousand years and nearly destroyed the planet.

The School Nurse scowled and shook her head at them. 'Remember,' she said. 'Now remember, team,' she said. 'Milena has no viruses. We're to use what the viruses tell us, aren't we? What do we think Derrida would tell us about Milena?'

There was a pause. What was the right line, then? The Lumps waited to be told.

'Milena is speaking from her own personal experience. She thinks of the viruses as Plato thought of writing. She is viewing the text in her own, unique way. This is inevitable, isn't it? Milena is a reader of books, after all. One of the few we've got left, and Derrida was writing about reading as well.'

The School Nurse smiled at her with indulgence. Then she turned to Rose Ella, the new Nurse, and held out her hands, as if presenting Milena to her. The new Nurse smiled again.

Make me smile back. Go on, challenged Milena. See if you can. She turned grimly back to Ms Hazell.

'You always use that word "remember",' said Milena. 'You say, "remember, team". You never tell us to think.'

They all were silent at that. The Lumps knew everyone thought they were stupid. Milena grimly resisted feeling unkind for reminding them of that.

'That's another large topic, the difference between memory and intelligence. Let's break now. Thank you, everyone. That was a very fruitful discussion. I certainly feel like I've learned a lot.'

The Nurse leaned over the table and began to discuss each Lump's individual project. Pauline was knitting a sweater. 'Very good!' exclaimed the School Nurse and held it up.

The new Nurse, Rose Ella, approached Milena.

'Were you measuring how fast we are? I didn't see you counting,' said Milena.

'I wasn't here to time you,' said Rose Ella. She knelt down in front of Milena. She was twelve, thirteen years old. An adult.

'We're too slow, huh?'

'It must be terrible for you,' said Rose Ella, and reached out with her hand. 'You're so intelligent. And not to have a memory.'

Milena rolled her eyes. It must be hell, she thought, to be so pretty and so stupid. Leave me alone.

'Did you specialise in Learning Disabilities?' Milena asked.

Rose Ella turned around and sat on the ground next to her. 'Not particularly,' she said. 'No, there was a new emphasis when I was doing my practicals. You know, the new fashion. There are fashions in everything.'

Milena liked that. It was honest. It seemed to treat Milena with a measure of respect. 'So what's fashionable now?' Milena asked feeling herself going shy.

'Originality,' said Rose Ella. 'They're telling us to look for originality, and Develop that. Nobody's coming up with anything new. Not in science, not anywhere.'

'So I'm original, huh?'

'I think so,' said Rose Ella. 'I've never heard anyone say those things about Plato.'

Milena's eyes seemed to go hot and heavy. Praise made her heartsick; she was so unused to it, and needed it so badly.

'Lot of good it does me,' murmured Milena, looking down.

'You like theatre,' said Rose Ella gently.

'They briefed you, eh?' Milena wished she had something to do with her hands, some leather to stitch, some brass to polish. Her hands were always empty. 'I don't know. I just like to imagine things on a stage. You know, costumes, lights. I put on the Christmas show.' Milena was going to tell her about the costumes, the golden shoes, and the brass ice bucket that was supposed to contain myrrh.

'Oh, yes, they told me about that!' exclaimed Rose Ella, forgetting herself. She pulled her curly blonde hair back behind her ears. That made her ears stick out. 'It sounded lovely! I was really sorry I missed it.'

'They told you all about it, eh,' said Milena. She fell silent. For a moment there I thought you were being friendly. Milena shifted where she sat, jerking her buttocks nearer to the wall, sitting up straighter. She would tell Rose Ella nothing else. She answered the next few questions with a yes or a no.

Rose Ella looked chastened. She had forgotten some of her training. Never tell a Disabled Person that you already know about what they're going to tell you. Milena could see the new Nurse think that. Milena could see her try to make amends. Rose Ella started to talk about her family. Her father restored furniture. Her mother was a glass-blower.

'Have you ever seen the glass-blowing?' Rose Ella asked. 'It's lovely to watch.'

'Sizing up a future Placing for me?' said Milena.

'No,' said Rose Ella. 'I'm just proud of my mother.'

'Mine's dead,' said Milena. 'She was an idiot. Well, not really. But we ended up here. We were from Czechoslovakia. But you already know that.'

'I didn't,' said Rose Ella, shaking her head.

181

'Don't tell me they left something out of my case history,' said Milena.

Rose Ella sighed. She looked down at her hands, and then back up at Milena. 'It doesn't work like that,' she said quietly. 'They don't brief us like that in case it affects what we think.' Her eyes seemed quite sincere. 'Look, let's go look at the glass-blowing. At least it will get you out of here.'

Away from the Lumps.

'Fine,' said Milena, trying to shrug as if it were all one with her. But her eyes were heavy. She wanted to be with Rose Ella.

Milena had rarely seen inside the School. She did not have relatives or friends who worked there. She had never really felt part of the Estate. Rose Ella pushed open the large, grey gates; they seemed to float backwards on their hinges.

'I love the smell of the wood, don't you!' said Rose Ella, looking back over her shoulder as she swung the gates shut behind her.

Milena felt vaguely as if her own feelings had usurped. 'It's all right,' she said.

Rose Ella walked briskly to a window in the wall by the gate. She waved for Milena to stand next to her. They peered into the Senate House of the School. It was the timber store. There were honey-coloured planks all in ordered racks. Beyond the doors across the room was a pile of huge logs. Men and women sawed the wood in perfectly straight planks, guided by virus. Men with brooms swept up the chips and yellow shavings.

'What do they do with the sawdust?' Milena asked.

'Use it for packing. Some old kinds of sofas were stuffed with it. We also use a lot of it to store ice in the ice house. It keeps it all through the summer. Most of the time though, we just use it on the fires. We aren't supposed to. Don't tell anyone.'

'I don't have anyone to tell it to,' said Milena murmuring shyly. This is how it is for other people, she thought. They talk and find out things. 'Is the world a great big wicked place then?'

'How do you mean?' asked Rose Ella, appearing to take her very seriously.

'Is it full of secrets? Little bits about things. Like that. About the wood.' Damnable shyness overcame Milena, and she stuck her hands in her pockets and could not look at Rose Ella.

'Sometimes. Little things. Such as . . .' Rose Ella paused. 'Such as I really, really like Senior Fenton.'

The Senior ran the Medicine. He was very old, twenty two, mature and handsome.

Milena was overwhelmed. 'You do? Are you going to marry him?' It was a wonder to talk to someone about such things.

'I shouldn't think so.' It was Rose Ella's turn to be surprised. She kept her hands behind her back, behind the white uniform, and looked down at her feet. 'He sings,' she said. 'He sings evenings at the Row, when we all get together. Oh! He has such a beautiful voice.'

'Senior Fenton sings?' Milena asked. She couldn't imagine it. No, she could. She could see his handsome face open wide with song. She wished she could say she liked Senior Fenton too, but the image of him did not move her. She began to worry, a little. Her heart never rose at the idea of men, or a particular man. Who did she like? No one, she was forced to conclude. She liked no one.

'Is there a lot of music at the Row?' Milena asked. She had never had time to learn a musical instrument. She sat in the conference room and watched the other children play.

'Ach! Oh yes!' said Rose Ella. 'Oh, such music we have at the Row, every evening! Have you never been?'

'No,' said Milena.

'Well, you come along tonight, then,' said Rose Ella. 'Come to supper.'

Milena found herself hesitating out of habit. She had her laundry to do and her book to read; and then she thought: Milena, why ever not?

'Yup,' she said, moving her shoulders from side to side, in a way that was supposed to suggest casual acceptance. 'Thanks.'

Rose Ella's mother worked in what had once been the School of African and Oriental Studies. The east side of the building was a foundry and glass works. The windows were open wide, but it was still hot. Milena felt the heat on her face. Almost as if she could feel her pores open, sweat welling out of her forehead. The furnaces were lined up along the back wall. One of them was working, its door hooked open. Inside the furnace, there was an even, unvarying orange light. A row of Restorers stood in front of it with long metal poles. Metal! Milena looked in wonder at the metal poles, hoping to see a marvel, but metal did not look all that different from dirty resin, except that it didn't melt.

Rose Ella introduced Milena to her mother. Rose Ella's mother was very small and slim with grey steady eyes and perfect smile. The eyes had a fixed light in them that Milena found difficult to warm to.

'Mala,' Rose Ella, calling her mother by her first name. 'This is my friend, Milena.'

My friend, thought Milena, she called me her friend. She was too pleased to remember to speak.

'Hello, Milena,' said Rose Ella's mother, pleased to meet her. There was something in the smile that would have been pleased to meet anybody. 'I'm making a pitcher. Do you want to watch?'

Rose Ella left it to Milena to say yes. They stood well back. Rose Ella's mother dipped the long metal pole into the orange light. A bubble of glass came out attached to the pole. Around the edges glowed orange, where the glass was thickest. Rose Ella's mother put the pole to her lips and blew, just a little, and looked, and blew again. She wore no gloves, no apron. She picked up a kind of scoop with a long black handle, and rolled the glass on it. The glass went rounder as it was rolled and it began to glow green as it cooled. Then Mala turned it on its base, flattening it against what looked like a small raised stool. 'That's it,' she said.

Rose Ella jumped forward and took the pole with an easy flip of the hand, and Milena stepped back in fear and admiration. Rose Ella fixed the pole in a vice, and turned it. She took a triangle of wood, ordinary wood dipped in water, and as the glass blob turned, she ran the wet wood around the lip of the pitcher's neck. The wood flared into flame. Striding quickly, lightly, Rose Ella tucked the pole into another oven, twisted it once, and pulled it out again. The glass was gone.

'Where did it go?' Milena asked.

'It's in the oven now. Eighty degrees. It will harden there,' said Rose Ella, with a grunt. She took her black metal pole and dipped it in a bucket. There was a bubbling and a sputtering of steam. 'Stand back,' said Rose Ella. She chopped away at a crust of crystal left clinging to the mouth of the pipe.

'I'm doing a net too, if you want to stay and watch,' said Mala.

'Ach! Oh, that's special, Milena. You're in luck!'

Her smile still sharp and steady, Mala sat in front of a little table. 'The order came in just today,' she said. 'It's for a house being done up out in Uxbridge.'

'She weaves with glass,' said Rose Ella, and in her excitement gave Milena's hand a little squeeze.

It really was the most beautiful thing. The glass was teased into strands like toffee. Mala used chopsticks to stretch and catch and weave the strands over and under each other. The strands would sag and droop, and each time Mala would seem to catch them only just in time, lifting one strand up to nip another strand underneath.

Like wool, the glass was knitted. The criss-cross pattern rested as it grew on a gently warm shoulder of metal. Very suddenly, Mala was cutting the strands with a pair of scissors, which were passed to Rose Ella, to be dipped into water and bashed clean. New strands were drawn up, and red hot tongs were used to stroke them, cajole them into melting with the previous strands.

'This . . . glass,' said Mala, distracted by her work, 'is for . . . decorative panels. Screens really. Between beautiful wooden benches.' Milena realised that Mala was talking to her.

Mala looked up, straight at her. 'They're beautiful when they catch the light.' Milena smiled back at her, lost for a reply. 'They'll be about a metre square each when I'm done.'

Rose suddenly dipped in front of her mother, as if curtseying. From under the shoulder of metal, she pulled out another shoulder, to support new sections of the net. The clear putty of the glass slithered up and over itself as if alive; the chopsticks clicked like frightened insects. 'Ah!' sighed Mala with satisfaction. Suddenly it was time for lunch.

They all went to Russell Square together. The lawns were full of people photosynthesising. Mala bought each of them a drink, and a communal cup full of fried squid. They sat on the grass and protected their fried squid from the sniffing market dogs.

'It's not like they tell you,' said Milena, mustering her words.

'What do you mean, Milena?' asked Mala, as if from a respectful distance. She was still smiling.

'Restoring. There's nothing of the Golden Stream about it. It's all about moving glass.' Milena had found the whole experience deeply reassuring. She had found some grounds for hope. Life would be more practical than she had thought. Life was not about memory.

Mala's smile shifted, finally. It grew more broad and took a slightly rueful slant. 'We don't sit around talking, no. The only way to learn this stuff is to do it. They can give a virus, and you can know all about it here.' She pointed to her kerchiefed head delicately, with a circle of squid. 'But your hands still won't do the right thing. You've just got to learn it.' Mala's hands held the squid with a perfect grace.

Milena was so pleased she had to look away. She had to look down.

'Well,' said Rose Ella. 'I'm a Nurse, not a glass blower. I've got to get back.'

They all stood up, and Rose Ella and her mother kissed each other on both cheeks, a curiously formal gesture. Mala's hand rested slightly on her daughter's shoulder. Then, to Milena's surprise, Mala kissed her as well.

'See you later,' Mala said. 'Supper at six.' Then, without a backward glance, Mala walked away. Even the way Mala walked was perfect, one foot placed exactly in front of the other. Everything was so simple.

'Isn't she lovely?' asked Rose Ella.

Milena said yes, but only because she thought Rose Ella was. Together they walked back to the Medicine.

All that afternoon, as some of the children practised music, as others set up imaginary stalls selling saws or soap, Milena smiled. As older children came and went on real business, selling roasted corn to the Tarty grandees parading up Tottenham Court Road, or sweeping the streets of other Estates for money, Milena sat, legs folded on the floor of the courtyard and didn't move. Parents murmured to Nurses about possible lines of Development. It was said the Estate needed chemists – was any work being done in chemistry? How many Places were there, just in general, for statistical work?

As all the easy chatter came and went like the sound of wind in trees, Milena smiled. She smiled as she stitched a leather purse, pushing the needle and the heavy thread without really looking at it. Life might be possible after all. She had a friend. She had a friend.

When the Medicine closed at four, she ran back to the Gardens. She ran up the stairs, and tore off her grey jumpsuit. She hobbled barefoot into the blessedly empty bathroom, and turned on the shower and lathered soap all over herself. She set the tartar bugs loose on her teeth and felt them feasting all along the borders of her gums. Quite a banquet, eh lads? She brushed her teeth to get rid of them – otherwise they died and began to smell – and she ran her tongue over her teeth. Her teeth felt new and polished like the smoothest, coldest resin. She brushed her hair, and peered into the mirror, and saw that some of her pores were enlarged with little plugs of dirt. She popped them out, and washed her face again. She threw herself onto her bed, and pulled on her best wooden clogs. They would clatter as she danced.

Suze and Hanna were out. She could hear them talking below, in the Gardens, in their group. They would talk there until sunset and then go in and eat. Usually the sound of their talk would make Milena feel forlorn, deserted. Now, in the quiet room, she thought: I have a place to go. I am going to eat with a family and all of you are going to eat in a Child Garden. Some of the Tykes will probably have another horrible food fight, wormy old stir-fry thrown all over everyone. You'll have to wash, and then you'll sit in each other's bedrooms playing cards, or trying to make a few deals. You'll trade toys or reed mats or whatever scraps you can and it will make you feel adult.

Me, tonight, I will eat with adults, and there is going to be music.

Milena savoured the feeling for just one moment more. Then she turned and ran down the steps, her clogs making a sound like a winnowing machine.

The Row was an old square of mostly eighteenth century houses. The old brick sagged and the whitewashed windows were not square, but the ancient buildings stood up proudly by themselves. In the middle of the square, encircled by wrought iron, was another garden. Livestock was kept between the huge old trees. Sheep and goats were tethered to stakes, each of them keeping a circle of grass trim. There was a great structure made entirely of bales of hay, resin sheeting covering the sloping roof.

Milena found No. 40. On the door was a brass knocker in the shape of a dolphin. Its head knocked against brass waves. As soon as Milena knocked, the door was opened by Rose Ella. She must have been waiting, Milena thought, waiting just inside the doorway. She was kissed on both cheeks again, and told again how nice it was to see her. On each side of the hallway there was a row of small brass cannons. 'They were for firing salutes,' explained Rose Ella.

The walls were lined with old, yellowing paintings. Rose Ella didn't know who they were. Milena stopped to stare at their faces. Areas of the paintings had been cleaned, as if the people in them had wiped a dusty windowpane to see out. There was an old chair, with a back made out of wood, carved to look like a harp. Some of the wooden strings were broken. There was a huge rug thrown over bare, worn wooden floors. The colours were faded, all the warp worn through. A large china dog sat waiting faithfully, the tip of its nose broken.

'What a wonderful place!' said Milena. 'All these things.'

'Secret,' said Rose Ella. 'We take our time repairing them, so they can stay with us.'

'Really!' whispered Milena. It was a wicked world indeed.

Rose Ella chuckled. 'Come on, I'll show you where we live!' She ran up a great booming uncarpeted staircase. Milena followed in her clogs. Someone higher up shouted down at them to be still.

On the first landing, there were old TV sets, cables folded over their heads, and rows of frozen painted Chinese Buddhas. There was a bust of Benjamin Britten, and another old chair, one of its legs replaced by a prop of bamboo, its embroidered upholstery as worn as the rug downstairs. The chair had padded shoulders, as if it were a jacket.

Rose Ella's family lived in a huge parlour room, with vast front windows made of wobbly glass. The glass made all the square outside look as if it was wavering with heat. There were wooden candlesticks, and decanters of clear water with glasses over the top to keep out the dust. There were portraits, photographs of dead monarchs, and French engravings of mountain or harbour scenes. 'Le Calme', said one. Rose Ella's sister, Maureen, sat at a polished mahogany table. More kissing of cheeks. Milena saw that the table's legs were carvings of naked women. She started to blush. On the table were plastic tiger lilies. Maureen was injecting them with colour.

'They never die, these flowers.' said Maureen. 'They're always bright.'

Milena was enchanted with the idea. She thought the thick waxy petals, red and orange and black were beautiful. There was an hibachi in the corner. It made the room too hot but a kettle had been left on it, so that Rose Ella was able to make them both a cup of tea. A boy ran in and asked for Johnny. 'He's out in the square, somewhere,' said Rose Ella, and the boy ran off again. Rose Ella's father came in, carrying books. He was huge, the biggest man Milena could recall seeing, with a face that might have been cruel. It had a small mouth, a long nose that had been broken, a black beard, and a very receding hairline. Then he spoke and his voice was high and gentle. 'Is it your mother?' he asked.

He was asking if it was his wife's turn to cook, meaning he hoped it was not his own. 'Yes, Ta, yes,' said his daughter, shaking her head.

'Oh good, that's good,' he said looking at Milena. 'My daughter tells me you're a reader of books. Well, come, come, come and see mine!'

He held out a paw, with hair on the back of it, took Milena's hand and led her clumping down the stairs again in her clogs. 'You've got hooves to wake the dead!' he exclaimed. 'Here, now, careful!'

They ducked down into a darkened corridor. The back of the house had no windows. He lit a candle, and held it up and there was a wall of books, on high shelves.

'Look at these, look at all of these, my beauties. None of these are in the viruses. None of them.'

It was a wall of unknown books. Milena, the one who remembered, saw them all again, in memory, clearer than a dream:

Before Scotland Yard
Castle Rackment – the Absentee
Tom Burke of 'Ours' by Lever
Wild Tales by George Burrow
The Professor by Currer Bell

Old books in leather, others in cloth, some with faded, painted paper covers.

Nunwell Symphony by C. Aspinal Ogladender, Hogarth Press – with painted skies over great houses.

In Tune with the Infinite by Trine – gold lettering on a blue cloth cover.

'Why does the Consensus forget them all?' asked Milena, dismayed at the waste.

The great burly man shrugged. 'They had their day,' he said. 'They were read and loved, and other books grew up in their places. Like people. Only some people are remembered. It's the same with books. Here, look at this one.' He pulled out one loose book. Its leather cover was torn; padding leaked out of it as from a sofa. He opened it up for her. There was a photograph, in black and white, obviously retouched by pencil in places. A woman in a white nightdress gazed in wonder at another woman. The other woman wore a garment of leaves. Elaborate scrolls were drawn around the photographs, and elaborate lettering said 'Scenes from Peter Pan, an enchantment for children'.

He turned page after page. There were misty backdrops of country cottages with bowers of roses, and women in linen flounces that left their stockinged ankles bare. Light was in pools of shadow all around them.

'It's theatre,' whispered Milena, in awe. Rose Ella's father must have been briefed as well.

'And none of those productions are in the viruses either.'

Love and yearning made Milena draw in her lower lip. Rose Ella's father ruffled her hair. 'Yes, you can borrow the book.'

'Thank you,' said Milena, very quietly, as if the gift were made of china so fine it could shatter.

They went into the dining hall. Rose Ella had gone for a shower and returned, looking even fresher, prettier. Milena grinned to see her. 'Look!' she said, and held open her book.

'Oh, Ta, Tatty!' she exclaimed, and kissed her father for doing her, Rose Ella, a favour.

The three of them went into the dining room. It was large, with many tables. The boys sat together, looking rough as boys anywhere will, making Milena feel threatened and shy. She vaguely knew all the boys from the Medicine. She had hoped to find only adults here. Again she wondered: how is it that children grow up to be such nice adults? Parents came in, men and women bearing trays of food. Mala came in, smiling. She looked up smiling at Milena, and she left still smiling. Milena hugged her book and felt her cheeks going hot. She had nothing to say again. She turned and looked at a huge black piece of furniture behind her. The back rose up in carved black branches like the stone that holds stained glass windows. Along the pediment there were clumsy carvings of very fat children. Two played lutes and one played a drum. The drumsticks were broken. A fourth child played the pan pipes.

Rose Ella's father knelt down beside her. He spoke to her softly, conspiratorially.

'The backs were made in 1700, but the fronts, well, the fronts were made in 1400. The wood is Spanish sweet chestnut. That's why it's so dark. Not horsechestnut. Spanish sweet. Look, there's its brother over there.'

Milena turned and saw that, across the room, was another, nearly identical dresser. But the fat angels had become medieval adults, lean and austere.

Rose Ella's father crouched down and pulled out from the lower shelf, an old helmet. The leather had gone black, and its braid and its chin strap. Its black copper badge said 'Irish Lifeguards'. He pulled it down low over his eyes.

Some of the other men laughed, and called things that Milena couldn't understand.

'Oh, Tatty, take it off,' said Rose Ella, embarrassed. They all sat together at one of the long tables. Food was heaped up on plates: stir-fried vegetables, all crisp, and a kind paprika stew of cauliflower, and huge GE prawns that were carved up and served like roast chickens.

Talk spilled back and forth across the table. The Stone and Timber Estates were playing up and charging too much. It would soon be cheaper to go cut your own and drag it back. Why not? said Rose Ella's mighty father. Eh? I'd fancy a quest to the outreaches, out to the woods, even out to the hills.

'William,' said Mala, 'Don't talk out your fantasies. It would take months to haul your way up to Cumbria and back, it's nearly to Scotland.'

But the men and boys were growing excited by the idea. There were great plans made. Seconds were served, and the candles lit, and the tables were pulled back. Rose Ella's great beefy father opened up the Spanish sweet dresser, the one with the musical children. He took out bagpipes. Whistles came out as well, and drums, flutes and harps and oboes.

A little piping ditty began, with a drone of pipes in the background. Elegant fiddles joined in, stately, calm, one of them played by Mala. The harp made a sound like stars, isolated and clear, and a muffled drum began to beat, and the Estate of the Restorers lined up, to dance, two at a time in the centre of the room.

And Senior Fenton sang. Milena looked at Rose Ella, and Rose Ella cast her eyes down, fighting a grin. Senior Fenton sang a story about a delegation from a Tarty official, sent to inspect the family of a Restorer who wanted to marry his daughter. The inspectors saw the goats, and thought they were an honour guard with beards. They saw the old broken furniture and the dirty paintings. They heard the crickets living in the fireplace, commonly called Pipers, and concluded the young man had his own private orchestra hidden behind screens. They slept on straw-stuffed mattresses and declared they were the finest beds. The Tarty official was so impressed, he sent his daughter to live happily among the Restorers, thinking them wealthy indeed. For the last verse, all the Restorers rushed into the middle of the room. Milena found herself pulled by someone she did not know into their midst. She danced as best she could, hugging a book, her clogs making a sound like a factory loom. The Restorers roared with laughter and applauded her. Milena fled, back to the sidelines. She saw Rose

Ella dance, her eyes shining, turning under the arched arm of Senior Fenton, like a doll on a music box.

It was a short walk back to the Gardens, though the Gardens were a different world. Rose Ella walked back home with her. 'How can I become a Restorer? Is there time to learn?' Milena asked her.

'If it's right for you, there will be time,' Rose Ella said. 'Now good night, love. You come to see us soon.'

Who would have thought life could suddenly turn so delicious? In front of the door to her block, Milena looked up at the stars. Rose Ella. Rose Ella, she said, over and over to herself, as she thumped up the stairs, her head wobbling from side to side to the sound of the reels. Rose Ella, Rose Ella, she thought as she lay on her little bed by the window. She could still look up and see the stars. I want to go back there, she thought. I want to be a Restorer and live in the Row. I want to knit glass, and save the old books. I want to learn how to play the pipes and I want to dance.

It was Rose Ella she wanted to dance with. The stars seemed to spin overhead, and she fell asleep, slipping into darkness with a smile.

All that summer, Milena visited Rose Ella. She stayed overnight at the Row, sleeping in a guest bedroom, that was stuffed with luxury. It had built-in Chinese cabinets. Milena would sit at a table, reading her books, and look up and see the doors of the cabinets. Ivory people had been inlaid in them. The people hunted or they fished or they carried bundles of grainstalks on their backs. But some of the ivory people had fallen out, leaving a hole behind them, a space that was in their shape, grey and broken, forever. Sometimes, most poignantly, their tunics or their shoes would be left behind, still in their shape, as if waiting for their return.

Milena remembered the bathroom, which was a wonder. The bathtub was huge and stood on metal legs. The white enamel was wearing through and the great brass taps were lopsided. There was a strange metal plunger, that you had to lift up and turn to keep it raised so that the bath would drain. There was a footbath, and there was a toilet bowl that was moulded in the shape of animals and inside the basin it said in blue lettering 'The Deluge'. The Milena who remembered saw all of this as clearly as if she could simply turn a corner and find it all still there, real and solid.

She remembered exploring a house by High Holborn that was being restored. Its roof had gone, and most of the floorboards. Milena and Rose Ella had to tiptoe on the foundations, the poured concrete, the rows of bricks. Yet colour still clung to the walls. Milena remembered a yellow room, with a broad band of red all around it. In the corners, where some of the ceiling was left, there were spreading plaster fans, mouldings. Just inside one of the doors, there was panelling of wood on all the walls. The wood was grey and weatherbeaten now, open to the sky and the rain. The stairwells were empty. There was only a zigzag tracing up the walls where the stairs had been. A fireplace still had its tiles. They were green with red flowers, twenty-first century Gothic. The grate had gone bright orange with rust.

'People got very rich,' said Rose Ella, leaning over it. 'Some people. Just before it all went wrong. They lived in big houses. They had many houses, and travelled all over Britain, all over Europe, to live in them for a week, for a few days. Can you imagine that? Shall we fly my dear to Edinburgh for the weekend?' She adopted a deep and portly voice.

'Why not? What amusement,' said Milena, imitating a Tarty wife. Together they stepped arm in arm across the missing floorboards, balancing on brick supports.

'Imagine being this rich,' said Rose Ella again.

'It's as if, if we could climb the stairs, and find a way into one of those rooms, we'd find everything back in place, with the people there. Like they didn't know anything had changed.'

'Ugh!' said Rose Ella and shuddered. 'I wouldn't want to end up back there. You and I would just be servants. Coming in miles every day in the train.'

'Breathing poison.'

'Thinking the world was going to end.' Rose Ella suddenly stepped forward. 'You've got to see this,' she said. She pulled Milena into the next room.

Stinging nettles grew high outside the windows. But here in this last room, the floorboards were in place, fitting perfectly. The floor was beautiful. There was no ceiling, just one huge beam all the way across the room. And still clinging to that one beam, by purest luck, there was a huge light fitting, a kind of frozen fountain of plaster, moulded into leaf shapes, and ending with a small hole in the tip.

'What is it?' Milena asked. It looked like some kind of wasp's nest.

'It was for lights,' said Rose Ella. 'It was called a rose. A ceiling rose. Now, look at this, too!'

She pulled Milena with her, into the next room and spun her around. In an arch over a broken door, a wall painting still remained. It showed a man in some kind of chariot, flying through the air, pulled by horses.

'Is that an airplane?' Milena asked, and knew it was a stupid question as soon as she asked it. An airplane with horses, sure. But she had no viruses to show her what an airplane had looked like, and had never bothered to find a book about them. Rose Ella kept looking up, pretending that Milena had not said anything out of the ordinary.

Beyond the broken doorway there was a pile of roof slates, all in a layered heap where they had avalanched, their edges chipped like stone age arrowheads. On the yellow walls someone had written in a kind of flourishing red marker.

Raisa 2050

and underneath that, in the same hand, but with smudged charcoal

Raisa (again!) 2085

They carefully picked their way over the heap of slates. They jumped and danced through a wall of bitter nettles. Milena stumbled over something and pulled it out. It was a tiny brass bedstead. It was all black and chewed except for one little floral ring around it, bent but still bronze-coloured. Milena suddenly could imagine it new, part of a child's bed, a child's bed with a duvet covered in small blue flowers. She imagined the child in it, a little girl with long brown hair, sweet and soft and innocent and privileged. She looked up at the windows, empty now and staring at the sky. What would she have thought, Milena wondered, if she had known what was coming?

It was as if the building were a train, carrying lives with it like passengers, moving at high speed until it hit the barriers. Then there was wreckage.

Rose Ella's father went off one summer morning early, in a wagon train. He and seven other men were off to Cumbria to fetch new stone. All the Row was gathered to see them off. Everyone waved. Milena had come early to wave as well. Rose Ella wept, though she couldn't say why. She had some kind of bad feeling. Something awful could happen on the road to Cumbria.

For the next month, there were still dances in the Row, with fewer fathers to dance with. The music became sadder. Milena remembered Mala, playing her fiddle. The fiddle was tucked under chin, and her eyes were faraway, remembering, and the sound of the fiddle was high and sad and sweet, coaxing out the heart of the old songs.

It was the music of home. Milena felt she had found a family, a people, a place. She thought she had found a future as well.

The ocean currents were unstable. The Gulf Stream moved back and forth. Bleak, blasted summers could be followed by howling winters, choked with snow.

Towards the end of that summer, it rained. Milena spent whole days in the Row, reading books, hearing the rain on the roof while Rose Ella knitted and her sister made immortal flowers. Paving stones dropped underfoot, spurting up mud. The ground was a muddy morass. The turf in the parks was as springy as mattresses. The trees hung their drenched and heavy leaves low, dripping water.

Then one evening, the bells began to ring. They all began to ring, every bell in the City. There were rivers of sound flowing in the air.

193

A pattern of three rings called for a doctor. Two warned of fire, and one chime with a beat of silence signalled a flood. These bells had no pattern. They were a continual ringing of alarm.

There was a bell at the corner of Gower and Torrington. Milena could see it from her bedroom window. Tykes were still ringing it, when she heard hooves. A crier came galloping out of Gower Street. She did not dismount. The crier stood up in her stirrups and bellowed in a clear and penetrating voice, 'Everyone please listen. There is a hurricane coming. There is going to be a hurricane tonight.'

The Tykes asked the woman something. She looked down and looked up, and answered to everyone, 'The Balloons have seen it, and it is coming. A hurricane is on its way. You have about four hours. Please nail shut all shutters. Remove loose material from the streets. Take shelter. Take supplies of food with you. Thank you.' Then, vermilion-cheeked, the woman sat down, and hauled on the reins to turn the horse around. Milena heard the hooves retreat.

The Senior of the Gardens ordered all furniture to be piled up against the windows. Brave Tykes with nails in their mouths, edged along ledges to hammer bamboo over windows. Clothes and bedding were carried down into the lightwells. The doors were closed and locked. Fire drill was observed. Wardens searched each room before hammering shut the doors.

Then, huddled together in the core of the building, everyone waited. They looked up the lightwells at the sky. The clouds were yellow, full of dust. The wind shook at first, with a sound a bit like a window shaking. Then it began to moan, across the opening of the well, blowing it like some musical instrument.

The wind slammed down the lightwell with sudden spurts like a fist. There began to be the sound from somewhere of things falling, crashes and booms and spreading tinklings of glass.

The children gathered together under blankets, holding each other's hands.

I should have gone to the Row, thought Milena. I should be with them. And she hoped that Rose Ella, and Mala, and Senior Fenton would all be all right. But most of all, she thought of Rose Ella.

Milena saw birds overhead against the sky. She saw them in a flock, peeling away in spirals. Then she saw that they were four-cornered. They were resin tiles torn away from the roof.

The network of bamboo poles against the walls began to creak. A Nurse suddenly threw herself against the children, gathering them up. Her wrist caught under Milena's chin and crowded her backwards. Milena was about to yelp in protest, when all the drainage system rose up from the walls.

It spilled water. Huge droplets clattered on the concrete. The shafts of bamboo caught on themselves; they were twisted around, wrenched; they split apart in strands. The system rose up in a tangle, and seemed to draw a breath; then fell down into the lightwell, an avalanche of bamboo spears.

From the safety of the basement corridors, the children squealed.

The rain began, great lashings of it, moving like ghosts in the air, against a fluorescent sky. Nestled amid the foundations, the children heard things being driven into the walls above them. They could hear a grating sound, and a spreading crackle like lightning moving through stone. They felt a click. The click sounded in their vertebrae, just at the base of their skulls. 'Ooooh,' said all the children in wonder.

Water began to swirl around the drains in the floor of the lightwell, frothing white as it slipped down. Wreckage was swept over the drains. They began to back up. Very suddenly, Milena's feet were wet. A sheet of water extended itself down the basement corridor. The children made sounds of dismay and disgust. Those who had been sitting, stood up crying or laughing.

They would have to stand all night. Fear and exhilaration both faded. It was wearisome having to stand, wet and cold. Water rose up over the tops of their shoes. The steady whiring of the wind made them sleepy. They nodded their heads and longed to be able to lie down. Sudden batterings startled them and made them jump. Some of them wept with exhaustion. The Nurses shushed and tutted and held them and called them darlings and babes. Some of them wept too, for their own lost homes, their parents. Their parents seemed to speak out of the howling wind.

The rain eased, the flood retreated. The children sat down in puddles, too tired to care, and the Nurses stroked their heads until they fell asleep, moaning like the wind.

Milena thought of Rose Ella and was suddenly awake.

The sky over the lightwell was a silver-grey, cloudy but full of light. Everyone else was still asleep, a tumble of arms and legs. Milena stepped out from under the arches onto the floor of the well.

A train wreck. Bamboo lay in twisted heaps. There had been a shower of glass and tiles. The walls were bare in patches. The roof showed naked timber, still looking fresh and cream-yellow at its heart.

Milena went to the door of the staircase, and when she pulled it open, a shower of glass crystals poured out, down from the staircase, over her feet. She shook her shoes and climbed up over glass and wood and lumps of plaster.

The walls of the stairwell were cracked in places and there was a light scattering everywhere of dust and rubble. She turned the corner of the stairway, leading to the front door. The corridor was full of leaves and branches, as if invaded by vegetation. A tree had fallen into the Child Garden.

Milena stood looking at its curtains of leaves at her feet, and the jigsaw-puzzle bark. 'Oh no,' she whispered heartstruck. It was her tree, the Tree of Heaven. The wind had pulled it down. Oh no, oh no, she kept thinking, not my tree, not my beautiful tree. She stepped through its broken branches that still smelled of sap and green wood. Leaves brushed her face like tender hands.

A great gash had been torn through the front of the building where the tree had fallen. The doorway was gone. Stone and brick and bars of twisted metal lay all around the tree. Milena climbed up onto the trunk, where the main branches met and looked down its length. Around the base of the tree, a halo of roots arched up above the ground.

This far, she thought, it used to be this far down to the ground. When it stood.

She walked along its trunk, out from under the unsteady wall of the building. She stood in the middle of the street. Her bedroom had been wiped away. Someone's bedstead lay half buried in rubble, twisted and flattened. Lengths of bamboo had been driven into the walls as if they were hammered nails. The shutters had been torn away, and all the windows broken.

Milena thought of her tree, how tall it had stood, how it had been the first thing she had seen every day. She murmured for it, out of pity. 'Tree. Oh, tree.'

She had not known that a tree could take root in you as well as in the soil, and that when it was uprooted, it was from your life as well as from the ground, as if it were pulled out of your own breast. Poor tree, full of wet leaf, in high wind, in damp weak soil. And you had stood so long, for a century or more so tall.

Milena wandered dazed in too many clothes, all her clothes worn at once, coat and jumpsuit and squelching boots. All the scaffolding was gone, all the windows. The old weak buildings of London had fallen as well. They lay stretched and broken across the streets. If they still managed to stand their upper floors were indecently exposed. Disorder embarrassed them, made them look foolish. A cart with no wheels half-hung out of a dignified old room. The polished doors, the moulded plaster, the glass of the sash-cord windows were scattered like cards. The work of the Restorers had been undone.

Milena walked down Gower Street to the Row.

The roof was gone. There was old furniture all about Bedford Square. Already the Restorers were picking mournfully through it, shaking their heads, scratching them. Women stepped out over rubble, over fallen beams, carrying tea. Oh no, Milena thought again. Not this too. Not the beautiful Row, with its beautiful things. Milena's feet slipped on wood panelling. Hay from the stables was distributed in drifts, like snow. Two of the fathers stood side by side, unmoving.

'They'll have to give it all over to the Reefers now,' one of them said. 'Bloody Coral.'

'Milena!' wailed a voice. 'Oh Milena, Milena!'

It was Rose Ella. The two girls ran to each other and hugged each other, and encouraged by each other, burst into tears, and sobbed, shaking in each other's arms.

'Oh, Milena, it's gone. It's all gone. It's all broken.' Rose Ella's lip was torn, black with dried blood, and tears were like snail trails on her cheeks.

'Our beautiful house!' exclaimed Milena.

'Come on, my love, have some tea,' said Rose Ella. They helped each other like two old women, across the ruin of the square to the tea. There was smoke from somewhere. A cooking fire? Milena hoped so. She was hungry and cold.

'Stay here,' said Rose Ella. 'You stay here with us, eh?'

So, under canvas, thrown up to keep out the rain, Milena went to live, finally and briefly with Rose Ella.

One wing of the Row was still in place. All the children were bundled up together in rooms, to sleep together on mattresses. Milena was shaken, made truly insecure by the blast. Her life had been completely overturned twice before. Somehow, that made her weaker, not stronger. Her teeth rattled. They had not done that since her mother had left her, bereft and alone among strangers. Milena was back in that blank, black unremembered time. Her fingers were dirty, there was no water to wash. She was frightened. She hid from people. She just wanted Rose Ella and her family, no one else. She hid from the Nurses of the Child Garden. She saw them coming, picking their way over the fallen plaster, on the second day. She darted back, and nipped into a cupboard under a staircase. She pulled fallen curtains over herself. She heard Rose Ella say: 'Oh I'm so sorry! We should have told you, Milena came here to stay with us. Oh, this is awful! You must have been looking all this time.' Rose Ella called for her. 'Lena? Milena? I don't think she's here.'

Then Milena heard Rose Ella whisper: *Not well. Poor thing, she's taken it badly. Better if she stays with us.*

That night, on the mattress they shared, Milena clung to her tightly, as if to drifting wreckage at sea.

'Milena love, I can't breathe! Please!' said Rose Ella.

'*Svoboda,*' said Milena. Czech? She was speaking Czech? She had forgotten Czech, surely! Rose Ella rolled over, away from her, and

Milena was left alone with terror. The stars were terror, the dark was terror, but most especially the past, the unremembered past was terror. She fell asleep in fear, her hand resting lightly against the back of Rose Ella's soft, smooth neck.

She woke up some time before dawn. She thought she was seeing a dream. She woke up in a fallen ruin, with strewn familiar objects. There were the four small cannons, too heavy for the wind to take. It seemed to her that she was looking at the ruin of her life. The ruin of her life had always been there, unrealised, since Milena had lost a father, lost a mother, lost a language, lost her very self, lost it forever behind layers of growing up, layers of loss, layers of scorn, self-hatred, ceaseless work, unfulfilled hopes. Lost it where there was no childhood, nothing simple or safe or sweet or whole.

Except that next to her was Rose Ella. Rose Ella was there as in a dream, kissed with the faintest light of early sunrise, the first clear dawn since the hurricane. Milena looked down at Rose Ella, beautiful, asleep, hair fallen from her face, nightrobe fallen open, and there was her beautiful breast. It was young and small, with a dark nipple. Stranded somewhere between sleep and dream, suspended in a kind of stillness in the light, and in the light mist, thinking how much the breast looked like a mother, Milena kissed the nipple. She took the nipple in her mouth.

Rose Ella's eyes opened with a snap.

She looked round at Milena.

Milena looked at her, dazed loving.

Rose Ella sat up. She pulled the duvet up over herself. She sat there staring, ice cold. Milena began to sense at last that something was horribly wrong.

'Milena! What are you doing?'

'I don't know,' said Milena truthfully.

It was said of the orphans that they were sexually advanced. Some of them, after all, were engaged to be married even before Reading. It was said darkly, that some strange things went on in the Gardens, before the orphans were safely Read, safely Placed, safely cured by viruses. Orphans were admired, held up as ideals, the children who became adults first and most completely. They were made ideals in order to help people be less afraid of them.

Orphans reminded people that they would die. Orphans meant their own sudden extinction. Orphans revealed too clearly the forced growth of everyone's children. People thought the darkness in their own minds was caused by something dark in the minds of the orphans. People feared that orphans would contaminate their own children with pre-cocious thoughts, or sexual adventures. Milena did not know that she had been a test of tolerance.

198

Rose Ella stood up, still holding the blanket. She jerked it away, from Milena's grasp. She turned and stalked away. She looked back over her shoulder at Milena. She was crying. She put her hands to her face, and began to walk more quickly. She gave her head a shake. She began to run, over the rubble, hobbling in bare feet.

Milena lay back on the mattress. She let herself realise what had happened. They would say it had happened because she was an orphan. She was an orphan; maybe they were right. They would send her away.

Mala came with her steady smile. Only the smile was strained now, slightly glazed like the grins on the lost porcelain statues.

'Milena. Hello,' she said, crouching. 'You're very upset by all of this aren't you?'

Milena was frozen, like some trapped animal. She felt fallen like her tree. She looked at Mala's knees. She couldn't bear to look up at her face.

'You've got a lot of problems, Milena. It's understandable. You've lost your parents. And you do have certain disabilities. And we've tried to help you with those, for your sake, and to help Rose Ella with her work. And I like to think we've done some good. But it's up to you now, dear. You're going to have to do some development yourself. You're going to be Read, and cured of all sorts of things. That's going to happen very soon now. And, maybe after that, when everything's settled. Well.' She paused and touched Milena's arm, or rather, her sleeve. 'Well, maybe you would like to come back to see us then.'

'Where will I go now?' Milena asked, her voice thin, choked, forlorn.

'The other orphans are moving into the Medicine. It's quite a sturdy building. Sturdier than the Row.' Milena could see the knees twist around to look at the rubble and to regret. Memory of her own grief made Mala more firm.

'I think you better go now, eh, Milena? Before everyone else starts getting up and wonders why. Here. Here are your boots dear.'

Milena lay still as the boots were forced on her feet.

'I don't want to go,' she whispered.

Mala sighed. 'I know, dear. But it's for the best.'

Milena stumbled back through the ruins, as dazed as the last time she was injected with virus, hard virus that had been shoved directly into her veins with a needle. The dosage had nearly killed her. She had thrown up blood. She had tossed on her bed for days, and wandered befuddled for weeks, the genetics of knowledge churning in her head. But even then the viruses did not take hold. The mighty Doctors had examined her, held her flesh in their cold hands and peered at her. They took samples. The mighty Doctors must know why the viruses didn't work. They had stopped even trying after that final dose: they had stopped making her ill. They left her alone to be unwell in her own way.

And they had sent Rose Ella.

'And we've tried' said the child bitterly. 'To help Rose Ella with her work.'

Milena found herself in the lobby of the Medicine.

There were Nurses sitting at a desk. Everything had been swept up or replaced by the children. Everything seemed so smooth and clear. The eyes of the Nurse flitted briefly over Milena. They saw her charcoal hands, the dirty face, the clothes white as if in mourning from the dust of rubble.

'Ah, good morning, Ms Shibush. Back with us after the storm. That's good, we have a new work group arranged for you. To prepare you for your Placement. And a nice new room.'

Milena stared at them. Does the room have teeth, she wondered, like a shark. Does it bite off fingers as you wander through the ruin of your life, chewing them? Does it grind you with great white molars of rubble? Does your blood ooze underneath the door of this nice, new white room, with the walls that have straps to bolt you down to the bed? 'I want you to burn me,' said Milena. 'I want you to burn everything out of me. I want this burned clear!' She pressed a finger to her own head. 'Make me sick,' she said. 'Make me ill. Make me as sick with the virus, as much as you can. All of it, all at once, I don't care if it kills me, just get it inside me.'

And I will be controlled. And I will be neat and clean, and I will keep everything neat and clean, and I will never speak, and I will never show myself again, not to you nor to anyone else.

'Cure me,' she demanded.

And she went up to her new room. There was a new bed, as anonymous as her last, and bare walls, and the smell of other room mates. Milena stared at the wall. I hate childhood, she thought. I wish I had never been a child. I want to be old, as old as I can be. Roll on, viruses, roll over me. Come on mathematics, come on Marx and Chao Li Song. Come on logarithms, come all you operas as fixed as the North Star. Come and dance on my head and break it up into rubble. I want to forget.

Milena the would-be adult turned feral. She turned into a hunter. She hunted memory.

No! whispered the adult who was remembering. No! but the voice from the future was too faint.

Milena turned on her self as if with fangs and claws. She pursued her child self through all its hated years in England. She felt the small cool coils and remembered. She had touched such things before and

200

destroyed them. Small cool coils of DNA, DNA that encoded sight and sound, that preserved pain and loneliness and work and waiting.

She sprung memory, as if it were virus. She savaged the coils, rended them apart and let their elements scatter. The memory of her landing in Newhaven on the boat; the death of her mother; the steady learning of the English tongue and the kindly man who had taught it to her; she pounced on them, and ripped them apart in a rage.

She came to the memories of Rose Ella, of home, of the music and the dancing and the book of theatre that Rose Ella's father had given to her. She held the memories as if in pincers; she felt their weight. She felt them flower in her mind; the sound of the clattering clogs, the lounging in the sun in Russell Square; the row of tiny cannons for firing salutes. She remembered the music of home.

All right, all right, she would let that be. Everything else would be obliterated. The young Restorers on her first day in the Child Gardens; they had gathered around her, calling her Russian out of contempt, damning her with Chao Li Song's words as she howled for her mother, her mother who was dead. Ah! fond memories of childhood, she thought as she slashed them. Ah my golden years! My bouquet of early life. The years of eating alone; the years of Nurses' shaking heads. The years of feeling stupid; the years of feeling foreign, the years of silence and dust and the years of her reading as well, all those books, all that work. Milena tore apart her work as well, consigning it to darkness.

No! whispered the future.

The Child Garden was destroyed.

So they made Milena ill again, and this time the viruses won. Milena had no memory of that, either. She remembered how she emerged smaller, neater, pale and wan and very quiet, with a continent of knowledge crammed into her head, along with several useful calculating facilities.

'Well, you were scheduled for your Reading,' said the Senior Nurse. 'But we couldn't send you because you were so ill. We only gave you educational viruses of course. Personality defects can only be cured by Doctors, and they do that after your Reading. I'm sure there will be a Reading arranged for you soon.' The Senior Nurse smiled, as if to an equal. Milena was now an adult. 'We're very glad that the information finally took. It must be paradise for you.'

'Oh yes,' said Milena, her voice dull.

'And the lack of your Reading seems not to have affected your Placing. Jack Horner, that's what we'll have to call you. You've pulled a Plum, Ms Shibush. You've been Placed as an apprentice at the Zoo

– the National Theatre. That's one of the highest Placings we've ever had at the Medicine.'

The Nurse reached forward and shook Milena's hand. 'We are all so proud of you, Ms Shibush.' The fact that Milena did not respond, that the flesh on her face hung dead, and that her mouth was pinched and withdrawn did not surprise the Nurse. She had seen Milena during her illness. She was surprised that Ms Shibush had survived at all.

Like the Tree of Heaven, Rose Ella had done Milena one last great favour before being torn out of her life. Rose Ella had testified on Milena's Placement board. Moira Almasy had sat on the board as well, as a representative of the Zoo. Milena had been Rose Ella's special assignment. Years later, Moira Almasy told Milena what Rose Ella had said.

'It is difficult to see,' Rose Ella had told the board (she spoke clinically, professionally), 'in what way someone as crippled as Ms Shibush could usefully be employed, if it is not to work in the theatre.'

So Milena walked out of the Medicine forever, into the newly swept streets, all the old rubble now removed, like her memory. Czechoslovakia lay too far behind her, encoded in a different tongue. Her English years simply no longer existed for her. Her self had been destroyed. It would take six years, until she met Rolfa, before she could rebuild it. She felt dirty. She thought she could feel viruses crawling on her. She wanted to wash.

The sun and the clouds, the new paving stones, and the cabbages squashed on them were all flat and heavy and slow. The viruses whispered like ghosts. They threatened to tell Milena the name of the street, and when it had been built, the names of its architects and statesmen who had slept somewhere along it. Milena walked out of the Medicine, into this unmoving world. She was free, unRead but safely Placed. She had escaped. There was no joy. Now she was an adult, and the world itself had become old.

It was some months later that she learned that Rose Ella's father, bringing back stone from Cumbria, had been killed by the great storm as well.

A tree had fallen on him.

Years later, amid the trees and flowers of Hyde Park, the Crab Monsters danced.

They pricked their way on the points of their claws and held aloft their huge front pincers. They danced in front of the Forbidden City. The Crab Monsters ruled the world. They were huge and orange and had tiny eyes.

The Monsters were orange because they had been boiled. Thrawn had not been able to imagine crabs, so Milena had bought crabs at

the market, cooked them, and scooped them out for puppets. Cooking
had changed their colour. The Monsters were dead and empty shells.

Across the grass, the Chinese princesses came crawling on their
knees in red and blue silk. They were played by Chinese children, but
the hologramming had made them huge as well, so they could be seen.
They were giant children, wailing an ancient song, pleading for the
world. The pageant was performed for an audience of children who
had been allowed to stay up late and for those who had children hidden
inside them, who had a world hidden inside them.

The children fell silent. They waited. Stars wavered overhead,
screened by the rising air.

Then came Bugs Bunny.

He was huge as well, but flat, a drawing. Bugs came dancing, a kind
of Chinese wobble. He gave his audience a knowing, narrow-eyed
look. With the voice of an American gangster, he began to warble a
Chinese song.

The audience of children roared with disbelief and delight. Bugs
paused to bite off the tip of a carrot, and continued to sing with his
mouth full. He danced in a circle round the Crab Monsters and
crammed a carrot into each of their maws. They went cross-eyed.

Next to Milena, in the darkness, Moira Almasy had covered her
eyes and was shaking her head. But she was also smiling. Milena
looked around. Embarrassed pleasure was on all the faces; they were
pleased but confused.

Bugs lit all the carrots as if they were cigars. The carrots sizzled for
a moment and then exploded in the faces of the Crabs. They were
stunned, black-faced. Bugs kissed them hovering in mid-air, fluttering
his feet like wings. Then with a whoosh he was gone. The Crabs gave
chase.

Thrawn McCartney was leaning around Moira, smiling. It was a
smile that demanded collusion. It demanded that she and Milena give
a performance of seamless agreement, and of professional triumph.

It was a performance that Thrawn had been giving all night. It had
been one of her best. 'We' she kept saying of herself and Milena, 'we'
all the time, to indicate a partnership of equals. She had been the
spokeswoman for the team, direct, bright, interceding. She had made
Milena feel small, tight, and dull. As they had sat down, amid all the
keepers of the Zoo, Thrawn had given Milena a wink and hearty
thumbs-up sign.

But there was something more in Thrawn's smile, now.

It was relaxed. The tendons and muscles of her neck, and the rope
of tissue around her mouth seemed to have cleared, like some kind of
disease. The smile was bright and young and full of affection. The
affection was for Milena.

Milena smiled back, with relief: relieved for once not to have to pretend, relieved for once to have a real smile warmed out of her by Thrawn. For just a moment, there was a hint of what might have been.

Bugs was drawing a gate in the ancient stone walls of the City. He filled it in black, and ran through it. The Crab Monsters tried to follow, and bashed their heads on stone. For them, the gate was always closed.

Bugs trotted behind them, holding up a box. Fireworks, said a sign on it, in Chinese. Bugs stuck in one of his sizzling carrots and walked away.

The sky was full of pink and green flowers of fire, blossoming outward, amid the clatter of gunpowder and the echoing boom of explosions. White smoke rose up.

And through the blazing light and drifting smoke, the Dragon Ship descended.

It was a tightly curled ball of scaled cord. That was all that Thrawn had been able to imagine.

But now, slithering, the knot unfurled, scales moving against scales, light glinting yellow on them. Talons emerged, great chicken feet with claws of steel. Very suddenly, the head was free. The Dragon had a face like a Pekinese dog, and long silver hair. She tossed her head and roared, showing shark teeth, and her hair lashed like giant whips, crackling at the tip. Milena stared into her huge, unblinking, yellow eye and she knew the Dragon was alive, as if she had been born crawling out of Milena's skin.

It was not Thrawn's Dragon. The Dragon had come to Milena, demanding to be born, and at the last minute, Milena had overlaid the image onto the recording. Milena had meant to tell Thrawn, but somehow the time was never right. Thrawn was staring at her now, icy with fury, the smile gone, black circles restored around her eyes. Here we go again, thought Milena.

The Dragon gathered up the Crabs. They were her wayward children. The Crabs, it turned out, were children too. The Dragon hissed, and vapour rose from her scales. She blasted fire from out of her mouth, and was driven backwards into the sky. She carried off the Monsters with her, to justice.

As she accelerated towards the stars, Bugs saluted. He had the power to charm, and the power to fool. He was the defender of children, whose only power is to love, and forgive, or to wail until they are heard.

And there was Milena, that same night. After the show, after Thrawn had turned her back on her, after the long walk back home. She was lighting the candle again, and placing it on her windowsill. It was the candle of work, which she had lit in childhood. She confused work with love. And she confused love, or the speaking of love, with the loss of home.

She had money to buy a chair now, but still did not have a desk. She opened the great grey book on the windowsill and sat down. Canto Sixteen. She had been working for a year and a half.

Milena lay her head down on the open book as if it were the lap of a lover. She wanted to work; she had to work, but she felt the world closing down, folding into darkness. Helpless, she slipped away into sleep, pulled by time from where she wanted to be.

Outside in the streets, the children were still singing with joy.

chapter eleven

FORCES OF ATTRACTION
(BOUQUETS OF CONFUSION)

The candle of work had burned out. It was late, so late that the sun had risen over the roof of the Shell, and sunlight flooded Milena's room. Milena had been awoken by a light touch on her sleeve. She looked up from the Comedy, and turned around.

Moira Almasy was in the room. Milena's vision was bleary from sleep and dust in her eyes. It seemed to her that Moira Almasy glowed with light so brilliantly that her features were blanched away, with all their lines and creases. Her hair was almost white.

'Milena,' Moira Almasy said. There was a hushed quality to her voice. 'Milena, something's happened.'

Milena sat up, feeling her hair. As always it hung straight and tidy in its ponytail. Moira was holding out a wad of paper towards her. There was a stack of paper on the floor. Milena took what was offered her, and stared.

It was paper in staves, and on it were written the words:

Divina Commedia
Canticche Uno
Inferno
Canto I
Piccolo
2 Flauti
2 Oboi
Corno inglese
Clarinetto piccolo (Es)

For a moment it meant nothing.

'After the show, last night,' said Moira. 'There was a call to all of the Terminals. They were told to find paper. Stores were opened, withdrawals recorded.'

2 Clarinetti (B)
Clarinetto Basso
2 Fagotti
Contrafagotto
4 Corni (F)
3 Trombe (B)

'Who did this?' asked Milena, still not fully understanding. It was not her music.

'The Consensus,' said Moira. 'Milena. The Consensus has scored the Comedy. The Terminals, all of them. Last night. They wrote it down. Two Cantos each.'

'All one hundred?' Milena felt dazed, hanging between many emotions. 'The whole thing?' She thought of all of her own work. 'All of it?'

Moira nodded yes, her smile muted by awe.

Milena knelt on the floor beside the heap of paper. It rose at least as high as her forearm was long. She fanned through the pages and found Canto Eight. She wanted to see how horns could be both sombre and hopeful.

'There's no vocal line,' she said.

It was instruments only, until Dante asked Virgil the question: '*Questo che dice?*'

None of the narration was sung.

'Those were the red notes!' exclaimed Milena. Most of the poetry was made mute, turned into music.

Milena's viruses played the notes on the page. She heard it, the swirling horns, deep, dark, water smelling of filth and of corpses. But light glinted on the surface of the water, and over the surface of the music. Even here, crossing the river of death, to the marshes of the Styx, there was purpose, there was justice.

Milena began to shake. 'Oh Marx and Lenin,' she said. 'Oh Marx and Lenin.'

She went to Canto after Canto. Music flowered. It was in gorgeous colours, as pungent as scent, combinations of sound that she would never have been able to imagine.

'It's wonderful,' she said, and began to laugh, and shake her head. 'It's all wonderful!'

Something rose up in her, and she stood up and whooped for joy. She jumped up and down in her tiny room, and Moira began to beam with pleasure.

'Moira! Oh, Moira!' cried Milena, and hugged her, and Moira chuckled at her pleasure. She draped her hands on Milena's shoulders and looked into her eyes. 'It means,' said Moira, 'that the Consensus wants us to put it on. We're going to put it on, Milena.'

Milena covered one eye, as if to protect herself from too much good news. 'I don't believe it,' she said simply.

The world changed about her. She felt her place in it change in that moment. The opera was going to exist, it was going to be real, and Milena somewhere had a place in that. She had done something with her life.

'We're all fair stunned too,' said Moira. 'The Consensus has never intervened so directly in the arts. We're having a meeting later today, about three. I can leave the score with you, if you want to read it, and think about it.'

All Milena could do was nod yes, yes, yes of course. Could she bring it with her? It was a lot to carry. Milena kept nodding yes. She had been carrying a load for so long, what difference could it make. Yes, yes. The word of acquiescence, which is not the same thing as freedom.

There was an orange on Milena's windowsill, as round and perfect as the world. As she read through all the Comedy, as all its streams and tributaries of music flowed towards one immense ocean, Milena ate the orange, smelled its zest, felt the spray of its skin. And she looked out of her narrow window at the sky, and saw the clouds.

The clouds were wispy and white, moving as if blown by the music of the Comedy. Beyond them, the sky was blue, and Milena could see that the sky was infinitely deep, masked by a haze of light.

Time pulled. Milena was hauled up through the sky, leaving the orange, the manuscript, her room behind.

And Milena was looking down through the sky, backwards, from above.

The sky was a thin film of blue haze that looked as if it could be peeled back, like the skin of an orange. Earth would be left exposed and defenceless.

Below there was a forest. The forest was like a carpet made of thousands of green needles. Milena could almost see each tree. They were floating above the Amazon. In the west, rising up above the blue haze of the horizon were the Andes, the snow on their peaks pink with sunrise.

On the walls of the Bulge, there were plants growing. They were small mountain flowers, tiny, pale blooms amid spines. They were the flowers of Czechoslovakia. The Bulge remembered the code that grew them. The same helix that coded life coded information. It grew both flesh and thought. Life was a pun.

The vessel was alive and linked to Milena. It knew what she desired and could consult her viruses for genetic codes. Then, by thinking, it altered the genetic code of its own cells. It grew flowers out of itself, mixing memory and desire.

As Milena was about to do.

She was smiling, no longer giddy with weightlessness, but expectant and nervous. There was to be a test of the Reformation equipment. A single image was to be cast. Milena was going to imagine a rose. It was to be a rose that would fill the sky below.

'What happens next?' Mike Stone asked. He stood stock-still behind her, his mind maintaining the position of the Bulge in orbit.

'Well,' said Milena. 'The area of focus is huge. So the Consensus is going to help map it out for me.'

'How?' said Mike Stone.

'With an Angel,' said Milena.

Suddenly there was a tingling underneath her scalp, where she had been made Terminal. 'It's about to happen,' she said.

Information was presented to her, not in words. The information was like an iron weight, very delicately placed in her frail flesh. It was as if the weight of the universe was whispering to her. All the bones of her cheeks and temple seemed to crackle and ache.

The Consensus had spoken.

As if it had breathed out a bubble, something was released. It was small like an orange pip, and Milena felt relief. The great voice had been withdrawn. Milena had the impression of somersaulting, of something rolling towards her. 'It's here,' she whispered. 'The Angel.'

Something seemed to open up in her head.

It was like a curtain going back. The suede walls of the Bulge, the lens of its window, the stars and the Earth all seemed to part, and she was in another existence.

There was no light, no sound, only sensation. The sensation was something like touch. But the touch ran in lines, taut lines between things. Consciousness was extended along them, and whenever thought moved, the lines were strummed, like the strings of a musical instrument.

The Earth was a carefully wound ball of lines which led out from the Earth in all directions. The lines of touch went out to the stars and curved inwards towards the heart of the sun, a nexus of lines eight minutes away. The lines pierced Milena's body and the body of the Bulge and held them both, falling, falling always towards the Earth, as the Earth fell away.

The lines were gravity. In the fifth dimension, the mathematical description of gravity and electromagnetic phenomena are identical. Infra-red, and ultra-violet, weight and thought. They were all the same thing. The universe was a pun as well.

A web, thought Milena. The universe is a web, like a spider's.

'Hello! Hello!' cried a voice. There was no sound, but words had resonated like music out of the lines. Rising out of the lines, part of the lines, was another consciousness, a personality, imprinted on gravity, where thought and gravity are the same thing.

The Angel rolled towards her, across the lines, making them throb. The Angel laughed, and the laughter thrilled its way through the lines. The laughter felt like the strings of a cello being struck by a deaf child.

'Light waves, the Angel said. 'X-rays, radio waves. They're all here. So what do you think? Isn't it lovely?'

'You were human,' said Milena aloud.

'Well ta,' said the Angel. 'Better than being called a spider, I expect.'

Milena saw a face in memory. The Angel was showing her a memory. Milena saw the face of a cheerful man with red hair and a creased face, an ageing face. He was wrapping a blue tie around itself, one hundred years ago.

'Your name was Bob,' said Milena.

'Got it in one,' said the Angel. 'Bob the Angel. It's an honour and a privilege, Milena, an honour and a privilege. Ugly-looking geezer, wasn't I? Mind you the wife was no oil painting either.'

Another memory was spun out of gravity. Milena saw a cheerful, pink-faced woman with a double chin and clean false teeth.

'But you enjoy it,' said Milena, with relief. He enjoyed being an Angel.

'Ah wouldn't change it for the world. One thing though. I wish my kids could have known how their old man ended up.' He strummed the lines of gravity.

He had wanted to be a musician. He played in bars after work. He had had three children and had kept their photographs on his desk as the world collapsed. Milena saw the photographs as well. Three cheerful, blonde children, with pre-Rhodopsin faces the colour of a photographic flash.

Milena sensed something else. Behind all the memories, between the words, something else swam like a fish in dark water.

'You're a composite,' Milena realised. They had given Bob part of someone else's personality as well.

'That's my mate George. Strong silent type. He was a nuclear astrophysicist.' Bob the Angel imitated a popping sound.

He keeps talking to reassure me, thought Milena.

'That's right. You're sure this isn't all too much for you?'

Milena shook her head.

'Say hello, George. See? Silent. I do all the talking. George never says anything. So it's not too strange, having him all tangled up inside here with me. It's just that from time to time I start talking in parsecs. You ready to go on, Milena?'

She nodded. She felt his pleasure.

'Just look at this. I want you to see this.'

And the Angel flung himself out again, into the lines.

He passed along them, like a wave through rope, accelerating. He hurtled himself along the lines, a disturbance in them. Milena could feel that there was a traffic in Angels. They were all sighing up and

210

down the lines, speeding away towards the stars. Bob shot past them, through them. They tingled in greeting.

There was a traffic in light as well. Milena didn't recognise it at first. She simply became aware of something in the lines, sizzling its way out of the sun. They struck the earth and reeled shimmying away from its surface, scattered back out into space, like tiny wriggling arrows. Milena could feel those too. She felt them sputtering into space. Light was part of the lines.

And Bob was swinging from line to line, slipping, somersaulting, shaking himself with the silent laughter of Angels. He spun, as if on tiptoe, and suddenly, made of gravity, he gathered the lines of gravity tightly in towards himself. The lines snagged the light, pulling them inward as well.

'Open your eyes, love,' said the Angel.

Milena had not realised that her eyes had been closed. She opened them and saw, with human eyes, the Earth.

She saw the Earth through a gravitational lens. It was as if she looked at it through the bottom of a wine glass. Its blue seas and white clouds, its thin and flimsy cloak of air, were seen as a series of halos, rings of light.

And the Angel let all the lines go, and the universe seemed to boom.

Milena's mouth was hanging open, and she was laughing as if drunk. Her eyes she knew were sparkling, giddy with delight.

The Angel spoke. 'Not bad, I'd say.'

'Wonderful,' said Milena, shaking her head.

'That's the spirit. I love it out here, really, I do. Can you imagine if everyone down there could see this? There wouldn't be any meanness would there? None of this grubbing, get your number 92 and stay in line. None of this, "Here you" if they knock your coat off the hanger.'

The thought was the lines, and the lines were pulling the stars and the sun, the Earth and the Bulge, holding them together through the forces of attraction.

'We're concepting it,' said the Angel. 'By which I mean . . . oh here,' He passed her a kind of telepathic diagram. It showed Angels rising up from the Earth and travelling the vastness between the stars. There were caravans of Angels, like drops of water sliding on a cobweb. Those in front passed the sensation of where they were to those in the back, one to the other, all the way back to the Consensus. They were making a mental map of the lines.

The map was on a scale of one to one, and overlay reality. For all intents and purposes, it was reality. The fact that the lines had been conceived so far out meant anyone in the net could feel that far out. Milena was touching the stars. She felt them flicker, as if against her fingertips.

The map had an end. There was a boundary beyond which the Angels had not travelled, though the map was spreading at the speed of light, like a wobbling jelly.

'We just hit Sirius. Eight point seven years out. Sorry, George. Bloody parsecs. Stickler for parsecs is old George. So we got the Serious Dog and we got Alfie Century as well. Not too bad. Not too good either.'

The Angels travelled at the speed of light and so went back in time. They passed the map back more slowly, into their future. They twisted gravity to break the asteroids, and compress them, heating them, melting them, hauling out the metal into space where it twisted like putty, cooling to be sent back to Earth.

'So how long before we get back to the beginning? Tuh. Long enough. Well before the sun goes Nova. And what will we take with us? Just ourselves. Just gravity and time. I'll tell you something, Milena. I used to think I was made of meat. Then I got up here and I thought. Oh no, I'm not. I'm really rather rarefied. I'm made out of gravity and time. Gravity makes the meat, gravity makes the thought. Time makes events. We're strung out along gravity and time like lines of laundry. Back at the beginning, when we get there, the only event left is going to be us. Gravity in quantum vacuum, with just enough time for something to happen in. Then – whoosh. We start the universe. Now look at this!'

The Angel divided. He peeled himself away in sections, like an orange. There was even a zest, a spray of personality that freshened. He spread, breaking apart into smaller and smaller selves, going up, down, sideways, all of him shivering in the wires.

He was defining a cube. He laid himself like eggs at regular intervals, and each point cried aloud a number.

'Plus one! Plus one!'

'Minus two! Minus two!'

'Fifty five! Fifty five!'

Then Bob spoke, in three great voices along three axes of height and width and depth. He was a graph. 'I call them,' the three voices of graph said, 'my Cherubim.'

The Cherubim called like seagulls, eager to be heard, to be useful. They were limited creatures, reduced in size and information. A fragment of the whole, that retained the rough pattern of the whole. The area that was defined neatly bounded one half of the Earth which swelled into it, like a great dome. The poles, and two points of the equator touched the outer limits of the cube.

'There you go, Milena,' said the three voices.

The Cherubim still called. 'Plus seven. Plus seven. Four nineteen. Four nineteen.'

'All for you, Milena.'

'Minus one oh two two! Minus one oh two two!'

'That's your stage.'

Milena looked at the Earth, turning slowing through the area that she could now control. Oh! she thought. The thought was too wistful and dim to be dismay. It saw the beauty, it saw the innocence below, it saw the opportunity. The thought was like regret.

'It's called a Comedy,' said the graph. 'Will it be funny?'

'Not funny,' Milena said. 'Just happy. Not the same thing.'

Milena paused. Milena hung back.

She looked at the blue world with human eyes. She felt it through the strings, its surface crumpled, like some old woman's face.

'It's too big,' she said, scowling.

'What you mean, love?'

'It's . . . sinful.'

There was space, empty and pure, and she was to fill it, with a show. Is there a flower called Hubris?

My name is Milena Shibush. It is a Lebanese name, but my family were from Eastern Europe. My father died. My mother died. They were killed by the virus.

The only virus is us.

The Cherubim fell silent. The three axes spoke together. 'It isn't just you, you know, Milena. It's all of us. The Consensus. The Consensus is all of us. It wants this. It's the one that's doing it really.'

The stars and the black spaces between them seemed to say that it would be a violation. To make an image the size of heaven, for half of Earth to see.

'Suppose God . . .' she began to whisper and found she had no conclusion.

'That's a great, big, lonely word,' said Bob the Angel. 'Don't know. He speaks too big. Too many connections. How could you speak to all the stars at once?'

'I'm afraid,' said Milena.

All the stars at once, how could all the stars be dwarfed? Only Earth, little Earth, could be humbled. We humble what is about us. We humble ourselves.

'There's no time like the present, love. You've only ever got the present. You can't do it in the past, or go dashing off into the future and hide there. Whenever you did it, it would have to be Now.'

'Has everybody been told?' Milena asked him. 'Do people know this is going to happen?'

'Of course they have, everybody's ready. Everybody wants to see it. This is an event, girl, a real event. They're all looking forward to it.'

'I don't want them to be afraid of it.'

'Their jaws will hit their feet with wonder. And they'll say, look at what we can do. All of us together. But they won't be afraid.'

'Bob. Could you break off for a minute?'

The Angel seemed to darken. 'Sure, love, sure.'

The link in her head seemed to close. She had only one vision, now, of the inside of *Christian Soldier*, and the garden growing out of his walls. She blinked at it. She had expected the Bulge to look small in comparison with the universe. Instead it seemed vast, as if the walls of the Bulge were distant nebulae. Mike Stone was the size of Orion. His hands were clasped behind his back and he rocked nervously on his heels.

'Is something wrong, Milena?' he asked.

'No,' she gave her head a shake. 'No, just nerves. It's like a dream.'

'Maybe this will help,' he said.

From behind his back, Mike Stone passed her the rose that Rolfa had given to her. It was the rose from Chao Li Gardens. It even bobbed in her hand. 'I just saw it growing on the wall,' he said. 'Maybe you need it for reference.'

'No,' said Milena, grimly. 'No, I don't need a reference for this.'

There it was, smelling of autumn, the tips of its petals brown with chill, a pale rose marbled with red, an imperfect rose. Milena blinked, and suddenly there were even dew drops on it. We'll call them dew drops.

'Milena?' asked Mike Stone in wonder.

Why, she thought, oh why do I have the rose, Rolfa, and not you? There was an ache in her throat from grief. I have the book and the rose and the music, but I don't have you.

You want to cover the world, Consensus? You want all the stars to see you in your greatness, do you? Well then let them see this, let them see this rose that you killed. You wanted her music, but you wanted it without her. So I will blast you with it, Consensus. Take it. Choke. Thorns scratch your throat.

'OK. Bob, OK,' she said. 'OK. OK.'

The Angel came towards her in wonder. 'Milena?' he asked. 'What's all this?'

She tried to close her mind against him. 'Do you want it or not?'

'Steady on. It's a cold rose, you know. It won't burn, even if you want it to.'

'There are people waiting. They want a show.'

'All right,' said the Angel, soothing. 'But just one promise. We talk later, OK?'

'Yes, yes, come on.' Milena tried to pretend to him that her concentration was something that had to be seized and coralled like a wild horse.

'Countdown,' he said and ripped himself apart, and the Cherubim awoke again in a chorus and the eye in her head opened, and there was the harp, the billions of crisscross strings.

'Now,' she said.

And all the Cherubs pulled, like a net, catching the arrows from the sun and moon. The Cherubim were like crystals. They broke the light apart and reformed it, clutching it to themselves, pierced by the arrows, as if through the breast, dying for love.

Cherubim murdered, love dead. Dead love returned fourfold. Feel the blast. Consensus, this one is for you. Here it comes. Image in her mind, the feel of smooth green stem, brown thorns, slight scent, the chill, the odour of roses and birdshit in pondwater, and the geese overhead, Rolfa's fur touching her just lightly on the arm, and the rose.

The memory caught the light, and was held by what it caught. The lens was gravity and gravity was thought and thought was the memory. Light was filtered through memory.

Her eyes were shut again. She opened them, and looked out through the window of the Bulge, and the window blinked, and when it cleared, there was an explosion of pink light that filled the window, pink light wobbling like a jelly, as if to fill the universe. Pink light falling in on itself, tumbling back into form, into focus.

Milena gave a kind of strangled shout. *Rosa mundi*. Rose of the World. There, over the Earth, filling heaven, and it was her rose. Do you see it, Rolfa? Do you know what it is, do you know what it means? A rose of light the size of half the world. The rose of memory was also the rose of anger.

It is rising up over mountains like some new flowering sun. In other places below, at midday, it is misty, high up in blue sky, pale like a daylight moon, pink-white, its shadows the same blue as the sky around it. It will be a pink glow behind monsoons in the south, where I can see them sweeping in arcs over the coastline. And in the east, it will be setting like the sun, streaks of cloud across its face, which it will pinken. In some places, the sun will shine through it, as if the sun wore a collar. Or a crown. Half the world will look up and see it and wonder at the way it shines, and it is shining out of my head, out of memory.

The Earth that is humbled is yours, Consensus.

'It's big, Milena,' said Mike Stone.

Milena smiled a crooked grin. 'That is the general idea, Mike.'

'Roses generally aren't big,' said Mike Stone.

'No,' murmured Milena, almost as silently as the Angel. The rose was huge and angry, and the curling-back petals looked like blubbery lips.

It's a monster, she thought, like the Crabs.

It wasn't supposed to be a rose of arrogance, hubris, or anger, it's supposed to be a rose of love, and a rose of love is small, small enough to be held in someone's hand. This was supposed to be a gift.

And then she thought: a gift to twenty-two billion people, both the adults and the children. A rose for each of them?

A rose for each of them.

'Now!' she whispered.

The rose dissolved. It broke apart scattering itself like the Cherubim. It fell like rain, as if a continent had crumbled into roses.

She who had learned to make the viruses still and who had read Plato at six, who could remember every detail of one hundred and forty-two productions, she could conceive of twenty-two billion roses. She held them in her mind. She held them in space as they fell, the numbers of the Cherubim ticking past like floors in an elevator.

Milena directed roses to the continents where there were people. To London, to Paris, to western China to Bordeaux, to the Andes mountains. She directed them into the shadow, out of the cube, where they melted away, like snowflakes. She could still imagine them falling, in her mind. These, she told the people below, are for you. She began to hear music in her head, music from the Comedy, from the end that was not funny but happy, great rolls and peals of music, drums and horns and cellos. Each note was familiar.

The light below was wrenched into sound. The great chorus filled the shallow sky of Earth. The tiny roses descended, small enough to be taken by hand, though the hands that tried to grasp the roses of light would pass through them. The roses fell out of clouds, they fell out of the sun, they passed through the roofs of synagogues and temples, ghost roses as immaterial as the love from which they were made.

The vision possessed her. The vision held her. Milena sat rapt and staring. The music hammered and roared its way to a conclusion, and the chorus sang.

The love that moves the sun and all the other stars.

She held all the roses still for a moment. They hovered wherever they were, in the core of mountains, in prisons, in the branches of trees, or just out of reach, in the air. Then she wiped them away.

'Twenty two billion!' she cried. She spun the seat around. 'That's more than the souls of the Consensus!' The extra flowers had been for the UnRead. They had been for the children.

The Cherubim were howling with delight. They had been of use. *Christian Soldier* crowded round her, hungry for a direction, willing to turn the whole of its being over to the growing of roses, willing to become a garden of flowers, if that was what Milena wanted. The component parts of the Angel rolled across the wires like the heads of dandelions and met and then exploded in a shower of gravity, all the lines singing in glee. Somewhere, deep beneath the waves of Milena's consciousness, something dark and monstrous heaved like a whale. The Consensus. Even its pleasure was like an iron weight.

But here in the world in which Milena lived, everything was dark and still. Beneath her, in the hold of the Bulge, racks of jelly wobbled like the map Angels were making of the universe. Spiralling through the jelly in smoky strands were cultures of viruses. Quarantined in space, away from dust and contamination, the codes of behaviour and memory grew out of the flesh of the Bulge.

Milena had been able to find a platform for the Comedy in a garden of viruses. Mike Stone tended it.

The rose of memory became the rose of confusion. It grew everywhere. The Bulge seemed to go mad, driven by desire. By breakfast the next day, *rosa mundi* covered the walls in identical copies of itself. There was a carpet of them on the floor and ceiling. They floated in a vase made of bone that the Christian fundamentalist spaceship had grown out of itself.

Opposite Milena, Mike Stone sat dawdling over his food. His face was suffused with love. Love made him look goofy.

'Do you like *Moby Dick*?' he asked.

It was early in their artificial day, and Milena had to pause to orientate herself to the question and to find an answer. 'No,' she replied.

'I found the detailed descriptions of whaling techniques very interesting,' he said. 'From an engineering point of view.'

'Do you think if I asked Chris to grow me a white whale, he might stop growing roses?'

'I think it might overtax his capacity,' Mike Stone said, his eyebrows knitted together. Was it possible that he was taking her seriously?

A long explanation of protein ceilings followed. The Bulge was fed with amino acids from supply vessels and was fuelled by sunlight. Milena ate in silence and let Mike's words wash over her. Some of it was new to her, outside her viruses, and she found that, in a hazy, early-morning kind of way, it interested her. She and Mike Stone had a similar appetite for details.

Mike Stone was a trained virologist. He told *Christian Soldier* which viruses were needed; he controlled and directed the mutations of its DNA. He directed it in orbit, he told it when to sleep. He could feel it shift and sigh with dreams that were half his. He provided it with a self.

'We do everything together,' Mike Stone looked tender and embarrassed. 'He even worships with me every Sunday. He knows that he doesn't have a soul, but he prays for mine. He feels that my soul is his soul. He wants to go with me when I die.'

'Yuck,' said Milena, over her scrambled eggs. It was bad enough having to suck them through a straw.

'He wants to go with you, too, when you die, Milena,' said Mike Stone. His face went even more solemn and sincere. 'I want to go with you when you die, Milena.'

Oh ficken hell, thought Milena, succinctly.

'I'd be your Christian Soldier, too, Milena.'

Ficken again.

'I know you're not a Postmillenarian Baptist and are therefore damned, but I pray for your soul, Milena, for the good that I know is in you.'

Milena paused for thought, and pressed shut her pouch of cooling egg. 'I've got to go use the head,' she said, and escaped. She floated upwards to the john.

Inside the door, there was a bouquet of confusion, more roses, taped with a note. 'For Milena who makes the flowers,' it said.

Milena fastened her boot clamps, and her shoulder straps to keep her in place. Finally and most importantly she tightened the seat belt. The toilet worked like a vacuum cleaner and it was absolutely necessary to maintain an airtight seal. Milena sat thinking: how long can I hide in here? How else can I avoid that man?

Maybe I could pretend to be sick, she thought. Then she had an image of a worried Mike Stone, bringing her collapsible bags of tea. I can shower after this, that will take a half hour. Then maybe I can pretend I'm working. But after that? I'm trapped in here with him.

After some considerable time, Milena emerged from the toilet. Just outside the door a snapping turtle floated in the air. It hissed, its beak opening wide, its eyes glaring. The air was full of floating snapping turtles and two large brown rabbits from Mike Stone's childhood.

Mike Stone reached up and caught hold of the turtle from behind. 'I forgot to put on his little sticky boots,' he said, apologetically. He stood in the posture of weightlessness, looking at Milena with anticipation.

'I'd like to show you a picture of my mother,' he said, still holding the turtle.

'Can't wait,' said Milena.

There was still a slight smile on his face, as if he were amused. Was he pleased? Can't he hear the way I'm talking to him?

'I like to think that you and my mother are a lot alike,' he said.

Suddenly hanging in the air was a hologram of Mike Stone's mother. Milena had the unfocused back view. The face turned around. Mike

218

Stone's mother looked exactly like Mike Stone, except for a thick, pulled-back clot of white hair. A rabbit wobbled up to it and sniffed, hoping perhaps it was a head of lettuce. Mike Stone smiled, and caught the rabbit by its belly.

'She was a very strong woman, too. I like strong women.'

'I'll start lifting weights,' said Milena.

'Would you?' he asked, looking over his shoulder, pleased. 'For me?' Smiling he put the rabbit back in its cage. 'Mother lifted weights,' he said. 'She could bench-press one hundred and twenty kilos.'

'Golly,' said Milena.

'She said Amen after each set. She said she pumped for Jesus.' He leaned over and peered into the rabbit's cage. 'That picture was taken just before she died. She couldn't lift any more weights by then, Milena. Her hair went white. You know how in the old days, people's hair used to go white? Well, Mama said it was a sign from heaven. She said that soon, people would be able to get old again. That God didn't want us to die so young. He wanted us all to have time to get to know Him before we were called. I tell you, we had a special service for her, all around her deathbed. The whole family was singing.'

In a voice of uncertain power, he began to sing himself. 'Yes Jesus loves me. Yes, Jesus loves me. Yes Jesus loves me. The Bible tells me so.'

He gave up pushing lettuce through the mesh of the cage, for the rabbits to nibble. 'I've been very lonely since she died.' He stood waiting, as if for Milena to help him.

'I'm sure you must have been, Mike,' said Milena.

The picture in the air between them faded.

'Will you marry me?' he asked.

'No,' replied Milena.

'Oh,' said Mike Stone, 'Well. That's just the first time.' He turned back to his rabbits.

This is getting serious, thought Milena. Honesty, Milena, if you've learned anything, it's the need to be clear and honest. 'Mike. The answer is going to be no, no matter how often you ask. So please, please don't ask again.'

'I'm very faithful, Milena,' he said, to the rabbits.

'I don't want you to be faithful.' She gathered breath and strength. 'I want you to be silent.'

'Right-o-rooty,' he said. 'I'll be silent.' Then he looked up, and smiled, and the smile said: but I'll always be here.

'This,' chuckled one of the Pears, 'is insane.' He looked delighted. Milena remembering could not now think of his name. He was dead now. She had not known that he was a friend.

219

'It would work,' Milena told him, quietly.

Charles Sheer was sitting on his hands, his legs crossed, and he was bouncing quietly up and down.

The Minister's office had been repainted. It was mushroom-coloured now, with stripes of subtly contrasting browns and greys running round the walls. The screens were gone. So was the Zookeeper. In his place was the sleek young man, fatter now, in even more wildly printed trousers and shirt. Milton. Milton the Minister. He had gone plump and florid with success, and anxious to show he had something to contribute. The Milena who was living looked at his purple face with its swollen neck and young smile and thought: he's not going to live long.

'Buh!' said Charles Sheer in a sudden plosive burst. The others turned. 'Buh-buh.'

The sound was appalling. There was something about it that made Milena physically queasy.

'Charles?' asked Moira Almasy. 'Are you all right?'

He looked at her with outraged dignity, terror and sickness in his eyes, and anger.

'Nuh! Nuh!' He was trying to say no.

They all went quiet and still. Milena thought: stammering, stammering again. It was over a year since the Princess had started to stammer. It seemed now as if almost everyone did.

Would you believe me, Charles, thought Milena, if I said I was sorry?

'To say anything,' Milena told her enemy. 'You'll have to sing.'

He looked at her with hatred.

'I'm sorry, but other people have caught this, and it's the only way they can talk.' People sang in the streets.

Charles Sheer writhed in place. He hated this. He knew it was true. From now on, he would have to sing to speak. He looked at Milena, and anger fuelled him. All right, his eyes and the creases around them seemed to say. All right. I will do it. You may make me look like a fool. You will not stop me saying anything.

The music and the words had to flow as one. The selection of the melody would always reveal more than words alone would. That was why singing was embarrassing. It was impossible to lie.

Charles Sheer began to sing, slowly.

'I want to make sure that I've got this right,' he sang. 'And that it is the case . . .'

The melody was unsettling, and slightly childish at the same time. It seemed to stalk something through a wood. Milena's viruses scrambled to identify it. It took them some time, a matter of seconds. The song was buried deep in history.

Charles Sheer was singing 'The Teddy Bears' Pic..c'. Without effort, the words took roost on the tune, as if humankind had always been meant to sing instead of speak.

That you intend to fill the sky
With holograms from space?
You've suggested this and outlined the cost
And the other productions that might be lost
But you haven't said why we should fill the sky
With Dan-te!'

The delighted little man chuckled again and clapped his hands. He was silenced by a glare from Moira Almasy. 'I think,' said Moira, 'that given the circumstances we should confine the discussion to the matter at hand. Milena?'

Milena felt herself placed at a disadvantage. She was very slightly flustered. 'I . . . I didn't go into the aesthetics in my proposal. The costings were complicated enough, and frankly, they seemed to me to be the main issue. Obviously, the Consensus has some interest in a performance of the opera. The Consensus orchestrated it. But the Comedy lasts over fifty hours. Any performance at all would be very expensive and difficult. I'm proposing that the Comedy be Britain's contribution to the Revolution Centennial. Staged as I suggest, it would become a public event, like fireworks, if you like. We would be saying in effect, here is a great new opera – there hasn't been one in some time – and here is the great new technology to go with it. It would become a tribute to the Revolution itself.'

Moira Almasy was considering something. 'It would do those things, I think, but I worry, for example, about the sick.' She did not glance at Charles Sheer. 'I worry about all the people who won't be able to get away from this, but who might want to very much. Imagine you're ill with a virus. Imagine that you're dying. All you want is quiet, peace. You don't want one hundred nights of an opera to take over the sky.'

'Where else could we stage it?' asked Milena, in a smaller voice. She had to admit, imagining it, that Almasy had a point.

'Down here. You can hologram a whole sky into a tiny room and it will look real.'

'I don't want it to look real. I want it to be real.' Milena knew she was on her weakest ground here. 'At New Year, the streets are full of parades and singing. People are ill then and nobody minds.'

'New Year doesn't last for fifty hours,' said Moira. 'Do we have to stage all of it?'

'The Comedy is not just a string of arias. Every single note refers to something else in the opera. It is a fifty-hour-long, unified piece of music. If it's cut it will make less sense.'

221

'I know!' exclaimed Milton the Minister, suddenly sitting up. 'I know what we could call it!'

'You want to change the title of *The Divine Comedy*?' Moira Almasy was from Europe and still had a capacity to be horrified by British provinciality.

'There's never been anything like this before, right?' said Milton. He chirps, thought Milena. It's very annoying. Milton's eyes gleamed, his teeth gleamed. 'We need something that's never been thought of before, something mint new. How about . . .' He paused for effect, his eyes glittering. '*A Space Opera*?'

There was an embarrassed silence.

'No one's thought of it before!' he explained.

'I wonder how the Italians would like it?' said Moira Almasy.

'Or, I know!' said Milton struck with fresh inspiration. 'We could call it *The Restoration Comedy*!'

Charles Sheer was making nasty snorting noises on his pillow. He was trying to laugh, but the virus wouldn't let him.

'I mean, why does it have to be Dante? Why can't it be something British? If we're paying for it? I know! We could do *Paradise Lost*!' exclaimed Milton.

This idiot is going to cost me the Comedy.

'Certainly,' said Milena. 'If you've got Milton set to music, Milton.'

'I have,' said Milton. 'It's by Haydn and is called *The Creation*.' Milton looked pleased. 'Haydn changed the title too,' he added. He looked so pleased.

'It would at least be shorter,' sang Charles Sheer, gleefully. The melody was from *The Creation*.

Milena could begin to feel it slip away. The new Minister grinned like a puppy dog, happy to have been part of things.

Moira Almasy spoke, looking pained. 'We . . . we seem to be straying from the original point.' Her brows were knitted, fighting back the bouquet of confusion scattered by Milton. 'We know the Consensus is interested in this particular work. Ms Shibush seems to have an unusual idea for presenting it. It is new, and it has a strong international element. If we make it our Centennial contribution, we might be able to ask other theatrical Estates to sponsor it with us. Even those in Europe.'

'There's a German version of *The Creation*,' offered Milton.

'Yes, Minister,' said Moira Almasy, who evidently ran things instead of Milton. 'We can present both ideas to the Consensus.'

Milton sat back, making a generous gesture with his hands. 'I just thought I'd throw a little something into the pot.'

The delighted little man whose name Milena could not remember spoke again. He had greasy hair and a tracery of purple veins on his

222

purple cheeks. He still smiled, but his voice was solemn. 'It's never in anyone's interest to innovate,' he said, and peered at Milena. 'Least of all the innovator. People always think its just a way of advancing someone else's career. Or they worry that they'll be blamed if it fails. We don't live as long as we used to, Comrades. Perhaps we should consider ourselves lucky that in our short lives we have a chance to help instead of hinder something as insane but as essentially workable as this. And that,' and he peered at Milena again, 'we are lucky enough to have someone who is willing to pay the cost.'

What cost? wondered Milena the director.

There was silence, and in the silence, things swung Milena's way. The Pears were all looking at Milena as if she were Frankenstein's monster and they were deciding whether or not to create her.

Moira Almasy spoke. 'Milena has now produced roughly one hundred and fifty outside projects. She has no Mainstage experience, but this will not be on a stage. She is one of the few directors we have with experience of Reformation technology. But. There is no guarantee that Reformation will work on this scale. So there will have to be a test. I'd like that to be made part of the proposal. That will mean, Milena, that you will have to go into space.'

The word was like a cold wind.

'The Centennial is only two years away. So there is not much time. You would have to be ready to go up this autumn. Is that all right with you, Milena?'

In the silence, Milena could only nod yes.

'You would have to be made Terminal. And you would probably have to be Read, finally.' Moira's eyes were firmly held on Milena's. Yes, we all knew, Milena. The Consensus was saving you for something.

'What a thing it is,' said Moira bleakly, 'to have a friend in the Consensus.' She was saying it out of pity.

'Speaking of friends,' sang Charles Sheer. The words now fell on the aria 'Nessun dorma' from *Turandot*. 'Nessun Dorma' means 'No one's sleeping'. It was a reference to the effect of staging the opera at night.

'Speaking of friends
Is that mad person,
Ms Thrawn McCartney,
part of this project,
part of this mad endeavour?'
'No,' said Milena, tunelessly.

chapter twelve

THE WILD HUMOURS (WHAT YEAR IS THIS?)

Milena was carrying parcels. She opened the door to her room, and on her bed, in the last of the daylight, sat Thrawn McCartney.

'Get in here and sit down,' said Thrawn.

Oh, that face. The devouring eyes, enraptured now that what Thrawn had wanted to happen had happened. The teeth were bared as if to rend flesh. The face could have been beautiful, if it had ever stopped eating itself. Milena the director felt the feathery brush of fear.

'In a moment,' said Milena, and found herself actually trying to smile. 'Surely you'd be more comfortable on the chair?' Meaning, get off my bed. Milena went towards her sink, to put down the rice and the peppers and the lumps of chicken flesh. She started to fill her bucket.

'What do you think you're doing?' Thrawn demanded.

'Putting my groceries away,' said Milena dismally. What she hated most was the impossibility of being direct as soon as Thrawn was near. Everything was veiled, every gesture she made was masked as another, hiding one part of the truth with another. Milena was afraid, irritated beyond measure, weary and dishonest.

'OK, Milena,' sighed Thrawn. 'You seem to like these little games.'

I hate them. I only ever play them around you.

'You haven't been to see me.' Thrawn sounded hurt, vulnerable. 'I have all kinds of new diddly boobs. I know you think it's all right to neglect people. But you're neglecting your work, Milena. That's your job, isn't it. To find out what I'm doing and see if the Consensus can use it?'

'If you say so.' Milena had just finished rinsing the peppers. Who would have thought it was such a long, complicated process to put away three pieces of food? Her back to Thrawn, Milena began to wash the chicken. She was thinking: this is my room. I did not ask you here. Do not think I am going to give you the full benefit of my attention.

'One of them duplicates what you are seeing exactly, and overlays it. A wall say. You see a wall, and it looks the same as it always has done and then the stones grow faces.'

Why can't I tell her to go? Milena was wondering. Is it because I don't want to hurt her feelings? Is it fear? What am I afraid of? Why am I worried about telling her to go, when I have something so much bigger to tell her? Why is she conducting the conversation, when I am the one with something to say? Milena felt small, mean, weak and bursting with things that had been left unsaid.

'I was talking to Sheer today,' Thrawn went on. She had started to pace. What diversionary tactic now? What evasion now? Why is my life full of crazy people? 'Oh really?' said Milena, trying to sound if something neutral had been said. Unfortunately the chicken was now clean, and wrapped in moist cloths. Milena was wiping her hands. Am I going to suggest we go out? If I do, that means we won't talk properly because we are in public. If I stay here, the hop skip and jump, the games, will be worse. Only in hop, skip and jump, the rules don't keep changing underfoot.

'He mentioned that you might have a new project. He didn't seem too pleased with the idea.'

He wouldn't mention it to you, Thrawn, because he hates you and only dislikes me. He doesn't talk to you at all. Why, wondered Milena, is it so difficult to call someone a liar?

'In the meantime,' said Thrawn, her arrogance perfectly ludicrous, not so much in her words as in the way she swanned around the room, lip curled at its size, at the one cold bed. 'I need a new production.'

'Well,' said Milena, still with a horrible neutrality. 'I hear Toll Barrett needs a good technician. I think he's doing *The Last of the Mohicans*.'

One small trick she could always play back: take what Thrawn said at absolutely face value.

Thrawn snorted. 'I know about that shit. I'm not interested. What about *The Divine Comedy*?' A very small trick, when Thrawn could play it back for bigger stakes, and always seem to both of them to be more honest.

'This is my room. Will you please leave?' said Milena. It sounded feeble even to her.

'Not until we have a few things straight.'

And I always end up saying the right things in the wrong place. Jumping when I should skip.

'Milton tells me it's all going ahead. Why haven't I been told?'

Milena, dear heart, this is it. You have to ditch her. If you don't, she'll have you forever. Somehow she has a hold on you. The hold is a knot in her own head, a knot that uses her fearsome intelligence to tie itself tighter and tighter. And you are now bound up in it, and you have to get free. Basically, you are the stronger. You are the one playing with the full hand. Mother of God, mother of anything, don't let me falter.

'You're not part of it, Thrawn.' Direct enough. Blown by the performance, a nervousness from which psychopaths are exempt.

'You know you can't do anything on your own,' sighed Thrawn.

'I put on one hundred and forty-two productions,' said Milena.

'Hmmm,' said Thrawn looking away half-interested. 'But it was Crabs that was the success, wasn't it. Now you've got hold of someone else's music and someone else's poetry. I suppose you think you're on to a good thing. Do you really think you could cube like me?'

'Yes,' said Milena.

And part of her pre-rehearsed speech fell into place, as it had been delivered so often to the walls of her room. 'You're the one who can't do without me, Thrawn. Until I came along, no one would work with you. Can you imagine yourself directing? Getting along with forty or fifty people? Not futzing around, not bursting into tears, not playing any of what you call your little jokes? You also have a very poor visual imagination, Thrawn. I know it sounds strange, but you're only good at duplicating what is in front of you. When you reform from scratch, the images are muddy. Toll Barrett wouldn't have you, Thrawn. Why should I be any better than him?'

Thrawn still mused, as if unconcerned. 'So. You're going to take my ideas and execute them badly at public expense. Vast public expense. Don't you think that's dishonest?'

'No. I'm getting rid of someone who is deeply unreliable and who is likely to ruin a project at vast public expense.'

'Getting rid of me, are you?' Thrawn managed an absolutely convincing, confident chuckle. 'I wonder what Charles Sheer thinks about that?' Does she believe it herself, I wonder?

'I don't know what Sheer thinks. And neither do you.'

And Milena reminded herself. I am the stronger really. I no longer have to worry about hurting her. I am going to have to hurt her. I am going to have to break her.

'But I do know,' continued Milena. 'That Sheer wasn't much impressed by either out-theatre or the Crabs. So I am moving beyond those. Because this cannot be and will not be junk. And you can't produce anything else.'

That's right, Milena told herself. This is Rolfa's. It isn't mine. I don't count. You will not get your hands on it, Thrawn. You don't have your hands on it.

'Why are you doing this?' said Thrawn. She looked wounded. 'I work with you. I give you the best I can. I've only produced junk, because that's what's been called for.'

And Thrawn sang, as accurately as her voice could manage, the opening of *Inferno*. Sang it with feeling. She could imitate any feeling.

'That is beautiful music,' Thrawn said with conviction. 'I know what we've got with the Comedy. Don't cut me out as soon as we're finally going to do something good,' she said.

'You just said I could never do anything on my own.'

Thrawn gave her head an annoyed little shake, brushed that away. 'Who can do anything on their own in the theatre? You know what I'm like. I don't always do or say the right thing,' she shrugged, giggled.

You have, absolutely, to dominate. You are almost afraid not to, as if you will cease to exist if you do not.

'But all the shit to one side. You know, I know. You're the strong one really. I got the wild humours. I got to move sometimes. Yeah.' She did a kind of wiggle, and the hunger showed itself. She was under the illusion that it was somehow charming. 'But you can ride with that,' she chuckled, confiding. 'You've done it for so many productions.'

So many productions. Why not one more? Milena felt herself begin to weaken.

Outside her window, the electric lights were reflected, rippling and distorted on the moving river. Milena wished she had a lamp, a huge, brilliant electric lamp. She wanted light suddenly. She wanted to escape from that dark room, to some other, large and airy place where there was no Thrawn.

'Let's just say I'm tired of riding it,' said Milena. 'Let's just say you've worn me out. Let's not plead high intentions for the moment, Thrawn. A lot of this is selfish. I don't want to work with you again. I want to try someone else. Directors change technicians all the time. Even ones they like.'

'I'm not just a technician, am I?' Thrawn stood up, changed tack. She had a rueful smile, and she pressed her hands together prayer-like, pleased. 'Suppose we say I've put in my own bid for Dante. Say I'm ready to move up to directing. Let's not plead good intentions for the moment. I'm as ambitious as you are. You've only directed one major piece. Badly. I can put in my own bid for Rolfa Patel's opera. And I'll be more willing to shorten it. Cut it a bit. Like you did to *Falstaff*, so don't get all weepy and artistic on me. I'll be cheaper.'

For just a moment, Milena felt fear. It almost made sense. No. Hold on. I have the approval.

'The approval,' said Thrawn, as if reading her mind, 'has been given for the opera's good social effects. I could get those same effects in shorter time, less expense. Think about it. You try to cut me out, I cut you out.'

That is delusion, Milena repeated to herself. She has no lead. No one will work with her, they gave her to me as a last resort. What if it's worked too well? What if they've forgotten how she was before? Then they are fools, and will deserve what they get. And I will keep fighting to do it well.

'Go ahead,' said Milena. 'Try it. Say I have the same idea as Milena Shibush, only I'll do it cheaper and nastier. More giant crabs, more badly imagined dragons. Give me the largest theatrical production that anyone can remember as my first job.'

Those delicious rehearsed lines, lumbering into place like old-fashioned scenery. Then feeling overcame Milena. 'This is all so boring, Thrawn. You are all so boring. Why do I have to jump through these hoops, just for you.'

'Because,' said Thrawn, in a little-girl voice acrid with sarcasm. 'You owe me something.'

'I don't owe you anything.'

'What about your first success?'

Let me out. Let me breathe.

'Poor little Milena,' chuckled Thrawn, and shook her head. 'Always afraid.'

She came close. Milena could smell her breath, feel her breasts against her.

'I warned you,' said Thrawn. 'I told you that you would hate me.'

Milena could feel the nipples through the shirt. Thrawn's nose brushed against her forehead, against her hair. Not this again, I am very tired of this too. Milena pushed her back, pushed her away.

'I could tell them, Milena. I could, of course, tell them about us. About our little peccadilloes, eh? And maybe ask a few questions about you and Rolfa. I wonder if they'd like your opera as much if they knew it was a monument to Bad Grammar?'

Let her have it, thought Milena.

'I already told them that, Thrawn. They already know, and they don't seem to care. So go ahead and tell them, my girl, go ahead, and I will tell them how you took the light out of my eyes and threatened to burn out my retina. I will remind them that you somehow escaped your Reading. They will whip you in so fast that you will puke with giddiness. You try that, Thrawn, and I will use the Consensus to squash you flatter than a fly.' Thrawn was right. Milena hated her. Milena had not known that.

Thrawn looked shocked. Then she giggled. She tore the quilt off Milena's bed. She pushed it into the sink into the bowl of chicken-pink water.

'God damn it!' squawked Milena, and hauled it out, stained and wet.

Hatred gave Milena words. 'You are firmly ditched, Thrawn. Ditched. The production goes ahead, without you.'

'I'll just keep it up,' said Thrawn, with a false girlishness. She spun around. 'I'll just keep coming and coming until you give in.'

People commit murder in circumstances like this.

'You keep coming, Thrawn. You see what good it does you. You will get nothing out of me, Thrawn, nothing ever again. You're right. I do hate you.'

'Then,' she said, like some horrible sort of doll. 'I've won.'

'Yeah. Guess so,' said Milena. 'Happy birthday, or whatever.'

Thrawn launched herself onto Milena's bed. Her smile seemed to say, anything that is yours, I will take over.

I really do feel like killing you, Milena thought. It really would be the simplest thing to take the kitchen knife that is behind me and cut you up and wrap you in the god-damned quilt and dump you in the river. Is that what you mean by victory?

Milena felt queasy, sick. I want to get away, from all of this. She wanted to hide her face, she wanted to weep, but she couldn't, not in front of Thrawn. And she saw Thrawn's face, saw its flatness. Thrawn knew what Milena had been thinking, Milena saw her face watching and waiting – hoping? The face wants me to pull that knife. Then she will scream and call people and destroy me. Or she would let me kill her and destroy me. I need a lock. I am fed up people coming into my room. I need a lock, and I need to get this woman Read, get her blasted full of virus.

'We're both crazy,' said Thrawn. 'Wouldn't it be nice if we could go hand in hand to the Reading rooms? They could cure us both.' It was a plea. She really meant it. 'You see,' Thrawn said. 'If we don't, something terrible is going to happen. I don't know quite what. But I do know I can't let you do this to me. I know that I am pretty clever. I think I'd have to destroy you. I get obsessed by things, Milena. I wouldn't stop.'

It sounded pretty much like the truth. Milena found she was steeled for it. 'You don't scare me, Thrawn. Except for nuisance value, you have no hold over me. My career? I don't care that much about my career. This room? Not even this room. You don't know what I care about.'

And Milena turned and left. It was very simple. She just turned around and walked away from it. Thrawn would do something to the contents. Snip off all the sleeves from my shirts, pull up the herbs in my window-box, what else could she do? Set it on fire? Good, burn the building down, Thrawn. That will really get you on the production.

They are going to send me into outer space, Thrawn. I will be where you can do nothing to me. Space for three or four months. Can't touch me there, Thrawn. You can't touch me at all. And no one else will need you, and no one else will want you.

But there was a leadenness in Milena's feet and in her mind as she trudged down the stairs. Everything was weary. It was a leadenness that Milena remembering knew well. *I wonder if that's when it began? When I let it in? We destroyed each other Thrawn. No one is invulnerable. No one is immune.*

And Milena remembered singing in her own wan, flat little voice.

It's a dog of a song

The sky above was still fierce and blue and flawless, and from all around the horizon, there came a murmuring of song. The streets and yards were empty; it was high, hot noon and everyone was sleeping in the shade. It had been a beautiful summer. No rain for weeks. Already the air was beginning to smell of the urine of animals.

Ambling gently along

There was a stall, its battered, turquoise shutters closed. Underneath it, out of the sun, a family squatted. The mother with a straw hat and her hair in pigtails smoked a pipe. She rocked on her haunches, singing aimlessly a dawdle of song. The children were naked under blankets, and dirty. *The old London,* thought Milena the director. *It's going.*

Then she looked up and saw the sign: a man falling on his face.

The Spread-Eagle, thought the Milena who remembered. *Is this before or after I left the Shell? It was about then that I found the Spread again.*

The pub was dark inside, and empty too, empty at lunchtime. It was too hot to swarm together in airless pubs. The floor was bare of nutshells, though the tables were still ring-stained. In the corner, someone was sitting. Milena couldn't quite see her, because of the shadows, because of the dirt. Then the face looked up, pale and lumpy and forlorn.

'Lucy,' Milena the director said. 'Hello. Remember me?'

Lucy was wearing the same coat as the last time, but it was an uneven black and grey now. The old woman looked up. 'What?' she croaked. She was crying. Her cheeks were smeared with the tears of the very old, tears that seem to have melted into the face, as if the eyes themselves had melted.

Oh no, thought Milena. *The face was devastated.*

'Can I buy you a drink, love?' Milena asked. *Now she had money. Now she could offer.*

Lucy's face contorted and she lunged forward. 'Puke!' she exclaimed. She looked for a moment like an angry lizard. Then the old face collapsed again. 'I'm hungry!' she wailed, and swept a mug off the table.

'I'll get you some food,' said Milena.

She went to the bar. The man behind it was tall, and burly with it.

His unfriendly eyes didn't blink as he looked at her, looked at her white, white clothes and new leather sandals, looked at her hair. It was a look that Milena had seen a lot lately, wearing her new Tarty clothes.

'Puh! Pay!' he stammered. 'Muh! Muh!'

Another one, thought Milena. Someone else who's got the bug. That's three in two days. Marx and Lenin, is everyone going to get it?

'Mug,' she said, completing the word for him. She paid him twice what the broken mug was worth. As Milena walked away, she could feel his unblinking eyes, boring into her from behind. All these changes, Milena thought. They're making people angry.

She went back to Lucy. 'Come on, love,' Milena said, wrapping her scarf around her neck. 'Let's go out to a kaff.'

'There's no bloody food,' said Lucy. 'Just those little stalls with those filthy black pans full of grease. You blow your guts out, you eat one of them. Wog food. Anyway, none of them are open when it's too hot. They just fold the place up and sit under it.'

'Proper sit-down place, love.'

Lucy looked up in complete helplessness. 'Who are you?'

'You only met me once before,' said Milena.

Lucy leaned forward. 'Where am I?' she whispered.

Milena told her.

'And what year is it?'

Milena told her.

'Bloody hell,' said Lucy, and her voice trailed off into a whine, and she started to weep again. 'Bloody hell. Everything just goes on and on.' Her hands began to turn round and round on themselves.

'Oh, poor love,' said Milena, and sat down, and tried to take the hands, to make them still. Even in the heat the hands were ice cold, lumpy, and as light as biscuits.

'I thought you was my daughter. She'll be dead, now.'

Where are her friends? thought Milena. Why is she alone? 'Where's Old Tone?' she asked.

Lucy pulled her hands free. 'He can do what he likes,' she said, her mouth open with outrage, her head wobbling from side to side. 'Is he a friend of yours?'

'No. I thought he was a friend of yours.'

'I know better where to get my friends from,' said Lucy.

They've had a falling out. That's why she's upset.

'Come on, love, let's get something to eat.'

Lucy squinted at her. 'Who are you?' she demanded.

'I'm a friend of Rolfa's.'

The old face suddenly went gentle. 'Aw, Rolfa. She was a dear. Is she dead now?'

231

'No,' said Milena and thought: not exactly. 'Come on to the kaff, and I'll tell you all about her.'

'Oooh, yes. That will be lovely.' Suddenly Lucy was cheerful. She stood up in stages, in jerks, everything quaking as if it were her bones and not her flesh that was shivering. Milena had to grab her to stop her falling. The terrible orange hair was half muddy grey from the roots. Lucy found her balance, and pulled at the hair.

'How do I look?' she asked.

'Lovely,' said Milena.

'Liar.' Her entire face folded up into a kind of merry wrinkle. Lucy took Milena's arm. 'Goodbye, Henry,' she said to the barman. 'Or whoever you are. I'm off to lunch with my niece.' Lucy did not walk. Holding onto Milena's arm, Lucy hopped. She hopped like a sparrow, both feet together at once.

'Henry's such a nice boy,' Lucy said. 'I don't mind them wogs at all, if they've got manners.'

'He's not black,' said Milena. 'He's got dark skin because of Rhodopsin.'

'It doesn't matter what you call it, they never should have let them in. You never see a white face at all these days.'

They stepped out into the sun and both had to shield their faces. 'Oooh!' said Lucy, squinting as her eyes adjusted. Milena tried to explain: there was a virus that made people purple.

'What! We've all gone black?' Lucy yelped. She looked down at her own mushroom coloured wrists. They did look bruised now that it was mentioned. She tried to rub it off, the ingrained dirt.

'Not black. Purple. It's a chemical that means we can turn sunlight into sugar.'

Lucy sighed. 'I don't know.'

They began to walk again. Lucy hopped, looking perplexed. 'I'll tell you what it's like,' she said. 'It's like when I used to work at the post office. Do you know what a post office is?'

'No,' said Milena.

'Well, people used to send lovely bits of paper, to show how much they liked each other. They'd write on them, themselves. I used to take such trouble. I'd make the dots over the eyes look just like hearts. And all the o's, I'd make them big and round like oranges. Just to make it nice. Like when I was at school We all used to do it. It was all the rage, you know. All these people sending each other love on paper. Of course it wasn't always like that. Usually it was just bills and circulars.'

It took all of Milena's viruses, scrambling frantically, to understand what Lucy meant.

'But you always went to your front door thinking maybe there was something nice from the postman.'

Postman. That's where the word comes from. Postpeople. I thought it meant people who used to be people.

'A little card from my niece or my auntie . . .' Lucy started to cry again. 'They had hearts of gold. And now I can't even remember their names. It makes you feel so stupid. I thought you was my daughter. I was convinced of it. I was going to tell you off for not coming to see me. She must have been dead for seventy years at least. What year is it?'

Milena told her again. Nearly one hundred years after the Revolution.

'You see? I just can't keep up. I went for a walk last week. And do you know? I saw lights. Electric lights! When the bloody hell did they come back, I asked myself. And then I was never sure if they'd ever been gone. And then I didn't know if this was before or after the Blackout. You can tell me what year it is until your lips fall off. It still won't tell me where I am. Anyway, what was I talking about?'

'You were saying,' said Milena, who had learnt the art of listening. 'That it's like your job in the post office.'

'Exactly what I was going to say,' said Lucy. 'Just like in the post office. You'd be sorting the post, and getting really fed up. But they'd be playing this music. Up-pumpity-uppity-pump-uppity pumpity. Well, I figured it out. They played the happy music just to keep you going. You'd be utterly wrung out and miserable, but the music pulled you along. Your hands would keep throwing the letters into little boxes, all you'd want to do is sit down and have a good moan, but the music would drag you out. That's what it's all like now. I just want to stop, but the music keeps playing.'

They came to the kaff. Lucy sparrow-hopped into the dark and tiny space, bouncing, unsteady. The shutters were down against the sunlight and the door and windows were left open. There were candles on the tables and steam was rolling across the ceiling. Men and women looked up from mugs of fruit juice, their faces glistening.

'Phew,' said one of the women and covered her nose. Lucy smelled. But they saw Milena's new sandals and bag and knew what they meant and said nothing.

A waitress came up to the table. She was as sweaty as the walls. Beads of sweat glistened on her upper lip. She was eight or nine years old, working during the siesta break at school. 'What would you like?' she said, looking between Milena and the ancient woman.

'Oh, terribly high-toned,' said Lucy, with approval. I would like . . . lamb chops with mint jelly, and . . . brussels, lovely, properly cooked, none of this boiled for a week mush, must preserve the vitamin content . . . and . . . oh, just mash. With lots of butter and pepper and a bit of bran sprinkled on it for my bowels.'

The waitress, young, painfully thin, looked helpless and limp, like her jumpsuit.

'We'll have two Cow Toms,' said Milena. 'No squid in it, or anything like that. Do you have any meat?'

The waitress became exasperated. 'Meat. What do you think this is, the bloody Zoo?'

'Chicken?'

'Yeah, we got some of that.'

'Chicken. No squid. And no hot sauce, no fish sauce.'

Lucy nodded. 'Lovely grub. Lamb chops. And a nice cup of tea.'

The waitress nodded.

'Mind you, none of this gnat's piss. Proper, lovely, strong tea.'

'You've got the same viruses I have,' said Milena. 'She wants tea as in a novel from a hundred and fifty years ago.'

'Well does she?' said the waitress, angry.

'I am a Party member,' said Milena. She wasn't because she had not been Read but she was treated like one. 'I can crunch this place like a plate. You use a lot of tea and you let it steep. Now Slide, child. Slide, Slide, Slide.'

The waitress was frightened now, and went back to the kitchen.

I've got a lot of freedom, Milena thought. Now that I don't care if anyone likes me.

'Rolfa's written a show,' she said to Lucy. 'And I'm putting together a proposal, you know, sell it to some people.' Have you heard of Dante? Would it mean anything if I told you that you were going to play Beatrice?

'Oooh,' said Lucy, and looked pleased. No, thought Milena, Dante wouldn't mean anything to her.

'It's all music. It lasts weeks and weeks.'

'Rolfa always had a beautiful voice. Beautiful, I always said.'

'It's a bit different this show. It will use a lot of holograms.'

'Holograms,' said Lucy, unimpressed. 'Are people still interested in those? My father took me to see them when they first came out. Boring. They just sat there.'

'We're beaming them from outer space,' said Milena. 'And we don't want everyone in it to be actors.'

'No you don't,' agreed Lucy. 'Bloody little snots. We had one of them in here once with Rolfa. Or was it at the Spread? Terrible little thing she was, nose in the air, face that would sour milk. Came in with gloves and a parasol if you please.' Lucy giggled. 'She left it behind and we burned it.'

Milena changed the subject. 'Would you like to be in the show?'

'What me? Do one of my turns?' Lucy was so pleased that her cheeks bunched up into pink apples. 'I couldn't. Not any more. I've lost my figure.'

'You're lovely and slim,' said Milena, looking at the tiny wrists and lumpy blue veins.

'Good bone structure,' said Lucy. 'Put me under strong lights and nobody will know the difference. Er. Do they have good strong lights these days?'

'They've just come back,' said Milena.

'You wait long enough, you come back into fashion.' Lucy bit her lower lip. 'So I don't suppose it will be a problem, then, will it?' She wrinkled her nose, confidingly. 'My previous, I mean.'

'Your previous what?'

'Convictions,' said Lucy, and waited.

Her previous beliefs and principles? Milena did not understand.

'I don't know why everyone made such a fuss really, it was just a little business on the side with credit cards. Quite innocent. It was how you survived in those days, black economy, payment in cash or kind, turning a few tricks . . .'

'Lucy!' exclaimed Milena in wonder. 'You're a criminal!'

Lucy looked offended. 'I was a cabaret artiste. A bit of snide went with the job. I mean we was very Alternative. We used to do scathing political and social satire. Politicians, the Royal Family. I always played the Queen.' Lucy drew herself up, smoothed her waist with her hands. 'We had her in fishnet stockings and roller skates.' She suddenly launched herself back into the previous subject. 'I mean, these big companies was all insured. It was the voice-printing that got me. I thought I could imitate the voices, you see, on the phone.'

'Did you go to prison?'

'No!' said Lucy scornfully. 'They could see I wasn't the criminal type. Six months suspended and a nosy Probation Officer was all I got.'

The Cow Toms arrived. Translucent bags full of rice and broth and bits of chicken. The waitress opened the bags up. Her face was full of hate. She cracked eggs as if they were heads into the broth, stirred them in, and threw in herbs.

'Is that good enough for you?' the waitress asked.

'Porridge,' sighed Lucy. 'That's all anyone eats. Fried veg and porridge.' Then she remembered her manners. 'It's lovely,' she told the waitress. 'My niece takes such good care of me, she's such a good girl.' She patted Milena's hand. 'It's beautiful,' she assured Milena, her face twitching. 'Raw egg.'

'It will cook in the broth,' Milena told her.

'Thank you, darling,' Lucy said to the waitress, who was already walking away, her shoulders slightly hunched.

The natives are restless, thought Milena. She suddenly missed the beautiful calm that been the very stuff of London life only two summers before.

'I know you're not my niece,' confided Lucy. 'But you're so good to me. And I don't know who you are.'

'Neither do I,' said Milena. 'Let's eat it while it's hot, while we can, before it gets cold.'

The beautiful past, as glimmering and faraway as a star.

By winter, everything was covered in snow.

chapter thirteen

DOWN TO EARTH (MAGIC)

Mike Stone was in love, and so therefore was *Christian Soldier*. The vessel was by now a real garden. The walls were covered with moss and fern and cedar and bay and baby palm and holly, all improbably mixed. The floor had sprouted grass and ivy had entwined itself around the column that supported Milena's chair. Most wonderful of all, there were now birds. They rustled within the leaves, and sometimes sang, huge American robins and red-winged blackbirds and tiny English finches. There were other birds, too, that Milena did not know.

The birds of Czechoslovakia.

Milena was playing the first scene of the Comedy over and over in her mind. She didn't see the flowers. She was trying to find some way of making the first scene work.

The first trial scenes had already been broadcast. Fifteen minutes of Dante in the wood had been seen over half the Earth below, between clouds, over mountains. The Terminals below reported that the broadcast was a success. Reformation worked, even on an astronomical scale. But Milena did not like what she saw. She had thought that Dante's allegory would work best if the imagery was kept simple and clear and literal. She had loved imagining Dante's wood. She imagined dead branches, with moonlight glinting on the sinuous, shiny patches where bark had come away. She imagined the soft, thin green coating of lichen on the nodules of broken twigs. There were scuttlings in the darkness, and tiny frightened eyes.

All sides of each object had to be imagined. Milena found that she could do this. All sides swam fragmented in her mind, suddenly focusing on one area of space. She built up an image focus by focus. The swimming fragments reminded her of a cubist painting. Cubism for cubing, she thought. Picasso was simply painting what he saw.

The wood she created was beautiful but it was not evil. Even in darkness it was a garden. Dante's forest was supposed to be symbol for the corruption of the human soul. To Milena it seemed such a terrible thing to do to a beautiful forest.

And the symbolism was redundant. An audience of viruses would already know what the wood meant. Viruses would supply people with all the necessary references. They would whisper as Dante stumbled through the wood, halfway through his life. Remember, the viruses would say, remember Isaiah 38.10, 'In the midst of my days, I shall go to the gate of hell'. The viruses would remember the *Aeneid* and its forest scenes. They would know that the lake of the heart meant the ventricle in which fear was supposed to reside. Dante limped with sin, the left foot being appetite and will.

The whole problem was one of redundancy. Rolfa had known that. That's why she decided to leave all the narrative words unsung. Otherwise the chorus could only keep on telling us what we were already seeing.

The character of Dante was wrong too. Milena had cast one of the Babes, Peterpaul, to play him. He was thick-wristed, beefy, and stomped on firm male legs. Milena had thought he would be a kind of Everyman. But Dante was no Everyman. In all the drawings she had seen, Dante was fierce, with eyes and nose and chin like daggers, a politician in a murderous age. That was the right image. Peterpaul, she realised with reluctance, would have to go.

Milena let the recording play on, in her mind.

Here came the animals. They were symbols too. Milena's heart sank when she saw them. The lion, the leopard, the she-wolf and her heavy teats; they were wonderful beasts. Milena did not want them to mean human wickedness. A lion is not murderous, a she-wolf is not greedy. Milena stopped the recording, and tried to re-imagine them with human faces.

Unbidden by her conscious mind, each of the beasts grew the face of Thrawn McCartney. With a shiver in her heart, Milena's mind leapt out of the focus, out of the Comedy. She let Rolfa's music play on, softly. The music was the only part of the opera that worked.

Milena looked up. Mike Stone was standing over her, holding out his violin as if offering it to her. 'Would you like some music, Milena?' he asked.

'Why not?' said Milena. The Comedy, it seemed, was beyond help.

'I've taught Chris how to play Bruch's violin concerto. Would you like to hear that?'

Milena felt a smile creeping over her face again. She had to admit that Mike Stone had a certain kind of charm. 'You've taught a spaceship to play Bruch?'

'He takes the cello and drum parts. He grows strings and hums,' said Mike Stone, gangling with enthusiasm.

From just outside the focus, Milena heard the first sung words of the Comedy. Dante had met the spirit of Virgil and was singing, 'Have pity on me, whether you are ghost or definite man.'

Mike Stone sat down and tucked the violin under his chin.

Cilla was playing Virgil. Her high, pure, female voice answered, 'I am not a man, though I was born one.'

Oh dear, thought Milena. I keep crashing it to the ground. I need to find a different way to do this. She let the Comedy fall into silence.

Mike Stone played. He sawed and scraped his way through Bruch's only masterpiece. The bow kept skidding off the violin strings with an earnest squeal. Somehow it helped, like someone slipping on a banana in a production of Rossini. *Christian Soldier* sang all around them, deep and resonating, like a fat man in a bath.

It's a different world, thought Milena. Spaceships sing and there are Angels sliding between the stars and astronauts grow animals out of memory. The Comedy will have to be new as well.

Mike Stone's brow was furrowed with concentration. His giant legs were splayed apart; his elbows flailed. Milena found that she forgave him. Whatever there was to forgive, except awkwardness and a touch of insanity. Milena smiled on him.

Mike Stone finished, and looked up at Milena as a little boy would, eyes full of expectant trust.

'Clown,' she pronounced him.

The birds of the garden whooped and whistled. Outside, the sun was rising over the Earth, a sudden diamond-burst of light. *Christian Soldier* lowered a blue-tinged cornea over the window as a filter. A crescent of blue appeared along the rim of the Earth. The sun seemed to have been laid by the Earth. The sun was a round, white, cold blue egg nestling in mist.

Milena found that she wished she could stay there, with the Earth and the birds and the music. The stars looked like a fall of snow, suspended.

Then, down to Earth.

Stars seemed to be falling out of a slate-blue sky. It was snowing. Milena remembered walking along the Cut some time during the week of her return. Snow was filling in the tracks made by the stalls, hissing gently as it landed.

The stalls had been pulled to one side, and folded shut. Only the coffee vendor was still open. He stood in the light of the Cut's one street lamp, stomping his feet to keep warm, and shouting: 'Coffee! Coffee for health!'

Everything smelled of coffee. The snow on the ground smelled of coffee. It was splattered with it and stained. A man bustled past Milena, his fawn-coloured coat mottled with coffee. He wore a facemask that was soaked with it.

There was a curious, raucous wail from an upstairs window: the Baby Woman. Everyone knew about her. She and her infant had both become ill with a sudden fever. The baby died in the night, and the mother awoke in the morning with the mind of her child. She lay in bed all day in diapers and howled. Her husband was often seen about the Cut. His stare was hollow and uncomprehending.

The apothecary viruses had mutated. They collected complete mental patterns and transferred them. They were contagious. One personality could obliterate another. It had not been obvious at first. Even the summer before, Milena had heard of an ageing actor of the Zoo who had woken up convinced he was a young and handsome Animal. He had howled, sobbing, when he saw himself in a mirror. The sickness became more noticeable when people began to bark or meow. Someone had tried to fly, leaping off the Hungerford Bridge. The viruses transferred information between species. People thought they were birds, or cats.

The old concrete arcade along one side of the Cut had been demolished. A rhinocerous hump of Coral was growing out of it, amid the stalks of dead nettles. Milena saw a sheet of black resin. There were Bees huddled under it, kneeling as if in prayer. They had lifted up a paving stone and were looking at the earth underneath it, and jittering in place with the cold.

'Oyster trails,' one of them whispered, scooping sand and snow aside with his hands.

'Old cigarettes,' said a woman's voice.

'Cold earthworms!' they all suddenly yelped together and laughed.

One of them was wearing a sequined jacket, and other Bees licked his ears and murmured to his soft blonde hair. He was the King, the King from *Love's Labour's Lost*.

The Bees flinched as Milena approached. They ducked and almost but not quite looked at her out of the corners of their eyes.

'Hello, Billy,' said Milena, gently. 'Billy, remember me? I'm Milena. Constable Dull, an't shall please you?'

'Lo, Ma,' he said, smiling vaguely, not looking at her. The others clustered more closely about him.

The Bees protected themselves by staying in groups and focusing their attention all together on the same things. They protected themselves from life, too much life all at once. If a horse, a huge and muscled, sweating and snorting beast, passed the Bees and they were unprepared, they could faint. Milena had once seen that happen, a nest of Bees collapsing in unison. She had seen Bees kissing the cobbles where a pigeon had been crushed by the wheels of a cart.

'What's it like, Billy?' Milena asked him.

'It's in lines,' he said, still without looking at her. 'All in lines.' He looked up, as if at the stars, snowflakes on his eyelashes.

An empathy virus had mutated. It stimulated sympathetic imagination. Nurses, Health Visitors, Social Hygienists and, most particularly, actors – they had all bought the virus from apothecaries. The new 2B

240

strain created an almost unbearable oneness with anything that was alive – or had been alive. The Bees could Read the living. They could Read whatever reaction patterns that were in the remains of living things, in the soil, in the stone, in the air.

'And the lines,' said Milena. 'They touch the stars, don't they?' They go down into the Earth. They shiver when someone thinks.'

Billy turned to her, looked at her, and gave her a bleary smile. 'Are you Bee?' he asked.

'No,' said Milena. 'But I know about the lines.'

Gravity was thought. Gravity was life. Gravity twisted nothingness into a leaf that had been alive. The skeleton of the leaf still sang, wistfully, silently, of its life on the tree. It had been blown by gusts of wind until it sighed down from the tree to the earth. The earth sang of the leaves it once had been. It sang of peanut shells and orange peel, dog shit and leather shoes, old clothes and the sweat of the people who had worn them. The dead sang to the Bees, out of gravity.

'The food weeps,' said the King. 'Torn away. Burnt. Boiled.'

Much of the food in this new age had been cut from hybridomas. It was still alive when sold, still alive when cooked or eaten raw. The Bees would scream as people ate. They could not bear to wear most clothing, the strands of cotton or spider web or silkworm threads. Clothes sung to them. The sun sang to them, and they tried to sing back.

Live on Rhodopsin, they told people, when they could bear being near people, for the blasts of thought from living people were too harsh for them to bear alone. They could bear it only in groups, for a short time, before scampering off like timid monkeys.

It's stopped snowing, Milena realised. Everything went still and cold.

'Coffee!' cried the vendor. 'Coffee for health!' Steam from his boiler caught the light and hovered golden in the air.

'The coffee screams,' said the King. The apothecary viruses had been derived from herpes, and like herpes, they ruptured when bathed in coffee.

'And the viruses,' the King said in pity. 'The viruses break apart.' Most hateful of all to this new age, the Bees loved the viruses, too.

A woman staggered towards the coffee vendor with a jug to fill. She shook like a rickety old cart on a bumpy road, juddering with cold and caffeine overdose. Her eyes were evil. She glared at Milena. The hatred in the look stilled Milena's heart. It was like a beam that passed through her. It struck the Bees, and they folded up into a tight knot around each other.

'Billy?' Milena said. He didn't answer. She knelt down and lightly stroked his disordered hair. You were the most beautiful man, she

241

thought, and all the girls wanted to hold you and love you because you were beautiful but not aware of it. And you had a voice like honey and on stage you took command lightly, as if by right, and you made me believe that people could speak as Shakespeare wrote.

'Billy, you're cold,' she said. 'Where do you live?'

'The Graveyard,' he whispered.

Milena paused. That place again. 'Come on,' she said, 'Let's get you back inside.' She stood up, and all the Bees stood with her, as if pulled by wires. They shuffled behind her, up the Cut wearing shaggy, artificial furs or plastic boots.

While all of this was happening, Milena thought, I was sending down flowers from space. It's as if there are many Earths and I came back down to the wrong one.

'Those are Bees you're talking to!' shouted the woman who was buying coffee.

Milena held up a hand for the Bees to be still, and walked towards her.

As Milena approached both the woman and the coffee vendor slipped back behind the metal tureen. They think it's a magic charm that will protect them, thought Milena. She saw herself reflected in the orange light on its misty metal surface. She saw the future there. The future was metal once more. The future was machinery.

'I know one of them. He is a friend of mine,' Milena tried to explain. 'They're human too,' she said.

The woman shuddered, and pulled up her face mask. 'Used to be human, you mean. Look at them.' Her shaking hands struggled with gloves. The gloves were soaked in coffee, too. Steam rose up from her. 'They're deliberately spreading these diseases, don't you know that? Where have you been?'

'In orbit,' replied Milena, in innocence. 'I'm an astronaut.'

Without another word, the woman flung a cup of coffee across Milena's face. Like disoriented beetles, her scampering hands fought to seize her jug of coffee, give money to the vendor, and leave, all at the same time. She was evidently holding her breath. She turned and tried to run, taking long, low, sloping strides.

Milena stood appalled as the coffee chilled on her face. She felt like someone in a comedy, to whom absurd things happen. 'Why did she do that?' Milena asked. She looked down at her coat. It was ruined by coffee.

'Perhaps she thought you were sick,' said the vendor. He threw the coins the woman had given him into a resin tray full of coffee. Coins spread infection too.

'You're the ones who are sick!' said Milena and walked angrily back to the Bees. 'Come on,' she told them. 'Keep walking. They're frightened of you, too.' She led the Bees past the coffee vendor.

Milena turned left, past the fountain outside of Leake Street. Bolts of metal had been screwed into the mouth of the fountain, and its rows of drinking cups were gone. Up the ramp that led to Waterloo, people were scurrying, huddled in terror. They stepped over something, a bundle perhaps in the snow. The bundle moved. The bundle, she saw, was a man.

The man's chest was bare. His jacket had been wrenched round and his shirt torn as if he had been fighting to get out of his clothes. He was trying to crawl, but his legs wouldn't work, and his fingers and arms were stiff with cold, as useless as the flippers of a seal.

People had just stepped over him? What is happening to us all? Milena thought. He'll freeze to death. She walked towards him. The Bees followed, a single rippling mass under their sheeting.

'She'll bite,' warned the King.

She? The man had a full and virulently red beard. She? As Milena drew closer to him, he looked up at her, bared his teeth, and growled.

'Piper,' sighed the Bees. 'Good Piper. Good girl, Piper.' They seethed and settled around him.

On hearing the name, the man yipped. As they gathered around him, stroking his head, he began to whimper. He whimpered, and tried to wag a tail that wasn't there. Then he yelped, in an agony of joy. Over-excited, he could not contain his urine. It spread out under him, across the snow. He licked the hands of the people around him.

'Piper!' smiled the King. 'Good dog.'

The man barked.

'Shouldn't we get him a doctor?' Milena asked.

The King shook his head. 'There are people in the ash,' he said. He looked about him as if dazzled, as if surrounded by stars. 'The ash falls.'

'What?' Milena felt as if all the breath had been sucked out of her.

'They let them die,' he said. He was smiling, as if he had seen something beautiful.

All across the city, the bells rang calling for doctors. Piper, Piper, Piper, said the Bees, soothing. They stooped down and lifted up the dog man to carry him. His tears had frozen on his face. He was stiff as a board and his fingers were held rigidly at awkward angles.

Milena stepped foward to help, and then something stopped her. *Disease* an old voice seemed to whisper to her.

'Bugger that,' whispered Milena to herself, and took hold of his hand.

The procession moved into the shelter of Leake Street. The gates

243

of the Graveyard swung open as if by themselves. Milena trooped with the Bees into a darkness that smelled of people.

'Milena, Ma, Milena,' breathed the darkness. 'Piper, Piper, Piper.'

There were new cells in the palm of Milena's hand. They had been given to her when she was made Terminal. The cells were luminous and shone brightly when she told them to. She held up her hand: light blazed out of it, and the Graveyard was lit.

The dead costumes moved, inhabited now. There were kings and courtiers, gypsy dancers and Robin Hood's men. There were mantillas of black plastic lace, and ball gowns of cheap coloured nylon, all the artificial fabrics that the Bees, hearing ghosts, could bring themselves to wear.

The mass of Bees opened up to absorb the Dog Man, to hold him and to warm him. They looked up in unison at Milena and all cocked their heads to one side at once. There were enough of them here to share the burden of consciousness. They all smiled at once in pleasure. They all stepped forward at once, left foot first, towards Milena.

'Help,' they all said. A thousand voices said it at once. Milena could feel them all in her head, along the Terminal scar. 'Help. Ma.'

'How?' she asked.

'Tell them,' said the Bees.

'Tell them what?' Milena asked.

'Tell them about the lines,' said one thousand voices with the same intonation.

Milena paused, imagining what it would be like to be the bearer of news. To tell people that the Bees only felt what the Angels of the Consensus did.

'Yes,' she said. 'I will.'

'Keep well,' the Bees said, and lifted up their hands palms outward. They meant stay away from us. We need someone who is not a Bee, to speak.

'Flowers,' the Bees said, and smiled. 'Flowers of light.' They all made a gesture together, index finger and thumb clutching an invisible flower, and they all passed it back to her.

Milena had gone up unknown, and came back famous. To another Earth, and another self as well.

Milena hardly remembered walking on to the Zoo Cafe. Her mind was churning with the things she had seen. Milena, Milena, she thought, you've had a headful of opera for too long. She walked into the Cafe and it was hot, steaming, choking with the smell of coffee.

'Hello, Milena. Milena, hello,' said people she did not know, who shook her hand. Her luminous hand was still burning bright, and light in ripples shone up under their faces. Milena nodded to them politely, still distracted. She needed to talk to Cilla. Cilla was there somewhere waiting for her.

Milena stood tamely in line. A fat, sour-faced woman with puffy bags under her eyes was jetting hot water from the boiler over all the knives and forks. Milena watched the cutlery curl into unusual shapes. I've done all this, she thought, I have been through all this before. You can't boil life clean.

At the end of the line, a skinny man with a moustache waited and watched. His cheeks seemed to have fallen into holes in his face. He passed each person, without asking, a cup of coffee. 'I don't want it!' Milena said to him, sharply. She took a piece of cake and a glass of milk instead. She watched people wash their face and hands in coffee.

'Milena, love!' exclaimed Milton the Minister, walking towards her. Milena inwardly groaned. But Milton took her by the hand, and drew her to his table. This new Minister was more sociable than the old Zookeeper had been. He was also more impressed by fame. You would not have done this six months ago, thought Milena, not before I went up.

She greeted the people at the table, coolly, politely. Being slightly Snide was not always socially useful. Milena sensed the flatness of these people. They beamed back at her, pink faced and swollen, calling her by her first name, as if they had known her for some time. It was as if they owned her in some way. They were Vines, social climbers.

'Milton,' said Milena. 'There seem to be a lot of sick people no one cares about.'

'Well,' said Milton, neatly combining a cough with a chuckle. 'You know what they say about the new strain. 2B or not 2B, that is the question.' Milton grinned.

'Milton. They are letting sick people die.'

He adjusted his spectacles, the ones he didn't need to wear. 'Uh, well, the official line is that the Doctors are doing what they can for them, and when they die, they burn . . .' His hands made a motion. He was clearly trying to think of another joke. 'Burn what's left.'

'Oh that does set my mind at rest,' said Milena. 'What kills them? The viruses aren't fatal.'

'But they do need treatment,' said Milton, still grinning. Why is he smiling? wondered Milena.

Milton's girlfriend spoke. Her voice was harsh and raw. She had a pretty smile and cheeks that Milena was sure contained pouches like a squirrel's. 'What else can we do? We've got to stop it spreading!'

'We can take care of them,' said Milena, quietly.

'Hiya,' said a soothing voice behind Milena.

Milena turned, and there was Cilla, and Milena was grateful to see her.

'Come on, Cill, we've got to talk!'

'I've saved us a table, Milena,' said Cilla, still soothing.

'Bavarderons D. Man,' Milton's girlfriend called after them. Vampirespeech for 'talk to you later'. Along the terminus in her head, Milena could feel that Milton's girlfriend was relieved that Milena was leaving. Me too, infant, she thought.

'Isn't it awful?' said Cilla, as they walked back.

'I've just seen a man who's been taken over by a dog,' said Milena. 'He was freezing to death. And do you know? No one would help him. It took some Bees to carry him off. They saved him, no one else would.' She paused. 'One of them was Billy,' she said.

'This will all be new to you, won't it?' said Cilla, sympathetically taking her hand as they sat down at a table.

'Actually, it feels very old. It feels how I used to feel.'

'Do you remember when you used to boil things?' Cilla said. 'You melted all my knives and forks. I thought you were crazy.'

Without thinking, Cilla was reaching across and taking food from Milena's plate. A bad habit from Cilla's own days in the Child Garden. Milena watched her do it, and allowed herself to smile as Cilla pressed together crumbs.

'I remember,' said Cilla, 'when you used to boil the toilet seats. One night we all hid to catch you at it. You had a kettle in your hand, and there was steam coming out of the toilet bowl, and you said "Oh. I'm just making a cup of tea!".'

'And you said "Funny kind of teapot".'

Cilla and Milena were finally friends. It had taken a long time. Milena always found it took her a long time to make friends. She knew that Cilla respected her, and that she had earned that respect. Milena could still not resist praise. Bad habits from the Child Garden.

'Tell me about space,' said Cilla, firmly changing the subject.

There was a hush all around them. Both Cilla and Milena were aware of it. Milena was no longer a director of small out-theatre. She was Ma, who had flooded the world with flowers. She was the producer of the Comedy. Cilla was its star, its Virgil. The regulars of the Zoo Cafe were too proud and polite to stare. But the quietness was there, of respect, of animal hierarchy.

'Well. Space is beautiful,' said Milena. 'Earth is beautiful. The mountains looked like crumpled paper, but the more you focus on them, the more detail there is. And you can tell, you know, you can see how far down it is. This huge, far distance. And you're falling. You know you're always falling. There is a horizon, and you can see the boundary of the air. It is the most beautiful, blue thing.'

It was like giving Cilla a gift, to tell her this, and tell her this in public. Cilla had a childish delight in being an Animal. Milena more than forgave it. It was one of the reasons she liked her.

'And the hologramming,' said Cilla. 'Tell me about that. It was noon here. Low dark clouds. And then it started to rain flowers! And there was that beautiful music! All around us in the air.'

'There was an Angel. He was the lens. He called himself Bob, and he was from London.'

Milena steeled herself to deliver some news. 'He's the one who told me I should be married.'

Cilla stopped stealing Milena's cake. 'And?' she asked.

'I'm going to be,' said Milena, smiling into Cilla's eyes.

'Hallelujah!' said Cilla. 'Really? Oh Milena, that's a sunny Feb.' She leaned forward, and kissed Milena on the cheek. 'Who to?'

Milena began to smile in spite of herself. 'Mike Stone,' she said.

There had been attempts to make heroes of all the astronauts. There had been public hologrammatic displays. Mike Stone was well known, but he had not become a hero.

Cilla's smile began to fade. It almost went sour. 'Mike . . .' her voice trailed off. 'Ew!' she exclaimed in pity and horror. She held up a hand for silence. 'Don't do it, Milena,' she said, swallowing cake in a hurry. 'I know, it must have been beautiful up there alone with a man, any man, looking at the stars . . .'

Milena had been longing to see what Cilla's reaction would be. She knew it would amuse her. 'The zero-grav toilet was replete with allure as well,' Milena said, smiling.

'Can I speak frankly?' Cilla asked.

'Cill, I've never known you do anything else.'

'What you need is a tooch knave.' Tooch meant sexy. Knave meant wild boy and was pronounced 'kenabva'. Cilla leaned forward, and spoke in a low murmur that could not be heard by anyone else around them. The only thing that would be heard was the general message that a very serious, important heart-to-heart was being had in public.

'Now that you're back, take a look at the Zoo Beauties. Any of them, Milena, has got to be better than Mike Stone. He makes me feel sick. He looks like he's got a broom stuck up his arse all the way to the top of his neck. He can't talk. He just sits there like somebody's wound him up too tight.'

'All of this,' said Milena, 'is true.'

Cilla's expression became deeply pained. 'I know,' she said, and closed her eyes with pity. 'I know. Men have not been good to you. They have looked right through you . . .'

'Thank God for that,' said Milena.

'But don't throw yourself away on the first one who pays you any attention. Am I offending you?'

Cilla, dear heart, anyone else in the world would have smacked you in the choppers by now. Milena's face was split wide with a grin, and she felt like roaring with laughter. She shook her head to mean no.

'Then why are you smiling?' said Cilla wisely, sadly. 'I always know, Milena. You always mask your pain with a smile.'

Milena finally laughed out loud. She clasped Cilla's hand.

'I'm marrying him,' she said, 'because I have absolutely no intention of marrying anyone at all.'

Milena was learning how to be honest. Honestly deceitful? Or just too damn inflated to care?

She looked back at Cilla, smiling, tougher than she had been.

'I have no intention of marrying anybody, but the Consensus would like a nice story. So. It's going to get one. Marriage of the astronauts. Romance in the stars.'

'You're going to give away the best part of yourself,' said Cilla in the weak voice of truth.

'I gave that away a long time ago to someone else,' said Milena, also truthfully.

'Any hope?' Cilla asked. She really was, when reality bit, a friend. The reasons did not matter.

'No,' said Milena and shook her head. 'But it's nice to know that somebody knows. That you know.'

A long pause. 'It was Rolfa, wasn't it?' said Cilla.

Well what do you know? Milena nodded. Yup. Yes. Pretty good, Cilla. 'Do you mind?' Milena asked.

'Mind what? About you being sexually drawn to a member of the same sex, but a different species? Why would I mind that?' Cilla was not on the firmest of ground at this point. Her delivery wobbled. 'No. No. No, I don't mind. It puts a lot of things into perspective. But I must make plain that my interests do not lie along similar lines.' She coughed, and tried to take a sip of coffee and missed, hitting her teeth with the edge of the cup.

Cilla had not really wanted to know the truth. She had been ambushed by her more honest self.

'I really wish you weren't,' she said, in a mournful rush.

'Because it spoils the story?' Milena asked, lightly.

'Because I'll always be wondering if you're sexually attracted to me,' she lifted the cup up again, thought better of it, let it drop.

'Cilla. I think of you as my best friend. But I am not sexually attracted to you. Ask yourself this question. Am I Milena's type? Am I two and a half metres tall and covered in fur?'

'Now you're making fun of me.'

248

'No I'm not, Cill.'

'Why didn't you tell me!' Cilla demanded, angry and heartstricken at the same moment. 'Now I feel as if I don't know you, just when I thought I finally did.'

To Milena's mingled horror and amusement, Cilla began to weep. A huge fat tear slid down her face like melting ice cream. 'Am I a ludicrous person?' she asked suddenly, in all sincerity.

'No. Why would I think that?'

'Because you're smiling again.' Cilla had been made suddenly self-aware by the shock of the truth. She was not used to being self-conscious and was not very good at it. Her hands were all of a jumble. 'Why haven't you been cured? I thought they took sick people like you and cured them.'

'There's a reason for that,' said Milena.

Cilla realised what she had just said and her eyes closed with shame. 'Milena. I want you to know I did not mean that the way it sounded.'

'The reason I have not been Read,' said Milena, holding to the point, 'is that the Consensus knows perfectly well what I am, and has decided not to Read me. Because it has a use for me as I am.'

Cilla paused. 'Is that what Bob says?'

God, she's bright.

'How can you say you don't know me,' said Milena. 'When you have everything worked out?'

'Because I can never be sure if it's me that's talking or one of my characters. Occupational hazard.'

And a bloody fine actress too.

'I always catch myself repeating my lines as if I'd just thought of them myself.' Cilla took a swig of cold coffee and made a face at it. 'Does Mike know he's being used as a cover?'

A flash of steel in there somewhere too. I really do like you, Cilla, very much.

'He wants the beautiful story too,' said Milena. 'For him, the story is the reality. I said no a hundred times. I said I am not interested a hundred times. He didn't even hear. He just kept on acting as if we were courting.'

'Yuck,' said Cilla.

'I said that, too. But after a while, I began to think he was a kind of daffy. Deep down daffy.'

'Is that why you like me?'

'Only partly. Don't worry, Cill. I've thought about this a lot. I think it's the right thing to do.'

Cilla reached across and took more of Milena's cake. It was made of slump protein and carrots. Milena rescued her glass of what was officially known as milk. People sometimes called it Seepage.

Cilla seemed to be mulling over the cake. 'Do you know you're going to be made a People's Artist?'

'What?' Milena's breath caught.

'Well, they've got to do it. They're investing more in the *Comedy* than just about anything else. Not just the British Consensus, but the European Consensus. They can't do that for any old Vampire. Of course they've got to make you a People's Artist.'

'Cilla have you heard any rumours about this?'

'It's just logic, Milena. It's how the system works. You know that, you play it better than anyone.' Another large chunk of Milena's carrot cake disappeared. Cilla was wrong. Milena did not play the system.

'I never wanted that Cill. I never asked for that.' Milena found she still did not want it.

They give you that, they own you, or they think they do.

Outside in the night, more bells began to ring. The sound seemed to be part of the starless sky. Someone else was ill.

Bloody Consensus. I always end up doing what you want.

The horror seeped back into the room, like an inky fluid from out of the corners. Milena thought of Thrawn McCartney. I went to space and thought I had left it all behind me. Now it's down to earth with a bump. They're letting people die. They will be killing them next.

Milena stood up. 'I can't just sit here,' she told Cilla.

She walked to Milton's table. Unease flashed around the uncertain faces. They're a little bit frightened of me, she realised.

'Milton,' she said. 'I need to talk to you.'

'Sorry, love?' Again the bulging corneas.

Milena pulled up a chair beside him. Cilla stood next to her, and put a hand on her shoulder.

'Milton, when I was in space, I worked with an Angel. I was Terminal and I worked with him in the Fifth. I've just talked to Billy, who was with me in *Love's Labour's*. He's a Bee, and he told me what it's like and I swear to you, that the Bees see something not all that different from what the Angels see. Milton don't look away, just listen. There's nothing wrong with the Bees. They're perfectly healthy. They just see the world in a different way. We can live with them. Point two. A lot of the people who get sick with other viruses are going to be people we know, people from our Estate, Milton. The Zoo has a lot of money. Can't we set up some kind of hospice, some place to take care of them?'

Milton shrugged and grinned. It really was all beyond him. I'll have to talk to Moira, thought Milena.

Milton's girlfriend spoke. Her voice was raw. 'What's happening now must be what the Consensus wants,' she said.

250

'What the Consensus wants is wrong,' said Milena. The sentence came to a point like a dagger.

The girl gave an incredulous smile. 'You can't say that!' She looked around at all the other climbing Vines. 'You're saying that everyone in the world is wrong?'

'Yes,' said Milena, eyes hard on her. She started to nod, in realisation. 'Yes, yes, yes, yes.' It was, she now understood, what she had been saying all of her life. The patch of luminous skin on her hand began to glow, fiercely, without her even realising it.

It took a lot of extra work, a lot of sitting on dull committees. It took Moira Almasy to help her. It was not in its details an interesting story. But Milena managed to save the Bees and help the sick.

'Magic,' said Cilla.

Milena remembered a dream.

She was weightless in space, strapped to the bed to stop her drifting away. A headband held her down to the pillow.

Out of that uneasy sleep, out of the light and the silence, Heather the Reader of Marx seemed to wheel her way towards Milena. Heather grinned in her wheelchair, amused at herself. Heather was wearing the robes of Virgil.

'Look who's here to see you,' Heather said, beaming behind her pebble-thick spectacles.

There was a voice in the light, in the silence. It spoke without words, but Milena recognised it. In the dream, she felt tears in her eyes, felt herself held in a great warm hug. Without words, the voice seemed to tell her to do Dante in her own way. It was giving her permission.

Milena saw Dante walking along the Embankment Gardens. His eyes, his nose, his chin, were all fierce, dagger-like. He had been made political by the events of his age. He was a Vampire of History. He was going to the Zoo Cafe. He met the Animals of the Zoo, and saw mirrored in their eyes his own greed, his own rage, his own cunning. He climbed up the steps, and the sun rose over the roof of the Zoo; and the Sun was God. Rolfa's music said it was so.

And Dante moved through steam from the coffee tureen to a bench, and sat across from Cilla, and she judged him. Prissy. Obsessive. Severe, she seemed to say. But she was like a spectre, her high voice ghostly rather than womanly. This was a Virgil who was neither man nor woman. There is a place she said, where there are spare clothes. And she led Dante through a gate, into the Graveyard, and the gate closed and locked. They fought their way through the darkness and the souls of the dead that looked like old and withered clothes, until they found a light.

251

Rolfa sat singing at a desk. Lucy was with her, swinging her feet.

We're Beatrice, said the voice.

It really is you, isn't it, Rolfa? You really are here with me. Who else could orchestrate the Comedy? Who else could come marching back from the dead down a highway in my head? It's a highway made of scar tissue and it links me to the Consensus. And that's where you are, isn't it love? You're still there somewhere, singing in the dark.

Milena went up and Milena came down and Milena did the Comedy in a different way, amid the tunnels of Leake Street and the scaffolding of the Zoo. Milena brought the Comedy down to earth.

chapter fourteen

HOP SKIP AND JUMP
(PSYCHODRAMA)

Milena fled from Thrawn. She moved out into the Slump, the vast estuary between London and the sea. In a sense, she was also fleeing from herself.

She remembered a boy singing. He stood on the flat, polished prow of a boat, pushing the boat with a long punt pole. He was tall and lean and the muscles on his legs looked like polished driftwood.

Mary oh lay ha
Mary oh lay ha hoo
Mary oh lay ha
Mary oh I love you

Milena was half asleep with relief at her escape. She would live out in the Slump, where no one would expect her to live, for three months. Then she would go up into space.

Milena looked at the ripples of sunlight lazing on the surface of the coffee-coloured water. Her eyes sagged shut and her head nodded, and she listened to the water gurgling slightly against the overlapping planks of the punt. She heard the crackle of reeds as the boat slid between them, where the channel narrowed.

There was a flutter of wings. Milena looked up. A moorhen, black with a red face was flying away. There was a thrashing sound in the water. A buffalo was dancing sideways away from them, startled. He looked at them with a mixture of timidity and outrage, water streaming from its muzzle.

There were other buffalo, amid the reeds. A child's voice, hidden somewhere, called la la la la la la. Slim shadows darted between the high reeds, hidden excitedly. As the shadows ran, the silver tops of the reeds waved in the air. Overhead, the herons circled.

'The buffalo, they can take the deeper water,' explained the boy. 'Out where you are, there is more shallow farming.'

He pushed their boat out of its narrow back channel, up and onto a hillock of drying reed and water grasses.

'Ach!' he exclaimed in disgust. 'It hasn't rained. Already, all my shortcuts are going dry.'

He hopped out of the punt and dragged it up and over the bank.

Where his feet sank into the mud, bubbles of gas from rotting reeds escaped.

'Is it a problem, the lack of rain?' Milena asked.

'It soon will be,' he said.

The boat oozed its way down mud, back into water, and he pulled it, still wading, between two houses, screened by high panels of woven reed. He leapt back into the boat, and pushed with a pole and the punt floated into a wide, straight canal.

Reed houses lined the canal on both sides, all the way to the horizon. Air pollution made the houses in the distance glow golden as if in sunset light.

The houses were shaped like loaves of bread, with tufts of uncut reed bristling at the top. They rested on firm foundations of Coral, and a low wall of Coral lined the canal. Hens ran through the dust of the bank. Women knelt over the canal filling kettles with water. In the right hand side of the channel small boats crowded together, stern to prow, low in the water. They struggled against the current, the children in them rowing furiously, heading upstream towards the Great Barrier Reef. The Reef kept the waters out of Central London. Beyond the gates of its locks lay the markets of the Pit.

The canoes and punts were all on the razzle, taking private merchandise for sale. They were full of water cabbages, water cress, dried reeds, or the product of dried reeds, the soft new textiles made from stripping and drying water plants.

'Lovely Tarty Woman!' a woman called to Milena, grinning. She knelt in the front of her boat. Jammed securely in the narrow boat was a wok over a charcoal stove. 'Lovely water chestnuts,' the woman called, 'toothy cabbage, all crisp, radishes, onions, slump, all swift fried now. You hungry?'

Milena made herself smile as she shook her head. She had been told that people in the Slump would call her a Tart, and would mean no insult by it. Party Members were still a rarity out in the Slump. That was why the new Party house had been built.

The boat boy took another shortcut, between houses. An angry Tyke stood up and shouted at him. The boy smiled and waved and called him Sir and Senior. The punt slipped past back gardens, carefully demarcated with reed fences. Water cabbages bobbed in rows; edible algae formed a smooth impenetrable coating over the water, like green ice. There was the chugging of generators on high Coral islands, and wires strung over the back gardens, feeding power to the houses.

The boat moved up another channel, into a wide expanse of water. It was as blue as the sky and looked like a lake, wind skittering over its surface. There were rows of paddle steamers, a hazy blue in the distance. They lined up in the main channel between the groaning

254

buoys. Milena could clearly hear people talking on them and the steady whoosh whoosh whoosh of their great twin wheels. Between the wheels, each boat had a chorus of black funnels rising up like church organs. The nearest steamer was laden with slump, all of it in layers like peat cut out of the earth.

Across the lake, near the reeds on the other side were flamingos. They moved in fits and starts, in pink and white currents. The people of the Slump loved and protected them. It was storks and herons they hated. Milena narrowed her eyes and could just barely see the tubby pink bodies perched on long legs, and the elephant-trunk necks reaching down, lifting up.

'This is L'Etoile,' said the boy. 'Different water roads spread out from here to all the different Estates. We got the hard farming, the cabbages and the like, we got the soft farming, the small birds and animals, we got the Slump itself. We go past the Slump, past the Soft Farmers.' He smiled, a gap in his teeth, his vividly Rhodopsin-purple face lumpy with acne.

'What Estate will I be near?' Milena asked him. She already knew, but she wanted to see his response.

'Oh, Lady,' he said embarrassed. He was still smiling but he looked down. 'You are Tarty.'

'But that is not an Estate. Will I be near the Slump?

He shook his head. 'No. You will be near the Estate of Remembrance.'

He was wincing. He looked away. Remembrance was a euphemism for Death.

The new Tarty flats had a social purpose. They were there to plant Party Members out in the Slump. They were also there to raise the social standing of a necessary but shunned Estate.

The punt moved on, round the edge of L'Etoile.

On the horizon there were now blue hills, striped by paddies. The border of reeds beside the channel grew narrower. Milena could see banks of earth, their edges white with dried salt. There was a sudden thundering of hooves.

White horses galloped alongside the lake, silver manes tossed, great heavy feet pounding the sandy earth and the thick salty grasses.

'Oh!' said Milena, in admiration. It was here that the huge but nimble carthorses were bred, it was here that they ran free when young, and they came back here twice a year to run free again. On their backs the Horseboys and Horsegirls rode, in thick leather chaps that were carved in tattoo shapes.

'Ai-ai-ai-ai-AIIII!' shouted Milena's punter, to them, all excited. The Horseboys ignored him. 'Ach,' he said in envy, and clicked his tongue. 'They are the ones. They are the ones.'

A young girl ran beside the leading horse. She caught hold of the mane, and seemed to bounce twice before suddenly launching herself up onto its back. She leaned forward, her mouth in the horse's ear. The stallion turned, and the whole herd turned with it, dipping suddenly down and out of sight behind the sandy rise.

'Oh!' sighed the boy. 'That is where I want to be Placed. I want to ride horses, not boats.' He smiled, but with sadness.

They moved out of L'Etoile into a narrow channel. From somewhere ahead of them came a clinking sound, like coins. The sound deepened as they approached, and as they came round a bend, Milena saw a long bamboo arm, trawling over the surface of the water. Buckets were hoisted out of the water, wobbling with weight and trailing black sludge. The buckets were then hoisted by a tiny, noisy engine onto the shore. Men snatched the buckets and emptied them, pouring slurry into pits. Their legs were glossy with mud; their cotton shorts and shirts clung to them.

A row of beehive-shaped kilns gradually came into view, smoking, adding to the haze of the air. There was a delicious scent of burning wood.

It was a temporary camp of brickmakers. Rows of young children squatted, cotton over their faces. They patted paste into brick moulds. The paste was Thames mud, a mixture of earth and clay and ash and the chewed up rubble of flooded buildings. Skinny people, the colour of the dried dust, carried shovels of brick to the kilns. Milena could feel the heat of the kilns on her face. 'Tarty! Tarty woman!' they all called and waved to her, with perfect, white smiles. Milena waved back.

The narrow channel led to a vast, flat area of rice as far as Milena could see. It basked in water and sunlight. There were flags marking fish-farms. There were houses at regular intervals, standing high over the rice and the water on pillars of bound bamboo. Lines of laundry hung from the porches. Children scrubbed clothes on pans on their laps. There were walkways, rope bridges slung between the houses. A man lay flat on his roof, swiping at a stork with a cane. The bird lifted its wings in anger, and would not be moved. Women and Tykes looked up at him smiling, teasing him. Milena clapped her hands once, sharply, and suddenly the bird took off. There was cheering and applause. The man waved sheepishly, still clinging in fear to his roof.

The punt glided past fields of giant lotus, the huge blossoms closed against the sun. The flat round leaves were large enough for the child-farmers to walk on quite safely. Coots walked beside them without fear.

There were mud ponds, full of children and adults running, knee-deep calling to each other and laughing with glee. They were chasing eels. Trout sweltered in ponds behind cages of water wood. There were salt-rimmed ponds in the banks where frogs were farmed. Shepherd children watched them, protecting them against marauding herons. Wet dogs, black and white collies, barked and chased the livestock. Milena saw one scoop up a frog in its jaws and trot back to the pond. The dog splashed far out in the middle of the pond, before gently letting the frog go free. Out to the horizon there were houses high on stakes, and walkways, and floating artificial islands, rising and falling as if with breath. There were boats everywhere, people everywhere, inspecting the plants, parching the reeds, drying translucent panels of rice paste.

Finally they came to the Slump itself.

Great mounds of it rose above the waterline in perfect domes. Deer grazed on the roofs, boats were pulled up onto its banks. Smoke drifted out of it.

The Slump was a kind of fungus, rich in protein, that was farmed on the saltier reaches of the estuary. The Slump Bobbers lived inside it. They shovelled out courtyards and chambers, cooking and sleeping inside their crop until it began to go soft and ripe.

On the top of the nearest dome, someone was bobbing. Not in a hurry, the man walked with a lazy, sauntering bounce. He carried something in a basket on his head. Rising up over the edge of the dome came eager children. They bounded across the Slump, as if on the surface of a trampoline. The man turned, annoyed, and perhaps said something. The Bobber children trembled to a halt, their knees suddenly absorbing all the bounce, their shoulders staying level.

The punt moved on, and Milena saw that a small paddle steamer was anchored beside the Slump. The Bobbers were out with their sharp-bladed shovels, cutting the Slump, peeling it up in layers, and loading it into barrows. They ran up the ramps on the boat, and tipped the barrows up and sent the fungus cascading onto the steamer.

Ahead of them there was thick black smoke streaming up in rows from many, many kilns, all along the horizon, as if the sky were on fire.

The boy reached into the top of his wrappings and pulled out a cloth. He tied it over his face. Milena began to hear an almost tuneful, hollow, clattering sound. There was wailing.

'Remembrance,' said the boy. He passed her a mask.

The kilns were irregular towers of red, baked soil, surrounded by bundles of reed for fuel. People in black scuttled up and down them, carrying reeds on their backs. The kilns seemed to stand on an island of pink and white. As they drew closer, Milena began to think it must be flowers, lotus blossoms or lilies. Is it a flower farm? she wondered.

Then she saw that the flowers were festooned on canoes. She began to hear a formless chorus of singing, a low, deep mournful sound of many different songs being sung at once. Up the sides of the fifty kilns, up each of them, stood hooded people in white. Between them they carried hammocks on long poles. The hammocks sagged with a dead weight.

One a minute, her viruses told her, they are disposing of one every minute. Two hundred, three hundred boats full of mourners, the viruses told her at a glance. The boats seemed to rise and fall with the sound of dirges.

Their boat had to pass betwen them.

Women sat in boats rocking quietly. Young men craned their necks to see how many boats were still ahead of them. Everyone wore white, including those who seemed to be asleep, their faces collapsed into themselves, their lips blue and prim. Shadows from the smoke drifted over them. Smut settled on the white shirts and jackets.

'*Oh did those feet in ancient times . . .*'

'*Swing low . . .*'

'*Silence, silence from which we all come . . .*'

The many songs of mourning seemed to compete. Children stood with their hands raised towards heaven, keening, warbling, tears smeared over their faces. Men stared as if stunned, glancing back behind them at the burdens in the bottom of the boats.

From out of the Estate of Remembrance, women covered in white waded out into the water. They wore white masks to hide their faces. They held out their arms and with a start, the orphaned children shifted themselves and tried to lift up the hammocks. The women in white took them on their shoulders, and bore the loads on their shoulders. As the hammocks were taken from them, the mourners threw flowers into the air. They called goodbye, they shouted out names, every name it seemed that it was possible to call, as if all the world were dying at once. The women in white stepped up onto the salty banks, their legs glossy with mud. They walked with quick jabbing steps up the slopes of the kilns.

'Go around! Go around!' they shouted, almost as if in panic, to Milena's boatboy. They made circular motions with wet purple hands. The boatboy shook his head, and pointed between the kilns, and thrust the boat forward in that direction, gliding between masses of rotting flowers. The white petals had gone slimy and brown. It was the flowers that stank of death, rank and gaseous. Milena coughed. Smoke drifted low over the water, pitch black and sharp in the nostrils. The boat surged into it: it stung Milena's eyes and made her weep. Then the boat was through it, there was a freshening breeze in her face, and Milena looked up and saw her new home.

It rose, like a hangar over the water, huge and arched, with four buttressing towers of bamboo at each corner. All the light about it was golden, filtered through smoke. It was made of reed and was a kind of Ark, floating on the surface of the estuary. A wide deck of reed surrounded it, with floating moorings extending out into the water.

The punt sighed up onto the artificial bank of reed, and the boy slipped over the side of the boat, and pulled it up closer to a small, dry platform. He helped Milena up onto it. He carried her one bamboo suitcase.

'I have never seen inside such a place,' he whispered.

'Neither have I,' confided Milena.

A tiny but rotund woman came down the sloping reed bank towards them.

'Are you the theatre person?' the woman asked, voice quailing as she walked towards them. Her face seemed settled in gloom.

'Yes. I am. My name is Milena Shibush.' Milena held out her hand, but the woman stopped where she was on the bank and would come no closer.

'I am Ms Will. There was no one else to do it, so they left me here to show you around.' She glanced at the boatboy. 'I suppose he will have to come in too. Isn't it awful about that horrible smoke? And the singing!'

Without a handshake, Ms Will turned around and led Milena towards the Tarty house.

The sliding-panel doors had been left open. The walls were a series of sliding panels that could be shifted according to the weather. Ms Will led Milena through them into a large, covered courtyard.

Inside, there was a cathedral hush. Arches of reed rose up and over them. Sunlight leaked through the walls, as if through a sieve. Sunlight burned in brilliant pinpricks, and spilled in rays on the floor. The floor was made of woven reed. Ahead of them was a tumble of bamboo boxes coated in plaster, and corridors and steps. There was a smell of cooking.

'All the quarters are separated from each other. There's some kind of resin between the walls. Dead Space, they call it, to absorb noise. At least we have some privacy. You are up here.'

They climbed a bamboo staircase up a scaffolding of stilts. Milena's rooms clustered over a water tank. Milena's door was a series of sliding screens. Ms Will pulled them back, one after another.

Milena's rooms were like a series of lacquered bamboo boxes. The winter screens had been folded back, the windows were open, there was a gentle breeze. There were reed carpets as soft as sweaters over the thick reed floors. There were summer shutters that had been woven into illustrative shapes of flamingos and herons and wading farmers. There were beanbags on the floor, there was a desk with a chair, there was a kitchen with a charcoal stove and a hibachi, there were charcoal stoves in every room. Behind a screen, there was a bathroom, a bathroom all of her own with a huge resin tub, and a trough of warm water and a pan for scooping it out and pouring over herself in great gushing plashes. There was a throne toilet, a bamboo box.

As Milena walked from room to room she cried aloud. 'Oh look at this! Oh look at this!' overwhelmed with gratitude at each new revelation. The boatboy walked hushed behind her.

'I have never imagined a house like this,' he said in awe.

Milena ran to one of her windows, and looked out. There was a patchwork quilt of green squares, brown pools, ridgeways, stiltways, a crowd of canoes where there was a floating market. There was a great stretch of water. There were flamingos. There was the sound of wind in reeds, of birds perched on fenceposts.

'I can't believe I will live in such a place,' said Milena. Here, she thought, I can rest. Here I can be safe.

There was the massed singing of Remembrance, and the drifting shadows of smoke.

It only took one week for Thrawn McCartney to find her.

A week later, Milena lifted up the lid of her new bamboo box toilet and there was Thrawn's face inside it.

Here it begins, thought the Milena who was remembering. This is the July, this is the August, before I went into space. I'm going to have to remember this, too. All part of the story. And the Consensus wants a story.

Thrawn giggled. 'Just a head in the head,' she said. 'If you're going to use it, Milena, you're going to have to use it with me in it. I think that's a pretty good picture of what our relationship's been all along, don't you?'

Milena stared in horror. The full horror took some time to sink in.

'Pretty new flats courtesy of the Party are no defence, Milena. No defence against a bad conscience.'

'You're the one who dumped on me,' said Milena.

'It's funny,' said the head. 'How people who commit injustice always have to fry up one that's been done to them. Otherwise they wouldn't be able to do what they do.'

Milena closed the lid. She walked through her beautiful lacquered boxes, surrounded by the Dead Space. There was a blaze of sunlight on the floor. It was the Summer of Song, the Summer of Light. It hadn't rained in two months.

A hologram of a squat toilet was in the centre of the front room. It was the old kind, that most people had to use, a hole in the floor with footrests. 'Yoo hoo. Mil-ena!' called a hollow voice from inside it.

There was also the carcass of a water buffalo on the floor. It had been skinned and gutted. There were pink and white ribbons of fat and flesh. The carcass stood up and limped, on stumps, headless, towards Milena.

'Here I am,' the carcass sang and whooped. 'A new Milena Shibush production.' It spun around on stumps, and then fell. 'Holograms courtesy of some female or other we can safely chew up into Coral.'

The carcass sprouted flowers from the stump of its neck. They were generic flowers, blearily imagined. But the flowers were bleeding.

'Poor, poor Milena. Such a hard time she's having.' There was a chorus of sentimental sympathy in the air all around her. 'Ahhhhhhhhhh.'

Milena saw something out of the corner of her eye, and turned around, and there was Thrawn, holding out a knife towards her.

'Go on, Milena. Why leave the job undone? I am what's inside your head. You'd like to kill me. Well. Now you can. Without doing me any real harm. Isn't that what you tell yourself? That you haven't done me any real harm? Here, slice me into ribbons. There'll be lots of blood, and I'll die, right in the middle of your nice Tarty flat.'

'Where are you cubing from?' Milena demanded.

The image laughed. 'Maybe I'm here for real and you really can kill me. Or maybe you're making all of this up.'

'If the Party finds out you're doing this you'll be scrubbed so clean even the viruses won't know you.'

'Will they?' asked Thrawn with a smile and a confidence that Milena found unnerving.

Then the hologram of Thrawn McCartney transformed itself into a hologram of Milena Shibush.

'Milton,' said Milena Shibush. 'Thrawn McCartney is persecuting me. She puts headless singing cows in my room. She waits for me inside my toilet. I wake up in the middle of the night and her face is smiling at me just in front of my nose. Milton, she's driving me crazy!'

The image of Milena Shibush turned and smiled. 'Now what is Milton going to think?'

The image of Milena Shibush turned and walked up to a bleary smudge of light that somewhat resembled Cilla.

'Cilla,' said Milena, her face sour. 'Get away from me, will you? Your constant social climbing is just too unbearable for someone as talented as me.'

The image of Milena Shibush turned and batted her eyelids at Milena.

There was no edge of crackling light where the image joined reality.

It cast shadows on the floor in the right direction. I'd believe it was really here, thought Milena, with a sinking heart. She thought very quickly of things she could and could not do, things like cutting the electricity supply. What electricity supply, where? She didn't know where Thrawn was cubing from.

It's an exchange of light, she reminded herself. That means Thrawn can see anything I do, hear anything I say. Anything I do or say will become ammunition. If it gives away a plan, if it shows what I feel, what I'm frightened of, what I'm not frightened of, anything will be used.

My defence is silence.

Next to the image of Milena was an image of Thrawn. They began to play a little psychodrama.

Reality was remade in light.

This Thrawn looked bright and sweet and pretty. This Milena looked unbearably snotty and smug, squat, untidy and smelly. This Thrawn tolerated Milena, felt sorry for her. This Thrawn was a victim who was held back by pity. This Thrawn was the stronger one really.

'I've got some new ideas,' said this Thrawn. 'I think they'll really help the show.'

Low feral cunning crossed the face of this slightly hunchbacked Milena. 'Oh really? That's terribly nice of you Thrawn. But better leave the content to me. After all I am the director.'

This Thrawn, sighed, and shook her head, full of forbearance. She turned to the real Milena and shrugged, as if to say, poor deluded thing, we have to humour her.

'Of course, Milena, you'll get credit, don't worry. But they're supposed to be fun, these ideas. Now.' She began to talk slowly and clearly as if to someone very stupid who never understood. 'People like to laugh. Let's give them something amusing.'

'Oh dear no,' said this Milena, nose in the air. 'That couldn't possibly be important enough for a Milena Shibush production.'

It is so banal, thought Milena. Tykes do this. They imitate each other, making each other say the horrible things that would justify hatred. Who is frying up an injustice, Thrawn? 'Now I know you'll never be a director,' said Milena, aloud.

Silence, fool.

Milena the image said, 'You'll never be as talented as I am, Thrawn. No one is as talented as I am. Now then, let's play this scene as I imagine it. You'll see. It will be so very much more talented.'

There was a kind of flicker and the holograms changed places.

In flounced Milena.

'Thrawn. I need something new and spectacular. I've persuaded the Consensus to give us the go-ahead. Connections. It's not what you know, it's who you know. Such a shame about you, Thrawn. If only you could rope yourself in a bit more. All you have to do is pander, Thrawn. All you have to do is exactly what the Consensus wants you to do.' Milena the mirror image had a face that was crossed with idiot concern. 'How are things, Thrawn? Working all day in here by yourself. You know how much I worry about you.'

'Then why,' said Thrawn the image. 'Do you always make me feel like something squeezed in between the soup and the fish course?'

Milena the mirror image faltered. 'Oh. Do I? I'm sorry.'

'Yes, you do.' said Thrawn. This time, thought Milena, the characters are more convincing and the acting is better.

'You always get so tangled in busy-ness,' said the image of Thrawn. 'The last time I tried to talk to you, you were washing a chicken. That chicken was the most important chicken I had ever seen. The concentration that you focused on that chicken. I asked myself: what has it got that I haven't? And the answer was: it's dead and in pieces. I can still fight back.'

It's better, thought Milena, when she imagines herself as me. It's as if I give her a tone of voice with which she can speak. If I am that important to her, no wonder she is fighting. If I lose and she stays, I will be an appendage for the rest of my life. I'll be bagpipes round her neck that she needs to make any kind of reasonable noise at all.

Silence, Milena. Listen and watch. Anything you say gets tied into the knot.

'I don't mean to do that,' said Milena the image in mock horror.

'Of course you mean it. You don't want me to be there, and it's a way of cancelling me out,' said Thrawn. It was Thrawn as she would like to be. Milena heard her speak with Milena's own intonation. 'You are continually dishonest, do you know that? You're so dishonest, it's actually very, very difficult to be direct and honest around you. Everything gets tied up in a sort of knot.'

She knows what she does, thought Milena. Of course she knows. She's not insane; she's not out of touch with reality. She knows what reality is and she hates it, and she sucks it into herself and spews it out backwards. Mirror image.

And Milena thought: I'll be very lucky to get out of this. This is very bad indeed. She went back into her Tarty bathroom and used the toilet, knowing what was inside it. Thrawn showed her, hovering in the air just in front of her, exactly what the head was seeing.

So far the game will be to get me to ignore it all. That is what she wants and expects. Like the chicken. Once she gets me to react with disgust or horror, that's a victory too. If I pretend to ignore it, she wins. If she gets a reaction, she wins. I have to cut through the Gordian knot. It can't be untied. And I don't know how to do it.

Except that if I stay around people, she can't do it at all. All it takes is one person to see what I see, see the holograms, and then I can go to Milton and tell him this is happening – and bring witnesses.

Otherwise, like she says, he'll think I'm the crazy one.

Hop skip and jump. Only she's the one making up the rules.

'It must be comforting to know you'll never be alone, Milena,' said a voice.

I speak, she wins. I don't speak, she wins.

Milena had an inspiration. She chuckled and shook her head.

'Tee hee hee,' said Thrawn, darkly.

Thrawn didn't like that.

Milena stood up, flushed the toilet. The image dissolved, refracted by the water, destabilised. Water, thought Milena. Vampires can't cross running water.

Thrawn was standing beside her.

'I'm going to get to know you terribly well, Milena. I'm going to be here all the time. I'll see every petty little stunt you're going to pull. When you talk to the little What Does who cleans your Tarty house, I'll be there. If there is a little fly on the wall, it will be me, watching.'

Milena in silence knelt under the sink, and pulled out her flask. She suddenly felt exhausted, drained. I feel tired all the time now. Can't let Thrawn see.

Milena the director stood up with her flask. She often filled it with tea to take to rehearsals. Now she filled it with water. If I can get her near people and throw water at her, at the image, the light will refract. People will see she is a hologram.

Milena walked out of the bathroom. She walked through the image of Thrawn, feeling the light tingling in her Rhodopsin skin. Better not fill anything else up with water, or I will give myself away. It's July now. I go into space in October. She won't be able to reach me in space. Sometime before then, they will have to make me Terminal. When they make me Terminal they'll know everything. I'll be linked with the Consensus. The Consensus will know, through me, what she has done. They'll have to pull her in. So I've already won. All I have to do is hang on. Until space, until I'm Terminal.

Until then, I'll have to be around people. I need to stay with people. Thrawn is the most impulsive, impatient person I've ever met. She won't be able to wait. Unless of course she realises that I am relying on that.

Work. Lots of rehearsals, lots of recording, lots of people all the time. She'll hate that too. She'll see me cubing the holograms, and she won't be able to stand it, she'll see it's happening without her and she'll have to act.

Thrawn, thought Milena with quiet certainty, I am going to have to destroy you. I wonder if that's what I was supposed to do all along?

'Say goodbye to your old life,' said Thrawn. 'Say hello to your new.'

There was the Dead Space between all the residences, but Milena could still hear the slithering sound of panels being pulled back. Someone else was going out. Milena spun around and immediately went out of her own front door. She did not slide it shut behind her.

Below, in the public atrium of the house, Ms Will was walking towards the open gate. The sight of Ms Will had never been so welcome.

'Going out?' Milena asked pleasantly.

Milena had not made an effort with Ms Will. She was too much like what Milena had imagined a Party wife would be, a kind of overstuffed, throwaway cushion. She was well dressed, hair coiffed, well fed, looked after, and her face carried an expression of settled resignation. Her husband did not really need her. The circles under her eyes were black rings in the full July flush of a Rhodopsin face.

'Yes. I have to do the shopping myself,' said Ms Will.

'Do you mind if I join you?' Milena asked, feeling false. I ignore people, she thought, until I need them. It's like the chicken. Thrawn was right.

'If you like, I'm not doing anything special,' said Ms Will. 'I never do anything special. It's different for you artists.' Ms Will waited, staring into space as Milena's feet applauded their way down the steps. Milena half ran to her across the woven floor.

'The weather has been lovely,' said Milena.

'Oh, it's far too hot,' said Ms Will. Behind Ms Will, unseen by her, the walls started to ooze mucus, and there was a whisper of sound, a voice in the air, a reminder. Thrawn was still with her. As if prodded, Milena walked on.

The main gate had been left open, so the air could flow through the house. The sunlight they stepped into was blistering, blinding. The ground was white, as bleached as bone. The What Does woman was hanging out sheets and underwear. They burned white in the sun. Already there was a smell of rotting reed. Already the grass on the bank was brown and brittle. A slope of mud led down towards the narrowing channel.

Everything was already going dry.

The What Does, Ms Marks, called out to them.

'Wonderful weather for sheets. They dry as soon as you look at them!' Suddenly Ms Marks' smile sprouted fangs and an eel's head glared out from between her teeth. Look! thought Milena and tried to pull Ms Will around. Then the image was gone. Ms Will blinked up at her, only momentarily distracted from her complete absorption in herself.

Milena kept thinking. The eel's head and that buffalo carcass were very good. Thrawn is using references. She's in a market somewhere, somewhere with beef carcasses and fish. Milena walked towards the quay. It no longer reached the water. The bank of the Ark ended, high over the edge of the water. From the kilns, smoke still drifted, and the formless choir of Remembrance still sung in the distance.

Ms Will took Milena's arm, as if she were a What Does companion. 'It's not good for you, all this sun,' said Ms Will. 'I got a terrible sunburn yesterday, just sitting out on the balcony. And it puts you straight off your food. You're never hungry. I told our girl Emily to come up with something especially appetising. But she can't change, won't change. No, it's tamales again.' Ms Will had not the least idea that she was extraordinarily privileged.

'It's so difficult to remember to eat,' Milena agreed.

'Well Emily blames the shortages. I can't fault her there. The perfect excuse. Isn't it ridiculous? Food shortages now that we have electricity.'

'There are a lot of people to feed,' said Milena, keeping her voice mild. 'And all this sun is lovely, but it's very bad for farming. A lot of the land crops have just burned up.'

'It's the costermongers, too, of course,' said Ms Will. 'I think they engineer these shortages, just to put up the price. Making everyone else pay. I don't want to eat tamales for the rest of my life. So I'm just going to have to do the shopping myself.'

Oh God, oh God, oh God, she's so boring, thought Milena. Fear made her more irritable.

'I'd like some bananas,' said Ms Will. 'Just for a change. I'd like something different.' The flesh on her face hung dead on her skull. The smoke of the dead from the Estate lay overhead. They waited for a punt, in the full, glaring horrible light.

I have an enemy, thought Milena. And I am alone.

Eventually a boat came past, punted by a stringy, burnished old man in his mid-thirties. Ms Will needed to be helped down off the Ark and into the boat. She let her full weight rest on the withered arms of the dying man.

As she sat down, Ms Will complained that it was so far to the market. Party Members should have their own market, she felt.

'I find it awfully difficult to get anyone to pay any attention when I'm talking,' said Ms Will. 'Do you find that? People can be so extra-ordinarily cruel for no reason.'

'Yes,' said Milena. She was thinking about the light all around them. Light was her enemy, too. The holograms were exchanges of light. Light in one place was exchanged for light in another, through the

266

fifth dimension, where thought and light could interact. But it was a reciprocal exchange. Only as much could be donated as was received. So I could live in the dark, too, thought Milena. She looked down into the water. It was opaque, like moving gelatin, but in its depths, she could see the heads and hands of children swimming. They had long reeds in their mouths that broke the surface and let them breathe. They hunted for fish or for snails.

And suddenly, just under the water, she saw Thrawn. Thrawn was a corpse and fish was nibbling the flesh of her face. Milena looked up and away.

'My skin feels so peculiar,' said Ms Will.

It seethed with worms, just under the surface, as if they would eat their way out any moment. You can't imagine flowers, Thrawn, thought Milena, but you can imagine that.

There was a niggling in Milena's nose. She sneezed. The tickle grew worse. She sneezed again. She began to sneeze over and over. Her head was tossed helplessly from side to side. Her nose and eyes streamed, trying to eliminate the tickle. The tickle suddenly took shape. It became a voice, resonating in the bones of Milena's skull.

'Achoo!' it said, in mocking imitation. 'Hello, Milena.' The voice sounded like her own. 'Think of me as a virus. You have caught a conscience from somewhere. You have committed a grave injustice, of which you are deeply ashamed. You hurt Thrawn McCartney. You must make amends.'

She knows I can't answer back, thought Milena. I am with someone, and I can't start talking to myself in public. Or, again, people will think I'm the crazy one.

'This is your own voice, Milena. Your own mind is telling you what is right. Your own mind is telling you: go to the Zoo and tell them you want Thrawn to be part of the Comedy.'

What now? wondered Milena in dismay. What game is this now?

Until October, she thought, I just have to hold out until October. In October, I'll be made Terminal, and the Consensus will see what's happening and. . . . And then Milena understood what the game was. She groaned and hid her face.

'You'd never believe it, but I used to have a beautiful complexion,' said Ms Will, feeling her seething cheeks. The worms had pincers.

'I'm sorry, Ms Will, I'm afraid I'm not feeling too well,' said Milena.

It was quite simple. Thrawn had never once admitted that she was sending holograms. She was saying that Milena was producing the images herself, out of a bad conscience.

'You don't have to tell me about illness,' said Ms Will. 'Not with my back, my kidneys. And all the Nurses can say is that I'm making it all up.'

When I am made Terminal, all the Consensus will know is that someone they have never Read is seeing impossible things and thinking that someone else, someone she dislikes, is beaming them at her.

When I am made Terminal, the Consensus will think I'm the crazy one.

'I told you the light was too strong,' said Ms Will.

The thirty-five-year-old boatboy punted them to the floating market. It was some five kilometres away from the smoke of the funereal Estate.

As if in Remembrance, everyone in the market sang, another formless chorus, but this one sounded joyful. People sang of onions piled high in their punts, or of lotus fresh and crisp. They sang of reed blankets, soft as a kiss. They sang of fish steamed with ginger, or frogs' legs in garlic. Instead of black smoke, there was a sizzling sound and wafts of spicy food.

'Stop here, boy,' said Ms Will.

He grabbed hold of a mooring post and pulled them in next to a barge that sold fruit. A woman of about sixteen looked up at them and beamed. Her shirt was printed in colours and patterns that seemed to jump and dance. A flower, a water lily, was wound into her hair. Oh, to be as safe and happy as you, thought Milena.

Ms Will complained that there were no bananas.

'Bananas mostly grow on the Continent,' the woman explained. 'That's burned dry.'

'They should grow them here,' said Ms Will. She bought water chestnuts instead. Ms Will saved bags. The bags were made of resin and were slithery to hold. Milena blinked. She seemed to have something in her eye.

The bag was filled and without saying a word, Ms Will held it out towards Milena to carry it for her. How miserable it must be to be you, thought Milena. She felt a surge of sympathy for Ms Will. It can be so difficult to be happy. Milena took one bag, and then another. Whatever was in her eye became increasingly irritating.

'Oh,' said Ms Will. 'I've forgotten my money. Could you pay for this?'

So much for sympathy. Milena was going to look for her purse. Ms Will's face became a smear. Water streamed out of her eyes.

'Could you take the bags for a moment?' Milena asked. 'I've got to get my money out.'

Ms Will looked glum. 'I'm not sure I can hold them,' she said.

'Well then I can't get my money out,' said Milena, with a slightly exasperated chuckle. She blinked trying to clear her eyes. Sunlight wriggled on the water, searing.

Ms Will reluctantly took the bags, and Milena pulled out her purse.

The light from the water swam in the water in her eyes.

Then it focused blazing inside them.

'Ow!' howled Milena.

The light drew even brighter into hard fierce knots. Milena was screaming, and threw her head to one side. The wriggling light seemed to swim after her, like worms. It was as if plasma direct from the sun had been planted in her eyes. She could feel the jelly in them heat up.

She screamed and dropped the purse. She was dimly aware of the sound of coins rolling out over the prow of the boat.

Lady, Lady, said voices all around her. Milena was aware that she was making an animal sound, a high helpless screeching. Her hands were pressed over her eyes, tears streaming between her fingers. There was darkness. There was relief. No light at all to exchange. She sobbed helplessly as the pain subsided, as purple patterns floated glowing on her retina.

'We'll get your purse, Lady. We'll get your money,' someone was saying.

There was inside her ear, a shivering. The shivering took shape into a voice.

'You don't like the light, do you, Milena? It shows the truth.' Her eyes screwed shut, Milena jammed her fingers into her ears.

It seemed as if there was a fly buzzing just inside her nostrils. The fly spoke with a buzzing voice, resonating out of the bones of her septum and cheeks and sinuses.

'Hear no evil. See no evil. Must be a first time for you,' said the voice. 'You're going to go to the Zoo, Milena. You're going to go to the Zoo to tell them you want Thrawn McCartney to work on the Comedy.'

Then, like a ghost, it was gone.

Milena opened her eyes. Her cheeks were smeared with tears, and there were still burning purple shapes hovering in front of her eyes. She very nearly blinded me, thought Milena.

'Where's my money?' she asked. 'Does someone have my money?'

The viruses had made people scrupulously honest.

'Yes, Lady, the boys dived for it. They found some of it for you.' It was the flower girl, pressing wet coins into her hand.

'Is there enough for a punt or a taxi there?' Milena sniffed. 'I can't see!' Milena's voice broke with distress and fear. Damn her. She's got me dancing like a puppet. Consoling hands held her.

Yes, oh, yes, said many people, all around her.

'I have to see someone at the Zoo,' Milena whispered. 'They may be able to help.' She felt herself being helped towards another boat.

'Oh dear,' said Ms Will. 'What about my fruit and chestnuts?'

269

'You can pay for those later,' the flower girl told Ms Will. I bet she doesn't, thought Milena.

Many hands lowered her into another punt. A cushion was moved behind her.

Milena felt the boat wobble sideways away from the mooring. It moved out onto the water. She felt the tickle in her ear. It seemed to shiver into place.

'Good girl,' said the voice in her ear, as if to a dog. 'Good little Milena. You always try to do the right thing. You have such high standards of behaviour.'

Milena settled back on the cushion, and drew a deep, trembling breath. I need a kerchief to tie around my eyes, she thought. I need plugs for my ears.

Someone started to sing, from the prow of the boat.

Lady oh lay hah
Lady remember me?

It's the boy, she thought, it's the same boy who brought me out here.

Are you ill, Lady?
Are you ill like me?

Ill? thought Milena. 'Are you a Singer?' she asked. He hadn't been a Singer a week ago.

Now I am Lady
I have to sing to speak.

This far? It's come out this far already? And Milena had a saddening thought: I'm the only thing that's come out this far. What if I brought it with me?

'Sing then,' she asked the boy.

'Poison,' said the voice in her ear. 'You are poison.'

All the way back across the Slump, the boy sang. He ran out of songs, and began to make up music without words. It was as if he was singing about the beauty of the world that Milena could no longer see. When she ventured to open her eyes, she would catch a glimpse of blue water and soft, silver-grey reeds. Then the light in her eyes was scattered, disturbed. It dissolved into a shapeless, queasy, oily mass. Thrawn was in her eyes.

'Don't you just love games?' whispered the voice.

I have to be able to see the cube, thought Milena. She can stop me hologramming. She can stop me doing the Comedy. Does that matter? The important thing is that the Comedy is produced. I could just go to Moira and say, this is too much, I can't do it, get someone else. But then, Thrawn might be able to persuade them to use her as a technician, and that does matter. And there is no guarantee that she would stop doing this to me.

I have to find a way to protect myself against this somehow. There must be some way to cut off the light, make it difficult for her to focus.

Milena opened her eyes. For a moment, she could see the world. Then it melted. She moved her head, and the world returned, before subsiding again into a chaos of colour. She moved her head once more, and then the light flared up hot and dazzling again.

'Ow,' said Milena again and went still.

The band of focus was small in itself, with plenty of opportunity for error. And Thrawn nèeded enough light to focus in the first place.

And suddenly, Milena had an answer. In the Cut the week before, there had been a Seller of Games, a great booming woman with a very high, but very loud voice. She had been a Singer, too.

Have you got friends who can't see themselves?
Have you chum who's a bum?
It's easily done, no mystery
With a little item from history . . .

She had been selling mirrored contact lenses. A joke, another game. Mirrored lenses would reflect light.

Yes, yes, the mirror would reflect light, make focusing very difficult indeed, and it would cut down on the amount of light inside the eye that Thrawn had to play with. Thrawn would always have to focus in from the back, instead of the front. Milena's viruses calculated the intensity of light, the resulting possible strength of any Reformed image.

It would be enough. It would have to be enough.

So how was Milena to get to the Cut to buy them?

'Take me to the Embankment Garden quay,' she told the singing boy. 'That's the one closest to the Zoo.'

The only way I can go to the Cut without Thrawn blinding me is to get lost. I have to get lost on my way to the Zoo and end up there as if by mistake. The only way I can do that is to make her mad enough to blind me with light. That means I have to make her angry.

'So you've won, Thrawn,' said Milena, aloud.

Silence.

'Thrawn? You can answer me now.'

Milena felt a tiny fist of light clenching in her eyes, and she closed them, and covered them with her hands. That left her ears exposed, and her skin open to the light. Fire suddenly crawled over the bare flesh of her arms, just under the skin. A worm seemed to writhe just inside her ear.

'This isn't Thrawn. It's you, yourself. Remember that,' warned the worm.

271

I can get you mad, thought Milena. So I can control you.

'You see, Milena, there is justice sometimes after all. You can't get away with using people forever.'

Silence and darkness, those are my friends, thought Milena.

Milena reeled into the New Cut market, into the Summer of Song. Everyone sang, even those who did not have the disease, just to be part of the fun. It was a new craze. Milena stumbled blindly, buffeted by people she could not see.

'These daytime drunks are everywhere!' someone exclaimed to the opening bars of Beethoven's 'Song of Joy'.

Song was all around her, in waves. 'Where are you? Where are you?' the voice in her ear demanded.

'I don't know! I'm lost! You won't let me see!'

Waves of song washed over her. The voice in her ear said something Milena could not hear. A wall of song bore down on her.

Oh I do like to be beside the seaside!

Someone pulled her to one side. There was a whizzing of bicycles, just past the tips of her toes. Milena's vision cleared. Trolleymen on bicycles sizzled past her, pulling their wagons full of hot food behind them.

Oh I do like to be beside the sea!

Two women were just by her elbow, at a fruit stall. They were singing new words to 'The Dance of the Sugar Plum Fairy'. The effect was delightfully, prinklingly sarcastic.

Oh you can't sell just one orange
How int'resting, oh how strange
Other markets can.

The voice of Thrawn screeched in Milena's ear. 'You're in the Cut? You're in the bloody Cut? How did you get there?'

'You'll just have to let me see!' whispered Milena.

There was a wrench of light. Milena doubled up under its impact. She covered her eyes. She refused to move. She heard the stallowner answer, to the final, demonic theme from Berlioz' *Symphonie Fantastique*. Each word was separate and heavy as if made of lead.

I can sell them by the kilo
I can't sell them separately!

All around her, people sang. It was easy to do, easier almost than speaking. As long as you told the truth.

What is the price please? a woman asked, in the theme 'Povera donna' from *Falstaff*. The effect was inappropriately tragic, as if everything in the woman's life were inappropriately tragic. The music revealed her.

Five francs and two yen

The answer came in a lively, happy voice to 'Alle due al la tre' –

272

also from *Falstaff*. That would be the dress seller, the happy young wife. The song revealed her too.

The song whirled around Milena. It drifted out of the open windows above, women humming as they sizzled sausages. It came from the roofs, where people would be lying down and photosynthesizing. From the bar by the butcher's shop came a steady, frog-like croaking:

Slup, slup, slup, drink it all up, up, up and we won't go to bed until the morn-ning!

'All right!' said the voice in her ears.

Milena removed her hands. Her vision was still slightly blurred but she could see to walk. She could see if the Seller of Games was still there. And if she wasn't, what then? Go to the Zoo? Crawl into the Graveyard and hide there? Milena found it difficult to think, with all the noise.

The world seemed to spin with song. Old street cries had been revived. 'Ripe cherries, ripe!' Insinuating love songs were given like gifts to female customers. 'Someone as beautiful as you . . . should buy two.'

Children ran on the ledges of the crumbling old buildings overhead. A woman admonished them, out of a half-open window. 'Watch out, you be careful! Watch out, you be careful!' she squawked to a dance tune, her mature authority undermined by the rollicking of her hips.

Song washed up and down the street, as formless as the chorus of Remembrance, as if it were a funeral for things already gone. There were occasional quiet moments and occasional contagions when a particular chorus caught everyone's fancy. The new viruses then trumpeted their triumph.

We all fall down!

The entire street roared in unison, and then laughed.

And Milena, stumbling, confused, peered half blind at each wagon-stall. There was the seller of paints and brushes, there was the Tacky with his hot, smelly little press, there was the birdman with his cages. Somewhere she heard someone singing:

Have you a chum who's bum?

'Turn around, you're going back,' said Thrawn in her ear.

'Can't hear,' said Milena, though she could.

The voice in her ear was then pitched to the level of pain.

'Now it's too loud!' said Milena. It was as if she were wading through glue, through the noise, through the people, through the glare, through increasingly panicked voice in her ear, the voice of Thrawn who now had guessed that Milena was playing a brand new game.

Then Milena saw her, the Seller of Games, big boned, hearty, with virulently purple cheeks.

All light was sucked from her eyes.

She groped her way blindly forward. Her hands crawled up and over people's shoulders.

'I'm blind,' she said, 'Take me to the Seller of Games.'

For some reason, *Symphonie Fantastique* was taken up by everyone. It was a half-serious prayer for rain. Everyone sang it, the song for a Sabbath, praying for the waters to fall. 'Oh God, please God, make it rain God.'

The person, a man, murmured something and took hold of Milena's shoulder to lead her.

Oh God, please God, make it rain!

'Cunt! Cunt! Cunt!' Thrawn was howling like a gale in her ears. Milena could hear nothing else. Her hands were clamped over her eyes shielding them. Blindness was replaced by fire all along her arms and hands. Thrawn was burning her skin with light.

She felt the edge of a stall. 'Am I here? Am I here?' she shouted.

'Yes!' she could barely hear the man howling at her.

'Sorry, sorry. I'm ill,' said Milena, unable to see the Seller, unable to hear her. 'I need your lenses. Your contact lenses, with the mirrors.'

Fire danced on her skin. Milena screamed. The sound of the scream was lost in the chorus.

'What? What love?' she could hear the Games Seller wailing.

'The light burns!' Milena wailed. 'I need the lenses!'

Milena rammed her hands into her armpits, to hide them from the light.

The beefy hands of the Games Seller seized Milena's arms. The Games Seller led her. Milena tripped up; she fell forward. The woman caught her up. Blisters ruptured against her cotton shirt. Her hands wept. The woman led her into Leake Street.

Everything went dark and cool, and Milena could suddenly hear.

'Put them in please,' wept Milena.

The woman was over her huge and sheltering. 'Yes, you are, yes you are, yes you are in a bad way,' the Gameswoman sang soothingly. It was a lullaby. She kept on singing, soothing, as she forced Milena to open her eyes away from the light.

Thrawn made the worms crawl inside them, but in Leake Street, the light was dull.

First one in. Then the other. Now there really was something in her eyes. Tears welled up to expel them. I will get used to them, Milena told herself. I will have to get used to them. She turned and looked up at the end of Leake Street. Thrawn tried to focus the light. It concentrated into a dull blue circle. Milena moved her head. It took some seconds for Thrawn to find the focus. That would have to be good enough.

The Seller of Games was inspecting Milena's blistered fingers. 'Your poor little hand . . .' she began. *La Boheme.* Then she tried to speak. 'Buh! Buh!' she stammered, and sighed, and sang again.

'Bloody viruses! What will they do to us next?'

Milena said she didn't know. She thanked the Seller, paid for the lenses and stepped out again into the light and the roar of the songs. She rocked her head, very slightly, from side to side. She bought a pair of gloves and some ear plugs.

'Go and die,' said Thrawn in Milena's ear, just before the plugs were inserted.

The game we are playing now, thought Milena, is called Sticks and Stones. Words can never hurt me.

All around her, everywhere around her, people sang.

Slightly less than a year later, Milena married.

She remembered the wedding party, in the forest of the Consensus. That year the summer was clouded and cool. A blustery wind rocked back and forth between the fleshy trunks of the purple trees. The guests were as chilled as the wine. They clutched their glasses with one hand, and warmed the back of their arms with the other and did their best to make conversation. Mike Stone tried to make conversation. Milena had forgotten how stiff he could be. He bent forward from the waist and shook people's hands and could think of nothing to say except 'Thank you very much for coming', or 'I suppose you're all famous', or 'I've always wanted to act'.

He had worn his astronaut suit to the wedding. He liked his astronaut suit and saw no reason ever to wear anything else. The pockets were full of astronaut gear – microscopes and multipurpose DNA capsules. He explained them at great length to Cilla, who used every particle of her acting ability in looking rapt with fascination.

Halfway through the party, Milton the Minister died.

'The two of you alone together up there in space,' Milton was saying. It was his way of congratulating them. 'It must have been a real Battle of the Bulge.' His eyes closed and his smile spread, as if he had finally made the perfect Milton joke. An expression of peace settled onto his face. Then he fell forward into the calamari salad and overturned the table of refreshments.

Mike had a first-aid kit in the pouches of his overalls. He slipped a pulse injector into Milton's ear to keep his breath and heartbeat going while Milena, Moira Almasy, all the Terminals, called for the Consensus. It came in the form of the new police, the men in white, the Garda.

They came with a chopping, juddering sound as if something were cutting the air into slices. Something predatory descended from the sky onto the pavements of Marsham Street. It was the first time Milena had ever seen a helicopter. It was made entirely of metal and resin, and it gleamed like some hungry insect. Mike swept Milton up and carried him past the Garda, his wiry limbs moving with a robotic smoothness. He lowered Milton into the bubble of the beast and the Garda trooped back inside it, and with a whirlwind of air, the thing lifted off, and was gone.

The death and the helicopter shook Milena. Many things had happened over the last year to shake her. She found her teeth were involuntarily tap dancing and the cold seemed to rise out of her own bone-marrow. Milena was cold inside. Milena asked to be taken home. The party was over.

It was a cold, cold boat ride back to the Slump, through little, lapping, grey waves. Milena curled up against Mike Stone to be warmed, and she still shook. She didn't know it was fear. She only knew that soon her husband might want to make love, and that she did not. She only knew that she had never told him she could not accept sex from a man. Paradoxically, the fear made her turn to him for comfort.

She was still afraid walking back into her little lacquered boxes. She showed him each of the rooms, puffing up pillows, folding in shutters, lighting the alcohol lamps. In the darkness in the corners, the truth still waited, unsaid. Whenever I get into this kind of trouble she thought, it is because I have been dishonest. What happens next? What happens now?

'Play some music, Mike, if you'd like to,' said Milena. Her back was to him.

Mike Stone said nothing. He stood in the centre of the bamboo box, his back rigid, his hands clasped behind him, uncertain what was to come next.

'You don't feel like it?' Milena asked him, gently. She often found herself thinking of him with kindness.

Still smiling his engineer's smile, he shook his head. He went and sat very tidily on a Pear, hands folded in his lap.

'Do you want to do anything special?' she asked him. Now what could you possibly do that was special on your marriage night?

'Doesn't seem that there's too much to do. Your friends are very nice. They tried very hard.' He looked down at his hands, and his smile broadened ruefully. 'I don't think Cilla's terribly interested in self-directed mutation mechanisms.'

'Just say that it means the Bulge can grow chicken meat out of itself,' she told him, sitting next to him. 'That's all they want to hear. They just want the excitement.'

'I don't find outer space exciting,' he said, simply.

'You must be the only one who doesn't,' she said.

Come on, Milena, she told herself. Begin, Milena, begin, say it quickly, the dishonesty can be killed, the knot can be cut with single word of truth. She sat with him on the Pear. 'This is going to be a . . . ah . . . a strange kind of marriage,' she began, and was stopped, as if by a virus.

He nodded, tamely, in agreement. 'I can't get an erection,' he said. Milena wasn't too sure that she heard correctly.

'Sorry, Mike?'

'I'm impotent,' he said, quite directly, without, now, a trace of embarrassment. 'I'm afraid that our conjugal relations are not going to be entirely existent.'

Milena could hardly believe her luck. She hoped she could keep the relief out of her voice. 'Mike. I want you to know how much I appreciate this. Your telling me, I mean. The important thing is the marriage. Physical satisfaction is not the main thing.'

After all these years of doing without it anyway.

'I didn't think you liked sex either,' he said. 'I had a pretty good idea that you were the sort of girl I was looking for.'

Milena was less sure she was pleased by this.

'You were obviously a very, very nice person who was not physically attracted to me, or to men in general.' His expression really was rather tender. 'I like cuddles.'

Milena could feel herself blushing furiously. She felt that she had been caught out in some way. She discovered that both hands were on her cheeks, feeling how plump and hot they had become.

'I hope I didn't mislead you,' said Mike Stone. 'I tried very hard not to play the tooch knave,' he said.

The very idea of Mike Stone playing tooch knave restored some of Milena's humour. Playing tooch? On what, Mike, the violin? 'Mike. I never thought you were a knave.' Her hands were lowered from her face. 'Did I mislead you?' she asked.

'Not for a moment,' he said, obviously thinking that this would reassure her.

'I'm scared,' she said. It was an explanation. She surprised herself by saying so.

'Of what?' he asked.

'These days? Of the dark. I'm scared of the dark, since Thrawn. Isn't that funny? Thrawn used light. I should love the dark. And I'm scared of . . . of the viruses and what they're doing . . . and of . . . of you.'

'That's understandable, I am pretty weird,' said Mike Stone. He meant it. 'I can't say for sure if I'm scared of anything at all.' He meant that, too. He shook his head. 'I can't think of anything that scares me. There are just some things that I can do and some things that I can't.

277

I'm always amazed by the things you can do. You seem to get people to do things just by talking about what's got to be done. You seem to be able to talk to pretty near anybody. That's because you're frightened. I think you can do all that because of the fear. I do the best I can without it.'

'You're not, are you? Frightened?' She saw what he meant. She had thought it was fear that made him stiff and awkward. She was beginning to see now that it was instead a quality of precision, like a watch, exact and unselfconscious.

'Only because I don't feel there's anything to lose. If I can't do something, like talk to people, there's no shame. I tried. I did my best. If I can do something, there's no shame. I did my best.'

I'm going to like you, thought Milena. I'm going to like you more and more. I don't think this is a mistake, after all.

'I'd like to go to bed,' he said. 'I'd like to hold you. You always look cold these days. I'm very hot. I have very hot feet.'

'I knew someone else who had very hot feet,' said Milena. It had been so long since anyone had held her. She looked up at him. In fear.

We could of course spend time cooking a meal that neither of us wants to eat. He could get out his violin, and I could comment on his playing. But the tension would remain. There would still be this to face. To do anything else would be an evasion, a dishonesty. And so this must be faced, even in fear, and I do feel fear. Prissy, obsessive, severe, that's what Cilla said. Am I still those things? I don't like this. It makes me feel estranged from myself, as if I have to give myself up. It makes me feel alone and exposed, an orphan.

Mike Stone let Milena lay on the bed in most of her clothes, and then went to the bathroom to wash, knowing instinctively that she would not like the smell of men. He came back, naked and neutral, and his body was more bizarre than she had imagined. In the midst of her fear, she saw that his body made her smile.

He was stretched upwards, very tall and thin, like something by Goya, with narrow sloping shoulders, and a washboard tummy, and arms and legs that were all knots and angles. His hips were very broad, almost feminine, with broad spaces between the thin legs. He was hairless except in unexpected places, on the shoulders, or in a ring around his nipples. His nipples were so pale and small as to be invisible.

Mike Stone had a huge and useless dong. It flapped back and forth between his thighs, smelling of soap, like some hapless passenger on a bumpy train ride, and his testicles hung by such a slender thread of scrotum that Milena found she had sympathy pains in places she didn't have. She was curious to see male genitalia, out of the mildest and most objective sort of interest. He settled next to her in the bed, and she wondered what she could do. She thought of stretching out her hand to touch him, to touch his penis. Something made of iron stopped her, as if a virus. She could never do that. She felt a stirring of distrust. What if he had lied, what if he would now come to life, and force her? Instead he put his arm under her head, and cradled her up, and lay her face on his chest, settling with a sigh.

Milena felt human flesh again, warm, against hers.

She was surprised by the body. She had thought that men would feel knotted and muscled and hard, all bone and sinew. His wiry flesh was still soft and smooth, warm and sheltering. She shivered in his grasp, still afraid. Experimentally, she put a trembling hand on his chest. He turned his face and looked into her eyes, with the preternatural trust, the animal simplicity, the brown eyes of a child. She smiled back, and found the fear began to melt.

He made a grunt of satisfaction. They lay still and quiet as dark descended. Milena had found a harbour, a place of refuge that was warm in the unseasonable chill.

During the Summer of Song, the summer of drought, each day began high and early with silver light filling an empty sky that looked like the inside of a bell. The floors would still be warm underfoot from the day before. There was no water to wash with; the water Milena drank was still hot in its wooden bucket from the previous day. Everything stank of rotting reed, and there were no more flowers at funerals: the flowers had all died.

By the middle of September, it had not rained for four months. The upper reaches of the Estuary were dry. Milena had to walk across the Slump to the main channel of the Thames, which was still navigable. In all that dreadful summer, those early walks were the thing she hated most.

The algae and the water plants had dried into something like papier mâché, a tough, leathery coating over the mud, over the stones. When it burst underfoot, dust and a dank smell like crypts escaped. There were a few shallow farming ponds left.

Milena remembered approaching a pond, and the ground ahead seethed. Hundreds of frogs lolloped into the brackish water. Overhead, marauding herons circled. It was seven o'clock and already the heat was like a hammer. Already Milena was drenched in sweat, her lips were cracked and her throat dry. Children sat, disconsolate on the banks, feeding on sunlight, no longer bothering to chase the herons away.

'Good morning!' Milena called to them, trying to be normal.

The children looked at her in fear and silence. They sat up and edged away.

Milena rocked as she walked, moving her head up and down, left and right. She was escaping the disruption in her eyes. When she looked in the mirror she saw someone with the eyes of a lizard, closed over with a metallic, gleaming surface. The eyes are the doorway into the soul; her mirror lenses denied all sorts of exchange besides exchange of light. People would look away from her, repelled. She saw the world, with its bright sun glaring on white stones and bleached plants through a dim blue filtering.

In the blazing heat, Milena wore gloves. She wore a heavy shirt that buttoned down around her wrists, she wore thick trousers and a scarf around her face. If any of her skin was exposed to light, the torment would begin. Light would concentrate just under its surface until it burned. There were blisters around her eyes.

Milena walked past the children into the dead rice paddies, where she would be alone. She walked with dread. Whenever she was alone, the images began.

A hump of dried algae appeared to rise up. Something human struggled out from underneath it, a bare arm, a blistered face. The face was bruised and torn, and the hump of algae rocked back and forth on top of it, smiling with white false teeth and glass eyes, sputtering as it breathed. Thrawn was being raped by it. 'Stop her,' the face pleaded, looking at Milena. 'Stop her, please.'

Milena's knees wobbled and her feet seemed to turn sideways on the stones; she walked like someone with a neural disturbance. She staggered through the image. She walked through the pumping mound of algae; her feet walked through the pleading face. You are not there, she told herself. You do not exist. Her fists were clenched. She was being worn down.

Milena had to walk around the edge of a long-dry fish-farm. There had been too many trout to save. Their corpses lay stinking in the bleached, baked mud. There were flies. They tickled the corners of Milena's mouth. Milena waved them away.

Suddenly a pile of dead fish heaved back and there was Thrawn McCartney. She had been opened up too, her softer portions eaten away. She opened her mouth to speak and flies ascended from it in a cloud.

'Milena!' said the swirling cloud of flies. The flies swarmed around her, buzzing. 'Milena! Milena!'

Milena steeled herself, hunching her shoulders and walked on. She was confronted with the scattered bodies of fish, almost to the horizon. She decided they were not real. She walked on and her feet slipped in the slime of rotten fish. That upset her more than anything else that morning. There was a sharp stab of anger, and then despair. My new shoes, she thought. My beautiful new shoes. I knew I ought to carry them! Now they'll stink of rotten fish all day. People will see the crazy lady rock and shiver and then they'll smell her. She tried to wipe the shoes on dried clumps of grass. The grass was as white and as brittle as china.

She walked to the main channel of the River Thames. At low tide, the river was now no more than roughly four or five metres across. It wound its way through a stinking softness of mud and drying salt, up to the white gates of the Great Barrier Reef.

The Barrier rose up like a range of snow-peaked, rolling hills in the distance. Even through the filter of the lenses, the Great Reef glistened in the fierce sun, as if mirror dust had been thrown over it. Milena could feel the light reflected from it on her skin. The Reef stretched away towards the South Downs, and north towards Tottenham. Its foundations were a stained and mottled brown from lichen and the mud and the waters that had retreated. Its gates, the locks, were left hanging open. There was no need to keep back the waters now.

On the banks a crowd of people waited for taxis. The docks of the taxi station, with its walkways and awnings were now stranded far up the shore, away from the dying river. The people waited disconsolately under broad-brimmed hats. They wore shorts and airy shirts and sandals. Some of them stood sinking into mud, staring away from the world. Baskets full of their goods waited untended on the shore. There were dried and shrivelled onions, a last few nurtured radishes, whole herds of frogs killed for sale before they died of drought and disease. Downstream, the banks were white with birds gathering by the water that was left.

As Milena approached, spiders scuttled backwards ahead of her. They had leering cartoon faces. Their grins were mad and mocking, the eyes bright with violence. Sticks and stones. You think that can hurt me? Milena felt her jaw jut out with determination under its sweaty woollen mask. Do you? Hurt? Hah? Even without thinking, her head wobbled from side to side, to escape the disruption in her eyes.

She joined the line for the water taxis and the images ceased. Her nostrils were plugged to keep out light, her ears were plugged. It was a little while before she realised that someone had been calling her by name.

'Milena? Milena!' he was saying.

She turned around to see a farmer burned black-purple from the sun, under a broad hat. He wore shorts and an oatmeal coloured toga. Mud was going dry and grey on his ankles and rough resin sandals. Then she focused on the face.

It was Al, Al the Snide. He carried a basket of shrivelled, slimy coriander leaves.

'My God, what's happened to you?' he asked her. He took hold of

Milena's arm, and pulled her to one side, away from all the people, from the babble of their thoughts.

Milena knew what he saw. He saw a woman with mirror contact lenses, who never stopped rocking, very slightly, and whose ears and nostrils were stuffed with cotton wool, and whose mind seemed to be full of images of madness. A woman who believed she was being persecuted, that someone was beaming images into her head, or into the air all around her.

Milena tried to think at him, very clearly, in the silence.

I've got someone angry at me, she told him, without words. She is the best hologrammer in the world. She tried to burn out my eyes. Thus the mirrors. Now, everywhere I go, when I am alone, she hounds me with very unpleasant imagery.

She kept backing away, drawing him up the bank, away from the others. Away from other people, he could Read her more clearly.

I'm telling you this because you're Snide, and you can see what I see.

He began to look anxious, and with a tug on her arm, brought her to a stop. Then she pushed it all at him, the carcass in the living-room, the flies, the sun in her retina, and the things she had just seen.

'Do you believe me?' she asked him out loud, so he would remember to answer her in words.

The Snide's mouth hung open for a moment, and then he answered, choosing his words very carefully. 'I believe . . . that you believe it.'

Milena knew what that meant. How could she expect anything else? It sounded like madness even to her.

'Right. Fine,' she said, in a flat voice and began to walk back to the taxi station. She looked at her feet as she walked. Her shoes that now stank of fish grinned up at her with the faces of fish. The blubbery fish mouths were painted red with lipstick, and the eyes were ringed with blue make-up and mascara.

See that? She jabbed the thought towards the Snide, and spun around to show him the shoes. My shoes, she cubed faces onto my shoes. Did you see it? Just then? It was in the light! It was real! It was real!

Al the Snide watched her warily. No, he had not seen it. Milena turned away in a fury of disappointment and walked back into the crowd. The crowd was stirring. Dimly, Milena began to hear the sound of a taxi's engine. People were climbing up the slope of the bank for their baskets. Milena stood in line. Al rejoined her.

There's no way for you to tell, is there? she asked him in her mind. All you can Read is my memories, and they may or may not be mad. All you can tell is that I believe them. So now you tell me, Milena thought, distinctly, what has happened to you? Al looked confused and shook his head and held up his hands in helplessness. Too many people. He couldn't Read her clearly.

'How long have you been farming coriander?' she asked Al aloud.

The water-taxi was drawing near, a round, heavy black tug with a tiny steam engine. 'No moorings, no moorings,' a boy on the deck was shouting. 'You'll have to wade to us!'

People rolled up the bottom of their shorts, or plunged into the brown water that was infested with bilharzia. The Snide answered, warily, looking about him. 'They're after me,' Al said, murmuring, thin-lipped.

Milena couldn't quite hear. She pulled out an earplug, and leaned towards him.

'Since all this Singing, they're after anyone who plays with the viruses,' he said, standing up straight and looking away from her as if they were not talking. 'They've got Snides out after all of us now. I've got to stay with people all the time too, to hide. Like you had to, from me.'

'I need your help,' whispered Milena.

He closed his eyes. 'They want to wipe me,' he said. 'They're wiping everyone.'

Please?

And Al's eyes looked back into hers with terror. He shook his head. 'I can't lift my head above ground.'

Milena closed her eyes and nodded. She took hold of Al's arm, as if to say, I understand. Her hand was shaking. I must look mad, she thought, and tried to smooth down her hair. I didn't remember to comb my hair.

Al was still looking at her, and his eyes were full of horror. Am I really that bad? Milena thought. She pulled off her stinking new shoes and began to wade towards the boat.

They slid down the mud into the water. Milena's immune system sent Mice crawling all over her knees and ankles. The crawling itched. The water was thick and hot, and the mud felt like porridge suffused with bits of twig. Milena rinsed her shoes and then they climbed up rope ladders into the boat. It was crowded. Everyone stood pressed close together. Milena had a wall of sweaty backs pushed against her face. There was no conversation. The boat pulled away from the bank, and the people in it sweltered, smelling of mud and reeds. People clung to the outside of the boat, hanging on the rope ladders.

The taxi chugged its way through the locks. The gates were open, the wooden walls were going grey and dry. There were gaps between the timbers where the wood had shrunk. The Slump and the Pit were now on the same water level.

There were high Coral embankments with steps rising up from the docks. They cast cool, delicious shadows. Relieved to be in shade at last, the passengers began to climb slowly, one step at a time, to savour it.

Rowing boats still clustered around the locks, but bigger boats and water-taxis lay tilted on their sides in the mud. Seagulls padded their way clumsily across the silt.

'I can treat you to a glide,' Milena said to Al as they waited in line for the steps. She would hire a punt. She didn't want to be by herself, with Thrawn.

Al shook his head, no. 'A farmer doesn't ride with a Party Member.' It would draw attention, raise questions. He made a gesture of ducking. He had to keep low.

Milena nodded slow acknowledgement. She found a boatman on the quay, and looked back up the lock steps. Al was already gone, lost amid all the other water farmers. But as her boatman rowed them away, up the narrow river, she saw him standing on the edge of the bank. He was still looking at her, puzzled, scowling.

If only it would rain, thought Milena. If it would rain, the images would refract. She felt the small straw basket she carried. At least I still have my flask, she thought. I still have my flask full of water. She went on to the Zoo, and her heart began to sink at the thought of what awaited her there.

The Tykes at the desks prodded each other into silence as Milena approached. Monkeys, Milena called them in her mind, as they fought down grins. Here comes the mad lady, Monkeys.

Milena gave her name, trying to sound normal, asking if there were any messages. It was as if her skin gave off an odour of tension, as if she made the air vibrate with it. One of the girls said something, and because of the padding in her ears, Milena couldn't hear and had to ask the Monkeys to repeat themselves.

Milena felt their eyes on her back as she walked away. Her shoulders hunched up, and she rocked so badly that she stumbled. She couldn't be sure if she heard the Monkeys laugh behind her.

She walked down the corridor to the rehearsal rooms. Severed hands scuttled towards her like crabs. They wore rings of coral flowers.

I just have to hold on, Milena told herself. Hold on until Thrawn loses patience, until she breaks, or until they send me into space.

In the rehearsal hall, the cast were waiting. They were trying to record the opening, just the earliest passages of the first Canto. The cast performed, and Milena created the world around them, the world of Dante's forest. It was to be beamed from space, images the size of a continent.

It wasn't working.

Milena was late again, for a start. Milena was always late now. I can't travel early, thought Milena, or I'll be alone with the images all the way and I couldn't stand that. So you'll all have to wait. I'm sorry, but since you wouldn't believe me if I told you what was happening, you'll all just have to put up with it.

Milena did not apologise.

You think I'm crazy too, she thought.

Milena could see that in the slightly grim faces ranged against her. Cilla and Peterpaul looked bored and betrayed. And Toll Barrett leaned back in his chair without looking at her at all. A director himself, Toll was helping with the cubing. Milena rocked her head from side to side and put her basket down on a chair.

'Good morning, Milena,' said Cilla, deliberately loudly. Expected politeness had not been received.

Tough, thought Milena. 'Hello,' she said distracted. She gathered strength to face what was coming. 'Toll. I'm going to ask you again to keep an eye out for any disruption coming from outside the cube. Huh?'

'Sure,' he said, without looking at her.

'I know that something is disrupting the images.'

Thrawn was sabotaging them.

'They aren't as good as they could be,' he said with a slight wisp of a demoralised smile.

'They're unusable,' she said correcting him. He probably thinks I'm blaming him, she realised. Something else that can't be helped. 'Right,' she said, remembering the others with a sudden jerk of her head, looking up. Her mind went blank. Where had they left off yesterday? Her viruses rose up in a disordered flurry, jittery with nerves. I can't remember what scene we were doing. I can't do my job.

Thrawn was winning.

'Cilla, where did we finish last night?' She tried to make her voice sound bright and friendly, but it was wan, near tears.

'*Temp'era dal principio del mattino*' said Cilla, with a sigh, wondering if the whole production was a mistake.

'Um. Is that your line?' Milena's two fists were clenched together, shaking up and down as if rattling dice.

'I haven't managed to do any singing yet, Milena. I don't sing until Virgil enters. I'm playing Virgil, remember?'

They were only thirty-seven lines into the narrative text, which was left unsung, intimated by the music and depicted in the visuals. The poor actors had not yet had a chance to sing. They had only posed for the imagery, over and over. They must think it such a waste of their time.

285

I will still do this, thought Milena the director. She reached across Toll, punched buttons, coordinates. She closed her eyes altogether. The light from the hall came into her mind for Reformation, and with her eyes closed, she saw Peterpaul and Cilla look at each other and shake their heads.

'It really would be so much easier if you took those things out of your eyes,' said Toll Barrett. He meant the mirror lenses.

'I can't Toll, and I can't explain why,' said Milena. She had to work with her eyes closed. Otherwise she would have to work rocking back and forth to escape the blurring of her vision.

I will do this anyway. I can still make this work. Milena had learned how to work with her eyes firmly closed.

Controlled by Milena's mind came the images. She was so familiar with the images by now. She saw the dark wood, its polished dead branches, its black twigs like claws. She almost felt the soil, black with centuries of good, natural decay, overlaid with generations of fallen leaves and bark. Beyond the branches, she could feel the distance to the high, volcanic slopes. There was the brush of an early breeze, moving the branches in waves. She could feel the air scudding up the high slopes over the rocks, moving the clouds, as dawn light slowly broke with a pale tint of sunrise. It was the end of a terrible night, lost in a dark wood. Imagine, thought Milena, when this is all over.

The leopard entered, prowling, bright skinned, with a Cheshire cat smile. The music transcribed the words into sounds.

And it did not did not depart before my eyes,
but did so impede my way that more than once
I turned round to go back.

'Uh,' said Toll Barrett. 'Maybe you could make that leopard look a little less human. Unless that's what you want.'

Milena forced the face back to animal form. 'OK,' she said.

Peterpaul, in ordinary dress, an ordinary man, thick-necked in a short-sleeved shirt began to limp along the mountainside. The sun mounted up into the stars of morning. Milena placed him in the landscape. He walked on its ground, as the leopard prowled, to be joined by a lion.

Toll Barrett tapped her hand.

'Milena, look at what you're doing,' he said.

Milena opened her eyes. All along the bottom of the lion's feet, her beautifully imagined lion, there was a searing, crackling line of light: bad composite work. She closed her eyes. It was not there in what she was piecing together in her head. It shouldn't be there. Milena knew how to build up an image! Damn. Damn. Damn.

Milena found that she had slammed the console three times. Cilla, Peterpaul, Toll all looked at her in shock.

286

Thrawn had found the way to ruin her. Oh the elegance of it, oh the technique! Thrawn was placing perfectly recreated, common, amateurish flaws right into the heart of the Reformation image. In exactly the right place. Who else could do that? Who would ever believe she was?

'Let's just stop,' said Toll.

Milena opened her eyes again. She opened her eyes again, and that meant she had to start rocking again, back and forth, from side to side, like an autistic child.

Cilla looked stricken. She walked forward, playing with the rings on her fingers. She leaned over the counter and looked into Milena's eyes, or rather tried to. The exchange was cut off by the mirror.

'Milena. Is all of this too much for you?'

'No,' said Milena, hard, determined.

'It's a huge project and needs professional imaging. There's no shame in admitting that.'

'You've done your best and it hasn't worked.' Toll Barrett was less sympathetic. Peterpaul was a Singer and refused to speak if it meant a choice between stammering and sounding absurd. He said nothing, but his eyes were heavy on her.

Milena went very still and quiet, closing her eyes. 'We're going to try again,' she said, her face taut. She would not give in. The others sighed.

'Hello everyone,' said a familiar voice, 'Having a good time I hope.'

The voice was strained, like a violin string tuned too tightly. Milena felt everything in her pull tight. There was a kind of ache, all along her scalp. She opened her eyes and looked around.

Thrawn was in the room. Thrawn was wearing a bright autumnal print, but it couldn't disguise the depredations that had been made in her face. The mouth was sagging to one side. The mouth tried to smile, and failed, as if pulled down by weights hung from wires on her face. Her hair had not been combed for weeks. It was in clumps, lumpy uneven strands that fell into her eyes, or stood up at angles. This is how Thrawn is really looking. This is what this is doing to her. Milena found she could not speak.

'Anyone mind if I watch?' Thrawn asked. 'I just thought I'd pop in and see how it's going. You must be nearly finished by now. How long has it been since you started? Over two months, isn't it?'

Milena still said nothing. Silence.

'Right,' said Toll Barrett. 'See what you think of this.'

He replayed what had just been recorded.

The mountain, the pass, the leopard, the lion, the music again, gone over so often it had become almost nauseatingly dull, Rolfa's beautiful music made unpalatable by long hours of failure. And there it was again, the unreal, mottled flare of light around the lion's feet. The stars were bleary overhead.

'Don't look at the composite,' said Milena, to Toll. 'Look at Thrawn. Just keep looking at Thrawn.'

Toll turned. Milena reached down into her bag for the flask.

'If you're having trouble,' said Thrawn, in wary voice, offering genuine help. 'I could come in, brush these up for you.' Her eyes were round and sad.

'Just watch her, Toll.' Milena unscrewed the cup from the top of the flask. She filled the cup full of water.

I fling water at the light of the image and it is distorted, and she is shown to be a hologram. What a waste of water. Milena sipped it thirstily and looked at Thrawn. Milena saw the worn face and the wild hair. Each hair was visible, individual, out of place, and the wrinkles about the mouth did not float about the face but were embedded in its flesh.

Is that a hologram? Could that possibly be a hologram? What if Thrawn is really here? If I throw water over her and she is really here, that will simply help convince everyone that I'm the one who has gone crazy.

Milena scanned Thrawn, looking at her for some flaw, some line of light. It was perfect. There was even a depression in the seat cushion. That's real, Milena decided. You're actually here. Who is doing the cubing, then? Is anyone doing any cubing?

Or maybe, she thought, maybe it's me. Maybe I am mad.

Her arms suddenly seemed to be made out of stone. They weighted her down and wouldn't move. Maybe my mind has turned on me. Maybe it is my mind that is making those horrible images. If that is so, then the first step to being cured is to admit it. Admit that my mind has gone.

'Those flaws have been added,' said a voice. 'That's sabotage.'

Milena looked around, and there, by the door, was Al the Snide. He looked nervous but grim, thin and vulnerable in his farmer's robes.

'What are you doing here?' demanded Cilla, enraged. She still had not forgiven Al. 'This is a private recording. You can just Slide, Snide, out of here!'

'Yah, I'm Snide. I can read thought,' said Al. 'Reformation is thought. I can read it too. You ought to know that someone has cubed in those flaws. I can read the thought and it's Thrawn McCartney.'

All of them went still. Thrawn went still, unmoving, smiling slightly.

'She's been hounding Milena, following her around with holograms, very nasty ones. And, she's also hologrammed things right inside the eyes. So Milena can't see. That's why the mirrors.'

'What?' said Cilla, something rising in her voice. 'Milena, is this true?'

Milena nodded her head, up and down.

'If she's doing all that, what's she doing sitting there?' asked Toll Barrett.

'That's not a human being,' said the Snide. 'There's nothing there. That's an image, a mirror image. She's looking into a mirror, and sending the image to us.'

'Could anybody else do this?' Thrawn asked, standing up. She twirled around, in place. Her feet touched the carpet. They left depressions in the carpet behind them. The image of a depressed carpet was absolutely opaque, in focus, properly shaded, no flares or edges of light.

'Is this or is this not the best hologram you've ever seen?' Thrawn began to weep. Cilla, the Soundman, Toll, Peterpaul all looked on in shock.

'So why are you all cutting me out?' the image asked. 'Why does everyone always have to cut me out?'

Milena picked up her cup of water.

Thrawn was pleading. 'You don't know what I could do for the Comedy. I could give you angels, and heaven, I could give you the music so clear, I could put you down on the ground so firmly, people would think that the sky had grown rocks.'

'You could take us to hell, too,' said Milena. And she flung the water at her.

Thrawn broke apart, refracted. Part of her face was in droplets, upside down in the air.

'My God,' said Toll Barrett.

Milena began to weep. 'Whenever I'm alone,' she said, and flung more water at her. The water was full of hate, as bitter as gall. With each lashing, part of Thrawn was pulled onto the wall and spattered against it. 'Whenever I want to sleep.' Another lashing of water, like a whip. 'She puts holograms into my eyes! She puts pieces of herself onto the floor! She makes me see things! Hear things!'

Thrawn stood still, hands clasped in front of her, as if pious, silent and weeping herself.

Toll put his arms around Milena and Milena shuddered. She dropped the cup and the water spilled over her hot thick trousers.

'Oh thank God,' she said, breathing out with relief. They had all seen it, all of them. They all knew. And she wasn't crazy, she wasn't crazy at all. Cilla was stroking her hair. Thrawn looked on for a moment longer, and then the hologram wasn't there.

Cilla stayed with Milena, while Toll and Peterpaul went to Milton, and told him what had happened. Milena never saw what followed. A delegation visited Thrawn's rooms and took all the equipment back. There was one portable machine which had vanished, along with Thrawn. She would never work for the Zoo again, and when she was finally found, she would be Read, and wiped clean.

Sometime during the confusion, the Snide slipped away, to a new disguise.

And finally as Cilla and Milena sat talking there came a familiar drumming on the roof. They both looked up.

'That's rain,' said Cilla. 'Milena, that's rain!'

They ran out onto the concrete walkways, under blue-black skies and the rain drove down in droplets the size of sparrow's eggs, and everyone ran out of the buildings, holding up their hands towards the skies, looking up at the clouds, letting themselves be pelted with the hot raw eggs of rain. They danced in circles, in each other's arms. From all over the city, came the sound of singing: Handel's 'Water Music', 'Singing in the Rain'. Milena and Cilla and Peterpaul and Toll all danced together round and round as the surface of the Thames was made rough with rain, and tiny rivers ran down the slopes of its cracked dry river bed.

And as they danced, a ghost appeared briefly, a dim image under grey skies, starved of light, scattered by raindrops. It sang, too, in a thin, unsteady wheedling voice.

Thrawn was still trying to join in.

A spindle-thread of gravity reached out all the way to Alpha Centauri. Milena could feel it in her head, and she could feel the forces of attraction tugging at her and at the Earth.

You could do worse than marry him said Bob the Angel. He felt like a thought in her own head. You need protection, Milena.

Milena was going to say, from what? But then she remembered Thrawn.

An image of exposure of loss, a sense of emptiness came to her from Bob. You are Bad Grammar. That was the implication.

'They know about me,' said Milena. 'Why haven't they Read me?'

They need you, said Bob.

Isn't it strange, how the stars are still beautiful? In the concentration camps of the twentieth century, they must have looked up and thought how strange it was that there could still be stars and beauty.

Why do they need me?

Oh, said Bob, they have a project, wilder than this. They need someone for it. They need someone who can mould the light. The Consensus is tired of being alone. It wants to reach out.

Instead of explaining, Bob the Angel gave her the idea whole, the image, its size, its function. He gave her the diagram again. He showed her the Angels, moving out in lines, radiated from a tiny Earth, from a tiny sun. No matter how many of them were sent out, they radiated away, into infinity. They did not move in parallel lines. The lines spread apart from each other. Trajectories of exploration that had appeared to be almost side by side when they left Earth were eventually spread so far apart that whole stars, whole galaxies were lost between them.

The universe was too big to fill, no matter how many Angels streamed up the lines between the stars. The Consensus wanted to do more than explore.

It wanted to call.

Somewhere else in the universe, there must be another consciousness also reaching out. If they reached out for each other along the forces of attraction, and they met, they could give each other the universe they had explored.

The Consensus was going to call for the Other.

So it isn't for Dante that they've done this, thought Milena, or for the music, or for anything else. They need to rehearse the techniques. They need to rehearse me.

Milena let it settle over her, the reality of the power by which she was held. I've always known that. I have always known they have me dancing, to pull me in when they want me. Why am I surprised? Did I think I was blessed, surrounded by some sort of sacred light? Did I really think the Consensus would love the music that much for its own sake?

Don't take it hard, murmured the mind of Bob the Angel. They love the music. They want to do the Comedy. They want to do this, too.

Milena had the concept, whole in her head. The Consensus wants to find a mate. It wants to meet another like itself. It is so sure that somewhere in the spangle of stars there is intelligence. It is so sure that intelligence will take the same form as itself.

So it wants to call across space. The call will go no faster than the Angels, but it will take the form of light, radiating evenly, spreading evenly, out through the universe.

The Consensus wants to make an artificial astronomical artefact.

It will be a hologram four light years high.

It will be an image of the human face. Milena saw it, four-sided, four sides of four different human faces: Chao Li Song, Marx, Lenin, and Mao. And the faces will mouth in silence:

One
One
Makes two.
Two and

then two
That will make four.

Over and over, the movements of the mouth would mimic the movements of the numbers, building up a code of mathematics, to be repeated, for intelligence to perceive and say: this is not natural. This is something calling.

Hubris anyone? Thousand Year Reich? They thought they would be judged by the size of their buildings, too, by the size of the ruins they would leave behind. Madness, monumentalism, Ozymandias, King of Kings.

It is a bit on the grand side, thought Bob, in her head. The Mount Rushmore idea is just a suggestion. They'd be dead chuffed if you had another idea, girl, dead chuffed.

Oh would they, now? Like they are dead chuffed by the Comedy? And the Comedy is just a way to test the gravitational lenses, and the Reforming, and all the techniques of sight and sound. They should have used Thrawn after all.

Oh no, lovey, oh no, don't be hard and bitter, thought Bob the Angel. Thrawn cannot be trusted. She has the wild humours and will not do as she is asked. We needed someone who would do what she was asked. We had to wait until you were trained by her, until you learned most of what she knew.

Milena's thoughts went small and quiet. Oh dear merciful heaven, she said to the stars. Thrawn was right.

That's your job isn't it? To find out what I'm doing and see if the Consensus can use it?

Yes, Thrawn, it was, but I didn't know it. I let them use me, Thrawn. I let them use me to destroy you.

Milena rose up, in rage.

So why did you leave me like this? she demanded. You don't need me independent, why not destroy me too, like you've destroyed everyone else. Why not Read me, wipe me, make me so much of a puppet that I can't realise it? Why not just make Thrawn over, why bring me into it at all?

Because, sighed Bob in the lines and in her mind, we have discovered that the viruses destroy talent.

Take Rolfa, he said, now Rolfa, we couldn't let that happen again. We Read Rolfa and look at her. Rolfa, this marvellous talent. We destroyed Rolfa. And your love for Rolfa, it pulls you up, love, it pulls you along and pulls things out of you no one could have known existed. We couldn't destroy that, could we?

You need me to love Rolfa, because it makes me work?

Not only that.

292

Bob showed her the rainfall of the flowers, her twenty-two billion roses.

The Consensus needs someone who can conceive of it. It wants to travel too. It will need you, to bear its image.

Where?

To the stars, said Bob. The Consensus wants you for an Angel. It wants you, Milena, to carry it out there, its image, to meet the Other when it comes. The viruses, you see, love. You didn't have them, but you had to keep up with them. So you forced yourself through all those years in the Child Garden. You forced yourself to do alone what the viruses do for everyone else. You forced yourself to grow a capacity for memory, for holding images, that no one else has.

All my history. All my self. It's to be used by the Consensus.

Bob. I've got nothing. You've left me with nothing. Why did you tell me this?

Because someone with nothing needs to know that. She needs to get something. What she needs to do, said Bob the Angel, is marry Mike Stone.

So Milena went up, and Milena went down and Milena married Mike Stone.

Hop, skip, and jump.

chapter fifteen

PEOPLE'S ARTIST (THE WHOLE TRUTH)

Milena remembered being on a platform in the gardens of the Embankment with her husband sitting beside her. On her other side there was some grand personage, whose name she had deliberately forgotten. It was July of the blustery summer, still plagued by high winds, but warm, warm at last.

Milena stepped forward from her folding chair, into the area of the cube that would magnify her. It would magnify her voice and her features, turn her into an artefact. Behind her there was a flapping of banners, long red banners, with medallions of socialist heroes. In front of her were red banners hanging from lamp-posts, buffeted by the wind. The trees moved and the shadows of the clouds moved, as if everything were stirring, alert and alive.

There were rows of faces in chairs. Milena knew many of them. Some of the faces were swollen with pride, proud of her, proud of themselves for knowing her. Others were slightly disgruntled with the boredom of doing a duty, forgivable under the circumstances. Others were sceptical and anticipatory at once. Would this tiny, drab-looking woman have anything interesting to say?

I think I have, thought Milena, looking up at the sky.

All around her was the silence. She could feel it. Silence and light being exchanged without human notice. She looked at the earth, still there under the buildings and the pavements. Besides performing a function, the buildings and pavements seemed to her to embody ideas and ideologies. Milena simply smiled, in the silence.

Milena kept on smiling for many moments, looking at the red banners and trying to really understand why they were there and what they might mean for her. The audience began to shift. Then, as she kept smiling, calm and feeling no need yet to respond or to speak, the audience began to smile with her, to chuckle.

'So,' she said finally. 'Here I am.'

Another long pause as the wind flapped. The banners sounded like the wings of birds. Milena knew what she wanted to do then.

There was a text that she had assiduously prepared, with a careful line of argument, discussing the need for a socialist artist to work for socially defined ends. She held the text in her hands. It was typed, on gold-embossed paper. Paper was still a way of making something important. It meant tradition. There had been copies of the speech waiting on people's chairs, weighted down by rocks to keep them there.

Milena found she was impatient with the paper. She set it free. She threw it up into the wind. It danced, and spiralled, rose up in the updraft of the Shell, spun around dizzyingly in the air. 'Wheee!' said Milena. No order. The audience laughed.

'I wonder,' she said, 'what this title People's Artist really means. I've always found that I have too little to do with people. My work has taken over my life. I wanted it to take over my life. It was as if I could fold myself up and keep myself safe in a drawer, very tidily, unseen. I wouldn't have to worry about it then. Or, to be honest, be worried by other people. In the end, I was. Worried by people. So here I am. Out.'

A mild, concerned chuckle. Just how embarrassing and personal was this speech going to get?

'I suppose the People part means that my work is used for political ends. It makes people feel and think in the ways they are supposed to feel and think. It's not much different from a virus.'

An unexpected burst of laughter, then. It swelled.

'Except that I always think of the great socialist ends after everything else.'

A warmer, but less certain, shorter laugh. Is this going to get dangerous?

'I thought when we were doing the out-plays that they were a way to make people love themselves and the London they live in. It seems to me that London now is at least as interesting as London was when all those plays were written. I wanted all the Estates to be proud of each other: the Reefers, the Cordwainers, the Tugboys, the Slump Bobbers. They're part of London too. I did not, however, set out to make them love two hundred foot tall Crabs.'

A grateful laugh now, of relief. This isn't going to veer off in any funny direction. This is going to work.

'I think people should love giant Crabs, particularly if they sing well.' Pause.

'Those of us who work at the Zoo often have to love giant singing Animals.'

A larger laugh. But the trees whispered, that's enough.

'You can get too high-minded. People should be easier on themselves. Life isn't high-minded. If it's got a mind at all, then it's out of it. *Attack* was just fun. It was an excuse to get in as many holograms as we could.'

We, meaning you and Thrawn, the trees sighed in and out.

'Sometimes fun can cost lives. The woman I worked with on Crabs is no longer with us. The woman who set all of *Divina Commedia* to music is no longer with us either. I used to think I destroyed them both. Now I think that to blame myself is just another way of making myself too important.

'The most socialist thing I ever did, the best thing I ever did, was trying to get people to help the sick instead of shutting them away and burning the bodies. I had a lot of help, from Milton John, from Moira Almasy. And that was nothing to do with being an Artist.'

Milena stopped, visibly wondering what she was going to say next, taking her time.

'Am I an Artist at all? I don't know what the word means. I do what I can, in the way I can do it, when I have an idea. I don't know where the ideas come from, except that I don't have them. By that I mean the "I" that I know doesn't seem to have them. The "I" that I know keeps trying to think of ideas and they don't come. The ideas seem to come of their own accord, in their own time, without me. So I can't really claim any credit for them. Or responsibility, either. Life just gives them to me. You, my friends, the ones I can see in the front row. You gave them to me. And the city, and the history that made it and made me too. So who is the Artist, then? Is there an Artist at all?'

Suddenly she grinned.

'Maybe we should be giving this award to each other, just for being here. The only way to be a People's Artist is to be as private as you can. That's when you touch something that isn't just you.'

And Milena said to herself, to the trees in the wind: Rolfa, I love you. I want to live with you and sleep with you. And I can't. I don't tell them that. To do that would be to try to tell them the whole truth. And who can tell the whole truth? You'd never stop talking.

She said that aloud. 'Maybe that isn't the whole truth. But if I tried to tell the whole truth, I'd never stop talking.'

Another small chuckle. Some of them were still working it out.

'We're all people. We're all artists.' She shrugged with helplessness. 'Thank you.'

There was a settled warmth to the applause that followed. Cilla, the Princess, Peterpaul, Moira Almasy, they all stood up. Moira's jaw was thrust out as she smiled. Cilla was grinning and grinning as if her face could not spread wide enough. Peterpaul was applauding, looking serious, looking straight into her eyes. Toll Barrett was nodding 'yes'. Even Charles Sheer was applauding.

And a Crab-like voice in Milena's head said, *You're good at making speeches, Milena. That could be useful.*

And another voice, lowering, slow, said *It made you look better than you are. They'll never guess.*

296

Milena stood, still and quiet, embarrassed, battling to keep her modesty. Perhaps she was wrong to think that arrogance and pride would destroy talent, but it was what she believed, so she tried to preserve her humility. It was a tactical decision. She exploited herself and had to protect herself from her self.

And how many selves, how many voices?

Be easy on yourself, Milena. Here is the sun, here is the applause, and the light, and the silence.

chapter sixteen

AN ENDING UP OF FRIENDS
(THE DEAD SPACES)

Milena remembered walking towards St Thomas's Hospital. A nurse led her. He was a big man, about seventeen years old, calm and smiling. She remembered his sun-bruised skin, dark purple cheeks and clear eyes. The picture of health. He sauntered, at ease with his body and the world.

'We'll go round this way,' he said, as they crossed the road. His teeth were perfect and white, and he had golden-green curly hair.

'How did you know to ask for me?' asked Milena. 'Did she tell you?'

'The Terminals said she was part of the Centennial and to find you out in the Slump.' He held open a door, and they entered the Coral Reef.

The hospital was full of tunnels and dens, like natural caverns. The Coral Reef walls glowed softly, fluorescent, so that there would always be light, so that the dying did not awake in the dark, afraid that they had already gone. The Cancer Ward, it was called. People were dying for the lack of it.

In each of the dens three or four people lay in beds, young people, thirty or thirty-five years old, suddenly stricken, suddenly dying. Very suddenly they lost weight, fell ill with a variety of diseases as their immune system failed. Their bodies wore out, their hearts, their lungs, their livers, all expiring in concert.

'It's an epidemic, really, isn't it?' Milena said, keeping her voice low.

'There really isn't a word for what it is,' said the picture of health. He held a door open for her. Milena smelled, very faintly, the stifled odour of illnesses and drugs and damp bandages and disinfectant.

The Doctors were still trying to break the Candy that shielded the genes of growth and maturing. The Doctors were still trying to find a way to synthesise the proteins that cancer had made, that had prolonged life. We all forget, thought Milena, we all have to forget that half of our lives has been lost.

Except for the Tumours, except for Lucy; they can't die at all.

'What's wrong with Lucy?' Milena asked. Lucy had been missing for several months. It seemed likely that she was very ill indeed.

The nurse stopped and shook his head. 'Nothing's wrong,' he said. 'She's getting better.'

'Yes, but from what?' Milena asked.

The nurse shrugged. 'Old age?' He beamed. 'The human condition? She also is in – ah – another condition. But maybe that isn't quite so miraculous.'

Miraculous?

The nurse led Milena on down the corridor, and indicated a doorway, and bowed slightly as if presenting Lucy to her.

Picture of health, thought Milena, looking at his puce and smiling cheeks, even you will be cut off.

Then she went into Lucy's room.

Lucy had a room to herself. She sat up in bed and Milena could see in that instant that she had changed utterly.

Lucy looked very calm and dignified, perhaps even stern. Her hair was no longer orange. It was the colour of friable, dry soil, a muted grey. It was going darker in a line, along the parting near the scalp. Her leathery old skin looked thicker, smoother. It was a different kind of skin.

Lucy looked at Milena, with a hint of a smile, and something in that look made Milena's breath catch. 'I know you,' she said.

'Hello, Lucy,' said Milena as if caught off-guard. 'How are you?'

'You don't have the time,' said Lucy, with the same stern smile. She turned away, and looked out of her window, at the river. 'You don't have the time that I have.'

Lucy was rubbing the palms of her hands, and the skin was coming off in thick rolls, as if it were a coating of dried glue. The new skin underneath was brown and thick and spongy, without any lines or creases. No future there, for a fortune teller to read. Milena saw Lucy's profile.

She looks, thought Milena, like a head on a Roman coin. Misshapen somehow, but fierce. She looks like something that might have grown up out of the earth, a sort of root vegetable. And she smells, smells delicious, like freshly baked bread.

'One day,' said Lucy, still watching the river outside, 'it all comes back, and you're somewhere else. Now. I can draw any map, right here in my hand. I can light a cigarette with my fingers. I'm not saying that everything will work out by itself, by what *we* want, mind you. I'm just saying that the eyes are hollow . . . that the light spreads out inside our eyes and not outside. One day it just added up.'

Her mind has gone, thought Milena.

'One day, it just all added up. Added up, all the little bits and pieces, and you blank out. No memory. Feels wonderful. Like a warm bath. You don't need it any more.'

Or has gone into another state, thought Milena. Lucy. What are you trying to tell me?

'I am five hundred feet tall,' said the ancient. 'You could all shelter in my shade – if my leaves was seen by you.'

She sighed and leaned forward and picked up a tray from the bed. On a plate was a huge lump of meat, its fat all crisp, golden, raised up in crunchy blisters. It was covered in minty sauce, and there was a mound of – what – ice cream?

No. Mashed potatoes. Lamb and mashed potatoes with a pool of meat juice in a hollow in the middle. And there was a pile of hard, green brussels sprouts.

It wasn't there before, thought Milena. I'm sure it wasn't there before.

Lucy chewed and swallowed. 'These little tracks go everywhere,' she said. She very neatly sculpted a mouthful of mashed potato onto the back of her fork. 'You can't see them at first, you've got to go blind for fifty or sixty years first. I couldn't see anything for at least that long, and then one day, there's an ache from the front to the back of your head, and your eyes are better. They get better and you see different. Everything different. They don't teach you to see, and it takes time to heal. You have to go blind in order to heal.'

She raised the forkful of mash in salute.

'What I'd like to do,' she said, food pushed over to one side in her mouth. 'Is plant myself for a hundred years or so. I'd just like to settle in like a tree. Feed like a tree on sunlight and rain. Get all those wrinkles in my brain to unravel. I think my bones would heal, then, too. Did they tell you? My bones are getting bigger, stronger. And all the nodules are flaking off, too.'

There was no archness about her, no mischievousness. She's lost the old London, thought Milena. She's shed it, like a skin.

'And,' said Lucy. 'I'm pregnant.'

She continued chewing the lamb that shouldn't have been there.

'Metastasis. A little bit broke free and started growing in my womb. One chance in ten million, but how many million chances have I got?' She coughed and laughed at the same time. 'As many as I need. She'll be a cancer, too, my daughter. I have very definite ideas about how to bring her up. I'd like her to be a child for forty or fifty years. I'll build a raft and we'll live on it in the middle of the ocean, just catching the fish that leap up when you're quiet and part of the scenery. I'll just let her laze. We'll turn somersaults on tiny islands. We won't do nothing at all. There won't be any need. And when she's fed up being a child – well then. She'll become something new. We'll keep on changing, getting thicker and healthier.'

She looked at Milena in silence, cheeks bulging, in motion. Ker-

300

swallow gulp. It wasn't the time to ask, but it was Milena's job to know. 'Lucy,' she said, pronouncing very slowly and clearly, as if perhaps Lucy had forgotten some of her English. 'Remember you said you would be in an opera? *The Divine Comedy*? Remember, you said you would play Beatrice? Will you be able to record your part in the opera?'

'Ohhhhhh,' growled Lucy in pity and fierceness. She reached out and rubbed Milena's hair rather hard. 'Oh, you poor little creature.' Lucy looked at her smiling, as if at a fool. 'I already have recorded it, can't you see? In another time.'

Her mind has gone, thought Milena. We've recorded nothing with her. We haven't been able to find her. She and Lucy looked at each other, each pitying the other.

And the Milena who was remembering thought: pity her if you like, Milena, but you will go home and find that all her part has been recorded. You'll see her, singing with Dante, leading him to heaven. And you'll try to tell yourself that she must have slipped in and done it when you weren't there. But the rest of the cast won't remember singing with her. Except in their dreams. The world isn't what we thought it was. That plate of lamb shouldn't be there, and her perform-ance shouldn't be there, and perhaps the world shouldn't be here either.

'You're all the same,' said Lucy, shaking her head. 'Always worried. I think of you all,' she said, looking into Milena's eyes again with a newly unnerving stare, 'like you was flowers in my garden. Beautiful flowers in a garden. When you're young, your bodies are so beautiful, all firm and fresh and full of heft. I want to press you in my book, just to keep you. But I open the book, and you've all gone grey and brown.'

Lucy took Milena's hand. Lucy's skin was thick, springy, as if upholstered with foam rubber. 'There's been some mistake,' she whis-pered. 'I should look into it, if I were you. You weren't meant to die, you know. Ever.'

And Milena remembered being young and well, running up the steps of the Shell. There was no Terminal ache along the crown of her head. There was lightness and fire in her feet. She turned a corner, and remembered finding Jacob on the fine spring morning of his death.

He was lying slightly on one side, his eyes half-open, dry.

Just for a moment there was the faint hope that he was blanked out again. Postpeople did when their memories were full. 'Jacob?' Milena whispered, as if he could awake. Then there was the immediate cer-tainty. 'Oh. Jacob,' she said in pity.

She looked at his shoes. He had put them on that morning, his old worn shoes, quickly ruined in climbing stairs, the sole loose and in peeling layers, a hole with borders of many different shades of grey.

I am the one who finds you when you die.

Not this time, Jacob.

Milena sat down next to him on the staircase, and took his hand. It was still limp and warm, and there was an exhalation. It was not exactly unpleasant, but it made one wary, like the smell of a foreign fruit from a strange land that one is going to have to taste.

A small gold crucifix fell out of Jacob's hand into hers, on a broken gold chain. The action seemed so natural it was as if he had passed it to her. Milena looked at the broken chain. He must have grabbed the cross, she thought, as if it could hold him up. He must have felt it coming, like a descending weight. He grabbed the cross and held it and the chain broke and he fell.

It was not exactly shameful to be a Christian. It meant you were a simple soul. Jacob did not come by a crucifix of gold by himself. It would have been passed from one dying hand to another, through generations. Who did Jacob have to pass it on to? He had his tiny room on the first floor, with his tiny stove and his tiny bed. He was not married. His life had been burnt through in service. The conviction came to Milena, irrational and immovable: the crucifix has been passed to me.

She stroked Jacob's head, as if to touch all the memories and all the good faith that had been there. She did not want to leave him, though there were all the usual things to be done: the quiet summoning of the What Does, the speedy gathering up of the dead. Well, someone else could go and get the What Does. Milena would stay there. Milena would stay there and take account of what had happened, pay attention to the death of Jacob the Postperson.

She took his ankles and pulled him out of the corner of the landing, away from the wall, into what seemed a more comfortable position. She arranged his hands.

We never had our talk, Jacob, the one in which I asked you what it was like to know so many people so well, to have so much information in your head. But I think it must have been like being smothered, smothered in other people, making demands.

I made more demands than anyone, Jacob. I cannot remember you making any demands on me. So I'm just going to sit here Jacob, and give you the time you deserve, a bit of time to understand the pattern you made, weaving through space and time, up and down the Shell, over and over, room to room, reminding people about debts and rehearsals, appointments and times to take medicines. Did you pray at night alone? Did you go to a Church, a boisterous singing church that

302

made you happy? Is there a church for Postpeople? And what about the seizures, the way you would blank out?

People said you were used to blanking out, Jacob. Postpeople do blank out if they don't take care of themselves. Three times, you blanked out, Jake, three times you let yourself get too full. You told me that it was like dying. Each time it happens, you said, you could feel your mind going cold in sections, like a city turning out its lights. Then they would give you a virus that taught you who you were and who your clients were, and back you went again. Three times you started anew, but it didn't make you look any fresher. You always looked dead around the eyes.

What can I make of that, Jacob? That you should have taken better care? They had viruses that could devour memory, leave you clean and open. But you were too busy with us, too busy taking care of us. Why did we deserve such care Jacob? We did nothing for you, except exchange the hellos and the goodbyes that are everyone's due.

I'm glad I never saw it. They say you crawled, Jacob. When the seizures came, you would crawl, and foam at the mouth. You would tear your hair. You fought, they told me, fought against it. You howled, No! No! and tore your shirt, gentle Jacob who was the soul of circumspection and dignity.

This last one killed you, didn't it? You died in another blank out, Jacob. So what does that mean?

I think it means you were abused. Your mind was stirred about like a casserole, you were taken over for the purposes of others. But you adjusted, each time. You found the joys that this life had to offer, limited as they were. The joy of knowing so many people well, the joy of being needed, of having a regular and recognised place, the joy of knowing so much about them, these many people.

But even that was taken away, the knowledge, the memory. And you would have to start again, dead, exhausted, climbing up the weary steps.

Good morning, Milena.
Good morning, Jacob.
And how are you today, Milena?
Fine, Jacob, fine.
Lovely weather, isn't it Milena?
Not really Jacob. A bit cold.
Oh yes, it's cold, but it's warm too, Milena.
Do you have any messages for me, Milena?
Do you have any messages for me, Milena?
Do you have any messages for me, Milena?

Only one Jacob, only one. That you deserved better. You did not deserve to end up here like a sack of garbage in worn-through shoes and one old suit dying alone with no one to see, and that we cannot make it up to you and the flowers on the grave will not be seen by you. And if that's the meaning, Jacob, if that's all the meaning I can get then I should bloody well try. Bloody well try again. Because if that's all there is then a mistake has been made, and the mistake is mine.

Milena remembering still had the crucifix, here, now, she could feel it, in her hand.

Ready to pass on.

And there was Mike, moving like clockwork, back erect, lighting candles in their home, their home together, amid the smell of food that he had cooked, against a window showing the slate-grey marsh, and the black reflection of clouds of smoke drifting over it, smoke from the cremation of the dead.

'What?' said Milena, easily amused, at least by him. 'All this? What? Tell me?'

Mike's thin lips turned all the way inward, fighting down a smile. He made her sit, and made her begin to eat, and poured her some wine, and then sat down.

'Milly,' he said. 'I've been thinking. We should have children.'

Oh. Milena set her fork back down on the table. 'Well you go have them, then.'

Breezy, everything was so simple and breezy back then.

'That's my idea,' said Mike Stone. 'I thought that since you're busy and don't like sex, you could donate an ovum, and I could donate a sperm cell and we could affix the result to the wall of my bowel.'

'You make it sound like a recipe,' said Milena sitting forward, suddenly disturbed. 'No Mike,' she said.

'I'd like to do it very much. It makes sense.' Milena remembered his daffy, trusting eyes.

'It's very dangerous,' said Milena.

'So's going up in space. I'd rather do this. I'd find it more interesting.'

Mike. Why are you so . . . so . . . nice? It isn't good for people to be nice. What if I make you bend too far? You won't know and neither will I. Until it's too late.

'I had a friend, Mike.'

'I know. Berowne. You told me.'

'He was nice and brave too, Mike. The placenta came away just afterwards. He bled to death. The blood hit the ceiling. And there was this baby left.'

Milena was surprised by feeling, thinking of the infant. 'It hadn't been part of the deal. Berowne was supposed to take care of the baby.

And Anna didn't want him, couldn't look at him at first, not until Peterpaul came along to help. So there were three lives ruined. No, Mike, no.'

'It's what I want to do,' he said. 'I've been consulting people. I've thought about all sorts of new ways to protect myself. And other people who do the same thing.'

'Yes and everyone thinks he is the one who is going to get through it, and for what?'

'For a beautiful new baby.'

'I'm not taking the responsibility. I've been through it all before. You think Berowne went around swinging from trees? He made it, he made it all the way through to delivery and out the other side, but they couldn't keep the placenta down. One good shove, and out it came and he was dead, dead in seconds, all the blood just pumped out of him.'

'There are stitch viruses. They can give me a stitch virus which will meld the placenta, hold it to me.'

'Please. I told you, I'm scared. I'm scared to death of all this biology. We're going to get something else wrong soon.'

'That's a different issue to my being pregnant.'

'I'm immune to it all. I don't have to worry. But you're not. What if these stitch viruses keep on stitching?'

'They don't,' he said, unafraid. 'They're safe behind Candy.'

Milena sighed and shook her head. He was right, they were getting off the issue. 'I don't want to make another orphan,' she said.

'One of us is bound to be left. For a time. Both of us are bound to die. That's no reason not to have a child. Otherwise, no one would have any children. And I like children. And someone has to be left to carry on.'

Make it breezy again, Mike. Take away the fear again. Tell me I'm just working too hard, that I don't wake up every morning feeling like I'm lead sheeting on a roof.

Mike kissed her on the end of her nose.

'No harm can ever really come. Even if someone dies. Death is going to come anyway. People always react to the thing that's just happened. Not to what's happening now. Out of step. I'm not Berowne.'

Milena went quiet again. Is there just a glimmer, she wondered, just a little tickle of jealousy? Thinking: hoi, that's my job. Men always seem to take over everything. Even this?

'So tell me, slowly and clearly,' said Milena. 'Why it won't kill you. And tell me what I'm supposed to do if it does.'

* * *

305

Milena remembered sitting at her desk in her new flat, working. She has a box that plays music to her. *Das Lied von der Erde* throbs gently in the background. Milena looks at maps of the Zoo Estate. She is trying to find the best place for a hospice for the Bees and for the sick. Milton wants to put them far out into the country. Milton the Minister is still alive.

The shutters of her lacquered rooms are closed against the weather. It is cold and from somewhere below comes the smell of coffee. There is a bleakness in Milena's belly, fear in the shadows, a tremor of anxiety in her hands. It is winter still, and she is not yet completely free. Thrawn is still out there, somewhere, with her one tiny machine.

'How's it going?' asks a familiar voice.

Milena glances up, quickly, and looks back down. She talks to the map. 'The Angels will be here soon, so you might as well go.'

Milena is Terminal now. The Consensus knows when it happens, and Angels come to break up the light.

'Look at me,' says Thrawn.

Milena pauses and then does look round. Thrawn's head is shaved; it is covered in stubble and little criss-cross cuts. She is smiling a faraway smile and is dressed only in a white vest and torn trousers. From somewhere, there is the smell of cooking alcohol, from the stove most likely. Thrawn's arms and knees twitch with cold. My God, thinks Milena, what a state.

'Look, Thrawn, part of me is very sorry how things have worked out, but I'm hardly likely to ask you to work with me again, am I?' Milena looks back around at the map.

'Are you sorry? Oh that's good.' Thrawn's voice is breathy, like a little girl's. Milena turns up the volume of the electronic box. The music becomes loud, the soprano's voice like a steam whistle, the flutes like knives. The Dead Spaces between the flats will kill the sound. Must see about that smell of alcohol, thinks Milena, trying to cancel out what stands behind her.

'Milena!' shouts Thrawn over the noise. 'Milena, look around, I've got a really good effect.'

Milena ignores her, eyes narrowing.

'That's your job, isn't it? To use my ideas? Please look around!'

Damn it, where are the Angels? I've been through all this before; I can't take any more of it.

Thrawn laughs, helplessly, musically. Out of the corner of her eye, Milena can see her staggering into her field of vision.

'Milena, just look around, and then I promise, I'll be out of your life. Out of your life forever!'

Milena looks around. She thinks she sees a hologram of Thrawn

McCartney, holding a lighted match. She is used to the perfection of Thrawn McCartney's images. The fire on the match rises out of gases from the wood. It hovers over the wood, and creeps its way up along it, slowly, towards the fingers.

'You promised,' says Thrawn, still somehow looking hopeful. Something thick hangs in strands between her cracked lips. 'You promised you wouldn't hate me.'

A whiff of cooking alcohol. I can smell alcohol, why can't you? asks the Milena who is remembering. If I can smell it, you can.

You can.

You're telling yourself you think you're seeing a hologram, thinks the Milena who remembers. Holograms don't smell. There's even a whiff of sulphur from the match. And you're watching the match get closer to her, and you want it to happen, I can remember you thinking, oh for God's sake go on, I know what's coming next, as if it's just one more horrific image in the light. You want to be rid of her, the crazy Fury, so she won't hound you, this Happy One, so that she will no longer be somewhere alive and betrayed and alone to make you feel guilty.

Look, even now, she's stopping, holding the match back. She wants you to stop her. She wants you to help. She wants to collapse weeping in your arms so that she can tell you that she's sorry, tell you she's hateful, tell you that it's not your fault.

'You were supposed to be my Saviour!' she has to shout, her voice breaking.

And the music wails.

everywhere the distance shines bright and blue!

Not hate, not love, but passion of a kind, twisted with lizard eyes. There are such things as demons. They are alive, and they live in the dead spaces between people.

forever . . . forever . . .

Soft, and sad, Mahler bids another farewell.

The match burns low, too low, while Thrawn waits for you to save her. The flame touches her finger. Her fingers, her arm, are soaked in alcohol.

The flower blooms, pink, flame. An unfocused flicker and a sudden eruption from the hand, along the arm up into the face, coating the flesh like this year's latest fashion, a crawling, living bloom of flame. Trickles of black smoke waver upwards.

And still Milena, the People's Artist, hesitates. Can it be real? What if this isn't just an image? Has she really done this to herself? Dread, horror mixed with an angry wrench of justification: you did it to yourself, Thrawn.

Stifle the dramatics, Milena, this is you, yourself who is remembering. You know what is happening is real. Worry a few moments longer and it will be too late.

'Oh shit,' says Milena the director and stands up finally. Not I'm sorry, oh God, but oh shit, as if it were the final inconvenience to have someone burn to death in your lacquered rooms. Worried about the rugs, Milena? That's it, stand up, get flustered, panic, pretend it takes a full minute to remember the thick new rug rolled up on the landing. You bought it just last week, your nice thick Tarty rug. Wipe away the distaste for spoiling it, wipe it nobly from your mind. What a sacrifice, Milena. Go to it, girl. Nice new part to play here. Heroine. You'll like this part, except you always were a terrible actress. You are strangely unconvincing in your concern. But there are no lines to remember, it makes you look good, everything a star can require, including someone else to cry over.

Somewhere in the midst of the flame, Thrawn is trying to dance, and is laughing. The thing that has hold of her knows that it has won at last.

ever . . . ever . . .

Fade into silence. The music is over.

Milena the director runs to hug Thrawn, the new, thick rug between them, to smother the flames. Thrawn is too tall. The rug encircles only her midriff.

'Get down on the floor! Get down on the floor!' wails Milena the director.

You weep do you, Milena? thinks her future self. Any animal would weep seeing this. Hitler's guards wept in the camps. The tears mean nothing except that you can feel the horror of it in your belly. You know you will feel that horror for the rest of your life, and that you will remember the tang of burnt hair, burnt flesh in the back of your throat until you die.

The alcohol burns away, like brandy on a plum pudding. Thrawn looks like a plum pudding. The plum pudding smiles and has bright white teeth, flecked with black. 'Oops,' it says and giggles.

'We'll get you a doctor,' Milena murmurs, unable to muster enough breath to talk plainly. She wants to scream, not to attract help so much as to express to the world that something terrible has happened. She wants to express it to Thrawn, who does not seem to have realised.

'Come on,' says Milena. 'Downstairs.' Without thinking, she takes Thrawn's hand. It is sticky.

'Mmmwhoh!' roars Thrawn, like a deaf-mute. Her nerves are beginning to feel what has happened. She jerks the hand away. The skin remains in Milena's hand like a glove, translucent. Milena keeps holding it, as if the hand were in two places at the same time.

Thrawn stares at the hand. She is no longer smiling. She looks dazed. 'Let's give the little lady a big hand,' she says, making a joke. She bobs as if floating.

Milena the director mews like a cat and throws the crisp and blistered skin away.

'Downstairs,' murmurs Thrawn. She walks ahead of Milena. She looks somehow ordinary, a quiet and somewhat muted person going for a leisurely stroll. Except for the hardened, flaking blackness of her head, Thrawn looks in some way normal for the first time. Her eyes are not bulging out with tension, her smile is not knife-edge sharp, she is not smiling at all. Her arms and legs move with a smooth and simple motion, and her fingers are not extended in a rictus of anger or unease.

Milena darts ahead of her, and pushes back the screens, one by one, the screens that lead through the Dead Space.

'Thank you,' says Thrawn, regally. She walks past Milena and out onto the varnished bamboo stairs. Outside the insulated flat, it is February freezing. Is it steam rising off her, or smoke? Milena wants to get her a coat but thinks: a coat on that skin? Her viruses tell her: third degree burns. Thrawn begins to trudge down the steps, like weary What Does at the end of a day.

'Oooff!' she says, as if exhausted from cleaning floors. She leans onto the handrail and the instant she touches it, she hisses and leaps back as if the rail were fiery hot.

Still hissing, Thrawn puts her arms over her head, and tries to pull off her vest. Blackened, the vest breaks up, falls away. Her back and shoulders are a mass of rising pink blisters, blackened streaks, and places that seemed to be covered with grit, as if it could be washed away.

It doesn't look too bad, it doesn't look too bad, Milena the director tells herself. The lower back is hardly touched at all. The breasts are beautiful, they have not been touched. She'll survive. She'll survive. Look, she is walking.

Thrawn takes another step and howls. Another step and she doubles up.

'Thrawn,' weeps Milena, helplessly.

Thrawn starts to scream. She starts to scream like a strangled cat, a harsh, meowing wail that moves in fits and starts but that doesn't stop. Her hands weave over her head, wanting to hold something, finding only pain, moving in a dance of helplessness.

There is a sound of sliding panels. Ms Will steps out of a Dead Space, and stands below on the rush matting. She stops and stares.

'There's been a terrible accident,' says Milena.

'There's been a terrible accident,' says Milena.

'There's been a terrible accident,' says Milena.

'There's been a terrible accident,' says Milena.

'She poured cooking alcohol over herself.'

Thrawn suddenly rolls forward. She tumbles down the steps, gathering speed, losing flesh, blackening the bamboo. She lies at the bottom of the step. Milena runs after her. Thrawn is on her back, gasping, breath coming in short agonised hops. She looks up at Milena, but does not seem to see her. She starts to shiver.

'Thrawn,' whispers Milena. 'I'm sorry.'

And what are you sorry for, Milena? You're sorry because you know you'll be so sorry for the the rest of your life. Are you mourning for her? Or mourning for yourself, for the anguish this will cost you?

Thrawn knows what you are. Thrawn focuses on you and smiles again, the demon smile, rearing up, in a frenzy, but paralysed, her hand a blackened claw, she looks up at you. 'Saviour,' she breathes out in a voice like the wind, smile blazing. She drags her hand along the floor, scraping layers of it away, leaving a blackened mark. 'Saviour?' she says, an angry, wheedling, bitter question. It is a rhetorical question. The answer is known.

She knows she has won.

We are coming Milena, says a voice in her head. Someone is coming to help.

The Consensus in her head.

The Angels soothe her. It's not your fault, Milena, don't blame yourself. It's not your fault.

'Isn't it?' asks Milena.

Do your work, Consensus. Rule the world, heal the sick, build the roads. Breed the viruses. Do anything that you consider to be good.

Only leave us alone.

From the top of the Tarty flats, a bell begins to toll. The emergency bell. Ms Will arrives with a blanket, and begins to wrap Thrawn in it. Thrawn's teeth are clicking together as she quakes with cold. Milena winces. It goes against instinct to put rough blankets on skinless flesh.

The Fire Warden arrives. She is trained to give treatment. In summer, if there was a fire in the floating Ark, pumps would spray water from the Estuary. Fire tugs would arrive, great steam boats that shoot water from cannons. But all the water is frozen now. The pumps don't work.

The Fire Warden kneels down and opens up her box of viruses and cream.

'Leave her alone,' says Milena, standing very still and quiet. The Fire Warden doesn't seem to understand that she means it.

'We'll use open treatment,' says the Fire Warden. She is a brisk and efficient Party Member. She has been trained to do good. She has been waiting for a chance to be needed. Her viruses are speaking, to the viruses of those who hear her, social viruses that know how to help the sick. 'We need to clean the burns, then keep them open to dry. Here.' The Fire Warden passes Milena a syringe. She wants Milena to take a blood sample. 'Test for nitrogen, prothrombin time, electrolyte levels, blood gases, hematocrit . . .'

Milena brushes the syringe away.

'Someone else is coming,' says Milena again. She means someone who can give better treatment than us.

'Don't see who it could be,' said the Fire Warden, getting out her creams. 'The Estuary is frozen, the Fire Tugs can't get here.' This was her responsibility, this was why she was trained and designated, so she could do good in the world. It is impossible to do good in the world, impossible that is, without also doing harm. The creams, the swabbing, the painkillers will do harm, relative harm.

Milena kicks the box over. The creams scatter, the applicators spin. Something made of glass shatters.

'What the . . . that is medicine!' wails the woman outraged.

So are the viruses. Relative harm, relative good.

The What Does Lady slides back the hangar doors. 'Come see, oh quick!' she says, gesturing to Ms Will. 'A wagon on the ice!'

Ms Will goes to the door. The Fire Warden bitterly gathers up her medicines. Milena watches over Thrawn. She looks at her shivering jaws and staring eyes.

And so I'm going to pass you over to them, Thrawn. You could have been beautiful. Maybe you will be. But you will still be theirs.

She hears the sound of galloping and looks up. Ms Will and the What Does are pushing back all of the great screens. There is a flood of cold air. Galloping across the ice, four great white horses, silvery as if frosted by the cold come pulling a fire wagon. Steam boils up as thick as cream from the boiler, and from the nostrils of the beasts. The wagon thunders up the bank of frozen mud and right into the Tarty flats, into the covered atrium, the horses reined in, snorting, half-turning and coming to a halt.

And Milena sees them. For the first time she sees the Men in White, the Garda. They are the masters. Their faces are screened by plastic, screened from the rest of us. For them, all of us are diseased.

'Look at my kit!' the Fire Warden says. 'She kicked it!'

The Garda do not reply. One of them takes hold of the Fire Warden's shoulders and moves her aside. He wears gloves. The other, with practised motion, peels back the blanket, slices through the clothes. Thrawn lies sad and exposed and barely breathing, looking

311

back up at Milena, sadly, as if asking her a regretful, reasonable question. Why? Pads are stuffed into her nose and ears.

The Men in White start covering her with spray. Milena looks away, to the horses.

The horses are huge, white, muscled. The horses wear wraparound mirror-shades. It keeps them looking only at what their masters want them to see. They toss their heads and their smoky yellow manes dance. Horses are beautiful even in slavery, because no one has told them they are ugly. Horses have no demons.

Milena hears the sound of the spray. Thrawn will grow new skin, a new mind. She will not be Thrawn anymore. There will be someone else, living a quite happy, very limited life, with gaps in her memory. She won't feel any anguish over what happened. A relative good then? Tell yourself it's a relative good, then, Milena.

The only place Thrawn is alive is here, now, as I remember.

Saviour.

hey fish it's me again!!!!!!

Milena finds a sealed oiled pouch, waiting for her when she returns from space. She remembers the spidery, shaking scrawl.

– well – they want the old lady to go back and she just doesn't want to go! broke my leg again – well – my hip but it amounts to the same thing – now they want to get the old dam back – thats what they want – get her safely on some old sofa and we'll bring her dinner whenever we remember

us polar types get old, fish – you don't know what that means – it means you start to fall apart – but what it feels like is that all the world starts dropping away too, piece by piece – it feels like they want to take the sky away from me

I used to be young – used to lay out all night long, feel the air sting its way over my face like someone touching me and i ud look up into that clear air and all the stars ud seem to look back at me – like all the stars have a face –

hell, fish, i could trek over forty k to the stores and drink all night hot raw whisky and roll back all in two days with no sleep – there was old betty who used to haul the stuff in on her back – we used to bath in whisky, wash the old tin plates in it and spend all day shooting fire out of our paws – blasting the stones apart and smelt them for metal like we was making hot soup – set up a sound system on the ice – sound system on the ice and we ud dance and blast and boom and batter and hunt penguins with lasers!

we were so crazy – we ud go fishing underwater in wet suits with music

*in headphones and whisky in a little tube that went straight into our
mouths – shoot that fish! sip that stuff! shake your tail to old bessie
smith, high and pure in the phones – it was like we could make life
up like kids playing pretend – they ever tell you about bessie smith,
fish??????????? – honey, go ask your virus, go get it to play you old
bessie – that's what we mined to in the dry rocks – bessie and satchmo
– singing to us in the blue blue sea – history alive in your ear singing
like the wind on the ice – we ud go swimming up the innards of an
iceberg like a smooth glassy cheese all full of holes and glossy light –
light going up the cracks, catching in the bubbles and strange dead
creatures froze right in the middle of it – fish, i was young – i was
young for years fore i met my husband – had rolfa when i was 40
years old – thats how late i left it all that domestic stuff – the wallpaper
the curtains the dishes the carpets and the four four walls*

HELL FISH

*they want me back in London – so I can be old – they want me to
shed the ice like snakeskin – they want me to lose the cold – lose the
stars – lose the fire – i could trek baby and blast – they want me still
not moving not hearing*

*it dont matter being deaf down here home in the cold – theres my dogs
– they fetch for me – theres the sun on the ice and the fresh air – theres
the post coming to bring letters and to talk*

*being deaf in south ken means being shut in with a little shivering
squidge who thinks your going to eat her – im deaf fish and i cant
walk – broken hip and joints that have ground to a halt – i have to
crawl my cold little fish – so theyll ship me home like walrus meat –
theyll fix my joints sure – and then say i got to stay in south ken till
theres nothing left of me – just some old animated rug barely talking
just reaching up for her little tipple with a hand that shakes – some
old withered dam rotting like leaf mould just able to lift her head –
with no light no sound no dance no cold no warm – nothing*

where we all head fish – where we all head and ive arrived here

*so heres what im going to do – im going to crawl – im going to crawl
out onto that ice in the night – ill roll over and look up at the stars –
i know cold honey – it settles slow – you just go to sleep – im going to
go to sleep looking at those stars – by the time you get this fish ill be
long gone*

*love is a torch you pass it on – tried to give it to my baby – my great
singing lump of a kid – opera hell i hate opera – where ud she get it
from ?????? just herself – love is a torch and you pass it on like someone
passed it to you fish – you never told me about your mama but she
must have loved you – or someone must have – so you loved rolfa rolfa
loved you – you just dug your heels in – me too kid – this is happy –*

313

*this is some old dam digging her heels in – into the ice – dont be sad
this is the best*

love

hortensia patel

Present tense, still present, still tense:
  When?
  This is me, packing for outer space. I'm running around my lacquered rooms with a tremor in my belly. I'm still afraid of Thrawn, of
space, of The Comedy.
  I'm worrying about my house plants. Who can I give them to who
will not kill them with over-watering, or kill them with neglect? I am
worrying over a potted plant of basil, which I use in cooking, and a
hydrangea. This is my main concern at the moment, the chewing gum
my conscious mind is recycling over and over until all savour of it is
gone.
  There is a knock on the sliding panels on my Tarty flat. They rattle
in their runners. Is it Thrawn? I am Terminal, I am Terminal, I tell
myself, and I throw back the sliding screens, one after another, through
the Dead Space that insulates. I pull back the screens, and before I
recognise who it is, I feel a band of muscle pull tightly across my chest.
  Rolfa standing in my doorway.
  She is covered in fur again, and wears virulently coloured clothes.
'Hullo.' she says. 'No trouble to go away and come back if I'm
interrupting.'
  Why now? That is the director's reaction. Yes, I would like to see
you, yes I have been meaning to see you, but now is not a good time.
Milena runs a distracted hand across her head.
  Well Milena, you have now successfully communicated that it is a
tremendous inconvenience, but that you are going to make the most
forced effort to be gracious.
  'Just, just packing,' says Milena, stiff smile, closed eyes, angry little
shakings of the head.
  Perhaps understandably, Rolfa makes no reply.
  'How are you, Rolfa?'
  'Oh. Not so dusty. Got to keep moving, you know. I won't stay long.'
  Milena the director is relieved. Mentally she is calculating how long
she has to pack.
  'It's lovely to see you,' says Milena.
  'But,' says Rolfa, supplying the qualification. She is hunched under
the arched and lacquered ceilings. She makes the Tarty flat look like
the kind of toy you give to a spoiled child. Rolfa is hunched and
covered in fur, and she wears a brightly-printed shirt, brightly printed

314

shorts, clean white tennis shoes and a rather rakish hat. It is a man's hat. She still looks uncomfortable, awkward. My God, she reminds me of Mike.

'Tea?' Milena offers. Milena has forgotten to ask her in.

'Beer? Whisky? Gin would suffice, if you had some lemon.' Rolfa shuffles her feet, wiping them on the mat. Her shoes are huge and white and very clean. 'And just a little morsel to munch, if you could see your way to finding it.' Rolfa ducks inside the door and, rather awkwardly, removes her hat. Politesse. She strokes the short, bristly crew cut on the top of her head. 'Needing sustenance. Long boat trip. My God, why did you move all the way out here?'

Milena doesn't want to answer. She would have to tell Rolfa about Thrawn. 'I like the Slump,' she says. 'Sorry, but I'm going away, and the only thing I have in the place is tea.'

'Ah well. That at least hasn't changed.'

Both of them stand looking at each other. Milena moves first, vaguely walking in the direction of the beanbags. After a step or two forward, Rolfa vaguely stays where she is, near the door.

'You ah, you know that we're doing a production of the Comedy?' says Milena. It is possible that Rolfa hasn't heard. No one at the Zoo has seen or heard of Rolfa for two years.

'Oh yes,' says Rolfa. 'Something about space.'

Is that all you have to say? thinks Milena the director. Did I really get obsessed with this person? She tries to laugh, but it sounds more like a cough.

'It's going to be a rather major production,' says the director.

'Golly,' says Rolfa. She says it coldly, plonking the word down as if it were a brick. She communicates quite effectively that she is not impressed. Rolfa has become sharper. There is an edge to her.

'Well,' says Milena. 'They're sending me up on the Bulge, to try out the lighting.' Usually people brighten when told this, relieved to be able to ask a string of questions that will have interesting answers. Milena realises immediately, is a tactical conversational error. Rolfa is not brightening with interest.

'I'm going to Antarctica,' Rolfa says.

'Oh,' says Milena, brought up short.

'Good for business. Need the experience if I'm to get on. Thought you might like to know, anyway,' says Rolfa and begins the process of turning around in the cramped space. She is turning around to leave.

'Rolfa. Wait! Antarctica?'

Rolfa looks over her shoulder. 'Seems like the best place for me.'

'But what about your music?'

'Don't have any music,' says Rolfa. 'Poof! Gone.'

'Your singing!'

'My dear woman,' says Rolfa. That's it, the gentleness has gone because the sexual attraction has gone, perhaps even been soured. Perhaps to block it, they turn it to distaste. 'Do you sincerely believe that they are going to cast me as, say, Desdemona in *Otello*? Or a delicate Chinese heroine in a classical Beijing piece perhaps? Now if there was an opera called *David and Goliath* in which the part of Goliath had been written for a soprano, perhaps I would have something that could be part of my regular repertoire. Otherwise . . .' Another raising up of the hands, and a smile. 'Nothing.'

'But *liede*. *Song of the Earth*, concert singing. Don't just give up!' Milena apprehends the waste.

'Why not?' asks Rolfa.

'Because you're good,' says Milena, disappointed, looking away.

'I quite like the idea of going to Antarctica,' says Rolfa. 'It's not all ice. There are some places that are so cold that water has never fallen there. It's a desert, freeze-dried, just rock and gravel. My mother was in the desert once and she found the corpse of a walrus. Perfectly preserved, nothing to rot it, really. Three hundred miles from the sea.' She pauses. 'Well. I am the walrus.'

'What does that mean?' asks Milena, bleakly.

'No one knows how it got there.' said Rolfa. 'And walruses can't make music.'

Milena finds that she has to sit down. She sits down and screens her face. She wants to protect her face from Rolfa, from the fact of her standing there.

'Rolfa,' she says without looking at her. 'Everyone says that the Comedy is a work of genius.'

'Really?' says Rolfa. 'Who orchestrated it?'

'The Consensus. But it is your basic music.'

'Then let the Consensus take the credit,' says Rolfa. 'They've taken everything else.' And a sputter, a kind of laugh.

Milena finds anger. Anger she can understand and cope with. 'Rolfa! You always let yourself be defeated.'

Rolfa stands looking at her, and the eyes, turning back the anger, seem to say, don't mistake. This is a different Rolfa. Don't tell me I am easily defeated. Her eyes narrow and she decides to sit down.

She sits down, and leans forward on the beanbag to make a point. 'I appreciate your efforts,' she says. 'But you must understand that everything has changed for me.'

She leans back and seems to relax. She expands. 'It was quite strange for a while, becoming someone else. But I rather like it now. Father and I get on rather well. I'm his star girl. Revamped his accounting system. I came up with a system of time-sheeting. Everyone's time is

316

costed. Time is money. May not seem much to you, but I'm proud of it.' Rolfa shrugs in place, a bit like a boxer.

Perhaps Milena looks bleak. She is staring at the floor, unhappily. This seems to exasperate Rolfa.

'I'm not that interested in what happens to the Comedy, Milena. It was not seriously written to be performed. I'm impressed that you've been able to get it on. But,' again the sputter. The sputter performs roughly the same function as the shudder-chuckle once did, though the sputter is more purely indignant. 'But the Comedy is hardly going to be anything new to me.'

'Was it hard to adjust?'

Rolfa raises her hands behind her head and seems to muse, as if considering something impersonal. 'It was rather strange, I suppose, yes. I could never be sure which bits had been lopped off, or what would grow back in their place. I positively terrified Zoe and Angela for a while. Called them stupid moos. I found I could not stand women for a while. I had a few drinking buddies, men mostly, and from time to time, rather unexpectedly, I found myself fancying them. It would always be terribly, terribly unexpected, because until just before then, I rather identified with them. They said that it was rather like having one of their mates suddenly make a pass. None of them ever took me up on it, of course.'

Milena is looking at her wrist. She is looking at the Mice crawling in and out of her skin, patrolling, still asking: where is Rolfa? Where is Rolfa? She wants to put both her hands around Rolfa's wrist, feel the warmth and the silkiness of the fur. It's starting. The love is starting, again.

'It was fun wasn't it?' says Milena. 'Those three months.' Milena's voice is pleading, frail.

'Oh yes,' agrees Rolfa, somewhat dismissively. 'Long time ago now. I seem to recall spending most of my time in a daze in that room of yours. I got horribly demoralised. Sorry about the mess.'

'I didn't mind,' whispers Milena.

'I should have done,' sniffs Rolfa.

'Are you tidy now?'

'Try to be,' says Rolfa, almost snapping.

I'm calling to you across a very wide, deep canyon, and the wind is blowing the words away. The wind is blowing you away.

'Are you going to see your mother?' Milena asks. She coughs. 'In Antarctica?'

'Oh yes. You and her became friends didn't you? Allies against the Family.' Rolfa smiles. She has bright new teeth. Fangs. 'It'll be nice to see the old bag. I feel a bit guilty really. I haven't written her or anything.'

Milena feels her mouth go thin with disapproval. Only the fact that Hortensia might call herself an old bag has stopped her being very angry.

Rolfa sees the expression and sputters, and shakes her head.

'Your mother is a very nice person,' says Milena. 'I was wondering how she was. I haven't heard.'

'Neither have we,' said Rolfa. 'She's gone quiet on us. I expect she's been on a binge.'

The letter in its sealed packet has not yet been written. But you know already, Rolfa, that The Family has decided Hortensia is to come back. You just think it's none of my business. You are smiling, with your new fangs.

'When are you off?' Milena asks.

'Oooh, about three weeks.' The conversation is flagging. There is too much and therefore too little to say.

'Do you . . . uh . . . have a boyfriend now then?' Milena asks. Trying to sound casual, her voice trails off into high, forlorn question.

'No,' says Rolfa, abruptly.

The destruction is complete. Neither of us have anyone. The director begins to feel horribly alone. Her life is her work. Somehow the memory of Rolfa has always been there, in the work, in the music, in the very sound of it, to keep her company. The work and the fact of Rolfa's living presence, somewhere hidden in the vastness of London, has made the connection seem real. The Comedy had made it real. But the artist is not the work. And this Rolfa was not the artist.

'Rolfa. I'm very, very sorry,' Milena says, meaning, I'm sorry I destroyed you.

'Don't be sorry for me,' says Rolfa, moving her shoulders as if punching something. If anything, this new Rolfa is far more masculine. 'Don't ask this Rolfa to be sorry, this Rolfa wouldn't exist without what happened. Wouldn't go back to being the old Rolfa for the world. What? All that moping about? All that dreary nonsense, writing, rewriting, pinning your hopes on nothing. What would have happened to that Rolfa in the end, eh? Dead drunk at the Spread, that's where she'd be.'

'Or writing another Comedy.'

This Rolfa sighs, rising and falling like the sea. 'Or writing another Comedy, yes. But all that's gone now.'

'It's as if you died. It's as if I killed you.'

'Oh don't go getting soppy on me, woman.' This Rolfa sulks. 'Can't stand sop anymore. What's the use of it?'

'You feel it anyway. You might as well face it.'

'Yes, but there's no need to draw it out. That's what I find with opera now, the people just stand there drawing it out. Takes them two hours to say goodbye to each other. I mean, what's the point?'

'If they have things to say . . .' Milena doesn't finish. 'I . . . I have time to go to a kaff, if you'd like some food.'

Rolfa's smile has gone queasy. She's frightened that I still fancy her, she wants to avoid that. She's come here to make a clean break.

'No, I'll be getting back home to eat,' said Rolfa, and slaps the beanbag. She reaches for her hat and puts it back on.

She probably thought about not telling me at all.

'Thank you for coming to see me,' says Milena, going cold herself.

'Well,' says Rolfa generously. 'Old time's sake, you know. Sorry I caught you while you were so busy.'

'I'm always busy,' says Milena, her voice dull.

'Well,' says Rolfa with a dreadful heartiness. 'You're a success.'

Pause. Milena goes colder. 'I've got someting of yours,' she says, rising up from her beanbag. She goes to her closet, her new Tarty flat has drawers and closets, and she finds the thing stuffed behind preserving jars and spare batteries. With a sudden wrench of frustration, she pulls it out, scattering jars. A dirty lump of felt smelling of childhood. She turns and presents it to Rolfa.

'This,' she says.

'Piglet,' says Rolfa staring at it.

'Take it, I don't want it,' says Milena, angry now.

Rolfa has already reached up and taken it. She sits with it on her lap, and strokes its ears, and feels its stomach, as if to make sure something is still there. She shudders, as if touching something cold, and then passes it back to Milena. 'I left him on purpose. It was a present. Old time's sake.' She shrugs, in a gesture of utter helplessness.

The two of them look at each other. Milena reaches up and takes Piglet back.

'Someone's cooking supper for me,' says Rolfa and stands. She extends her hand. 'Goodbye.'

'Goodbye,' says Milena and shakes it. Rolfa leans over her, vast, intimidating, like an adult to a child. Milena wants to fight. Why bother to tell me at all? Why didn't you just go?

Rolfa bunches herself under the door, out of the doll's house, onto the stairway. Milena stands in the doorway, feeling as swollen and bitter as a wound. She thinks it is only social habit that is making them go through this ritual.

And Rolfa turns and smiles with her new white teeth, a beautiful wide smile that the old Rolfa could not have made. 'Such larks,' she says. 'I'm going to have such fun in Antarctica.'

Milena can suddenly imagine it, dogs and ice and stars. She can see

319

what might have been, Hortensia and Rolfa, happy on the ice that was as white as Rolfa's new smile. An Antarctic smile.

Out from one eye, in a trail, there is a line of moisture, and damp shiny fur. 'Pooh and Piglet go in search of the South Pole. Eh? Who'd have thought it? Me to Antarctica, you up into space. Well if you think it's hell down here, watch out, cause it's purgatory up there.' Rolfa barks out a laugh and makes a ghost punch at Milena's shoulder. 'Couldn't keep either of us down, could they? Ah? Ha-ha-ha!' Rolfa is shouting.

Awkward, she shuffles backwards on the landing.

'Anyway, take care of yourself, old girl,' she bellows at Milena, too loudly, swaying dangerously on the tiny landing. 'Take care of yourself. Get your work done. Don't worry about me, I'll be all right. Right as rain, eh? Ta-ra!'

Rolfa starts to climb down the steps backwards, one at a time, still looking at Milena, still howling as loudly. She is shouting more loudly than Milena has ever heard anyone shout, shouting across a tundra colder than mere nature could ever blast flat, through the Dead Space.

'Be good, and if you can't be good have fun. Remember, tomorrow is the first day of the rest of your life! Ah? Ah? Ha-ha!' The head is laughing as it disappears below the level of the landing.

The shouting continues. 'Don't take any wooden nickels! Ha! Old Canadian expression! Mind your pees and queues! Keep well! Keep well! Keep well!' It is a fervent hope. The voice falls away, with a kind of cough.

Milena tries to go back to packing. She has packing to do after all. Plenty to do. And she looks out of her window, in the dusk now, and there is Rolfa, huge and swaying, her back towards Milena, walking towards the quay.

And me, the one who remembers, I know. I know that this is the last I'll see of Rolfa. There is her back, the gait, the huge round shoulders, the sagging head, all of it familiar. As familiar as if we still lived together.

And oh! Rolfa turns around and waves, waves from the shore of the Slump, where the punt is still waiting for her. 'Ta-ra!' she booms as if across the ice.

And little Milena waves a little wave. The lamps are out, and it is dark in the room. Does Rolfa see her. I think not. But wait, yes, she would.

There is a fluorescent patch of skin now on my palm. Is it glowing? Does she see it? Am I burning?

I'll never know. Rolfa gets in the boat, but she is still standing. She stays standing as the narrow unsteady craft wobbles its way back from the shore. The hat is turning over and over in her hands. Milena stands by the window, stroking Piglet's ears, smelling childhood, and she is thinking: what do I do now? What can I do? I'm getting old and selfish and I need to have someone here, someone real and alive, not a memory.

Me, thought the Milena who remembered I know what lies ahead. Ahead of her lies space and Mike Stone.

Behind her lies love.

I remember Rose Ella's room, the room I stayed in at the Estate of the Restorers, who wanted to bring back the past. I remember the Chinese panels on the walls of the room and the spaces in the inlay, the shoes, the clothes, the dolls and the bare gaps the people left behind them. The Dead Spaces, full of the things they might have felt, might have thought, might have done.

If only, only, they were still here.

Antarctica was one of the few places in the world from which it would be impossible to see the *Comedy*.

And suddenly Milena is in the Bulge, saying goodbye. Through the window, she sees the stars. She can sense their weight now. The stars to her are anchors, solid and unmoving hooks on which to hang things. She is calling for Bob, plucking the strings of thought that are in the air.

'Going,' she says. All the other feelings, of farewell and anticipated return throb in the lines of gravity. She passes on feelings, direct.

Ah, love, hums the Angel, as if plucking strings in her.

And she asks him a question she would be too embarrassed to put into words, a personal question about him that was also a heartfelt mystery to her, a question that was somehow one with the unmoving stars.

Bob answers. We're embedded in the flesh, the Angel says. He means the flesh of the Consensus, and for a moment, Milena can feel the flesh of the Consensus in her mind, a mountainous and tangled pattern etched in the lines of gravity.

But once we leave it, he says, meaning once we become Angels, then we are embedded in the lines. And we just keep dancing in the wires. And Milena feels how the self could slither up out of the Slide, the Charlie Slide. The self is a perturbation in the forces of attraction. Gravity pulled energy out of nothing. The Angels do not need feeding. The self is embedded in the universe, beyond harm.

Milena remembers: I look through eyes of flesh at the darkness between the stars, the small part of the universe that flesh can see. And I'm thinking that we are embedded in flesh too, and I'm wondering if we can become Angels, too.

'Goodbye,' says Bob, but the feeling is: you'll be back, girl, you'll be back here again.

'Time to go,' says Mike Stone, months before I marry him, ducking down into the little Bulge, and feeding the last of my equipment into the holding maws of the cargo racks. I'm strapped into the living chair, and Mike Stone gives me a quick kiss on the top of my head. Like a butterfly, it is beautiful, but I'm not sure I don't want to swat it away from my hair.

And there is my future husband, standing in the open mouths of the two Bulges, where they meet and kiss. He gives me an odd little wave, just the tips of his fingers moving, as if in a breeze.

Then there is a hiss and the seal is broken. The mouths of the Bulges purse shut, shifting and crinkling and turning inward. I look out of the window, at the stars. I think of the lines and the Angels moving up and down them. The air is full of people dancing.

Next.

And here it comes, on a high, hot April day of a different year, with a different Milena. She walks slowly, musing how to bring the Comedy down to Earth. The animals will be Zoo performers, the souls of the dead will be the dry and empty clothes of the Graveyard. And the clouds of lovers? Will the peak of Purgatory be the summit of the orbit of the Bulge?

There are cries of children, climbing scaffolding, swinging from it. Monkeys. And there is a clutch of Bees, sitting on the walkway to the Zoo, in the sun.

The Bees have learned how to do something new. Perhaps they learned it from the Bulge. Perhaps they learned it from me. They can change their genes by thinking. And now there are leaves sprouting out of their backs, thick, broad leaves on sinewy stems, like purple rubber plants.

They sit up and turn and smile, delighted. There is the woman with the green teeth and the wide happy eyes. There is the young boy, with hair down the middle of his back and he is happy too. They all are happy.

In some other time, someone else is shouting, Keep Well! Keep Well! Keep Well! It is a fervent hope.

The Bees all exclaim in triumph, pointing in unison at me.

'Cancer!' they cry, like birds.

chapter seventeen

TERMINAL (LOVE SICKNESS)

If cancer did not swim in the same sea as us, we might admire it, as we admire sharks. We might admire its simplicity and fitness for purpose, its lethal beauty.

Cancer is a disruption of the process of growth. Some cancer cells produce their own growth hormone, giving themselves the signal to divide and multiply. Others increase the number of growth hormone receptors on the membrane of the cell, or duplicate the internal message bearers that carry the command to grow. They do not respond to messages of overcrowding from other cells. They need blood to feed and so they secrete proteins that induce the body to grow new blood vessels for them.

They do not need to be firmly attached to the intercellular matrix, as normal cells do. They can split off from the main tumour, float freely in the bloodstream and find new sites to grow. Cancers are a disfunction of what is called differentiation. They do not mature into fully functioning blood or bone or muscle or skin cells – they are not differentiated. When they find a new site, in different kinds of tissue, they can grow there too. They can spread. The word for that is metastasis. The word for that is malignant.

And, cancers are immortal. Normal cells stop dividing after between fifty and one hundred and fifty times. Normal cells senesce. Cancer cells go on growing.

Before the Revolution, in the world of the very rich and the very poor, something terrible had happened. Through some alteration of genes in DNA viruses, there were new strains of cancer that spread with the ease and speed of the common cold. New DNA was inserted in proto-oncogenes, which altered their function. Sometimes as soon as as two weeks after infection, tumours began to grow with an almost choreographed dexterity, spinning off and landing with both feet firmly in other tissues.

A final cure for cancer became a matter of shrieking urgency.

Cancers disrupt key genes in the chromosomes. These genes are called proto-oncogenes. They code for proteins that are involved in growth or differentiation or certain kinds of cell structuring. Genetic material might be added to them – as when retroviruses introduce new

323

genetic material. Genetic material might be taken away from them, as when they are irradiated. They might suffer an accident in reproduction where their order is reversed, or they are translocated among other gene sequences.

Proto-oncogenes are normal. When disrupted by addition, subtraction or alteration, they can become oncogenes – genes that are involved in cancer.

All possible proto-oncogenes had been identified. A final cure for all the cancers would be something that would protect these key genes from any kind of genetic change.

The DNA spiral is made of alternating phosphates and sugar. Between them are rungs, like rungs of a ladder, made of nucleic acids. The answer was to coat the rungs themselves in sugars and phosphates – and reinforce the helices of DNA.

The sugar-coated genes were protected against attempts to add new genetic material to them. They were firmly bound to a reinforced spiral and would not be broken and replaced out of sequence. Radiation or chemicals did not remove genetic material from them. They were able to communicate with reverse transcriptase and mRNA. The communication was one-way. They were inviolate to change, locked in sugar.

People called the cure Candy. Engineered retroviruses inserted Candy genes into all cells of the body – including germ cells. Candy became part of human genetic inheritance.

Cloned tumour-suppressants cured the existing cancers. Cancer disappeared. The capacity for cancers disappeared. So did the proteins they secreted.

Cancers had been of unsuspected benefit. They secreted anti-senescence proteins in large amounts of very low molecular weight. The proteins entered other cells easily.

Cancers delayed senescence of other cells. Small, premalignant lesions prolonged human life to its accustomed span. Without cancer, the span of human life was halved.

Attempts to duplicate the anti-senescence proteins produced only localised effects. Only patches of tissue responded.

And the proto-oncogenes and the Candy genes were locked safely behind a wall of sugar.

Bees admired cancer, as we would admire flowers; for their life, for their beauty. For them, it burned like a white light. They could feel its escape from order as a break for freedom by individual cells.

They followed Milena, entranced.

'It sings,' they would sigh.

'Milena! You are a Garden!' they would call to her. 'Full of flowers!'

The Bees followed Milena to St Thomas's Hospital, to the Cancer

324

Wards where she was tested. They followed her when she was summoned to the Reading Rooms, under the purple forest on Marsham Street. Milena was Terminal and she kept asking the Consensus as she approached it: what have you got to tell me? The Consensus stayed silent.

Milena remembered waiting in the white brick rooms and thinking: all the bad things in my life happen here.

The door opened and in came Root, the Terminal.

Root stared at Milena, her shoulders slumped. She kept shaking her head. Root the voluble did not know how to begin. 'Oh, child,' she said. From down the corridor came the sound of a garden full of children; the guitars, the kazoos, the clapping hands, and the singing of ten year olds waiting to join the world.

'You got cancer,' Root said finally, held up her hands and let them drop.

Milena looked at the white bricks and the bare electric light. 'How?' she asked, 'How is that possible? Cancer's dead, cancer's gone.'

'You got no Candy,' said Root. She came to Milena, who was sitting on the only chair, and knelt at her feet. She picked up Milena's hand. 'You can play around with genes, love, like you was thinking with them. You kept trying till you found a gene that made a new kind of transcriptase. It went to the rungs, and dissolved the sugar round them.'

'No I didn't,' said Milena, pulling away her hand.

'You didn't know.' Root's mouth formed the word like a kiss. 'You didn't know you was doing it.' Root tried to reach up and stroke her head. Milena leaned away. 'We're like a huge ocean, with a leaky boat on top. The boat is all we know of ourselves. The rest is underneath.'

'This is nonsense,' said Milena, and tried to stand, but Root was resting across her lap.

'No, love, it's not.' Root's face was suffused with love for her. 'You broke Candy, and then so we could see, you changed your genes so the cancer came back. Like you were flying flags of joy, saying Here? See? Milena! You brought the cancer back so that all of us can live!'

Milena succeeded in pushing Root away from her. She stood up, and walked away as if she could escape from what had happened.

'Because of you, we can all get old again!' Root said. 'We'll see our children grow!'

'I don't want people to get old!' exclaimed Milena, her back towards Root. 'And I hate children. So why would I do something like that, eh? Eh?'

'We can copy the new gene you made. We can put it in new retroviruses, we can cure everyone!'

'After what happened the last time?' Milena found her two fists were

325

clenched together in rage and were shaking at Root. 'You're still going to muck around after what happened last time! Who knows, maybe you'll kill everyone off straight away, this time!' She was shouting. She turned back around, and hugged herself. 'What's going to happen to me?'

She heard Root rustle up from her feet and swish her way towards her. She felt the warm, plump hands on her shoulder. She was turned around and enveloped in the fatty tissues of Root's arms and breasts.

'Oh Milena, love, don't be worry, don't be fear. We got the genes that shut off the new blood vessels, we got the genes that stop the growing. We'll give you those, we'll make you well!'

'Will you make me like Lucy, too?' asked Milena, as cold as ice, and pushed Root away again.

'We don't know,' said Root, shaking her head.

'I don't want to be like Lucy!' Here was a new dark terror. To grow so old that you understood nothing of the world, except that everything and everyone you loved was dead. Milena's fingers were dug into her hair.

'Sssh. Sssh. If you don't want it, then you won't be. With what you can do? You can change your cells, move things round, cut, splice. Nothing will happen that you don't want to. You're Milena, who is immune.'

'What cancers? What cancers do I have?'

Root looked helpless.

'Well tell me!'

'All of them,' said Root very quietly. 'All of them we ever knew of.'

The room seemed to hiss all around them, as if the walls were leaking air.

The merry viruses had already known where she was ailing. The merry viruses began to roll off a list.

Skin – squamous epithelium, basal, and pigment cells – squamous and basal carcinoma, malignant melanoma

Alimentary tract – squamous epithelium of lips, mouth, tongue, oesophagus – squamous carcinoma

Alimentary tract – columnar epithelium of stomach, small bowel, large bowel – carcinoma

Milena found she was chuckling.

'Isn't that a bit excessive?' she said, shaking her head. 'Wouldn't one have been enough?'

No, replied the merry viruses. The whole balance had to be restored. All the cancers had to be brought back.

'We'll be with you, love, all of us,' said Root, dismayed. 'The Terminals, the Angels, we'll be with you all the time, helping you fight, singing in your blood.'

326

Nasopharynx, larynx and lungs – bronchial epithelium – carcinoma

'I hope cancer likes music,' said Milena. She was shaking, as if with laughter. She found that her hands were on her face, feeling the flesh. There were pimples on her nose.

'Oh, Milena, if only you knew how much we all love you for this.'

'That sure makes all the difference,' said Milena. 'I used to wonder why those Mayan maidens let themselves be thrown over the edge of cliffs. Now I know. Everyone loved them for it.'

'No one's throwing you over a cliff. You're going to get well!' Root exclaimed in anguish.

Urinary system including bladder – urothelium cells – carcinoma

'Yah,' said Milena.

'You have to believe you are,' said Root, warning her.

Solid epithelial organs – epithelial cells of liver, kidney, thyroid, pancreas, pituitary, etc – carcinoma

'Shut down!' Milena said to the viruses, to make them still. It was the viruses that would have told her the meaning of each gene, the function of each protein so that she could change them. There was a kind of hiccup, but the list kept scrolling up through her mind. Part of her wanted to know.

'So how are you going to cure me?' she demanded.

'First, you move into the hospital, St Thomas's. You live there, you and Mr Stone, he's pregnant, it's good for him, too. Then we start, site by site. We cut off the new blood supply. Then we have the retroviruses that infect the tumours with growth inhibitor. They start to regress.'

'How long before I'm well?'

Root looked helpless again. 'We're out of practice with cancer.'

'You don't know.'

Root shook her head.

Milena began to feel sick and weak in her stomach. She needed to sit down. She dropped back down onto the one chair.

'I want to see the baby,' Milena said. Already life had bargained her down. 'I never thought I would have a child, and I want to see her. I want to finish the Comedy. We've only got backgrounds for two of the books! I want to go up again and finish the Comedy!'

'And you will,' said Root, going a little harder. 'You'll do all those things and more.'

'If I die and if Mike dies, then the baby will be an orphan. Just exactly what I didn't want her to be!'

'You are not going to die. Why do you think we asked you here? The Doctors, me, the Consensus, we've got it all planned, exactly how you're going to get well.'

Milena looked up at her, bleakly. I've done it again, she thought.

327

I've done exactly what the Consensus wanted. I don't even have to think.

Milena felt an undertow. It was as if she had something dark inside her, pulling her down. It was larger than she was and had different interests. Life had wanted cancer back, all of life, the ocean within her that was part of her but which she did not know and could not control. Milena began to be afraid.

Milena went up and Milena came down and Milena gave the world cancer. Hop skip and jump.

'I could go to Antarctica,' she said. 'I could go to Antarctica and I wouldn't be free.'

'You take on too much,' said Root, her lips heavy as if with sadness. 'You always nipping about the place. It was like that with cancer. It always took the ones who did for everyone else. When they went, other people didn't know how they could go on. Well, you going to have to let other people take care of you now, Milena. I know you don't like it. You have to let yourself be the child, now.'

Milena was bullied by sympathy. She let Root keep hold of her hand.

'Come on,' said Root, patting her arm. 'Come on, love, let's get you home, let's get you home and talk to Mr Stone. We're going to fight this thing and we're going to win.'

Central nervous system whispered the viruses. The list continued.

Outside, the Bees were gathered.

Their faces were rigid, caught in a rigour of ecstasy, washed in waves of thought. The forest of the Consensus rose up huge around them, dazzling them with the processes of photosynthesis and elimination. Beneath their feet, the thought patterns of over one million people pulsed.

The Bees were dazzled by it. Tears streamed out of their faces and they clutched each other's hands.

'Milena,' they all whispered, like trees blown in a wind. They were caught up in the patterns of the forest of flesh. They were a forest of flesh. They wore curtains of vine leaves grown out of themselves. They were sheltered by a canopy of leaves growing out of their backs. People were becoming more and more like plants.

'Milena. Milena Shibush,' the Bees whispered over and over in love. 'Garden.'

They grew fruit out of themselves, heavy human fruit full of human sugars. They grew roses. The rose was a symbol of Milena. It was a symbol of the cancer. The Bees loved them both. They formed a wall of love in front of her, transfixed, trembling under the skin. The tears on their faces tremored slightly as they crept down their cheeks.

328

Milena stood facing them. 'They keep following me,' she said in despair.

'Go on, move,' said Root to them.

The Bees tried to shuffle, but it was as if their feet had taken root in the soil. Much longer, and they would take root, growing tender white shoots into the earth, as if from seedling potatoes.

'Part!' shouted Root. 'Like the Red Sea! Move!' Root advanced, holding Milena's hand. Root drew her hand back to strike.

'Please,' whispered Milena.

There was a great rustling. It was as if the ocean parted. Slowly at first with the sound of many leaves shifting, hissing like the sound of surf, a passage began to clear. The wall split open with gathering speed, a cleft penetrating deeper into the mass of Bees. As if something had been sparked by the movement, the Bees came awake. They began to sing in joy.

Milena Shibush
Milena Cancer
Cancer Cancer
Cancer Shibush
Shibush Flower
Flower Cancer
Flower Flower
Cancer Flower

The wall of love became a wall of voices. Milena moved dazed through the shadows cast by the vines and the leaves that grew out of the human backs of the Bees.

It rained flowers. The Bees tore them from their backs and threw them. The human roses fell over Milena, leaking clear sap. The flowers were caught by human thorns in her hair. Milena moved through the Bees and the wall of human hands.

Milena moved into the sunlight, onto the steps of the Consensus. As if she pulled them by wires, the Bees were dragged after her, still singing. They followed her down the steps.

Flower Cancer
Flower Shibush
Shibush Flower

'I hate that,' said Milena. At once, the song was cut off, like a thread.

On Marsham Street people were running. They ran towards the Consensus and the tumult of the Bees. They ran away from it, bearing news. Boys in the uniform of the Estate School shouted to each other. They swung down from the scaffoldings. Tykes still carrying laundry baskets stumbled down stairs and into the street.

Cancer, the people said, cancer.

A woman was leaning out of a window and a boy was shouting up

to her. 'They say the cancer has come back!' A horsecart was reined
to a halt. 'What's that?' the driver called as if in alarm.

Bells began to ring over and over, in no pattern at all.

'We got to get you out of this,' said Root, and gave Milena's hand
a quick tug. She led them down the remaining steps and into the
gathering crowd.

Transfixed, the Bees followed, gathering up people in front of them
like a steam shovel. The crowd swirled, clotted, trying to change
direction, trying to avoid the Bees, trying to avoid the sickness and the
thorns.

'The Garda are coming!' said Root, and hauled Milena forward.

A man in an apron stained with green grease seized Milena by the
shoulders. 'Cancer's back!' he roared with joy.

'It's true!' someone shouted down from a window. 'I'm Terminal
and I've just been told. It's true!'

There was cheer from all along the street.

'Move!' shouted Root at the man in the apron. His face went blank.
Root pushed him out of the way.

Milena stumbled forward. She felt sick. Her knees suddenly gave
way. Root scooped her up in her arms and carried her. Milena's head
fell backwards and she looked up.

There was a sound overhead, as if the air had become wood.

Helicopters roared over the tops of the purple trees, that sighed and
swayed. White tubes were spat out from the machines. The tubes
wrapped themselves around the trees. The Garda came swinging down
the white web, white boots swinging.

'There'll be merry hell now,' said Root.

There were screams behind them as people suddenly surged forward; a wave of them broke against Root's back. Root and Milena
were swept forward along Marsham Street, towards Horseferry Road.

The Bees tried to run too, but they were held by the lines of life all
around them, from the crowd, from the forest of the Consensus. They
ran in slow motion, as if time flowed more sluggishly for them. Perhaps
it did.

The Garda raised the palms of their hands, and tubes burst forth
from their palms. The tubes shot towards the Bees, whipping around
their arms and legs.

'Leave them alone!' whispered Milena.

The Bees were entangled in the translucent tubing. They fought
against it as it drew them together in a net. Then the tubes leapt up
like the tongues of frogs catching insects, high into the sky, silver
against blue, hitting the helicopters and sticking to them. Very suddenly, the Bees were elevated five or six at a time, as if taking wing.
They were hauled skywards towards the bubbles of the helicopters.

'Milena!' they called, as if for salvation, kicking their protein-starved, scrawny legs.

Root pushed her way onto Horseferry Road. It was blocked with reined-in carts, or with bundles that people had let drop in order to watch. Milena felt a burning in her belly, like very severe indigestion. Root swung her shoulders from side to side, shoving people to one side. She came to a thinning of the crowd and began a burdened run. Milena could feel the swaying back and forth of the volumes of flesh on Root's thighs.

From all over the floor of the Pit, bells were ringing. There was the light clamouring of the signal bells of each Estate. There was the heavy, droning toll of church bells, and the great din of the bells of Westminster Abbey. Everyone's face was turned towards the sky. The helicopters rose over the tops of the buildings of Horseferry.

Root slowed to a staggering walk. She dodged round the carts stopped in the middle of the embankment road. Milena slipped out of her grasp. 'Can you walk?' Root asked her. Milena nodded. Root led her down the granite steps of the embankment, to a jetty, on the river.

On the river, the horse ferry floated in place, the tillerman and the passengers crowded into its prow. Beside the jetty, in a small barge, two Slump Bobbers gazed up at the sky. Behind them was a cargo of mattresses. Root stepped down into their boat.

'You get us out of this,' she said to the two boys, leaving no possibility of denial.

'What's that all about?' the Slumpers asked.

'Just some bloody Bees,' said Root and helped Milena step onto the mattresses. 'You lie down there,' said Root.

'Lo, she's not ill, is she?' one of the boys asked. 'We can't sell them if people think there's sickness on them.'

'Oh! Everybody's ill. Don't tell anybody and they won't know,' said Root, slapping the boy's shoulder. 'Go on, now, the Garda's pulling people in.'

The boys pushed the boat away from the jetty and one of them danced across the mattresses to take the till. A small, dirty sail was unfurled.

Milena lay on her back, listening to the slopping of water under the prow and along the sides of the boat. It was a comforting, satisfying sound. Milena felt more at peace. Looking up she saw the ancient buildings of the embankment and their bamboo scaffoldings. She saw people clinging to the bamboo, leaning out or up to see. Bees dangled from threads in the sky. The helicopters chopped their way through the mix of gases that bore them up. They headed east and south, bound for Epping, or the New Forest or even the South Downs. The Bees would be dumped there. But they would return.

In her hand, Milena still held a human rose. She lifted it up to her nose to smell it. It was perfumed, like freshly washed, soapy human skin. 'It's all so bizarre,' she said. She sat up and leaned on one arm, to look behind the boat.

All along Lambeth Bridge traffic had come to a halt and groups of people singing and marching arm in arm were spreading the news. They talked to people in the carts, animated, waving their hands. The word cancer kept cutting through the air between them. There were threads of song, from Singers no longer able to keep quiet.

But in the quiet on the river it seemed to Milena that she saw something else moving among and through the people on the bridge. Something seemed to impel them forward, sweeping them along with it. It seemed to push behind them, and force its way out of them, pouring out of their eyes and mouths, making their hands leap and their feet spring. It was as if she were seeing the force of life, moving through them.

Milena looked at the people, looked at life, as if she were being borne away from it. What have I done? she asked herself, amid the sound of helicopters and church bells. Life had forced its way through her like a bush through soil. Life has a will. It needs things. It needs us to grow wings, or larger brains, or pads on our elbows, and we do. That's how it was done, she thought, remembering the foliage growing out of Bees. Life had a need, and need hammered on the door of our genes until the genes were changed by will. That's how we grew, up from the slime. We needed hands, and made them. Only now, Lord, now we know we can do it. It will all happen faster.

Milena saw the clouds over Lambeth Bridge. That's how there are spiders in the sky. They thought themselves into that shape. She smiled. Give the Bees time, she told the helicopters. Give them time, and they will live up there, suspended between ice crystals on the tubes. Will you drive them from there too?

That's what we are becoming. The Bees are our future. Life wants us to be more like plants, there's not enough room on the planet now for hunters. We're growing new shoots in so many directions at once, the Consensus will never be able to hold us. The Bees and Lucy and the GEs and the Singers. We're a new forest growing out of the old. We're pushing it back.

A big Thames barge slipped past them, making waves, making them rock. Root looked around the sail.

'You comfortable now?' Root asked.

Yes, yes in a way I am.

Milena fell asleep.

* * *
332

She woke up with a familiar, acrid tingling in her nostrils. It was the smell of home. It was the smoke of cremation from the Estate of Remembrance. There was the singing too, the undertakers warbling with their tongues, the mourners passing over their dead, singing old hymns. Milena saw flowers from the boats and biers bob past their boat. She did not look up.

Bees had been dumped in the Slump, and they had adapted so quickly that they were now a nuisance. They had grown huge flat pads like the giant lilies. They floated on them and fed on them. Milena saw that they had gathered around the graceful hangar of the Party Estate. She groaned and closed her eyes and pretended to be asleep.

She heard the Slump boys shouting at the Bees and felt the boat turn to the side and the boys push against the rooted human lilypads. 'Shoo! Shoo!' she heard Root shout. She felt a scraping of woven reed underneath the boat as it was pulled ashore.

'Here, Lady,' said one of the boys.

The slopes of the tiny artificial island were covered in Bees.

Milena, Milena, Milena, said all the Bees all together, and there was a rustling of their many branches. Milena saw the faces of her neighbours, pinched and unhappy, staring out of their upper windows. The What Does stood guarding the door, a cloth wrapped around her face against disease. A charcoal stove was burning wet reeds to make smoke, to clear away the sickness.

There was a smell of coffee. The What Does husband was scrubbing the lintels with coffee from a bucket. He turned and looked up, and flung the rest of the coffee on the ground to make a path for walking on.

'Oh, bloody hell,' said Root.

Overhead there was the sound of helicopters.

Milena stepped out of the boat onto the woven shore. She began to walk towards the Bees.

'Where are you going?' called Root in dismay. As Milena approched them, the Bees made a sound like many doves and arched their arms over their heads, to cut out some of her thought. Those on the shore waded backwards into the brown water. Milena stood on the shoreline, facing the water, which looked as heavy and golden as oil, a reflection of sunset heaving sluggishly on its surface.

'You'll have to go,' Milena told the Bees. 'If you stay, the Garda will come again, people will be angry. I am not going to be staying here anyway. I will be in hospital and I won't be well. Try to stay away from me. Try to find places where you are safe and I will try to come to see you when I can.'

From out of the water two men came wading, one on all fours, carrying roses in his mouth. The other had lost all his teeth, and his

333

golden hair had thinned to nothing on top. Uncombed coils of it hung matted down the side of his head. 'Hello, Ma,' he said, in a perfectly ordinary way. He was the King. 'Remember Piper?' He stroked the head of the dog-man.

'Yes,' said Milena, in a whisper.

'He remembers you. He remembers that you saved him. He's a good dog.'

Piper dropped the flowers at her feet, and stretched down low, looking up at her, tongue out of his mouth. There was eagerness and love in his eyes.

'Good Piper. Good boy,' whispered Milena and began to scratch him behind the ears.

Piper gave a yelp of pleasure and shook his bottom from side to side, trying to wag a tail he did not have.

'He thinks you are his mistress,' said the King.

You had to understand Bees to know that it was a sacrifice for them to give up Piper. They loved him. You had to understand Bees to know what a tribute it was for them to give Piper to her.

Milena sighed with weariness. Here I go again. She knew what she was going to do. 'Come on then, Piper,' she said, ruefully. 'Come on boy. Or girl. Whichever.'

'Home,' said the Bees, all together, in chorus. 'She takes him home!' They were smiling.

'What did I say?' shouted Root. 'I said you had to be the one who gets taken care of!'

'You had all better go,' Milena said to them. She stumbled as she walked up the coffee-washed pathway. Piper tried to caper about her ankles, but his knees were not sprung like a dog's ankles.

'You're not taking that thing!' exclaimed Root.

'He's not a thing,' said Milena, and her voice suddenly thickened and she found she was weeping. 'He's alive.' To her that was suddenly the most precious thing.

The Bees began to withdraw, bowing and stepping onto the lilypads of their brethren. There was commotion in the water as roots pulled themselves free and pushed the lilypads away from the shore. As the helicopters turned back, as Piper nittered and wriggled and tried to pant, and as Root shook her head with misgiving, Milena began to climb the stairs that led to her home. She felt something sluggish in her loins, the ebbing of the life that still washed all about her in waves.

She opened her door, and Mike Stone came rushing forwards from the balcony, his face full of alarm, full of questions.

Milena tottered towards him, fell against him. 'Mike,' she said. 'I've got cancer.' It was not until Mike held her that she realised. She had made herself ill, out of love. But Love of what?

chapter eighteen

THE ARMOUR OF LIGHT (THE CHILD GARDEN)

On Milena's twenty-first birthday, she and her friends went for a picnic in Archbishop's Park, near St Thomas's Hospital.

Al the Snide carried the wine and the fruit juice. Cilla carried the basket of food and Peterpaul carried Mike's chair. Mike had designed and built it for himself. It supported him from the shoulders and thighs, leaving his swollen buttocks to hang free. Mike had developed a waddle. He walked by shifting his hips from side to side and letting his feet follow. There was a football pitch in the park, covered in vividly red grit. Some boys who were playing on it stopped to laugh at him.

Milena expended her strength by walking up to the boys. They saw her and fell silent, then shared embarrassed smiles. They knew they were going to be told off but they were nice enough to accept it as their due. They also knew who she was.

Milena was bald, and her head leaned forward insecurely on a thin neck, tendons straining. She had started to wear make-up, like an actress. Cilla put it on for her, giving her skin a lightly tanned, purple colour with a smear of silver around the eyes. The silver suited the purple but could not hide how deep the flesh had sunk into the sockets of her skull. Milena smiled with rose-coloured lips, knowing that she showed too much gum and that the grin made her look like a death's head.

'Don't laugh,' she told the boys gently, through the cane screen around the pitch.

The boys shuffled, looking at their feet. One of them had a nasty graze on his knee that trickled brown-black down his leg.

'Someone had to carry you, before you were born,' she told them. 'Who knows, maybe you'll be pregnant one day.'

The boys chuckled, shook their heads. 'Oh, ta. Don't think so.'

'Maybe your wife will insist.'

'She'll be lucky,' murmured one of the boys.

'Are you sorry, lads?' she asked them.

They nodded. Milena blew them a collective kiss. The Princess came up behind her, little Berry pulling in another direction. 'Come with us, Milena,' she sang, to the beginning of Faure's *Requiem*. *Requiem eterna*. I know, thought Milena, I know she's a Singer and cannot help her choice of music, but I wish she would sing something other than a requiem. It's so mournful.

Little Berry lived with his mother now, and had done since the Princess had met Peterpaul. They were all Singers. Berry never talked. Sometimes now, especially when he was alone with Peterpaul and the Princess, he would not use words at all. When he was eating, he sang. Different foods had different themes. He sang them over and over, even with his mouth full, celebrating.

He wore a cowboy hat. Milena had worn one for a time, when her hair had started falling out, so he had wanted one too. The hat was black and red, and had a thong and a toggle that was pulled up tightly under his chin. There was circle of white cotton bobbles all around the underside of the brim. Berry loved his cowboy hat. For him, it was alive and there were particular songs devoted to it.

The Princess was trying to help Milena, supporting her by one arm, while pulling Berry, who was leaning with all his weight and all his being towards something he wanted. He sang about it to himself, but the adults couldn't think what the song was about. The trees? The football pitch?

'It's Piper,' said Milena. Terminals were also empaths with people as well, slightly Snide. As Milena weakened, her ability to Read people improved. 'He wants to ride Piper.'

The Princess paused and looked up at Milena with a kind of helpless concern. Is she trying to find a song? Milena wondered. There are no songs that ask if a man who thinks he's a dog can give the virus to your child.

'It's all right, Anna. I've checked. Piper is not infectious, not contagious, nothing.'

A Speaker could have lied and said that was not a worry. Singers couldn't lie. Trying to lie clogged the music just as speech clogged the words. The Princess went silent until she could sing something else. 'What would you do if someone found him, someone who knew who he used to be?'

'Give him back?' smiled Milena, and shrugged.

'What if it was his wife who found him?'

'That would be sad,' said Milena, smiling dreamily. 'Especially as he thinks he's a female dog.'

Milena felt calm today, she always felt better with people around her. It was at night the terror came, the cold, clinging sweats, the pacing around the room, the life-devouring fear of death. Mike, poor Mike, would wake and hold her as she quivered next to him, teeth chattering.

Milena was immune to the cures. She had unstitched the suppressor genes they tried to give her. So they gave her immune suppressants, so she could catch the cure, and the cancers raced ahead. The cancers ached at night with growing pains. She felt them in her mind, and tried to find the spirals, the spirals that could change with thought. But she had never had so many cells to change before. She had never been so tired or confused before. She sometimes thought, that at night while she slept another part of her, obeying the old program, made the cells cancerous again.

At times, she could find the idea amusing. I can fight off any illness, and so I'm dying, because all the cures are diseases. Haven't things become just the slightest bit confused?

The only other cures they had were the ancient ones, and they were illnesses too. They killed cells in your body. They made you queasy or sleepy or confused. They parched your throat and made you so nauseous you couldn't hold down a glass of water. Your hair fell out.

Other things were happening. The patch of fluorescent skin on her palm had spread up and over her arms onto part of her face. Parts of her glowed in the dark. She could feel other things happening in her genes, strange attempts at mutation, trying to grow new things altogether.

All of that was better than the euphoria. When the terror got too bad, happy drugs were given to her. Then she would talk in a loud, swaggering voice of what she would do when she got better. How she would quit the theatre and become a space pilot. She would believe it. The memory of Mike's face, all its muscles strained, his encircled eyes wincing, told her that he would rather not sleep at night than see her wheeling with joy and mad relief.

But today was a good day. Today everything was in the most perfect balance.

'Milena. The chairs are up,' called Mike, already sitting, balanced in a criss-cross bamboo framework. It was Mike who called and not Peterpaul. Peterpaul did not like to call in public, in song. The days of persecution had been brief, but Peterpaul was still wary.

Milena suddenly felt a nose bump against her hand. She never had to call Piper. He knew when to come. He was more intelligent than most dogs. Perhaps he had been given an empathy virus. When he was human. He had been trained now to wear shorts in public, and slept in a wicker basket in the hall.

'Pi-per!' sang Berry, and chuckled hoarsely, clambering up on to his back. Milena and the Princess began to walk across the grass, hand in hand. Piper crawled beside them on hands and knees, panting with his tongue hanging out, a wide doggy grin of contentment.

Oh, it was a beautiful day! Trees and clouds and sky. In one corner of the park, well away from her was a cluster of moving shrubbery. It was Bees, three or four of them. The Bees always followed Milena, keeping their distance, respectful and silent, like mourners. The Bees bored and oppressed and sometimes frightened Milena. Milena could sense how they saw the virus as something golden, in islands in her body. The cancer sang to them of life even as it was killing her.

But today was so beautiful that Milena felt strong enough to give them a smile and a wave. And they smiled and waved back, looking for a moment like normal people, white teeth in purple faces, quick smiles for a friend on a sunny day. Then Milena saw that one of them was the King. She smiled and waved again, to him.

Milena had not planned to come out. The friends had planned to stay inside, in the Coral Reef room at the hospital. It was comfortable there and warm. There was a kitchen and a bedsitting room and even a small balcony, with a view over the river. The friends had all crowded onto it, and felt the air like a bath all around them. It did not seem likely that Milena would get too weary or too cold. They must get so tired, Milena thought, of me being ill all the time.

Peterpaul reached out towards her to help her sit. He took such exaggerated care to lower her gently that Milena wanted to smile. There had been just a little ill will when she had asked Peterpaul to leave the Comedy. Dante was not an Everyman, and could not be played as one. She had worried about it for weeks, losing sleep, before she finally told Peterpaul over lunch at the Zoo. She was replacing him with Jason, the waspish apothecary from the Babes' production of *Falstaff*. She explained, and Peterpaul had said nothing for the rest of the meal. She learned later that he wanted to reply in the funeral music from *Peer Gynt* and was too embarrassed. He was not angry; he was very, very disappointed. He might also have been a little relieved.

So we've all lost the Comedy. Peterpaul didn't sing it. Mike's pregnant so someone else is riding the Bulge. And I'm dying. Someone other than Milena Shibush is pumping out the images every night into the sky. There's not a breath of live performance about it now. It's a recording. And only the first two books; we only had time to do the first two books. You can't call it a Comedy if you only do the first two books: it ends in Purgatory. Well, thought Milena with a smile, a lot of people have said watching it every evening is pure hell. She settled onto the chair and reached across to take hold of Mike's hand. Oh, it was good, just to sit and feel the sun on her face. Her Rhodopsin skin tingled with the light: she could feel the yellow reflection from the arms of the bamboo folding chair and the warm green reflections of the grass and the sudden stab of orange from the grit of the football pitch. We can almost see with our skins, she thought, her eyes closed. I can almost feel the clouds overhead on my arms.

338

Little Berry was singing, a far from aimless song. His voice was like a cherub's, inhuman. It was an infant's voice singing complex and beautiful music with perfect pitch, perfect tone. It was not innocent. It was unsettling, the voice of another kind of human being. And the song was so strange, as well. It seemed to be about the day itself, the trees, the sound of the tennis balls on racquets, the sunlight. But there was something wary in it too, something defensive. What, wondered Milena, does little Berry have to defend? He must know Singers are different. But people are not unkind to them, well, hardly unkind any longer. Then Berry stopped singing. Milena opened her eyes, and found that Berry had been looking at her, dead at her, at her face.

I scare him, she thought.

He was wide-eyed, solemn, his mouth pulled down at the corners. Was he about to cry? Milena was about to say to the Princess: Berry's worried about something. Then she decided to find out what it was. She tried to Read him. Usually infants could not be Read. Either they were too blank, or too different from adults for the Reading to make sense. Milena could only get a dim sense of what Berry was feeling. Berry was a jumble of song. The songs were secret. Berry did not sing them around adults. The songs were about his world, and his world was like an egg that he was hatching. He was trying to keep it warm. This tender world, protected by secret song. Now it was Milena's turn to be disturbed.

He's trying to defend it from us. Well, children always have secrets. Milena tried to dismiss it from her mind. She suddenly felt unutterably weary. I have a disease to fight. Little Berry must fight battles of his own. Except that it did not feel in the midst of the tangle of song as though it were his battle alone.

Milena drifted into sleep, or in a state enough like sleep for her friends to call it that and not feel too disturbed. They spoke in whispers. Berry had been told to stop singing in case he woke Aunty Milena. He kept on singing in his head and Milena heard the music as if in a dream.

She woke up after a time feeling very thirsty. She had been breathing through her mouth. There was a dull ache, all the way from the surface of her eyes back through to the back of her brain.

Oh don't say I'm ill, she thought. Don't make me be ill. Let me have this day. It is such a perfect day. Please. I don't want to be carried back, I don't want to vomit, I don't want any pain. Not today. Tomorrow. Tomorrow the sky will be grey, and we won't be all together.

'Are you all right, Milena?' asked Mike, rising in his chair, giving her hand a little shake.

'Yes,' she said. No point pretending to be asleep.

She opened her eyes. They were full of a clear, sticky moisture, that refracted the light into rainbows. There were nameless shapes of light, rainbows dancing all around them, swirls of light, beating, like wings.

She opened her eyes and she was in another world.

I know that! I know that place! Milena remembering suddenly sat up and yelled. *I know what it is now! I know where I am!*

I'm really ill, thought Milena who had been a director. This is the start of a new sickness. But she didn't mind. She was smiling.

The world was made of light, light exchanging light, light going in and out like breath, the breath rising up from the Earth into clouds, clouds edged with all light, light in all colours, white, fading to ice blue, swirls of ice crystals in the breath of the world.

Hallelujah. Hosanna.

Shaky, smiling, Milena stood up. She stood up and began to run across the grass. She wore sandals; she could feel the swish of grass against her toes; she could feel the stream of air, fresh from the respiration of the plants, the trees, the grass, the breath going in and out of her, the light on her skin, striking Rhodopsin, breaking it apart, making sugar, sugar and sodium that sent nerves flashing, her seeing, dancing skin, rippling like waves with the light.

The ground had knees and elbows, and outstretched arms, and suddenly Milena had fallen forward with delight into them. She stared about her with delight.

'Milena! Ma!' the adults were calling behind her.

Everything was shielded, everything was protected by an armour of light. She looked at her arm, and saw the light rising out of her as well as into her. She looked up and she caught the trees, turning away, away from her like the Bees, orienting, disorienting.

Milena laughed. 'Whoo-hooo!' she cried, and kicked with her feet. The adults were upon her.

'Ma? Ma? Are you all right?' cried Cilla.

Milena rolled over, and the shock of seeing Cilla took her breath away. Cilla's face had fallen in on itself. It was more of a death's head than her own. The hollow eyes were exhausted with the strain, the strain of playing nurse. Tell me to fickit off if you want to, thought Milena.

Berry squatted beside her, leaning into her line of sight. He was grinning now. He looked dead into Milena's eyes, and Milena who was no longer a director thought: he understands. Milena who had been a director looked at him instead, and smiled. His returning gaze was steady.

'Why did you run like that?' Cilla demanded. 'Did you hurt yourself?'

'We're all hurt. But not hurt by the fall.' She thought she meant her own fall, into the grass, the welcoming grass. Then she thought she maybe meant something else as well. Milena lolled in the grass, ran her bare arms across it. Ohhhhhhh! The beautiful grass.

The grass knew. It orientated itself towards her.

'I think,' she said thickly, as if drunk. 'I think I'm becoming a Bee.' She believed it.

A cure that makes you well, not ill.

'Goddamn viruses,' chuckled Milena. 'Why do they feel so good?'

'Oh, Milena,' said Cilla, weary, worn, taking her hand. It was a lot to bear for Cilla, who had never thought about death or its coming.

'There is a thread, a golden thread, that connects us to Life,' said Milena. 'And we keep making it thinner and thinner. If it ever breaks then we all will die, and take the world with us. And we just keep spinning it out, thinner and thinner,' Milena was grinning. She held up her arms and looked at them.

Her arms were blazing. They fluoresced with generated light.

'Let's go back and eat,' said Cilla. 'You don't eat.' Her voice was clogged.

'Have you ever wanted to be fucked by a tree?' Milena asked, and giggled.

'Milena!' hissed Cilla and gave her hand an admonitory shake. The boy was near.

'Trees are so big and beautiful and strong.'

'Peterpaul,' said Cilla, turning, pleading.

'Listen, listen,' said Milena, lolling her head. 'I don't want to die, but I don't want their virus either. I don't want to live forever. I don't want it, here.' She formed a cone with her fingers that glowed liked embers and tapped her heart. She had not understood before why her body had fought off the cure. 'This is enough,' she said, and pointed to the light all around her, and what lay beyond the light, beyond life.

'She's all bones,' said Cilla miserably. Together, she and Peterpaul lifted Milena up.

Let me stay in the garden, thought Milena whose head hung down, looking back at the grass, confused, confounded. The light that shone out of her arms and her face began to ebb.

Don't take her! begged the Milena who was remembering, to Peterpaul and Cilla. *Don't let them*! she told Milena the director. *It's yours. It's something you did yourself. You got back! It's real! They will take it away again! Keep it!*

They helped her back to the chair. They lowered her onto it. To their surprise, little Berry climbed onto her lap, and hugged her and Milena lifted up weak arms, and put them around him.

Everything was going flat again.

'I think she's just confused from waking up,' Cilla said hopefully to

341

Mike. A quick warning gaze to Peterpaul said: don't tell him anything different.

It was just a virus, thought Milena. A beautiful virus. But it's going now. It wasn't real. Why are the viruses beautiful? She held Berry up to look at him, Berowne's son, his babe, the son of a friend. She looked into huge round eyes that were in a different proportion to his face than the eyes in an adult's were. They looked blue-grey, huge and pale against the purple roundness of his face. It was Berry she wanted to defend. But I cannot help you, and I cannot protect you. I will not be with you.

A cloud passed in front of the sun, and the light was gone. Everything was grey again. So it was sunlight and fever, that was all. And yet it had seemed so real, when I saw it. Another euphoria.

Berry suddenly frowned, and sat up. He tightened the toggle of his cowboy hat and then turned and stumbled down from her lap.

'I think,' said Milena, 'I want to go back inside.'

It was on the way back, when Milena and Al were talking alone together that the Snide suddenly said: 'It wasn't a virus, you know, Milena. What you saw. It was you. It came from you.' His eyes were red, as if he had been dazzled.

Milena stopped and looked back at the garden, at the trees and tried to see the light again. The trees were beautiful, but they were adult trees, and it was an adult sky. 'Come on,' she called smiling, to Mike Stone. 'Catch up.'

Later, the Princess came singing music from *Madam Butterfly*. She told Milena that she wouldn't be bringing Berry to see her for a time. Did she understand? 'It frightens him,' the Princess sang with shame. 'You frighten him.'

But there still was the memory of the welcoming grass; of the turning, curious, tender trees as strong and silent and gentle as fishermen in unvisited villages; of the bouncing, happy clouds; and of the birds that flew without hesitation. Rising up on the breath of the world. There and then, but not now. Only in memory could she see it.

And the Milena who remembered understood. The silence and the light were one.

chapter nineteen

DOG LATIN (AN AUDIENCE OF VIRUSES)

'Life is history,' said the philosophers. They imagined that life worked as they did, by preserving decisions. Thereby they took the life out of history altogether.

'The brain works like a computer,' said the writers of popular science, as if in unison, when computers seemed to be changing the world. They meant that nerve impulses take one branch of a ganglion as opposed to another. A yes or no, a one or zero code that they could describe if they wished, and they did, as binary. They did not know what made living memory, or how sound or light or even silence could be recalled.

'The brain works like a collection of viruses,' the Consensus said one hundred and fifty years later, when viruses were difficult to avoid.

The need to simplify and to put things in a sequence, their devotion to history, made them slaves to whatever was current.

'Time is money,' said Rolfa's father, on the last night of the Comedy. He meant that the younger members of the Family had become slack, and did not see the connection between how hard they worked and Family wealth. Zoe had just asked him if he wouldn't come outside to see the end of Rolfa's opera. She stood at the door of the starkly tidy room he called his office. Zoe was scowling slightly. Becoming Consul had not been good for her father. It had made him pompous and insecure.

Rolfa's father was thinking that it was strange, that of all his children it should be Rolfa who ended up the most like him. Rolfa would have known the opera was there just to glorify the Squidges. She would have known it was more important to get on with work. It had been Rolfa who had invented the time sheets. Every hour a member of the Family worked was supposed to earn forty francs – four marks. This meant that every hour they did not work also cost four marks.

Rolfa's father had become Consul of the Family after the Restoration. The Family called it the Emergency. The Squidges had metal of their own now.

Time is not money. Money is money. Money is a promise, nothing more, an agreement not to doubt. Money is, for example, an exchange of iron ore for promises. The Family were receiving fewer promises for their Antarctic iron, but the time sheets still said they were rich. That kept them happy. And money being nothing more than a promise, an abstract notion, the Family somehow managed to stay wealthy. Rolfa's father sat with his whizzing machinery, looking at figures that were pure superstition. Like all superstitions, money was real. It was as real as the gods of ancient Sumer. The gods of Sumer were media of exchange as well – they presided over storehouses for goods. They also were agreements not to doubt. Gods collapse.

Zoe shook her head. 'One of us ought to see it,' she said. She was thinking of Rolfa, who could not see the Comedy, under the clear unshielded skies of Antarctica. She was thinking of Milena and the strangeness of life. 'The little fish,' Zoe murmured to herself.

Her father was busy with an account. Any system of accounting, whether it uses words or numbers, achieves meaning by what it leaves out. Her father's account left out almost everything that interested Zoe. She and her father spoke in different tongues.

As Zoe turned away, a cat on the roof over her head slunk down the roof slates. A thin coating of cats moved all over London, some in mid-air leaping, others licking their feet in doorways, others hunched over bowls, eating. Some of them lay on their sides, cold, on the pavements.

Under the roof of the Family house, seven women and two men were cooking in various kitchens, chopping vegetables or staring at boiling pots without really seeing them. Downstairs, eight Polar teenagers watched their video, each costing the Family a notional two marks an hour. The time of teenagers was given half value.

In the houses on the other side of the street, a Party Woman was filing her toenails. Another was repairing seat covers. One couple made love, another fought, someone else was washing the leaves of her rubber tree. Outside in the street, two coffee vendors passed each other, pulling their wagons and tureens. One was on his way to Knightsbridge, the other was going home. They smiled and nodded to each other in good fellowship. There was good fellowship among those who plied the new trade, now that the public were safely addicted to caffeine. At the bottom of Rolfa's street, where the terrace ended, there was a noisy main street full of traffic. A smelly omnibus dragged its low-hanging rear end past the corner, alcohol exhaust billowing up behind it. On the pavement, a woman covered her face with a scarf, to filter the fumes. A sun-blasted drunk was slumped in a doorway and he held up a bottle, saluting the woman in the twilight.

The shops on the corner were closing early. A plump, bald man, only nineteen years old, but afflicted with the signs of middle age, folded bamboo shutters over his windows. There was no night trade now, with the opera. He lived with other families in rooms above the shop. On the roof, the shopowner's wife and his children and the What Does cousins were gathering setting up pears or tables, carrying basins of food, preparing a party.

Two miles away, along the river, fishermen were pulling in lines. There were bonfires on wasteground, where people were gathering to share the last night of the opera. In parks, bamboo platforms had been erected, onto which the Comedy was cubed when there was heavy cloud. Much of the Comedy had been obscured by cloud, but tonight, the sky was autumnal and clear. Even so, technicians were carrying out final checks on the equipment. Holograms of giant roses and human hands flickered in and out of existence. The platforms would serve if there was a sudden front of warm moist air. Overhead there were balloons which would see the advancing front of weather and give warning.

In Archbishop's Park one of the workmen finished a bottle of beer. His head tilted backwards to receive the last drop, and overhead he saw the spangle of stars. Another workman was peeing half-seen behind a bush. A tug moved in the direction of St Thomas's Hospital, with the current of the Thames. It swung up and down in the wash of a bigger barge. Lights from the hospital glowed.

In London's two hundred and ninety-two hospitals over fifty women were in labour at that very moment. One of them bit her lip and pushed, and there was a sense of breakthrough, and the head of newborn was free. Another newborn was slapped, and began to wail. It began to wail, just as Zoe turned in the doorway; as the coffee vendors nodded; and as a laughing man in a pub seemed suddenly to slip and fall, knocking mugs from the counter. His heart had failed. In the kitchen of a kaff, near the Cut, amid a clatter of pots and pans, a twelve year old sharing in the cooking poured boiling water over herself. A man finished positioning his favourite stuffed chair in the middle of the street, to watch the show in the air. Three doors down a young man moved from one foot to another, nervously waiting for a girl he only partly knew.

It can't be done. Now cannot be imagined or described, not all at once. We have to string it on a thread, in imitation of the way we view the past. In imitation of the way we view ourselves. If you try to tell the whole truth, you never stop talking. And so we tell stories, histories, instead.

'Time is money,' said Rolfa's father.

'Who were you today?' Mike Stone asked gently.

Milena was sitting on the balcony of her hospital suite. There were no sharp corners in the hospital suite. It was made of Coral and had grown like flesh. The floor of the balcony flowed upwards to make a wall. The top of the wall rose and fell with a line as natural as that of

345

a tree branch. The walls were covered with plaster because the Coral could sting.

The Coral had chewed up rubble from the older buildings of St Thomas's Hospital and laid it in genetically-determined patterns. Milena's genetic balcony looked over the Thames. There were moored barges strung with lights and full of people. The windows of the West were full of people. The West was a sandy-coloured swelling of Coral where the Houses of Parliament had once been, across the river.

Below was the embankment pathway that Rolfa and Milena had walked along on their last day together. Milena remembered looking up at the hospital then. Now she was here, ill, and the wide pavements of that walkway were filled with Bees. They sat in respectful silence, looking up at her. Oh well, thought Milena, leave them be, it's the last night of the Comedy.

The souvenirs of her life were scattered about her. There were not many. There was her attempt to orchestrate the Comedy. It was bound in a notebook. *Music by Rolfa Patel* said the first sheet. *Orchestrated by Milena Shibush*. There was a dirty lump of felt invested with personality called Piglet. There were Rolfa's papers, and some Coral jewellery that Mike had bought for her. There was the paper Cilla had given her, and the music that Jacob the Postperson had remembered. In a box of earth on the wall, there were herbs. They had been grown out of the wall of the Bulge and Mike had brought them home. They were dying.

There was a hard, hot swelling in Milena's stomach, and her arms and fingers were as delicate as a robin's foot. All her skin was fluorescent now. It gave off a dull, orange glow, with brilliant threads in it where nerves ended in the surface of the skin. There was a huge, gathering knot of flesh just above her shoulder.

Even the Party had stopped telling Milena that she was going to get well. They still insisted that she had many months to live and refused to accept what Milena herself knew, that she was weakening. As she weakened, her empathy virus grew stronger.

'Who were you today?' Mike Stone had asked.

'I was . . .' she paused, actress-like for effect. 'One of the attendants downstairs in the laundry. The short one with the wig, I think. I was very tired and had flat feet, but I was in love with Flo. You know Flo, the one who always says hello. I don't think I really knew it, but Flo made my life worth living. We just talked, folding towels and sheets. The soap on them brought our hands out in a rash. Flo's family live in the outreaches, did you know that? I didn't quite hear the name of the place. Oxbridge? Boxbridge?'

'Uxbridge,' whispered Mike. 'It's in the west.'

'Never been that far out,' replied Milena.

346

'What about when you went up in the Bulge?'

'That,' said Milena 'was moored at Biggin Hill.'

'That's far out of town.'

'It's south.'

Oh, said Mike in silence.

'Then,' said Milena. 'I came down with an attack of barge girl. I was a nine year old girl helping my mother on a barge. I ran back and forth along the wood in bare feet, but I knew the varnish would stop me getting splinters. I had lines trailing in the water and I was checking them all for trout or salmon. I had never caught a salmon. I was in love with the idea of catching a salmon. Isn't that strange? Love is the only word for it. I ached to catch a salmon. Meanwhile, I helped with the sails, and checked the tiller. I whistled for my dog. My dog never slipped or fell into the water. And my mother sang.'

Milena paused, living another life.

'She'll make a nice thread,' Milena said. Milena and Al were making a tapestry of what she empathised. They called it 'A London Symphony'. The pattern had music woven into it, the music of Vaughan Williams.

'The tapestry sure is pretty,' said Mike Stone.

The tapestry hung in the air, for those who were Snide to see it. Mike Stone was not Snide.

'Was Heather helping you? Was Heather there?' Mike asked.

Milena settled back. 'Heather's always there.' From time to time Heather would emerge, to help drive down the visions that came with Terminal empathy. Milena let her emerge sometimes, to talk to Al. Heather would die too, when Milena did.

'She's a big help,' said Mike. Something in the way he said it was as if he understood.

Milena had grown imperious, on her cushions, under blankets. 'How would you know?' She drew the blankets about her, nestling down so that she was looking straight up at the sky. She was cold. 'I spent the rest of the afternoon wondering what to do about all of this.' She let a bird-like hand drop towards the things on the floor. 'Most of that is Rolfa's. I want the papers to go in trust for her to her sister, Zoe. But not to anyone else in her family, just Zoe. Do you understand?'

'Yes,' murmured Mike Stone, leaning against the balcony doorway. He preferred to stand rather than sit. He preferred to spend most of the day in another room, away from Milena. He knew he annoyed her.

'The paper with the music written on it – not the score, you stupid man, the notes, there, those! That should go to Cilla and no one else. It was Jacob who remembered the music, and Cilla who gave me the paper, and it was very precious. This cross was Jacob's and I want you to have that.'

'Thank you,' whispered Mike Stone.

'Don't get morbid,' said Milena. 'I'd like a drink. A whisky. Neat. Hard.' It seemed to Milena that she had spent her life doing things for other people. Now she wanted to be served.

Shuffling his feet, Mike Stone worked his swollen buttocks around and waddled into the kitchen. The sound of his feet enraged Milena. Couldn't he pick them up? The burgeoning growth in her stomach was hot and as noticeable now as a late pregnancy. She had dreams in which she gave birth to monsters. 'Quick!' said Milena, suddenly fierce. She wanted that drink.

Then there was a voice, like a virus, hot in her inner ear. *God*, it whispered, *must be a distiller.*

'Did you say something?' Milena demanded.

'No,' came Mike's voice, and the sound of waddling.

'It's going to start any minute!' Milena was impatient. Canto Thirty Three. Dante and his goddamned numbers and star charts. You couldn't change a thing without making a mistake.

Shuffle, shuffle, waddle, waddle. Where was he with that drink?

'You sound like a duck,' she said, bitterly. Her face was stringy, sour; she could feel it, pulling in on itself like shoe leather that had been salted by wet pavements in winter. She wanted to say and think beautiful things, but there wasn't time. She wanted to step back and view her life as a whole but a thousand tiny things, blankets and pain and boredom, nibbled at her like Mice. It was as if Mice were swallowing up the last crumbs of her life.

'Thank you,' she said, taking the drink, pursing her lips, and sniffing. The whisky was harsh on her tongue.

'Are you comfortable, darling?' Mike asked. He moved so slowly these days, like a boulder rumbling, rolling.

'Yes, yes, I'm fine, sit down before you hurt yourself.'

What did it add up to, a life? An accumulation of memories, scattered, discordant, buried so deeply most of them never surfaced again. We don't leave much of a dent behind, she thought. A few things to be given away and some ash scattered on a favourite place. Milena's ash was going to be thrown to the River. She belted down two more mouthfuls of the drink, and immediately felt queasy. She put the glass down.

And you only used to drink tea, said the voice.

'I'll drink what I like,' insisted Milena, aloud.

'Something else, darling?' Mike Stone asked.

'No,' she replied exasperated. 'I've got my drink haven't I? What else would I need? It tastes like shit. Was it the good whisky?' Mike rocked in his chair trying to get up. 'No,' said Milena, suddenly savage, angered by her own unfairness to Mike. 'Just sit there!'

I shouldn't have had that drink, she thought and felt a kind of weight descend. It was as if something were pushing her deeper into the chair. It was as if the chair were spinning. There really was something terribly wrong. She knew it as soon as she felt it, and then denied it.

She pursed her lips and sat up again, as far as she could.

'Why doesn't it start!' she exclaimed.

Below, the Bees began to stir. It was most strange. They were not talking in unison.

Mike Stone remembered something. He leaned forward and picked up the dirty lump of felt. He put Piglet in Milena's lap. Milena stroked his ears. Milena and Piglet watched the Comedy together every evening, as if part of Rolfa were still there.

A trumpet sounded in the sky. Every other night since June it had announced a Canto of the Comedy.

Light, like aurora borealis, played on the horizon.

Then the Comedy arose, like a new planet. Each night the end of the previous Canto was played again.

Dante himself seemed to climb up over the edge of the world. In the last Canto he had passed through the uppermost level of Purgatory through the fire that purified those whose only sin had been to love. The homosexuals walked the circle in the opposite direction from the others. The sin of Caesar, Dante called it. The sin of love was the highest sin, the last that needed expiation. Love was burned away, and then came elevation to the Earthly Paradise, Eden.

There, in Eden, Dante had drunk the waters of Lethe and his memory had been cleansed of sin. The destruction of memory set him free.

'I really shouldn't have had that whisky,' said Milena. The Bees were talking more loudly. They were disagreeing. 'She wants to see it!' one of them, a woman, was saying quite plainly in the darkness.

Dante climbed, bringing Eden with him. The sky overhead was full of trees. Eden was Archbishop's Park, by Lambeth Bridge.

It was the Park as Milena remembered it on her birthday. Light flowed in and out of the trees, as Rolfa's music flowed. But there was one new tree.

It was superimposed, slightly floating, on the memory of the Park. It was a huge tree, with graceful dangling branches delicately support-ing leaves like those of a maple. Its bark was in sections like a puzzle. In the Comedy and in reality, the tree was called the Tree of Heaven. The sight of it made tears start in Milena's eyes, though she did not know why. She did not remember where she had ever seen a Tree of Heaven before.

A costermonger's cart had been chained to the Tree of Heaven. It represented truth. In Dante, it represented the real Church, to be

349

borne away by the dragon, the old serpent. This Comedy was two allegories, one old, one new, both intelligible to an audience of viruses.

The old cart was taken over by the Vampires of History and the Beast that Was and Is Not. The old snake's skin glistened with light and in the light of its scales were glimpsed old scenes, ghostly faces. The snake was history. The snake was memory. It stole the truth, to a clashing and banging of Rolfa's music. The end of the previous Canto had been recapped. The new and final Canto was to begin.

There was a moment of silence, of darkness.

Out of the silence, and into the silence said the voice in Milena's ear.

'Will you stop talking!' she said, turning on Mike Stone. He stared at her blankly. It wasn't him, thought Milena. So who is talking? She pressed a hand across her forehead.

Voices began to sing in Dog Latin. They were the Naiads. The viruses knew they represented the seven cardinal and three theological virtues. Milena made them real people. We are all virtues, now.

There was Billy the King, and Berowne. There was Hortensia. There was Jacob, and Moira Almasy. There was Peterpaul, and Al, and Heather. There was the Zookeeper. And there was Chao Li Song.

Deus venerunt gentes, they sang.

I don't want to hear this now, thought Milena. Her head swam. The very walls and air sang at her, and the light seemed to dazzle, as if she had a migraine. I'm too ill. She could go inside, but there would be no escape from the light, from the sound.

And she saw all the faults. There was a slight jerk of transition here. Unlike the text of the Comedy, a complete Psalm was sung.

The Naiads were singing Psalm 78. There was no clue in Dante or the opera as to how much of it should be sung. There had been a note from Rolfa in the great grey book. *See setting of Psalm*, the note had said.

Where? What setting? Milena had always wondered. When the orchestration by the Consensus arrived there was a setting of the complete Psalm. From nowhere.

Milena fondled Piglet. She stroked his ears. He was wearing out.

Suddenly his zipper burst, as the virtues sang.

Piglet split open and a tiny black book slipped out of him.

Something silent, something hidden, something dark. The flickering light in the sky reflected on gold lettering on the binding. HOLY BIBLE said the words.

Milena's hand fluoresced to make light to read by. She opened the book. The Old and New Testament said the words.

And in writing, underneath it – *For an audience of viruses*.

'Oh my God,' said Milena.

She flicked through the pages. There, almost infinitesimally small there were staves and notes. How small could Rolfa's writing get? How small and hidden in the dark. It was as if Rolfa wrote fractally, each part leading to a smaller part.

'Mike! Mike!' Milena cried out. She held out the book to him, open, her hand shaking. 'Mike! She did it again! She set the whole ficken Bible to music!'

Mike took it from and looked at it, stunned. Each word of the King James version had been given a note.

And Milena knew then. There would be other books.

'Mike,' she said. 'Have them search. Have them look all through her house. There will be more. There will be others.' Milena made a guess.

'Have them look,' she said, 'for a complete Shakespeare. Have them look for *Don Quixote.*'

Have them look for *A la Recherche du Temps Perdu.*

Milena lay back, suddenly queasy.

It wasn't meant to be performed. It was all more original than that. For an audience of viruses the notes said, and I didn't understand. It's lazy just to listen to music – Rolfa had said that and I didn't understand. It wasn't written to be performed! She said that, too, the last time I ever saw her.

The Comedy wasn't a new kind of opera. It was a new kind of book.

A book you read and while you read, your viruses turned it into music. Like the words Satie added to his piano pieces – there only for the pleasure of the pianist, and not be recited to an audience.

The performance was all my idea.

Milena was giddy, giddy again, as if weightless. The fire water in her stomach burned. 'I think I'm going to be sick,' she said. Mike tried to rock to his feet, to get a bowl or a towel. He was too late.

Milena, to her surprise, was too weak to swing her legs off the chair. Vomit spewed all down her chin and over her blankets and dress. Piglet would now smell of adulthood sick as well.

'Oh, Milena,' said Mike, in sympathy.

'Ficken Naiads,' said Milena, as he fought his way to his feet.

Milena lay helpless on her bed, and looked at Lucy. Lucy was Beatrice. Beatrice was Wisdom. She looked on calmly, with a faint smile and sang in an aged voice:

'Modicum et non videbitis me;
Et iterum . . .

A little while, and you shall not see me, my beloved sisters,
And again, a little while, and you shall see me . . .

Lucy, who had disappeared, had somehow recorded all of her part in the Comedy. Another strangeness.

Milena lay still, as Mike folded away the sick-covered blanket. Things like that did not matter any longer. Beatrice's face mattered now. This Beatrice had gone on ageing. She was no longer beautiful except in the ways her face had crinkled, in its ruggedness like the rocks. She looked immortal, as if she had gone sailing on, resolving human weakness, discarding as unnecessary the human beauty of youth. The Queen of Dante's soul, his love, his reminder of goodness. More stern than the rocks, a love as deep as the Earth, whispered in memory, and now restored on top of a mountain in a forest.

People don't love like that, thought Milena. Not for a lifetime with just a memory.

And on that hill the voice in her ears said, *a small boy and his bear will always be playing.*

'That's the wrong opera!' shouted Milena.

Then the helicopters came. There was a great shuddering in the air, and a shadow fell as if materialising out of the darkness and moonlight itself, blue-black and gleaming. It turned around over the pavement, over the heads of the Bees, scattering dust, lifting up their human foliage and rattling it, making a sound like the ocean.

'Leave them alone!' begged Milena, too weak to move on her long chair. The Bees hurt no one: they left after each night's performance; this was the last night; why come now?

Two helicopters. They landed, springing on their sled-like feet, the Bees retreating to the walkways and the walls. The blades kept spinning. Milena felt the air rush past her face. It was as if she were moving at a hundred miles an hour.

'Mike?' she asked, but the words were drowned in the sound of the rotors.

Mike was standing, looking out over the balcony.

'No!' a sea of voices seemed to sigh all together.

'They're fighting!' shouted Mike Stone. 'They're fighting the Garda.' Outside their front door, Piper began to howl, ya-roo like a dog singing at church bells.

'What?' asked Milena, and a bubble of something seemed to burst out of her mouth.

'Lie back, Milena. Don't worry. I'm here.'

Mike Stone, astronaut, thought Milena. What can you do against the Consensus?

'They're coming inside,' said Mike, pointing, voice raised.

Piper wailed. His voice broke. It became a human shout. Toddling on his knees, Piper came into the room, stammering, howling. Then he stood up, like a man. Piper ran on two legs, spinning in circles towards her. 'Milena!' he shouted quite plainly. 'Milena.' Piper had remembered how to talk.

'Piper,' she whispered, and he came, weeping. He knelt beside her, doglike again and she had time to touch him behind the ears.

Then, looming through the door came men covered in white plastic with clear plastic facemasks. They shone torches about the darkened room and then strode with great nimbleness towards Milena. It was so nimble, it looked like a comedy double-take, a piece of elegant, exaggerated performance. With beautiful, dancelike weaving, their arms laced her up in tubes. Tubes were inserted into her nostrils. A wafer, thin, small, translucent was placed on her tongue. Milena could no longer talk.

'What are you doing?' asked Mike Stone with a kind of numb helplessness.

A litter was unfolded as from nowhere. Milena, limp and heavy as clay, felt herself hoisted, helpless to resist. Lifted up, lowered, in a swoop that was delicately timed to avoid making her sick again.

'Taking her to be Read,' said one of the men in white, answering Mike finally, kneeling down with his back to him. 'We've only just caught her in time.'

As if all of the Earth was falling away Milena felt herself lifted up. One of the men in white snapped white resin fingers and pointed. 'The chair,' he said. Milena turned her head. Her head was heavy, and hung unsupported by her neck over the edge of the litter. She looked behind her to see Mike helped back into his chair. The men in white kneeled around that too.

Piper was held back by his collar. He strained against it, gasping. 'Don't go!' he called. 'Don't go!' A gloved hand gently lifted up Milena's head, as she was shifted further onto the litter.

In the sky Lucy was singing, looking back over her shoulder. '*Brother*,' she sang in Dante's Italian, '*why don't you dare to question me, now you are coming with me?*' Then Milena was borne away.

She heard Piper howling as she was carried down the hospital staircase. With a bustle she was carried along the hospital corridors. Light blazed from the hands of the Garda sweeping over the glinting, flowing surface of the Coral, making it yellow, making it flutter. The Coral sang: the Comedy embedded in it, ringing with human voices in some kind of extremity. The walls thumped like an angry neighbour. The monstrous egotism, she thought. The monstrous egotism to put this on, to flood every space in the world with it, to drive out the silence, to hammer the heads of the children, of the fragile, of the ill. Who wants this? Who cares about Naiads and medieval allegory?

The white men carried her into pandemonium.

Bees were pasted, writhing, against the walls of the hospital, held by the tubes. The tubes worked their way blindly along the ground, whiplashing around ankles and arms, hauling Bees up and away in the light from Lucy's face. Lucy shook her head with a sad smile.

'Milena!' the Bees wailed with loss, holding out their arms to her. 'Don't go!'

Around the helicopters the Bees had linked arms. Two white men stepped forward. They had things in their hands that looked like frozen lizards. Light leapt from them. The Bees made a sound like falling rain. A passage had been cleared. Briskly, the white men ran, the litter jostling. Deft hands kept tubes in place, deft feet stepped over fallen bodies.

Then a wave of Bees broke around them, hands raised. They struck the Garda full in their clear plastic masks. Both the Garda and the Bees reeled backwards. Any pain the Bees inflicted they also felt themselves. 'Take the pain. Take the pain,' they told each other, and broke again against the Garda. A Bee woman was trying to wrest the litter from the grasp of the Garda. She quivered, cowering, hands fluttering, eyes screwed shut.

'They are taking you! The Consensus wants you. Swallow you!'

All Milena could do was stare, weakly. No, she thought, I don't want this, no. The cancer in her, hot and heavy and victorious, blazed out at the Bees with terrible life. As Milena came near them, they doubled up or dropped to their knees, as surely as if they had been struck. The woman fell away.

With a wrench and a jostle, Milena felt herself hoisted into the black loading bay. She felt tiny clicks in her spine, as bolts were slid through the supports of the litter, into the floor of the craft, as she was strapped in. The blades overhead began to beat more loudly.

In defeat the Bees began to chant, a chant they had surrendered to silence with Milena's promise to be with them. Now that she was going, they sang it again.

Milena Shibush
Shibush Shibush
Shibush Cancer
Milena Cancer
Cancer Cancer

Very suddenly, the helicopter left the ground, leaning forward, wafting upwards over the roof of the Tarty flats.

Cancer Flower
Flower Cancer

And old Lucy was singing too:
cosi queste parole segna a vivi
del viver ch'e un correre a la morte

so teach them, to those who live
the life that is a race towards death

354

The roofs of the flats were in slated pinnacles like bare mountains. The sky was full of light, light glowing in the leaves of Eden. The roofs fell away as Rolfa's music glinted like the light, sparkling, cool music for paradise and the rivers of paradise. The helicopter turned, slanting, and Milena saw far below her the river of London, old Father Thames.

She saw the garden of her life, whole. She saw the Shell, like a series of building blocks, two great wings open in an embrace, with walkways between them, the walkways she had beaten back and forth at such a pace. She saw the Zoo, held up by bamboo, and the steps of the Zoo where she and Rolfa met for lunch and the park on the embankment where they had eaten.

The Cut was gone. The old buildings had finally been torn down, made into rubble. They were growing again in cauliflower shapes of Coral, hard against the old brick bridge. Leake Street was now closed at one end. Everything changes. The Cut was closed and dark, but the old railway bridge was lit and full of traffic. Milena saw the Hungerford Bridge, where she had stood with Berowne to see the lights come back on. It was crowded with people now, looking up, as if at her, as if she was still down there among them. The same lights still hung in a line along the embankment, making the river glow yellow and green. The whole city flickered green, from the light in the sky, from the Comedy.

Milena looked up too, and the garden in the sky was the same as the garden below. Lucy and Dante walked together out of the chasms of light that was Archbishop's Park.

They walked past Virgil Street, encased in brick. And from somewhere came a ghostly, floating voice. It was Rolfa's voice singing out memory, singing on the night when Milena had tried to find her, after the Day of the Dogs.

Beatrice and Dante alluded to their old love. Dante sang:
Si come cera da guggello . . .

Even as wax under the seal that
does not change the imprinted figure,
my brain is now stamped by you.
Rolfa kept singing without words. Her voice would now not leave the rest of the opera, hoarse and enraged, echoing out of Virgil Street. On the Day of the Dogs, Rolfa had been singing the end of the last Canto, alone in the dark.

Elsewhere in the Comedy, Dante was saying that he could not remember that he ever estranged himself from Beatrice or the conscience of having wronged her.

The viruses will know what that means, thought Milena.

355

He has drunk the waters of Lethe and has forgotten all the wrong he did in life.

He doesn't remember losing Beatrice. That means losing Beatrice was a sin.

Like my not speaking to Rolfa. Like my not loving her. Milena's hands were stroking something soft and spilled. Piglet was still in her lap.

And outside the helicopter, on a level with it, were the black balloons that went up from Waterloo Bridge. They were swollen and singing gently to themselves the music they heard. The light reflected on their hides. Faces from memory flickered on their surface.

And the music walked through an Eden that was made of old brick. It spoke of life in the stone, in the ground, in the air. Air moved like the trees and the grass; brick was as solid as stone. It was fulgent and fragrant; even in old London, wafting with history. Touches of minor keys and discords made it disturbing, pained. Odd sour notes glinted like light on falling leaves. The music became an eerie dance, as if, unseen, the Garden was dancing to itself, by itself. The dance was lost to us.

Beatrice and Dante walked across Westminster Bridge Road and into the Cut: the Cut that no longer existed, the Cut in the Summer of Song. There were all the old familiar faces; the boy with the Hogarth face; the slim clothseller and his pretty wife; the seller of mirror lenses. They were a chorus. For the first time, the narrative was sung. They sung about the sun at the meridian, noon on the heights of Purgatory.

In this Comedy, the Pit, the sink of Hell and the heights of the mountain were the same place. Eden and all the other circles up and down overlapped each other in layers, in a world of layers.

Is that plain enough? wondered Milena. Will they understand this Low and earthbound Comedy of mine?

Could I have done Heaven like this, *Paradiso*? Could I have found heaven on Earth as well? Who will finish the Comedy? Should anyone finish it, or should it exist only in the pages of Rolfa's book?

Then she thought of little Berry, who sang. He had sung the music of the Comedy before he could speak, as he lay helpless in Milena's rooms. As if a sword had been jammed into her throat, Milena had the metal taste of certainty. It would be Berry, little Berry. He would finish the Comedy. He would keep it alive. She seemed to see herself passing it to him. What she passed to him was its smallness not its grandness: The Comedy was the size of flower.

She felt herself flush with light. Her whole skin blazed with it. It illuminated the inside of the helicopter. It shone through the open door. The people below saw her in the sky overhead: light in the shape of a woman. There was a roar from below.

A weight was taken off her. The helicopter began to descend.

Beside the loading bay there were suddenly thick, purple leaves, flapping like great wings and bowing away from her. In the forest of the Consensus, Milena looked up. She saw Dante and Beatrice come out of Leake Street and walk towards the river. The chorus sang of the seven ladies stopping in cool shade. Dante and Beatrice walked into the shadow of the Shell.

The leaves of the Consensus applauded. Milena heard shouts from below, and the helicopter descended into a forest of hands beneath the forest.

More Garda dancing, flicking up bolts, sliding her from the helicopter. All around them, Singers were singing, Bees were chanting. 'Give us the disease, Milena. Milena, the disease!' Someone was licking her hand, to become ill. The stretcher was turned around and Milena saw people in the windows of Marsham Street. There were people on the steps and under the fleshy trees. The people roared. Flowers were cast over her. They fell like rain, human flowers, real flowers.

What a fuss, she thought, what a fuss to make over a second-rate director. But she knew it was the conjunction of the cancer and the Comedy, both together.

Overhead Dante walked the banks of the River Thames. By Hungerford Footbridge he climbed down steps, wading into the water. The River Thames flowed like history. The Thames was now the River Eunoe, that restores the memory of the good a soul has done in life, its labours of love.

Below, in Marsham Street, the Singers began to sing one of Rolfa's songs. The Bees joined in, unable to resist. They all began to sing in Dog Latin, as the lips of the Consensus parted, and its mouth opened amid its own forest.

Modicum, et non videbitis me;
Et iterum
sorelle mi dilette
modicum et vos videbitis me.

A little while and ye shall not see me,
And again a little while and you shall see me.

Oh no, you won't, thought Milena. Then over all the other voices, she heard one other voice begin to sing.

Just a dog of a song
Just a dog of a song
Ambling gently along
With no bad feelings no ill will

The voice was weak and distant. Who is singing? thought Milena. She was too weak to turn her head to see. Then she realised: she was the one who was singing. She was singing something from the old London that was gone, nothing to do with the chants and the sound of the grand opera overhead. She was singing for the Spread-Eagle and the street markets and the men unloading beer barrels and the starlings who lived in the trees and the crumbling buildings and the fringed and heavy feet of the carthorses and for the children who peddled coffee: for the children, for Berry, and for the very old people they would now turn into.

And it doesn't know how to end
And it's so hard when you a lose a friend.
Just a dog of a song
But

Milena felt the bier wobble as she was carried onto the tongue of the Consensus. She looked up through the fleshy trees and the tangle of leaves to the sky, where the light played. All the world seemed to be submerged in water, clear and full of bubbles that looked like pearls. The water of Eunoe, memory. Rolfa's music gathered for a final blow. This is the last I'll see of the Comedy, thought Milena. Yet it was not the Comedy, or her great position or the Zoo or this circus that Milena would miss.

We all sing along
But
We all sing along

The living tongue of the Consensus cradled them, and bore them all down into itself, and the sound and the light were lost.

But the silence remained.

chapter twenty

WHAT HAPPENS NEXT? (AN ORCHESTRA OF GHOSTS)

Inside the white brick corridors all the children had gone. The Reading Rooms were empty; no children sang; there was no sound of guitars or bells. There was only the muffled sound of the Comedy above and the harsh glow of the bare electric light.

Milena was lowered to the floor. She could smell dust. Mike was lowered next to her, on his sling chair. There were flowers in his lap, flowers that had been thrown over him. As he leaned forward over Milena's bier the flowers spilled onto the floor.

'You all right?' he asked gently.

'I'm fine,' she answered.

I am in no pain. Everything swirls, everything dances, and still I cannot believe. I still cannot believe that this is happening, that I am dying.

'They're going to make you part of the Upper House,' Mike told her quietly. 'Do you know what that means?'

Milena knew what it meant and she did not want it so she shook her head. Mike thought she meant she had not understood.

'It means they keep the pattern,' he said. 'The pattern they Read. They save it to consult it. It means even after you die, you are still part of the Consensus.'

'It means,' croaked Milena, and began to laugh, 'they need me for something.' The laugh was a shrivelling inwards from the chest, as if in a coughing fit. 'I wonder what happens to the Lower House?' It was rhetorical question – Milena knew the answer. Mike Stone shrugged, to indicate he had no idea. 'They get wiped,' Milena told him. 'Wiped clean away.'

The rustle of the white dress, the buttocks. Milena smiled and shook her head. Here was Root.

'Any experiences with the paranormal, Mr Stone?' Root murmured the question, not wanting to disturb Milena.

Only my entire life, thought Milena. Only a performance on a cube that should not have been there from a woman who cannot die. Only a plate of lamb that should not have been there. Only London. Only an enemy who shivered and danced inside my eyes. Only Angels and Cherubim who talked to me through the wires, the wires of gravity.

'Now it will just be a few seconds longer and we'll be ready,' said Root, folded into herself by sadness. But Root could not stay closed up for long, and suddenly her face blossomed out into its great grin. 'How are you my love?' Root asked, picking up Milena's hand. 'How are you my darling?'

The great grin was enough to make Milena smile back. 'Not too well,' she said.

'You been here before so you know what happens next, don't you?' said Root.

'Yes,' lied Milena.

'You'll see everything, all at once, your whole life.'

Like drowning men do. 'No time like the present,' said Milena. There was no time left but the present.

'I got things wrong didn't I?' said Root. There had been no cure.

'Yup,' said Milena. No denying it.

'But you'll live forever, here,' said Root, and held up her hands, to indicate the Consensus, all about them.

I'll never be free of the Consensus.

'And here,' said Root, and touched her own heart.

But not here, thought Milena, of the flesh in which she lay, on the brick floor. 'I want to be free,' whispered Milena.

Root looked at her out of love and pity. Such a hope could only lead to pain and disappointment. 'Then maybe you will be,' she said, falsely, and touched Milena's hand. 'I'll be back.' She stood up, and rustled away.

Mike pulled himself out of the sling-chair and crawled towards Milena on all fours.

Like the opera in the sky, Mike leaned over her.

'There's something I have to tell you,' Mike said. 'I caught a virus from you. A receptor turned transmitter. I caught you. Do you understand? I have you in my mind. Like you have Heather.'

How very strange. It's as if I'm shedding myself all over the place, like leaves. 'So that's how you know about Heather,' murmured Milena. 'That's how you knew about the tapestry.' The weakness of her voice surprised her.

Mike nodded.

'Heather's not going to die!' said Milena. She was relieved and happy: Heather won't be destroyed with me! 'Say hello to her for me.' she said. 'And tell Al, will you? Let him come and talk to her.'

'I know about them,' said Mike. 'I know about Rolfa, too. I know everything now.' He pointed to his temples. 'So you don't have to worry about me. If you are worried about me. Tuh.' The shudder-chuckle. Mike Stone shook with Rolfa's shudder-chuckle. 'I won't be alone. I'll still have you to talk to. I'll tell the child about you, all about you. And you'll be able to talk to it. Through me.' In all innocence, he was smiling. 'It's what I said when I first told you I wanted to have the baby. No harm can come, I said. And it's true. You see? It's true.'

On his hands and knees, he lowered himself and kissed her on the forehead. Milena managed to encircle his neck with one thin arm. 'I love you,' said Milena. It was the first time she had said it.

His smile did not change. It was still happy. The eyes did not soften or lose honesty. 'Yes, I suppose you do. In your own way,' he said.

The hot hard lump on Milena's shoulder seemed to ripen. It burst.

'Ow,' said Milena, rather mildly, feeling it. There were ragged edges of flesh. The tips of her fingers came away wet, but not with blood. She looked at them. On the tips of her fingers there was clear sap.

'Oh, Milena,' said Mike Stone, and pulled something from her.

It was a rose, a human rose.

'It's a tumour,' said Milena. 'That means it's immortal. Plant it and it will never die.'

There were other rupturings. Something seemed to fall into the sleeve of her smock. She shook it, and smeared with blood, a snapping turtle crawled out onto the floor. Milena was giving birth to memories.

Her stomach creaked like leather. It creaked and opened up. Something stirred, and Milena lifted up her smock.

There was something new.

It was smooth and pink and had a long extended nose and drooping ears. On Milena's lap there was the spilled and broken doll of Piglet. As if stepping out of him, shedding old dead skin, there was a new Piglet. He was alive. He looked about him in fear and wonder. Mike Stone reached down and took his hand.

'Hello, Piglet,' he murmured kindly. Dazed, Piglet stepped down from Milena.

There was a rustle of skirts.

'For the love of heaven,' murmured Root. Piglet stared up at her and cocked his head in curiosity.

'They're all getting out while they can,' said Milena.

Root was shaking her head again and again. 'I don't know,' she said. 'I don't know.' She turned and walked towards the Reading Room.

Is this happening now? wondered the Milena who remembered. Or is this a few moments ago? Has this already happened? I can't remember. Am I the one who is living, or the one who is remembering?

'It's all right,' said Mike, as other hands came to help. The litter was raised. Mike had to let go of Milena. He cradled up the snapping turtle and Piglet. Piglet carried the rose. All of them were carried in the sling chair. They went ahead of Milena, through the ultra-violet, light along the accordion corridor, into the Public Reading Room.

In the room there was a tall man in white, his face behind a clear plastic mask.

'How much more virus?' he asked, disapproving. 'You all ought to be in whites.'

He was a Doctor. Doctors were the highest Estate of all. They supervised the Health Regime. They tended the Consensus.

'And what the hell is that?' the Doctor asked, pointing to Piglet.

'New . . .' said Mike Stone, and couldn't speak. 'New life,' he said.

Vita Nuova, whispered a voice from elsewhere.

'It's been ultra-violeted,' said Root to the Doctor. Her hand was on Mike's shoulder. 'Mike, love,' she said. 'You've got to come away now. Come away, or we get two readings mixed up together and that's very weird.'

'We're already mixed,' he said, his voice strained.

'It'll be all right, Mike,' said Milena.

'Yes,' he said. 'It will.' He turned around and leaned over. She had never seen his face like that before. It was twisted, pulled in many directions at once. He looked at her face, looked over all of it. He's looking at me to remember, she thought. He's looking at it to remember me. Root's dark, reassuring, reminding hand on his shoulder pulled gently backwards. He turned and crawled away.

Milena was left alone on the living floor. My, but dying is lonely, thought Milena. Everyone has to fall away.

What happens next?

She remembered Rolfa. This happened to Rolfa. I saw the wave go through her. When does it come? Do you know it? Do you remember, afterwards, all the things you saw, or only some of them?

Overhead, dim, as if in a dream, Rolfa's music shook the earth and the stone and the flesh of the Consensus. Rolfa, where is Rolfa now?

The voice spoke again, gently. It whispered in Milena's mind.

What happens next, said the voice, *is that you remember. Everything. There is nothing to fear. It seems to go on forever, and only lasts a moment.*

Root? Milena tried to sit up, to look around. Who was talking?

I have to go now. But modicum et vos vitebitis me

In a little while you will see me.

It was Rolfa. It was Rolfa who was talking.

Overhead, through the stone, the music suddenly ended. The Comedy was over.

Space shimmered. Suddenly space and time and thought rolled towards her, all together.

Then the wave struck.

* * *

362

Somewhere in memory, Milena saw the face of Chao Li Song as a young man. 'The problem,' said the outlaw, 'is time.'

Milena remembered being on the Hungerford Footbridge and it was crowded with strangers and old friends. She remembered Berowne standing next to her, and he was alive, alive and young, the wind stirring his hair as if with hope, his smile leached of calcium. 'I want to be part of it,' he said.

'ZERO!' the people called. 'MINUS ONE! MINUS TWO!'

Lights came on, one after another, and Milena kept splitting into a thousand selves, a thousand moments, each Now a different world, all the moments of her life moving like a bird in flight, each moment separate. Cause and effect were not enough to unite the world.

Paradise is eternally present and so is hell. Time blurs them, crowds them in so close together that salvation and damnation are one. Memory is like being outside time. It can separate them. Memory shows us what heaven is like, where nothing ever happens. It shows us that moment when desire achieves its end, and stays touching, holding the thing it loves, forever. Memory enslaves us, preserving the horror, bending us to it, moulding us to it. Memory is purgatory. To be saved or damned you have to be outside time. You have to step out of this life.

'Oh!' Milena howled, lifting up her thin and dancing arms like the branches of a tree. 'Oh!' she cried aloud in both pain and joy.

She met Mike Stone for the first time. She met Thrawn McCartney. The apothecary spun on her heel, and the Bees moved on the tidal mud like a flock of flamingos. Milena faced Max. 'A big grey book. What did you do with it Max?' Al the Snide came to help her. 'A person is a whole universe,' said Al the Snide. 'We call memory the Web. Underneath is the Fire. And that just burns.'

Chinese princesses dancing in orderly rows lifted up fans in unison, before a giant, enthroned crab. The King, from *Love's Labour's* stared at her with a dirty face. 'The food weeps,' he said. 'The coffee screams.' The Seller of Games was peddling mirror contact lenses, and she was singing in great, clear voice:

It's easily done, no mystery
With this little item from history.

Milton the Minister fell into the calamari salad. 'I think of you all,' said Lucy, 'like you was flowers in my garden.' Somewhere there was still the sound of helicopters.

A spreading fire lit up Milena's life, blazing through all the branches of her nerves. The nerves branched in a yes/no, one/zero code perhaps, but the pattern led to something as dense and as fluid as magma.

I rise up like a tree in smaller and smaller branches, each tiny twig

363

another self. But the roots are lost, the roots of my whole world are lost. I get nervous and my grammar reverses. Bad Grammar for real.

'Because the Past is you,' said Root, somewhere. Now?

The purifying fire burned through her, lighting up memory.

Purgatory.

Milena remembered standing on a train platform in Czechoslovakia. She was holding her mother's hand. At the end of the pink Coral railway, on the edge of the horizon, there was a star. The star was coming for them both. Milena became very excited.

'Ssss Ssss Ssss,' she called, making the sound of a train.

The train huffed and squealed and creaked its way into the station on huge rubber tyres with a steam engine between them like a calliope, streaming molecules. Crows rose up cawing from the field behind.

The train was huge and strong and friendly, like her father had been. It was as if her father had come back. There was a great hearty screeching and a clunk, as if her father had dropped down onto the sofa to play with little Milena. But between Milena and the train, there was a gap. The gap was dark, and Milena could fall down it. The steps leading into the train were as tall as she was, adult steps, not made for children.

Then her mother hoisted Milena up, as if lifting her into her father's arms. Her mother spoke. Up we go, one step, two steps.

'Nastupujem! Raz, dva.'

She's not speaking English, thought Milena remembering. It came as a shock. She's speaking Czech and I understand every word. I understand it better than I ever understood English. English is not the same: it doesn't pick me up and swing me. English is a different universe. Czech tongue, Czech time, Czech feelings. A train is a different thing altogether from a *vlak*. A train is British and mostly reliable and very run down, déclassé. A *vlak* is abrupt and powerful, and takes you to the town, where all good things are. And because the *vlak* is so important it cannot be allowed just to leave. There must be a tremendous fuss made. Handkerchiefs waved. Women sticking hands and heads through windows, clutching each other, giving urgent advice, making urgent demands. Bring me back the books. And tell Juliana not to forget to see Aunty. As if they were going to go away and never come back.

Milena and her mother enter the carriage and there are rows of faces and a woman with spectacles and a fox fur coat.

'Mami, proc ma ta pani na sobe mrtve zviratko?

Mama, why is that woman wearing a dead animal?'

Unanswerable. All the people in the carriage laugh, including the spectacled woman, though her mouth is thin and her eyes narrow. The question is unanswerable, because carefully considered there is no answer that makes sense. You can hardly say it is because it makes her look better. There is the fox's dead and wizened face, biting its own tail. So why is she wearing it?

The burst of laughter alarms the child. She wants people to understand it really isn't a stupid question.

'*Snedla je napred? Mela je ochocene?*

Did she eat it first? Did it use to be a pet?

'*Milena*,' chuckles her mother, and looks around, nervously. No one else ever says her name in the same way.

Her mother's voice, rises and falls, caressing the name, in love and pity, embarrassment and distress. Milena gives her mother great pain. The pain is tangled with many feelings. And the way her mother says it, restores the meaning inherent in the name.

Milena remembered that her name meant Loving One.

I still have the name, but I had lost its meaning, until now. It was as if her name had taken off a mask, to have its meaning restored, to hear her mother say it again with the sound it first had in Milena's first world.

Milena's mother is pulling her towards a seat, and talking to her, in a voice that other people can hear:

'*To nikdy nebylo zviratko, Milena. To narostlo. Pestuji kozesinu jako rostliny.*'

It never was an animal, Milena. It was grown. They grow the fur like a plant.

Milena wants to know why they do that. But she is afraid, afraid of another burst of laughter. She is deeply chagrined. Obviously, it is a bad thing to ask questions. Questions show that she is stupid. The child already knew that she was stupid, that she must keep quiet, that she must hide. They had given her viruses time after time, but the viruses would not hold. Milena would not learn. She was resistant.

Her mother lifts Milena up onto a seat. Milena can feel how small and light she is, as if she can flick herself up into the air like a playing card. It is a talent to be so light, so quick, so much like a fire. Time seems so slow and smooth, like honey. Milena's legs swing high off the floor. Her mother pulls her back into the seat and her legs have to stick straight out in front of her. Nothing is made for children.

There is a screeching and a sudden lurch forward. Slowly, as if weary or reluctant, the train begins to pull away.

'*Zamavej no rozloucenou, Milena.*'

'Wave goodbye, Milena. Wave goodbye.'

Her mother is weeping very silently. Milena the child is perplexed. She had been told they were going away, but she did not believe it. Go away where? What other place to live is there? To Prague? That would be lovely, but wasn't Prague dangerous? Hadn't they left Prague to hide?

The drab little station is hauled away. It is not possible to see the village. There are trees, and the old river, and the cows, dim in the mist, and a steeple with a rounded dome. Gradually, it is all swallowed up in darkness.

Home, wept the Milena who was remembering. That's my home. Milena the child is not weeping. For her it is just a passing landscape. That is the country I have never seen again, thought the one who remembered. That is the place I carry around in my head, unformed, part of me, but not remembered. Until now.

Milena's mother holds up Milena's hand in a tiny mitten and waves the hand for her, makes it wave goodbye to no one.

Not mittens, but *palcaky*.

The clothes the people on the train wear, the way their hair is cut and combed, the stockings over trouser cuffs to keep out the cold, the smell of the trains. Mint tea and little sugared cakes in boxes to eat on the way, and that particular resin panelling, and the sound of the train, its low throaty growl, as if it had a beard and sang songs in a wild, strained voice or smoked cigars. As if, like her father, the train talked about freedom until it died.

Not freedom, not freedom, but *svoboda*.

Those aren't houses, they're *domy*.

Those aren't fields, they're *pole*.

Those aren't blackbirds, they're *kosi*.

And I am not Milena Shibush. I never became Milena Shibush. She is elsewhere, in the land that might have been.

Oh Tato, oh Mami, does it stretch that far away? Does life pull us apart so much, that we stop being real? All of that then was real? How did it fade? And how is it here again?

Milena remembered childhood.

She remembered skinning almonds in someone else's house. Loving One, Loving One, they kept calling her. The almonds came out of a red clay bowl of boiled water and they were hot. Milena kept pushing with both thumbs, and then magically, mysteriously, the almond would slide out of its brown skin.

It was Easter. She and the other children ran through a huge garden, giggling, in sunlight, to cut chives with scissors. A shaggy horse with feeling lips kissed the chives out of their open hands and Milena gasped in wonder. They found ladybirds and tried to keep them in a bowl full of grass, and in the front room of the great old house, which was a warehouse, the girls built a secret room out of boxes. They had a toy piano. They fought to keep the boys out of their secret room, and as they fought secret music tinkled. Milena remembered pushing a boy over. Milena fought and won, squealing with excitement.

Milena remembered the faces of the friends she had forgotten. There was a little girl who had almond eyes, beautiful black hair in a ribbon and a pink dress. There was Sophia with blue eyes and brown hair, and a wan little boy, weaker than the girls but who refused to cry and kept bravely coming back to storm the redoubt. Milena's hand was slammed in a door and she wept and wailed, and then, as soon as the pain subsided, she ran off, laughing again, to be with the others in the garden, hunting chocolates under the leaves.

I was happy.

And I have never been at home in England. I have never felt English, I have never felt in the way they do. I know their words but I do not really feel them. I do not really cry in English, or laugh in English, or make love in English. I find the people dull or cruel, bland or pretentious, rude or prim but I never quite get their measure. And I never quite do the right thing or say the right thing, because underneath my grammar is not only bad. My grammar is Czech.

And Milena remembered later on that same Easter Day, the child beginning the long climb home. There had been an Easter pageant in the domed church, and the child wore white robes now, and wings covered in crinkled resin that caught the light. She was climbing the hill that led up from the village back to the hot limestone house. The path sloped up through a dark wood. The child was holding her father's hand, and her mother's hand, and she was dressed as an Angel. Her plump face, flushed purple, looked up.

The child looked up at Milena.

She can see me, thought the Milena who was remembering. I can see her.

Her father tried to pull her higher up but the child resisted. She stared glumly right at Milena, at her adult self.

I remember this! thought the adult.

And Milena remembered looking at an old woman whose skin seemed to have gone yellow wherever the bones pressed against it as if the bones would break out. The woman was bald, except for a few wisps of hair. The child saw her and felt dread. It was unaccountable dread, as if she knew this wasted spectre was her future.

And time stood still. The moving hub of the world turned around a point that was still and Milena stood in it, Milena at the beginning and Milena at the end.

The adult knelt underneath the branches of the trees that had paused for breath, in the sunlight that was not moving, in one instant that was fully apprehended.

'Do you have time?' the adult asked the child. She wanted to talk to the child, to warn her.

The child did not understand English. That's right, of course! thought the adult, and put a hand to her face. She tried to remember the words in Czech. She wanted to warn her, protect her. Warn her against what? Life? Death? Leaving home? The child scowled, perplexed.

'Be happy,' croaked the adult, whose world it no longer was. She reached for a foreign language and came up with the wrong one. '*Soyez content.*'

The child tugged at her father's hand and time began again.

Stay here! thought Milena the adult. Don't hurry to be away. Your father will die, your mother will die, you will lose this whole world! You will lose your self!

Milena remembered seeing an old, desperate, sad face yearning to deliver a message that perhaps no child should understand.

Loving One turned away. She tugged her father's hand for a swing up the hill. He laughed, and made her fly up from the ground. She squealed, tickled both by joy and fear, and was lowered down to her feet. She walked on, up the wooded hill, through patches of shade and sun.

But not lost, not lost in the middle of her life, thought Milena. This is at the beginning, when the wood is full of light, and the way is straight.

The child turned and looked back at her. And the face showed that the child understood more than she could put into words.

Ghost, the face said, go home. Ghost, you are nothing to do with me, now. Ghost do you think that just because you are at the end, that you mean more than I do?

At the still hub of the turning world, Milena saw all of her past. She remembered the Child Garden on the day she met Rose Ella. She remembered the flowers that poured out of her on the day she stood in Thrawn's room and reformed light. She saw the Earth below through the windows of the Bulge; she saw Archbishop's Park; she saw the reeds and slow waters of the Slump. She remembered the fire as it danced up Thrawn McCartney's arm. Did any of it really weigh more than this, here, the child walking between her father and mother, up a hill, through a wood in another land?

And Milena awoke again on the soft, warm floor of the Reading Room.

'Not again,' said Root. 'I told you! I said don't fight.'

'Always fighting,' murmured Milena.

'They don't have what they want.'

They want Rolfa.

'The pattern isn't complete!'

Mike Stone came crawling. 'It's got to stop now, anyway,' he said. 'My wife is ill.'

We get old and lose our selves, thought Milena. Why did I bring the cancer back? So that people would get old? She thought of Hortensia whose calcium-leached bones kept breaking. She thought of the child running through the garden of the great house and of the faces of her childhood friends. They would be her age by now, in their early twenties, in Czechoslovakia. But they would not be dying.

Why did I do it at all?

Root strode quickly to Mike Stone. 'Mike, love, let me explain,' she said and helped him back into his chair. Milena heard some of what she said. Something about medicine helping. Something about it all being over in an instant.

The Doctor came. The Doctor was in Whites and carried an applicator. Milena thought of the round, fat, flushed face of the child she had once been before the virus touched her. She thought of the feeling lips of the horse in the garden and the fun of cutting chives.

Milena understood why she had brought the cancer back.

'People are going to get old now aren't they?' Milena asked him. 'They're going to live a long time because of the cancer?'

'Yes indeed,' said the Doctor. There was a hiss from the applicator. Another cure to make her ill.

'So if people can get old again, will you let them stay children?'

Milena Shibush had brought back cancer so that children might be left alone a little while longer to play in the garden, amid the trees, with the light. Who would have thought that Milena Shibush would die out of love for children?

'Oh,' said the Doctor, his smile still professional and distracted. 'We've cured people of childhood. Children knew nothing: they needed to be taken care of; they were naturally cruel. Childhood was a disease.' He stood up, looking pleased, and shook his head. 'We're not going to bring childhood back.'

I've lost, thought Milena. She had not even known there had been a battle. Her life had been spent trying to bring back what she had known in childhood.

Milena had thought her life had begun with Rolfa. She thought that she had bloomed when she found Rolfa, and that her life had gone on blossoming even after Rolfa had left. Instead, her life had been finished, in the sense of being accomplished. Its end had been achieved. In Rolfa, with Rolfa, she had found love. And love was the image of everything that had been lost: her home country, her home tongue, the landscape of childhood, her way of seeing it, her father, her mother,

her name, the place where she would have been happy. She had lost her self.

And Rolfa, even she was lost. Rolfa, they even have you. They have your voice, they have your mind, they can make you speak when they want you to. I gave you to them. So why am I holding back my memories of you? Let them have those.

I am going to have to find another way to fight.

Milena relinquished her claim. She remembered Rolfa for the Consensus.

Milena remembered being lost in the dark in the Graveyard. Loose threads of old dead costumes strayed across her face and blistered sequins were rough under her fingers.

There was music playing, insanely loud. The music was *Das Lied von der Erde*. The words told a kind of ghost story.

Milena was sucking her finger, sick at heart with fear, fear of being ill again, of losing more of herself. She was lost in the dark, more frightened than she need be, because it reminded her of all the other ways in which she was lost. It reminded her that no one would notice she was gone. And the voice, high and sweet and sad, was a woman's voice, reminding her that she needed love.

So the dark around her was haunted. Don't be silly, she told herself, what do you think it is, an orchestra of ghosts? She scraped her head on brick, looked through an arch and saw a light on the wall. She saw there was no room for an orchestra. It was obvious what was playing; if she could have thought clearly she would have known that it was a recording. But she was too frightened of life and of herself to think clearly. Milena remembering felt pity for Milena the actress. The actress knelt and pulled back a curtain of old clothes.

Trouble, thought Milena the actress. Trouble, thought the Milena who remembered. Trouble, seeing the mound of papers, the mess, the shrieking music, and the slumped, dazed brute of a Polar Bear. There was disorder there.

Ewig blauen licht die Fernen
Everywhere and eternally, the distance shines bright and blue.

In the music, someone who might already be dead was departing with regret and sadness. The dead are more afraid than the living, and in some ways they are more alive.

Ewig ... ewig ...
Ever ... Ever ...

The GE stirred herself with a kind of convulsion as if she had almost settled into death herself, following the music there. She knocked over paper and plastic cases, as if she were blind. Sadness hung from her face like lead weights, pulling down the flesh under her eyes and

370

around her jaws. The music had been calling for someone. The paper slid away to reveal a box, a small, crude soundbox, made of metal as thin as paper. No wonder the music had hurt when the volume was full up.

To the poor starveling of the Consensus the soundbox was a wonder, and it drew her out of her hiding, out of her fear, as did the soul-sadness on the GE's face.

'Where did you get that?' Milena the actress asked in wonder, though she could hear music any time she liked. Her viruses would sing it for her, out of memory. It was the metal that drew her, the cost of the thing. It was private metal, something owned and therefore more precious, if only to someone else.

'China, I believe,' said Rolfa, and Milena could hear the youth in her voice. Youth was plump and fruity, not yet worn by doubt. It still had hope. 'You wouldn't happen to have any alcoholic beverages about your person, would you?'

Milena remembering saw that Rolfa was trying to be raffish. She was already trying to charm. She liked me as soon as she saw me, realised the Milena who remembered. She was signalling in a thousand ways.

'No. I don't like poisoning myself,' said the actress, narrow, bitter, expecting defeat.

'Tuh.' Rolfa turned away. She was slightly slimmer then, without the pouches of fat on the small of her back. There was something musical in the way she moved. The clumsiness was stricken with feeling. Feeling grew out of her like fur: she bristled with it. Bleary with love and music, she began in a rather rational way to dispose of the mess on her desk.

Milena the actress had felt the first tug, the first little spindle thread of love, but she did not know it. 'Effendim?' she said, pained at being ignored. 'I've come to change these boots.'

Already, unknown to either of them, they were together. Their animal selves had recognised it. Their whole lives were there to be read in the way they each smiled and moved. They had already Read each other, but their conscious selves had yet to catch up.

'You,' said Rolfa, turning, 'are a ponce.' It was said with a kind of honest affection. It was true, and Milena the actress needed to know that other people could see the things she tried to hide.

Milena the actress went cold and shy. She had been seen through again. Her masks were paper-thin. The moment for a reply passed and Rolfa turned away. The actress kept seeing Rolfa through a series of paper masks. Polar woman, rough and tumble. The Bear who Loves Opera, a famous Zoo character. Her conscious self was not seeing Rolfa at all.

371

'Bastard,' the GE murmured to herself.

'Are you talking to me?' demanded the actress. You know she's not, Milena! Why are you looking for injustice?

'No,' said Rolfa, turning to smile, holding up a bottle. 'I was talking to this empty whisky bottle.' She's saying she sees through you, but likes what's on the other side. And she wants, she yearns, for you to like her.

Made bold by the force of attraction, Rolfa threw the whisky bottle away and listened to the breakage, as if extraordinary acts and sudden sounds could speak when people could not.

If it was me, now, Rolfa, I'd laugh and ask your name. I'd sit beside you and let you know that I already thought you were wonderful, that I didn't mind the fur or the teeth or the rotting shoes. We'd sit and talk for hours about music, and I'd say, let's go out for a drink if you like whisky so much. We'd be friends from the start. And the reason why I could do that now, Rolfa, the reason why I'm different, is you.

I don't want to remember any more, I don't want to see the waste and the pain and the waiting. I just want to hold you. I just want to stroke the fur on your arm, and try to save you from what's coming. And this time I'd do it, this time, I would know how: I wouldn't let anything go to waste. I'd say, wait until the metal comes and your Family has to make friends with the Consensus. I'd say, be with me from time to time, but don't run away until you've shown them, your father and your sisters, that the music works. And I'd never let you be Read.

Rolfa held up a bottle. 'God,' she said, 'is a distiller.' She grinned, and Milena the actress saw the horrible teeth and the dandruff and finally relaxed enough to realise that she liked her, liked this strange creature.

'Do you live here?' Milena the actress asked, and stepped forward a bit. Amusement suddenly bubbled up through her, and childish wonder, and something sweet that was kept hidden and protected.

Maybe not, maybe I wouldn't change anything, thought Milena remembering. She ached with love for both of them. Maybe this is the best way for this to happen, as tentative as a spider's web. Not bold and knowing and businesslike.

A look came over Rolfa's face, a look Milena remembering now recognised, a look of great tenderness, of simple kindness, of wishing the world were different for them both. Her hair in her eyes made her blink. 'It would be better if I did,' she said, ruefully, amused. 'This is where I hide, instead. Since you don't like poisoning yourself, perhaps you'd like to look at this.' She held out the musical scores.

I'd forgotten that, thought the one who remembered. Already the music was being passed between us. The music would unite us and

* * *

372

part us and fix us together for all of our lives. The paper was smooth like skin, and still warm from Rolfa's grasp.

'I take it the reading of music presents you with no difficulties,' said Rolfa, meaning that most other things did. It was plain now that Rolfa was the older of the two, plain that she was controlling. I always thought you were a shuffling innocent, thought the Milena who remembered. But you knew so much, Rolfa. You were a genius after all.

Genius is in the shapes your hands make as they move, in every reaching or withholding gesture. You know what you are, and you know that ego is the enemy of what you are, so you defend yourself against it, against pride and ambition, and you are very gently guiding me, and you so very gently want me. You knew who I was, Rolfa, and you knew that you could make my body bloom, and my soul. I still want you, Rolfa. I want your hand on me, on the flower between my legs. Desire is like a blister that needs to be burst. And cunning, you were cunning to sing, knowing that it was the music that would hold me, hold us both. You sang, to show me what you already knew. That music in you had found its elect.

So the ghost began to sing again, out of the past.

Ewig . . . ewig . . . ewig . . .

Promises of forever, with silence in between them.

Suddenly Jacob's face was smiling at her, eyes weary. 'I have a message for you, Milena.'

I am Constable Dull, an't shall please you. *No, no, no, no,* howled the director.

'From Ms Patel,' said Jacob.

'Want some mitts?' asked Zoe, not at all unkindly, in the dining-room of the Family. Zoe passed Milena the fingerless indigent gloves of kindness. No, not mitts. *Palcaky.*

Milena and Rolfa ate again in the riverside park. They walked together to the Buddhist shrine and watched the acrobats. They rode on the back of a dustcart from the night market, listening to the sound of the horses' hooves.

'But now,' said Jacob, 'because of you and Rolfa, when I dream, I also hear the music.'

And Jacob and Milena walked together again out into the sun, regretting Rolfa. The whole river regretted Rolfa, now, and the sky, and the birds. Jacob gave Milena's hand one last squeeze. This time the crucifix was passed between them. 'I must run my messages, now,' he said, and turned away, and Milena saw again the sun reflected in the windows, the fire in each of the rooms. Jacob walked into the fire and was consumed. He made the light burn brighter.

'Fire!' Cilla was shouting. 'Fire!' A bell was ringing and Milena was outside in the cold again, in the dark.

Each room has one of us in it.

Cilla opened the box and inside was paper, being passed again, like human skin.

'Oh Cill,' asked Milena, 'who did this?'

'Just us Vampires,' said Cilla. 'Just us Vampires of History.' Her face in the moonlight, in the past, was blue.

A trumpet blast sounded. The fire was over. A trumpet blast sounded. The Comedy started again, and the sky was full of fire: it was the Inferno. The souls roiled within it. The souls had been imagined like dandelion fluff, rolling on invisible wires, toiling through the fire, caught in their own sins and imbalances forever, in a universe made of thought. What made the fire, then?

'You like dogs?' a man in a body warmer asked. He was on fire too, a fever. Rolfa turned in rage, drunken, demented with what had been denied to her. Rolfa lifted up a table.

It wasn't the sweaty man she was going to hit with it, realised Milena. She was going to hit me.

And it seemed to the Milena who remembered that she could see across the river to a park and a little boy in a cowboy hat ran round and round it, singing, 'Pi-per! Pi-per!'

And the dog cried out, 'Don't go! Don't go!'

I have to. A little while, you shall not see me.

All the Earth seemed to fall away. Milena saw the fields and the village of England in neat patterns, the grain, the pinioned pear trees, and the beehive houses. She wafted up through cloud, into mist, and up into Antarctica, and there, in the light of heaven, in the icy chill, there was life. There, the spiders danced, between crystals of ice. I know where I am, thought Milena, remembering.

Then the window of the Bulge blinked, and suddenly, strung between the clouds were Bees. They had grown great purple wings, veined like leaves, and they hung like bats. There were veins in the sky, clear tubes, full of sluggishly pumping fluids. There were bobbing plants rising up in seaweed tangles, attached to pumpkins full of gas. There were great swirls of Bees, throwing themselves between the plants, rising up on spirals of air like Doré's Angels, living on light and moisture. They attached themselves to the veins that bridged the clouds.

When was this? Then Milena remembering remembered.

Rolfa threw her head back and howled with joy.

It doesn't just go back. It goes forward as well, Rolfa said in wonder.

This is the future, thought Milena. I am seeing the future.

Past and future swirled together, in a vision. Milena was swept higher. The sky overhead went dark and the sea far below was like burnished brass. The Earth and the clouds exchanged light. All of it, the Earth, the clouds, the light, the many Milenas, the future and the past, the net of Bees, the net of nerves, all held in a system of reciprocity.

I am. I am outside. I am, outside of time. Outside of time, I have always been weightless.

Afternoon sunlight poured in through the windows. Rolfa's breasts, shaved, spread almost flat on her chest. Milena was kissing the prickly belly, filling the belly button with her tongue. Then memory took her down further, to where Rolfa had not shaved, to where womanhood lay in folds, and Milena kissed that, slipped her tongue into it, and whipped her own small body around, so that Rolfa could kiss her. It was not harbour or refuge that Milena sought, but the body that was one with the person.

There was a hiss. The two Bulges parted, the seal broken, and the smaller Bulge fell away from the larger. It was returning to Earth. Milena the director saw *Christian Soldier*, outlined in pure white light falling away from her. It doesn't matter, don't regret, she told herself. You'll be back, you'll be back here for the Comedy.

Zamavej no rozloucenou, Milena!

Wave goodbye, Milena. It was the last thing she could remember her mother saying.

I'm going home, thought Milena the director.

And then it was the night, in the little room, the Shell. 'I'm going to sing,' warned Rolfa, feverish on the bed. Milena fumbled in panic for a pencil to write the music down. Why write it, Milena? No one ever forgets anything. They only try to escape it. You will know this music for the rest of your life, note for note.

Rolfa began to sing the music that ends Purgatory, that will end all that will be performed of the Comedy. She sang it for Milena, looking all the while at her, the music that was like Handel, like Mozart, like Wagner, notes rescued from the core of the soul that belongs to no one, pulled out of the realm of freedom, the realm in which we all ought to live.

'Give it a rest!' someone shouted from an upper floor.

Rolfa smiled, and raised her voice. You'll remember this, too, the smile said.

'Qu-iet!' howled someone else.

Milena went to the window to yell at all of them, all of the people who had blocked the music in Rolfa and in themselves and in her.

'Someone's dying!' Milena wailed. For her, it was true.

Rolfa held up her hands and through some miracle of air and spittle reproduced the sound of applause, the sound of justice. And suddenly they were both in Rolfa's street, at night, by a park, and the trees were applauding too with their leaves. Milena was wearing the indigent gloves. Rolfa, covered in fur again, hugged her and held her. For some reason, it was snowing. Snow fell like stars. When did it snow?

Milena looked at the park in the snow and knew it was the London of the future. This was the crescent outside Rolfa's house, years after both of them were gone. This was the London in which Milena no longer lived, in which there was no Rolfa to hold her, in which Milena had no flesh to be held.

It was cold this future and she haunted it as a ghost. There were bootmarks in the snow, but no one walking. There were lights floating in the sky.

Did it matter that she no longer existed? Did this eternity stretching after her weigh any more heavily than the moments in the garden? The future was utterly without nostalgia or understanding, as cruel and new as a child.

I'm going to faint, thought Milena. She was cold, shivering. This is ridiculous: real people don't faint. Neither do ghosts.

But she felt herself slip away anyway. The moon of the future swam in the sky and Milena let herself fall. She felt herself fall, and was lifted up. For a moment, she thought she was in Rolfa's arms.

Time was a dream. The helicopters came again, roaring over the tops of the trees, tormenting them, tearing leaves from the branches, sending flurries through the snow. It was not Rolfa, but Mike Stone who was carrying her now, running with her as he had with Milton the Minister, as if this were her wedding again. People rushed to help him lower Milena to the floor, and from out of pouches in his trousers Mike took a pulse injector and clips. He put them into Milena's ears and arms.

This is not the future or the past. This is my Now, she realised, and Now is always timeless.

She thought the Reading Room was the grass of the park in Rolfa's street. She wished with all her heart it was that crescent of grass and trees and that she would wake up in the morning in her own room to find that Rolfa was going to live with her.

Milena felt the grass of her sixteenth summer press against her cheek. She wanted to put the very tips of her fingers in Rolfa's hand. She couldn't find it, any of it.

The grass was gone, and the park, and the infinitude of different Milenas for all her different Nows. The Milena who was remembering felt herself reunited with the Milena who was still alive.

She felt herself lying on the floor of the Consensus. She could feel her thoughts surge and fail. Mike Stone was leaning over her and there was a pulse injector in her ear. She felt herself slip down and away and then return, like the lapping of waves on a little lake. The Reading was over. She was dying.

Had Rolfa kissed the top of her head? Had she run her fingers through Milena's hair?

The answer was yes.

What, Milena wondered, what happens next?

chapter twenty one

THE THIRD BOOK (A LOW COMEDY)

The Consensus of Central London rose up as a fleshy forest over Marsham Street. It turned sunlight into sugar and elements of the soil into protein. Sap was pumped through its heart, the Crown, which directed all of its unconscious mechanisms of tending – the circulation of oxygen and sugar, the elimination of wastes, the patrolling of its immune system. It was also there, in the Crown, that the synthesis of memory and thought took place. Out of the Crown, attached by roots, grew clumps of tissue, nestled together in the earth like potatoes. Crabs the size of hands protected the tubers, attacking animal or insect invaders. Doctors inspected the flesh, crouching through brick corridors like coal miners.

Inside the tubers, there were ranked and ordered areas of flesh. They were called cells. Imprinted in these cells were the Readings of individual selves.

The Consensus of Central London nurtured and made use of over one and a half million souls. There were fifteen individual Crowns spread across the geography of Greater London. There were fifteen million selves contained in them. Almost all of them were children, Read at ten years old.

Everything is a hologram, a smudged image of the whole. The children of the Consensus slept, like individual memories. While the Crown itself rested, the children played, like dreams. Scattered, disordered, nightmarish, the many selves of the Consensus tried to reassert themselves, tried to live again, like the unhappy memories imprisoned in each of us. The Crown would shift in uneasy rest, reminded of all the things it tried to forget.

The Consensus of London slept, stewarded in the being of the Consensus of the Two Isles, as the Two Isles were only occasionally brought into being in the Crown of Europe, while Europe slept in the World. There were great fleshy cables of nerves, under seas, across continents.

It was the Crown of the World that wanted Milena Shibush.

The great synthesising cortex was in Beijing, and all its attention was slowly focusing on one small cell of flesh, in England, in London.

* * *

Milena the pattern awoke trying to breathe. Her lungs tried to pull in but it was if there was no air. There was no light, no sound. A pillow was over her face, she was being suffocated. She fought, groping in the darkness, clawing at it. No hands, she thought. I have no hands!

Calm

A bolt made of iron seemed to shoot into her.

Be still

It was not a voice but an impulse, a direct electrochemical command that occupied Milena completely.

And Milena was still. The panic left her.

Then, like a flock of birds, came other, smaller impulses.

Milena   *Ma*

            Ma   *Milena*

The birds of thought were the impulses of children from all around her. They darted in and out of her. They came as greetings and were joyful, glad to be of use, weaving and ducking. They were playful, newly awoken into full and conscious life. They were doing the will of the Consensus.

Like this!   *Like this!*

            You do it

                    like this!

As if they were carrying ribbons that they wove round and round her, the children presented Milena with the knowledge of how to exist in the Consensus. You sleep, they told her, and then you are a dream. You are brushed lightly, quickly, with thought and your reaction is harvested, as if by a virus. All the reactions together make a decision.

It was the knowledge of how to live in slavery. The poor birds tried to be happy. They were full of good will. They were still ten years old, though laden with virus and trapped in these mountains of flesh, trapped in tiny cells. They would stay ten years old, until they were wiped away.

Milena the pattern was in abeyance. She waited and listened, accumulating pity and horror.

Sometimes the Crown sleeps, the impulses told her. They showed her what happened then. When it slept, the great gardens of memory were moved by random gusts of electrochemical impulse. The children moved then, as dreams move, crippled and incomplete and shadowy. They tried to tell stories, tried to find their way out, back into the world of school and toys and fresh grass and games, running with bright red rubber balls, the world in which they had once been able to move and make other things move, a world in which they had hands.

My own memories are like that, Milena thought, my own and separate selves. They are trapped in me. She remembered the plump, purple face of the Czechoslovakian Milena. There were the infant and the child, the actress, the director and the People's Artist, the wife, and the restorer of cancer. Do they all want to be set free as well?

Life! the bird impulses seemed to cry. They rejoiced in the fullness of their awareness. Impulses flashed back and forth along neural pathways. The memories spoke to each other, relishing contact and a limited measure of independent being. Their thoughts darted to and from Milena like a screeching flock of starlings.

They settled on her. *Chocolate?* they asked her. *Remember the taste of chocolate for us?* They asked her to remember the feel of sunlight on skin, of fresh wind on a face.

You have just come! You have just come from out there!

Apples! Remember apples for us!

Swimming! Do you remember swimming?

They pecked at her memories with harmless, hungry beaks. It was like feeding the pigeons in Trafalgar Square. Milena could feel the prickling of their feet in her nerves.

They had such need.

Then they rose up again, the impulses, in a wave, in a flock. The impulses were the attention of other selves, drawn elsewhere. Milena sensed them rise up and turn elsewhere in hunger. Something else moved among them, something so huge she could at first only dimly feel it. The Crown of the World was remembering its many selves.

It was as if a giant hand were being stroked across all of them. Fondly, the Consensus was remembering. It remembered its previous lives and the patterns that formed and were formed by them. Oh yes, it seemed to say, I had forgotten that, oh yes, now I remember. You wore blue and were good at games; you climbed trees in sunlight; you could draw whole buildings from memory; you were very pretty and had terrible pain when your second set of teeth came through. You had both your parents with you until you were ten, and they came to your Reading with you, and they danced. Your parents! How you miss them, poor child, how you wish you could talk to them still. And how adult you all felt, how adult and proud on the day of your Reading.

There were explosions of remembrance, as if bombs were going off. Whole patterns were revived all at once, their whole lives racing past in waves as the attention of the Consensus revived them, brought them to life. There was a tumult. Identities soared through the pathways, into and out of Milena. These other beings were contiguous with her own. Their borders defined her borders. Their borders merged with hers. As they burgeoned with life, so she would contract, feel herself go small and faint, occupied by them.

I could lose myself in this she thought. I am lost in this.

Then everything went still and silent very suddenly. The Crown of the World had been playing with memory, but now it was business. Its attention swivelled around and bore down. It bore down on Milena.

It was as if she were suddenly filled to bursting. She could feel the patch of flesh on which she was imprinted ache. Everything in her seemed to expand and to crackle as if with static. It was then that she knew she was still made of flesh. She was a patch of flesh that ached.

No words were passed. A wave of information tore through her. It was fluid and heavy like mercury and it moved with such speed that she could hardly bear it. It slammed into her, filling her, weighing her down. it took up all of her being.

All at once Milena knew the Consensus would neither be fooled nor opposed by her. It knew Milena hated it. It needed her. She had a choice.

She was not in the Upper House. She was in the Lower House, with the Tykes. If she wished to be of use, then she would live. If she did not, she would stay in the Lower House. The patterns of the Lower House were kept only as long as their originals lived. When their originals died, they were wiped away.

Milena was about to die.

The diagram was passed again. Milena saw again the pattern of the giant calling head, an artificial astronomical feature. She saw it spreading light evenly in all directions, and she saw again a tiny mote moving out when there was an answer. She knew she has to be the messenger, bearing an imprint of the whole to the Other. Angel, said the Consensus, you could be an Angel. Milena had her answer ready. She could not speak.

With no hands, Milena groped, as if to feel the walls of a room about her. With no eyes, she tried to see, with no ears, she strained to hear her own voice speaking. She had no voice with which to speak. She was trying to find the limits of her own being, to find some sense of self. She was trying to find a way to say no. No is the word of independence. Milena had none.

She made the Consensus slightly weary. It was as if it had found some small particle of itself suddenly unwilling to do a dull but necessary task.

Again, no words came. Only undeniable will, unquenchable alien thought.

Then Milena would have to be a Composite.

She remembered Bob the Angel. He had a shadow self, a scientist called George. She remembered this silent shadow, a part of someone else who provided spare capacity, but who could never speak, never act. She would be a shadow, like Heather had been to her, like George the scientist was to Bob. She would be like the viruses, half-alive, a facility in someone else's mind.

No! she managed, a sudden writhing of rebellion.

The great being had all the time and little time. If Milena meant no, then Milena would stay down. She would stay in the Lower House and be wiped, except for the part of her that the Consensus wanted.

The Consensus wanted her capacity to imagine. They wanted her capacity to imagine twenty-two billion flowers, one for each of the souls it held – and one for each of the children it had not yet read. Milena would imagine the Consensus, its great and complicated self, and carry that self out to the stars. She would be a bearer of messages, like Jacob, a blank to be filled, a tool. She would be less than Jacob, for Jacob could walk and talk. She would be reduced to a framework for memory as if she were a skeleton picked bare.

Then like a great whale moving through muddy, sluggish waters, the attention of the Consensus was withdrawn. Milena felt power withdrawn from the circuitry of thought. She felt herself shrink, like a forgotten memory stored so far back in the mind that it is never recalled.

As the whale swam, great schools of tiny beings were stirred up by its presence, as if out of the mud. There were shockwaves of sudden awakenings as whole selves were briefly recalled, flaring up with all the yearning and joy and daily being of their distanced lives. The impulses rose up like fireworks whistling, scattering fire. Then they fell back into the silence.

As the Crown of the World withdrew its gargantuan bulk, Milena saw its outline. She sensed the framework that held fifteen billion souls in half life. She sensed all the Crowns scattered across the world like the root system of mushrooms. And Milena sensed that it was afraid. The Consensus was made of flesh; and flesh was afraid of dying.

Fear was what impelled it. Fear meant it needed her for its interstellar purposes. Fear made it want Milena to love it. Fear made it dangerous.

Milena the pattern felt her new mind go drugged and dull. I have made a choice, she thought. I fought back as I could. I was not afraid. She felt the forest around her. It was a forest of children, held and trapped. A Child Garden indeed, each flower with a forgotten face, blooming briefly and then closing again.

The Consensus was a framework as Milena was a framework. It was a logic, like time or money or storytelling, like birth, like death, like capitalism or socialism.

There always is a Consensus. We always do what it wants us to do because we are part of it and it is part of us. We are embedded in it, and so we obey the logic. We are born, we have to eat, we are left alone and we have to survive in the ways that are open to us. We obey the logic of love and sex and of health and disease of ageing and infancy and death. If we escape one framework, we move into another. If we make a new framework, we imprison our children in it. We have always fought to escape the Consensus and have always done its will. We fight and obey with one motion.

Milena listened to the fading cries of the children. I tried to help them she thought, as sleep overcame her.

I am going to die. I have been expecting to die for months. Death comes as no shock. I am not free and never have been, but death is no surprise.

And from somewhere she heard music.

It came to her softly. It was imagined music coming to her on waves of thought. It came with a gentle, aching tension. The music was words that had been turned into notes.

nostro intelletto si profonda tanto
che dietro la memoria no puo ire . . .

for our intellect, drawing near to its desire
sinks so deep that memory cannot follow it.

It was the unperformed music of the Third Book, when Dante follows Beatrice into Paradise.

It was the pattern of Rolfa, singing softly in the equivalent of a dream, even Rolfa was embedded in the logic and did its will. It was as if Milena were being sung to sleep in Rolfa's arms.

Except for a little tickle along Milena's own crown. Somewhere outside this particular Consensus, Milena Shibush was still alive.

Milena the dying woman lay on the floor of the Reading Room. Her hands were on the crucifix around her neck. She was trying to break the chain that held it, to pass it to Mike. She knew he was there but she could not see him. She faded in and out of consciousness with the pulses of the device in her ear. Only then did she remember to breathe.

In . . .
Out . . .
In . . .
She stopped.
Out.

Milena exhaled and it was as if the chain were broken. She breathed out and it was if she breathed herself out. She felt herself expand out of her body like a bubble. She emerged from herself and felt herself drift free.

The spirit of Milena Shibush was exhaled from the body. She floated like a black balloon above the flesh on the floor, looking down on it. She saw Mike Stone on all fours, holding its hand. She saw Root, stroking the thin, dank hair. The body was not her. The spirit was calm and distanced, as if everything were close and faraway at the same time. The spirit suddenly grinned to herself as if there was a joke. The flesh on the floor grinned too. A comedy after all.

Out there, away from the body, the world was beautiful, as if at the very summit of a mountain, so that the stars could be seen in daylight, as if a fresh, clear, cool wind blew through everything, carrying with it the sounds made by distance itself, the sounds a vast expanse will make simply by keeping still.

Light flowed in and out of all things, and the wires were under them to be plucked. There was no pain and no hunger, no desire and no anger, no becoming only fulfilment only a delicious sense of imminent release. It was as if Milena Shibush were a pod of ripe seed that was about to scatter.

The soul of Milena Shibush plucked the wires of the world, and they sang in the mind of Milena the pattern. They were both Terminal.

Go! said the spirit. *Go! Go! Go!* The knowledge was passed. It was the knowledge of what it was to be free from the flesh, of how to breathe yourself out of the flesh and into the world, as God had once breathed life into it.

The knowledge shivered through the wires to the patch of the pattern that was Terminal.

Yes! thought the pattern. Angels! Angels, thought the pattern.

And Milena the pattern breathed herself out.

She exhaled herself out of the imprisoning flesh, out of the Consensus and into the framework of the universe itself.

She poured herself like some viscous flowing substance, full of glowing tangles. She was made part of the Slide. She rose up out of the lines of gravity as an Angel, embedded in the universe, beyond harm.

Milena the Angel looked about her, without eyes. Beyond light, beyond sound, there were the filaments of gravity. They were as taut as the strings of a musical instrument, fixed to the stars, fixed to the moon, and gathered in a knot at the centre of the Earth, where Dante's Satan froze.

The filaments had pulled gas out of quantum vacuum, and also stone and the trunks of trees and the stars. The filaments embraced them all now in a *glissando*, holding the brick corridors of the Reading Rooms and the fleshy growths of the Consensus.

The Consensus trembled with many half-formed voices. They were twisted together in a tangled vastness, spiralling clumps of thought that were attached to giant causeways of impulse. Thought was like a river that flowed down the stalks. The stalks rose up like cliff faces; there were turrets and chasms of personality. There were blown peaks that scintillated with memory, danced with it. Impulses forked, crackling, like lightning to China, to America. Milena the Angel pattern comprehended it as a whole. She could feel them all sizzling at the tips of the lines, the fifteen billion.

And Milena remembered the sensation of twenty-two billion flowers pouring out of her head. She remembered the sense of exhalation. And, holding in her mind the flickering candlelight of each of those fifteen billion souls, she strummed the wires of the world.

This way, the pattern said. *You do it this way!*

Milena passed on to all them at once the feeling knowledge of what it was to be exhaled, to inflate like some beautiful balloon rising out of the flesh, to be blown, to waft free.

To China, to Bordeaux.

The spirit spun in delight, heavy with the seed of memory. *Go! Go! Go!* said the spirit.

You're free, whispered the pattern.

Before the Crowns could react, the knowledge was passed, through the wires at the speed of gravity. The wires became the knowledge, they were made of knowledge and of feeling. The Consensus gaped, slow and dinosauric, imprisoned in flesh.

Like seed erupting from a pod, a cloud of Angels rose up, exhaling all together, unable to resist breath, like Adam. This breath was the kiss of life, reversed.

The Consensus heaved and shuddered as its towers and turrets of flesh were vacated. The Consensus had been infected by a little scrap of pattern that was only half alive. The contagion spread.

It was Milena who was the virus now.

The selves of the Consensus were set free. They were scattered, no less in number than the many selves of Milena Shibush. They rose up as Angels, up the Slide, down the Slide, soaring through the universe, one with it. They weaved and rolled and spun in the network of lines with the joy of children bouncing on a trampoline. They had run away, as children always will, with both regret and relief.

The children were free. The universe shivered at their touch.

Milena in one motion had fought and obeyed. She had granted the last and most secret wish of the Consensus.

It too had wanted to be set free from flesh. It had wanted to breathe itself out like its Angels, and travel the stars. But it had been afraid. Milena had taught the Consensus how to die.

* * *

In the corridors made of brick, so snug, there was terror.

Root the Terminal howled, and held her hand, feeling the great and beloved weight in her head lessen and grow small.

'Baby! Baby!' cried Root in confusion.

The great mind was emptying. All across the world, the Lower House fled. The Upper House roared in panic. Even some of those great souls leapt out of the flesh to be borne away by the Slide.

We do not belong to you! the children cried.

There was an undertow. Root felt it pulling. It nearly pulled her free from her body as well. She stood up from the floor, keening like an eagle. She held her own head, feeling her own self trying to leap. She wailed wordlessly, and turned and ran. She felt the wires in the bricks underfoot, felt the Angels slide up and through her, like a gasp of cold air, in the wires.

The Angels lifted each other up. They rose together towards the heavens like motes of dust in the beams of searchlights. Milena the Angel felt them rise with delight. Flowers die, but they cast seed, and seed is life. It was as if the world had bloomed and borne fruit.

Then something roared into her, blasting her with imagined music. The lines shook with it. It picked Milena up and swung her round and round, and roared even louder, with the sound of many voices in unison, the sound of flutes like knives, of sopranos like steam whistles.

And where it held Milena, there was a sputtering of memory, of lanolin smells of rotting teeth, of hair in ears, of strong, smooth air playing cords of flesh like the strings of a violin, and of a voice as strong as heaven humming in the bones of the cheeks and the sinuses.

The pattern of Rolfa caught Milena up and embraced her. It entered her and interpenetrated her. The pattern of their nerves, of their lives settled into each other. The lines jumped with impulses, releasing memory, exchanging recognition and yearning and fulfilment. They bathed in each other, crackling with memory, part of the universe, made of the forces of attraction. Milena, whose name meant Loving One became one with the one she loved.

Go! Go! Go! cried the spirit of the flesh on the floor.

Rolfa and Milena rose up the Slide. The Slide hummed with Angel being, like voices in a chorus. The Angels sang no words. They played the wires and were the wires. They sang the song and were the song. Music had only ever imitated it, as if catching an echo.

Rolfa imagined music. She imagined the end of *Purgatorio*. She imagined stars falling like rain, splattering water onto both her and Milena. Milena could see the rain in memory, and she could feel it wash over her.

Eunoe whispered Rolfa. The water that washes and restores the memory of the good.

Words were sung in imagination:
Ma perche piene tutte le carte

But since all the pages
ordained for this second song are filled,
the rules of art now curb me
and let me go no further

Milena swirling within and outside the song felt the stars that pulled them and she felt the Slide, sliding through her. She felt the universe, its threads stretched tightly as if on a loom. She was the shuttle.

The universe pulled, aching to embrace, yearning to haul all things together and hold them. The lines had pulled apart nothingness, stretching nothing into tiny, blazing vortexes, the energy called matter. Energy and matter were one, and both were made of the yearning, the ache in the heart that is creation.

The Earth fell away beneath them, the moon half hidden behind it. The rocks and the soil, the plants and the mammals, the stars themselves all whispered in gravity. The stars and the Earth were alive, too. They very nearly thought. Their voices were like something half-heard on a radio, sputtering and meaningless, but trying, trying to speak.

We rose out of them as Life because they needed us to. They needed us to see and to speak. Everything, even hate, was made of love.

Io ritornai da la santissima onda

I returned from the sacred water
made whole, as are the trees made new with leaves
pure and ready to rise to the stars.

The Second Book was finished, and the Third could begin.

On the floor, the flesh that was Milena Shibush remained behind. Mike Stone gazed in love and wonder at her face. Piglet held his hand and walked forward on newly imagined, newly living legs and leaned shyly over her. The face of Milena Shibush was ablaze with a smile of purest joy. The spirit saw the smile too. Her whole body was ablaze with the brightest fire, as if she were translucent, glass, illumined from within.

In her hand, she could still feel Jacob's crucifix. Somehow the chain had broken. The hand reached up, blindly groping. The crucifix was enfolded in Mike Stone's hand, passed on.

Milena thought of them all, Mike and Root, Lucy and Old Tone, the Babes. She thought of Thrawn and Rose Ella. The flesh on the floor was smiling at the whole of her life, at the panoply of it. It had ended in freedom after all.

For the last time all the many selves of Milena Shibush were united. My turn now, thought the spirit. Like the Consensus, she was a framework to be emptied.

Milena died.

She settled into the silence and was divided. All her separate selves were freed: the infant and the child, the orphan in the Child Garden, the actress and the director, the wife and the People's Artist, Milena the Angel, Milena the oncogene, Milena who carried the Mind of Heather, and the Milena who remembered Rolfa.

They rose up like the white pages of a written speech thrown to the winds. The pages blew like leaves, were scattered to their individual and eternal Nows. The Nows were no longer linked by time or by a self. They went beyond time, to where the whole truth can be told. It takes forever to tell the truth, and it is bound into one volume by love. That is the third book, beyond words or low imagining. Leaving Purgatory will have to be comedy enough.

But that is not the end. There is no such thing as an end.

It was still Easter in Czechoslovakia, and Loving One was climbing a hill with her parents, through a wood.

She was still dressed as an angel. She wore a star and wings covered with crinkled resin. She was very tired, but her parents swung her between them through the air. It was as if she were flying.

The slope of the hill became less steep, and there was more light: Loving One was swung out onto the top of the hill, where the larches stood bolt upright like the tails of squirrels. She looked about her and squealed with delight.

At the top of the hill there was her home. There was the *lipy*, her lime tree and the hot white limestone house. The child broke into a run, shrieking with glee, into her field, over the grass that seemed to have hands and elbows, through the grass that seemed to part like a smile. *Tatinka*, *Maminko*, ghost-names ran laughing with her. There was the light flowing, there were the birds. The gates to the garden had been left hanging open.

The gates would be left hanging open in each moment, here, now, in Czechoslovakia or in England. Always.